About Rain Hunter

Rain Hunter is a writer of post-apocalyptic science fiction. Having spent years as a materials researcher, Rain intricately weaves scientific precision into the stories. "I've had a fun lab run over the years and might have picked some degrees on the way," laughs Rain. "But the most important thing for my books is that the science has to be real. No more can-and-know-it-all characters! If I know how to cook meth from baking soda and cough syrup, I won't be able to start a rocket engine, full stop. Even in fiction!"

Rain is a huge fan of the zombie genre, both in movies and books. "I'd kill to be a zombie extra in a film. Even if they smash my brains out in the first two seconds. Sign me up anytime."

About the European Synchrotron

The European Synchrotron Radiation Facility (ESRF), Grenoble, France, is a high-energy electron accelerator producing x-ray radiation for various research applications from biology ("squishy") to metallurgy ("rocks"). ESRF was open in 1994 with 15 operational beamlines. As of 2025, it operates 51 beamlines.

The ESRF Ring is 844 m in circumference (for example, Wembley Stadium has a circumference of 1,000 m).

ESRF hosts more than 2,500 user experiments annually and is financed by the participating countries, including France, Germany, UK, Russia, South Africa, etc.

THE SYNCHROTRON

RAIN HUNTER

Cover design by Rain Hunter

First Edition

ISBN: 978-1-0682043-2-6

For more information, visit: www.rain-hunter.com

Email: rain@rain-hunter.com

Warning

Besides occasional details and descriptions typical for the postapocalyptic genre, this book contains the word "fuck" **53 times**. The English language doesn't seem to have a better word for the end of the world.

Some of you will find that 53 are not enough.

Then – bring your own.

Contents

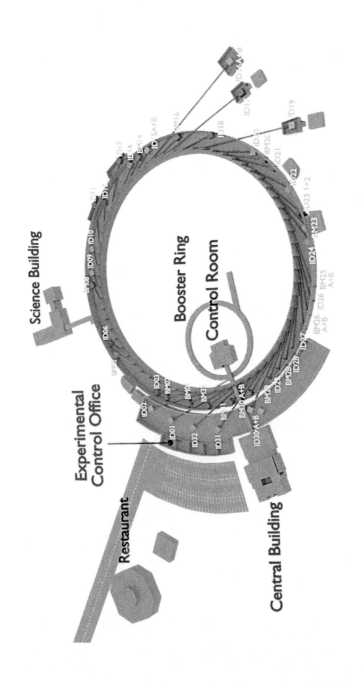

Prologue

I've always thought that the end of the world would take some time. The planes would return to their hangars to sleep, the cars would run out of fuel and stop going places, and nobody would care about the FTSE index anymore. The world would roll to a full stop, and Nature would slowly reclaim its rights over the years.

But no.

Nature has a different plan.

When the world ends, I stand in line at the synchrotron restaurant. The steak sizzling in front of me does not inspire much enthusiasm. The French call it a minute steak. Only cows that died Before Christ are eligible to contribute to this culinary adventure.

Lily is in charge of the dead cows today. She is young and pretty, barely out of school, and has hair so red it looks like the fire has spread from the stove. Lily places the steak on my plate and gestures at the bottle of wine on my tray:

"Nothing a drink can't fix," she says, her French accent cuddly and comes with its own wink.

Before I can grab the plate from her hand, a guy in a chef's apron bursts out of the kitchen, rubbing his eyes. I wonder if he's been splashed with hot oil, but then he lunges at Lily and rips into her throat with his teeth. Her blood splatters on the steak. Her scream dies in a choke.

The chef lifts his head from her neck and stares at me with milky, impenetrable eyes. That second, the world ends.

I am twenty-six, almost engaged (I know Steve bought a ring last week), with a PhD in chemistry and a brilliant scientific career ahead of me.

Ha.

I dump all my hopes in the scrap bin and run. Tomorrow, when the world starts again, I'll pick them back up.

But tomorrow never comes.

Chapter 1. Hunger

1.

It's time to decide who we eat first.

Edsie is bulky and muscular, but we will probably find his lean, old muscles hard to chew. Tanya seems softer in places, but she is tiny. Max is almost two metres of skin and bones.

On the plus side, if we eat Edsie, I won't need to listen to his snoring and blabber anymore.

Yes, let's eat Edsie.

Kidding. For now.

We shared our last food – a Twix bar – a week ago, splitting it into six equal pieces, mindlessly swiping the tiny biscuit crumbs onto the floor. Today, I'd kill for every one of those crumbs. Since then, our bellies have been growling, and our hopes – dying. As if the horrors outside were not enough, we're doomed to starve to death.

It could be worse, Kay reminds me, ever the faithful, cross-wielding-and-God-calling optimist. At least we still have a handful of tea bags and tap water – drinkable but smelling of chlorine.

Who doesn't love a five o'clock brew?

If I don't eat something soon, I will stop thinking of my colleagues as people and start thinking of them as food.

Just like those monsters outside.

We haven't seen or heard any of them since Monday. Woken up by hunger in the middle of the night, I climbed out of my makeshift bed to fill up my water bottle. Through the glass panel in the door, I saw a guy I didn't recognise creep out of the BM26 control room and head towards the stairs. He didn't notice me wave at him.

I wondered what he was up to. There was nothing upstairs in this sector of the Ring apart from a dozen locked offices and a tiny staff kitchen with a mini fridge, a kettle, and a toaster. Too late for that, anyway. We cleared the kitchen straight after the hell broke loose – a handful of stale crackers way past their expiry date, a Twix bar and a large piece of stinky rotten cheese. A day later, we re-identified the cheese as "authentically mouldy" and devoured it despite its looks and smell.

I had turned around to climb back into my makeshift bed when the guy slammed into our door – reinforced glass, thanks to Odin – screaming for us to let him in. I was about to move the slab of concrete blocking the door when a monster leapt onto his back and plunged its teeth into his neck. As they went down, my eyes briefly met the blind, milky eyes of the zombie. It couldn't see me, so it couldn't recognise me, but I knew who it was – Eleni, the kitchen lady who used to serve breakfast in the campus restaurant from six-thirty to ten every morning.

The man screamed in agony, his nails scraping against the door in a doomed attempt to get in. I turned away, crawled under the table, and plugged my ears to block the sounds of slurping, scratching, and agonised sobs. No idea how long it lasted; it could have been five minutes or five hours.

A hand on my shoulder made me jump and bang my head on the tabletop, but it was only Dan. He looked down at me, a sea of sadness in his eyes.

"Is it gone?" I whispered, not rushing to leave my shelter.

He nodded. "We need to move the body before the others turn up. They've made so much noise, the whole Ring has heard it!"

We pulled on purple nitrile gloves and opened the door, pushing the body out of the way. It left a thick red smear in its wake, and Kay hurried to our small chemicals room to fetch the bleach spray and paper towels.

With Max's help, Dan rolled the body over.

"Do you know this guy?" he asked Max.

Max, pale almost to blueness, shook his head. "I... I don't... It's... hard."

It *was* hard. There wasn't much left to identify in the lump of bloodied meat and bones that the monster left behind.

Ignoring the twisting inside my stomach, I pulled the smartwatch off his wrist and scrolled through until I found his name in one of the stored messages. "Andy."

Max shook his head again. "There was no Andy among permanent BM26 staff. I guess he was a visiting researcher like you."

I stood guard, watching out for any signs of monsters attracted by the commotion. The narrow corridor passing by our beamline brimmed with condensed, visceral silence, ready to break at a careless sound. My heartbeat slowed down, and my breathing became deeper as I stared into the depth of the corridor, half-mesmerised by the darkness and the danger it radiated.

Kay and Tanya washed the floor, and Edsie helped Dan and Max to wrap Andy's body in a black bin bag. Then they dragged it inside, into the small chemicals room adjacent to our control room and locked it up. The following day, we would take it to the wet chemistry lab – a few beamlines down the Ring. Our monsters seem to have enhanced hearing and sense of smell to compensate for their poor eyesight, so they get attracted to the smell of the rotting body. The chemistry lab stinks with, well, chemistry, so it would hide the stench of decay.

At least, it worked for the other two bodies we stashed there.

We barely made it in time because, less than five minutes after we finished and retreated to our beamline, the first monster came sniffing around our door. It was covered in dried blood and goo, a horrible reminiscence of the human it used to be. Half of its scalp was dangling down the left side of its face, covering one milky eye.

Tanya ran to the sink to throw up.

Within a few minutes, the monster shuffled away, following the scent of its luckier colleague. We waited to make sure others did not follow it and then climbed back into our beds. No one went to sleep – even Edsie, unfamiliar with the concept of human empathy, was tossing in his winter coat next to Dan.

"Do you think they saw it all?" Kay asked after a bit.

"Who?"

"The guys from BM26?"

"Maybe," I said and snuggled deeper into my coat, wishing my weakened body would produce a little heat. "Why?"

"They didn't even come out to help us pack him in," said Kay.

I shrugged. "Would you? The man is dead. What difference would it make, since we've done the cleaning?"

"But what if… what if there's no one else with him? What if he was the last of them?"

Unlike Tanya, who spent three consecutive days flooding the control room with tears, Kay was not big on crying, but her voice was shaking now. Andy's death was not the first we'd witnessed, and his body wasn't the first we'd dragged away in a bin bag. But this time, it touched deeper. He was the last living person we had seen in days, and now he was gone, too.

Maybe, they're all gone. Steve, too.

No, I wasn't going to cry. I bit my lip and squeezed my eyes shut so tight that the fireworks started behind my eyelids.

"It makes sense," Dan said. "Nobody would be so stupid to go alone if he had a fella."

His words sank into a heavy silence.

Kay voiced what haunted us all. "What if we are the last, then?"

Edsie snickered. "If that's the case, it's all about quality over quantity, then."

"Of course not, since you are here," Kay snarled, spitting the bitter "you" at Edsie.

Andy didn't turn – the dead ones don't come back, only those scratched or bitten. The monster ripped through his neck and then worked hard to get to the guts, twisting his ribs out of the way with its enormous strength. Those beasts are after the spleen while it's warm and pulsing; after that, they are uninterested, leaving wrecked bones and leftovers of flesh behind.

It's been five days since Andy's death – still no monsters in sight. Humans, either.

We've started to hope the zombie apocalypse is over and the world forgot about us while celebrating. This could happen, right? They probably don't even know we're here.

Here.

Kay, who has a naughty habit of peeking over my shoulder while I write, insists that I record – for the benefit of the future generations (please let there be future generations!) – who we are and what we are doing in this forsaken place.

Were doing… in the days before, when we were scientists, and not a bunch of terrified losers.

This is the European Synchrotron Radiation Facility (ESRF), located in Grenoble, a proper shithole of France. (Apologies to anyone from Grenoble, and congratulations if you are still alive. Come and say hi.)

We call it the Ring.

Yes, you guessed right. It is circular.

I bet you've heard about the Large Hadron Collider. It is a synchrotron on steroids for smashing particles into each other. Our Ring is a more delicate kind: it makes electrons run superfast and sweat out X-rays. In science, you can learn a lot about things if you shine light through them, but if you shine very powerful light, like X-rays in our case, you can get a hell of a lot of amazing data.

Twelve days after our arrival, it's only hell and no data.

X-rays come out of the main storage ring and into the workstations called beamlines. There are forty-three beamlines at ESRF, all configured for different types of experiments – from soft and squishy proteins to hard rock.

Picture yourself inside a shipping container split into three sections: the optics room, the hutch, and the control room. The optics room is the closest to the racing electrons, with large mirrors and lenses that direct the X-rays into the hutch. Everything in that room is so fragile and expensive that you are not allowed to breathe in its direction unless you are a beamline engineer with a pre-formulated breath.

The X-ray show happens in the hutch, but the crew runs it from the control room on the other side of the hutch. A fifteen-inch concrete and lead wall keeps the X-rays inside the hutch. It works the other way around, too. If it's good enough for radiation, it will keep the monsters away for sure.

Hiding in the beamline while the world collapsed seemed a good idea at the time, but after almost two weeks of squatting next to each other in the control room the size of a one-car garage – don't forget to count Edsie as three people – it feels less of a refuge and more of a prison.

I suppose we could take over the hutch, but it is so packed with equipment that it looks as if a spaceship has crash-landed there in an ugly entanglement of metal, tubing, wires and a scatter of screwdrivers – a sad view, considering we never got to run our experiment of the century.

Dan is telling me that nobody gives a shit about the experiment anymore. Instead, I should tell you who we are and provide sufficient description details to enable a smooth identification of our bodies. At first, I wonder why it matters, but then I think of my mom and dad. Their bodies have never been found, and although we held a funeral, sometimes I am still waiting for them to walk through the door...

Okay. Right. Descriptions.

The bald man with a big tattoo of a football on his left arm and a skull on his right arm is Dan himself, a senior chemistry lecturer from Birmingham Uni and my former PhD supervisor. Yes, he might look like he got out on parole yesterday, but in reality, Dan is on track to become a full professor by his fortieth birthday in six years.

Or, looking at our current situation, maybe not.

The over-pumped steroid fanatic with grey hair is Edsie, also from Birmingham. Edsie is short for Edward, but I don't recall anyone ever using his full name. Gym workouts are the only work he recognises, irrationally combining them with binge drinking until he passes out under the table. At fifty-four, he's more likely to die from liver failure than ever get promoted.

The blonde woman in her fifties with a massive cross dangling on her chest is Kay, a senior lecturer from Glasgow University and my current boss. She came to England from Yugoslavia at the beginning of the noughties, so she was, in a twisted way, the most prepared for the End of The World, having lived through it once already in her home country.

The tiny Asian woman who sleeps next to Kay is Tanya, from Vietnam. Her official position is a technician, but I call her a magical lab fairy – no one can soothe an upset lab chiller or vacuum pump the way she does. Maybe, because chillers and pumps don't try to take advantage of her quiet and unassertive personality. Imagine, as soon as Edsie heard she was a technician, he ordered her to fetch him a sandwich from the train station café.

"TECH-NI-CIAN, Edsie!" Kay repeated for the stupid in the room. "Where in the word does it say 'waitress'?"

Even in the absence of loud titles, Tanya is worth triple her weight in gold – no surprise that Kay would slay and wound for her. I like Tanya and could also be her friend would she ever allow anyone to become close to her.

The younger, lanky chap with purple hair is Max. As a beamline scientist, he's local and came as a part of the synchrotron package – to make sure we didn't break anything during our experiment.

The average-looking, dark-haired, pale-faced female human who sleeps under the computer table is me. I know this description doesn't help much for body identification, so I scribbled "Anna, ID26" with a permanent marker on my left elbow.

No, it won't come off in the shower (what shower?).

No, this is me trying to stay positive.

Have you ever thought about how surviving through the end of the world would be such an intimate experience? Of course, I would love to share it with the most important person in my life, Steve, but instead, I got the joy of these five.

It could have been worse. It could have been just Edsie.

We don't know if our loved ones are still alive. The last time I spoke to Steve on the phone, I was heading down to the restaurant, intending to treat myself to a glass of wine and a minute steak after spending two days locked up in the lab.

"From what I've heard about their steaks, the word "treat" might not be appropriate," I told him.

He laughed, his husky laughter making me warm and fuzzy inside. "Be careful, Ania; if you don't stab the steak straight away, it might run off your plate."

Can't believe we were discussing our dinner plans while the world was on fire!

The networks went down in the first hours of the Apocalypse, but we still have electricity – thank you, progress, for giving us solar-powered backup generators. Dan thinks the switch from the main grid to the backup generators, accompanied by a short black-out, caused a crash of the Wifi system inside the Ring. Fibre is more robust than cell networks; maybe we could...

Not anytime soon.

We keep our phones charged, but without a network, they are as good as coasters. But in the darkest nights, when the hunger is the worst, Edsie's snoring is unbearable, and the heartache feels lethal, I hug my phone with Steve's photo on the screen and pretend I am snuggled next to him.

I pretend, for a single heartbeat, that the world is still going, and in a few days, on Friday the twelfth of February, we will finish our experiment and take a train home.

Friday the twelfth of February is today. No one is going home.

Before I start hyperventilating, let me focus on the facts. Dan says that when emotions are bigger than you, facts never are; they are short and precise.

Octopuses have three hearts.

A day on Venus is longer than a year on Venus.

Although zombies are a fictional concept, there are "zombie" ants that are infected by fungus and jump off heights, killing themselves.

Ah, crap, ignore this last one!

It's not correct to call these monsters "zombies". Look, I've watched a lot of Hollywood movies, and movie zombies want your brain but won't snuff the rest of your flesh and guts. Our guys are very single-minded and want only spleens, so the term "spleen-eating monsters" suits them well.

Tanya thinks the virus is a Chinese invention, like COVID-19 or bird flu. I've heard lots of funny theories about where the COVID-19 virus came from, but I thought that bird flu was, well, of avian origin. "You never know what they are cooking," she responded when I said as much – a rare time when our gentle, sweet Tanya showed anger.

No point in arguing, is there?

We caught some information before the internet died and pieced together the rest from our own observations. Once you get bitten or scratched, you have a few hours until the early symptoms. First, your eyes get hazy, your iris turns milky grey, and a thin film covers the whole eye. Next, eyesight reduces to shapes and silhouettes. When your eyes fully turn white, you have a few minutes to say bye to your humanity. After that – animal instincts and nothing else.

Hunger – this is what drives them.

Kay suggested that when you get infected, the virus attacks the spleen, since they crave it so much after they turn.

"I've heard that's what modern science thinks about vampires. They couldn't produce haem-carrying proteins, so they had to source them from the blood of their victims."

Ehm… I wonder what branch of modern science studies vampires – Who funds it? Where does it source its test subjects? – but the whole idea sounds plausible. Something is driving those buggers straight to the spleens; no waffling, no licking around.

Ah, wait a sec! Is there a science that studies zombies? Zombology? Zom-biology?

Our folks do not develop supernatural strength or speed, so you can fight them like any regular human. This is good news. Now, the bad news: their hunger makes them angrier and less susceptible to pain. Their blood also clots quickly, so they don't bleed out if you injure them. That is why so many misshapen, tortured, twisted monsters are walking around the Ring with their limbs missing.

More bad news. Their nails grow faster and stronger than human nails, turn into claws and rip through clothing as if they are made of metal. They have their human teeth, but have you seen what damage human teeth can do to human flesh?

Think of Andy. There was barely any Andy left when the monster had finished, just twisted bones, ripped muscle and…

Facts, Anna!

When two cats fight, the loser cat turns to leave first, and the winner cat bites him in the bum.

Okay, where was I? The Ring is the most powerful X-ray source in the world, and the experiments conducted here are often ground-breaking. This time, our shot at the Nobel Prize was about pal—

Cat's bum, it's a scream.

And it's coming from the hutch.

Ignore it. Edsie makes this kind of squealing high-pitched sound. The last time I heard such a squeal, Edsie saw a spider in the hutch and imagined that X-rays would turn the poor thing into a hairy seven-foot monster.

"Anna, bring a woolly hat!" Kay shouts.

Oh wow. Has someone decided to venture outside? Or are they trying to push Edsie out?

"She's turning!" Edsie squeals again.

Turning? Do they think the hat is going to help with that?

"Anna, for fuck's sake!"

2.

I ran into the hutch to find everyone crowding around something. I pushed Edsie out of my way, but he grabbed my hand.

"What's wrong with her, Anna? Why is she doing that? Is she turning? She is turning! She is turning!"

I squeezed between Edsie and the experimental table to see what was happening. Surrounded by the towering chillers, Tanya thrashed on the floor, convulsing as though possessed; thick white foam was coming out of her mouth; her eyes were rolled up so I could see the whites; her legs hit the chillers with loud bangs. Dan wrapped them in his coat, gently restraining them. Kay rolled Tanya onto her side and pushed the woolly hat under her head, trying to keep it from smashing into the equipment.

Kay was pale, her hands shaking, but she acted calm, as she had done this many times before. Even though Tanya was hitting her with her hands, Kay leant over and whispered something into her ear, stroking her head.

Dan brought more coats and cushioned Tanya around with them. Soon, she started calming down, her movements less frantic, her breathing more controlled. On cue, we all moved slower and spoke quieter.

"Has she turned?" Edsie's voice snaked into my ear.

I jumped, startled by his proximity. "Are you an idiot, Eddie? She is having a seizure, not turning into a monster!"

Kay lifted her head and looked at us. Her eyes were full of tears. "She ran out of her meds a few days ago. Three, maybe four. Without them, her seizures will get worse. It also doesn't help that Tanya is hungry. Low blood sugar triggers her episodes."

Oh, Odin! That explained all the late-night bananas Tanya munched on in the lab while nobody was watching. The Health and Safety guys would have had a heart attack if they discovered, but they didn't because, during the unsocial hours every morning, I took those banana skins out of the lab bin and tossed them in the staff kitchen bin.

"Oh, fantastic! She will not just starve to death, but she will do it dancing!"

"Edsie!" Dan and Max hissed at the same time.

I'd suggest feeding this asshole to Tanya if I didn't know how toxic he was.

Meanwhile, Tanya relaxed into an exhausted slumber, her shoulders steadily rising and falling, the strained grimace leaving her face, a breath at a time. Kay kissed her forehead, unwilling to leave Tanya on her own.

"She will sleep for a bit. I will stay with her." She waved us off.

We tiptoed out of the hutch and closed the door behind us. As if he was most traumatised, not Tanya, Edsie ran straight to the drawer with alcohol. Wine and cognac seemed to be a must-have to run experiments at ESRF, so every control room had a not-so-secret stash of booze. I guess that's why Dan and Edsie preferred the French synchrotron to the English Diamond.

"What were you all doing in the hutch? One can break a neck out there, not five of you!" I asked Max.

He shrugged.

"We had an idea that maybe we could try to build some sort of transmitter out of the equipment we have there."

"What? Building a radio out of chillers and temperature probes? It's like making a rocket from a washing machine!"

Max shrugged again. He had never been very chatty.

"The question is not what we were doing," said Dan. "The question is what we are going to do now."

I sank into the chair, suddenly exhausted by this unexpected issue. I liked Tanya, and even her gentle patronising – "Can you please turn off the pump if you are finished with it?", "Anna, are you planning to wash your glassware, or do you want me to help with that?" – didn't annoy me. But in our situation, any person who couldn't establish full control over their body and could go off at any moment was a potential survival threat – to themselves, to us.

She's not a threat, I reminded myself. She's a friend, and if we don't do something to help her, she will die.

"I didn't know that she had epilepsy," I admitted with a sigh. "And I've been working in the same lab for a year. Looks like the meds kept it well under control for her."

"And food," Dan pointed out. "Can't say which of them is more important in her situation."

I nodded. "Both."

The silence settled for a long time while everyone considered what it meant. Edsie continued slurping his wine, but that was normal; I had never detected any thinking activity in that man.

Kay walked out of the hutch, and we all stared at her as if she was a surgeon who left the operating room to tell the worried family that the operation was successful and that soon, they would be able to see their loved one. But she went straight to Edsie, took the bottle out of his hand and downed the rest in one go, despite his weak protests.

"We don't have much time," she told us after. "Without the meds, it's like her brain has a loose switch that goes off randomly. The longer she's off the meds, the more episodes she will have."

"I suppose you won't get the kind of drugs she needs in a first aid kit, will you?" Dan asked.

She shook her head.

"I know where to get some. I… my… there is a girl from the Ops team. She has epilepsy, so she keeps carbamazepine in her office," said Max.

"That's it, then! Where is her office?" Dan hopped off the table he was sitting on, ready to go.

Max sighed.

"Where?"

"Central Building."

Kay looked at us in confusion. Since it was her first time at ESRF, she couldn't place where the Central Building was… It could have been in Miami, with our luck.

"Look. A Skylight Bridge connects the Central Building to the upper Ring Hall, so we don't even have to get outside," said Max.

"Yeah, but what about the monsters that are inside?" asked Edsie.

Max shrugged.

"We can't not go," I said, scared of the silence that settled after. "Tanya won't survive without the drugs."

"We can make it to the restaurant from the central building," Dan added. "A couple of people with backpacks could bring enough for a few days, maybe even a week!"

Nobody wanted to be that couple of people. I expected Kay to volunteer, considering the bond between her and Tanya forged over years of working together, but she turned away from my gaze. Who was I to judge? Although I liked Tanya, she was not on my list of people to die for.

Heroes were a thing from the movies, not real life.

Like zombies, right?

In the absence of volunteers, we decided to pull straws.

Or rather, Post-it notes. Kay scribbled a small X on two out of five, folded them into nail-size bits and threw them into her woolly hat. First, she pushed the hat to Max and then to the rest of us. I picked out the last note.

My hands shook as I stared at it, too scared to unwrap it. Beside me, Kay fingered her cross, her lips moving in a silent prayer. What was she praying for? For a blank Post-it for herself? Wouldn't that go against the very idea of Christian self-sacrifice?

Max cleared his throat, drawing our attention. "I am volunteering." His note was still folded. "I... nobody here knows the Ring like I do. I have to go."

"No, you don't, man," said Dan. "You don't have to sacrifice yourself because you work here!"

"Eh, I thought we were talking about getting food and meds, not sacrificing anyone?" I muttered.

Why did I suddenly feel like a doomed oil driller on a killer asteroid?

"Max should go and show the way to the Central Building!" Edsie said behind my back.

"Shut up, Edsie!"

Dan put his chair in front of Max and leant over to him. "Look. You are the last person who needs to go. Hell, can you imagine what you will see out there?"

"I need to," said Max.

"Man, don't you remember what happened to Andy?"

Max shrugged as if it didn't matter, but I could see the pain in his eyes – it did. The Ring had been his home for a few years. Those monsters in the Ring used to be his friends or colleagues.

I didn't even want to think of the dead.

"If he goes, does it mean that one of us doesn't have to?" Edsie asked, waving his folded Post-it.

Jesus, let's eat him.

"Why are you so quiet? Don't you have anything to say?" I turned to Kay, annoyed with her for not speaking out.

Kay looked away, her hand reaching for the cross on her chest.

"Dan is right!" I tossed my Post-it in the paper bin. "Max shouldn't go. I will go instead of Max."

"I will," Dan said, staring at his unwrapped Post-it note.

It wasn't a "no, I" bravado. The "X" was in his voice.

If Dan had to go, I was going, too. He was on my to-die-for list after everything he'd done for me, so it didn't matter if my

Post-it had an X. I already had a large red X written all over me. A walking target. Bite here.

Edsie sighed with relief, crumbling the blank Post-it in his hand. Kay whispered a quiet, "Thank you." Hers was blank, too.

Oh, hello. I didn't even need to open my note. Welcome to the X Club.

I patted Dan on the shoulder. "Well, man, isn't it convenient? We both volunteered. We both go. But don't worry! After all these years, I will be honoured to die next to you!"

"Eff off, Anna!" He crumpled his Post-it and threw it at me. It bounced off my forehead and landed in the recycling bin.

Oh, well. Let's call it a good sign.

3.

Thinking of it, my first trip to the synchrotron wasn't lucky either.

I had already secured a PhD position in Edsie's group and was writing up my Master's thesis when Dan invited me to join him and Amrit, his postdoc, for an experiment at ESRF. I couldn't believe my luck! With four Nobel Prize winners among its users, it felt like an invitation to an elite society. And so early in my career, too!

Halfway through our stint, I got a WhatsApp call from my aunt. She told me that Mom and Dad's yacht had been caught in a severe storm and sank off the eastern coast of Australia.

"They haven't found the bodies, but the wreck was bad, Anna. There is no way they could have survived," she said.

We dropped the experiment – all three of us – and took the first train back to Paris and then via London to Birmingham.

It was a strange time, and I didn't know what to do next. If my parents were dead, should we hold a funeral? But what would we bury? What if we held a funeral, and they were not dead? What if they were stranded somewhere uninhabited in the middle of the sea, waiting to be rescued?

My head was exploding from all the questions, and in the chaos and confusion, I struggled to grasp the hardest truth – my mom and dad were gone. No more cosy family dinners when everyone shared their daily wins and losses, summer picnics in the local park or cool autumn evenings we enjoyed in the back garden huddled around a firepit. I hoped that when the time came, my dad, mom and I would share these little family traditions with my kids. But they would never see their grandchildren born, Dad wouldn't take me down the aisle, and Mom wouldn't cry happy tears at my wedding.

Aunt Liz insisted on having a ceremony and a wake. Lots of people came to say sorry about my loss, but the more I heard, the more annoyed I got. What loss were they talking about? My parents were on the yacht, finally living the life they had always dreamt of.

They'd planned their Big Escape for years, but it wasn't until my last year at uni, when I secured my PhD position and a healthy scholarship, that they found time and money to embark on their journey. I was a big girl, and they didn't have to worry about me anymore. They were excited, like kids at a fun fair, promising to send cards from every corner of the world they travelled to.

"Just to make you jealous, kid," Dad said before boarding the plane to Sydney.

I received four cards from them.

The fifth one, with a smiling cartoon koala, arrived two days after the funeral. Written by my mom's hand, with her usual "Love, always" at the end, it tore open a black hole in my heart. After that, all I could do was cry – no eating, no sleeping... Steve stayed by my side, day and night, even when I swore at him and begged him to leave the wreck of me. That's how I knew he was the One.

Dan showed up ten days after the funeral. He walked into my room, ignoring the mess and the smell (shower didn't make it to the to-do list, either), and told me to get up and pack my stuff.

"I got us some more experiment time, but we must hurry to be there on time. New street, half twelve tomorrow."

I couldn't grasp what he was talking about.

"Well, we didn't finish last time, did we?"

What an ignorant dick! All he cared about was his stupid experiment! And he used to call himself my friend! I screamed, threw a full cup of tea at him and told him to go to hell with his bloody synchrotron.

The next day, I was at the New Street Station with my suitcase packed, waiting for the twelve thirty-four train to Euston.

Science brought the purpose back to my life and healed me. I promised myself I'd build my life so that Mom and Dad would be proud of me, even though I cannot share it with them anymore. Would they be proud of me now when I feel so scared and useless?

One day later, I asked Dan how he knew what would pull me from that black hole.

He smiled. "I guess we are not that different, Anna. A while back, when I was in a dark place, Lesley introduced me to science... It changed me, made me a better person. Sometimes I think I wouldn't be alive if she didn't show up for me then. The dark place would have me."

He'd told me before that in his teens, he was a runner boy for a local gang, following the steps of his two older brothers, both of whom ended up in jail. "I didn't think I was good for anything else," he explained. It was Lesley, then a teenager herself and later – his wife, who convinced him that he was more than his small-town upbringing and the jail time he would face one day. She invited him to study together and soon discovered that he had a talent for chemistry.

Lesley had saved Dan, and later, Dan saved me. This time, I also had a strange conviction that we could make it through as long as we stuck together. As if he was my talisman. Or maybe I was his.

And let's not forget Max, the true volunteer in our suicide squad!

Max's self-preservation neurons must have short-circuited – how else could you explain this stubborn insistence on coming? Dan even suggested spiking Max's drink with sleeping pills to make him miss the departure of our Doom Party, but we couldn't find any pills. The other option, knocking him out with a heavy blunt object, didn't gather much support either.

We memorised the evacuation plan by heart. It showed the Ring with all its beamlines, offices, toilets, adjacent car parks, and assembly points. The skylight passage connecting the upper level of the Ring with the Central Building was eight beamlines away – a sixth of the circle. Almost nothing on the map!

The map didn't convey the actual state of the Ring: a chaotic hybrid of a dump with a warehouse. The beamline containers stand so close together that you could jump from roof to roof. Random storage boxes, fork lifters, platforms and cabinets are scattered around the beamlines like fungi sprouting from a rotting log; narrow metal staircases, scaffolding, tangled pipes, and wiring entwine every available surface, like strangling vines overtaking a jungle. A slim walking path squeezes along the perimeter, encircling this chaos of clutter and metal.

How do you survive in this maze when every nook and cranny could harbour monsters?

"How many do you think are out there?" Dan asked, always thinking quantitatively.

"At peak time, there were around a thousand people in the Ring. When the bad news hit, most locals went home to their families. This takes away two, maybe three hundred people."

Dan nodded. "In the worst-case scenario, everyone who stayed is now either Team Zombie or Team Dead."

"No," I corrected. "Worst case, they're *all* after our spleens."

Thus, it would be the three of us against seven hundred monsters. Not bad, not bad… if we were Bruce Banner-type scientists, Hulk and all, and not the regular kind, weakened by two weeks of starving.

I've picked myself an emergency axe for a weapon, but I'm starting to wonder if tomorrow I'll be able to swing it at all. Maybe, I should go for a nail gun, like Max. But knowing me, I'll probably end up shooting my own foot. Or Dan's.

Dan has a lab wrench for opening liquid nitrogen cylinders. It is the size of a baseball bat, and from the way Dan swings it, I can tell he's got plenty of experience with bats. Not sure about the balls – I don't think they were a part of that experience.

While we were gearing up for war, the rest of the team prepared a send-off party. We walked out of the hutch to find a banner made from A4 sheets that read "Good luck!" and in smaller letters, "We are thinking of you!" There were five glasses of wine on the table, and as we got closer, Kay and Edsie tossed handmade white confetti into our faces, giggling.

They were already drunk.

This isn't a party for us, I thought in disgust. They are celebrating that we are going, not them.

I checked on Tanya, who was peacefully asleep in her coat under the table. She'd had another seizure an hour ago, worse than her first one. She bit her cheek, and the foam on her lips turned blood-red. After it passed, we rolled her away to rest. Kay was right – she didn't have much time left without the meds.

It's for Tanya, I told myself, not for Kay or Edsie.

Having a party to send us off on a mission we might not survive felt like a mockery, but then I thought, what the hell! It could be my last party ever – I might as well get wasted, hook up with some random guy in the toilet, and struggle to remember it in the morning.

What a fantastic plan!

The full-bodied French merlot slipped heavily into my empty stomach, and it growled in protest. "That's not what I ordered!" Don't worry, darling, I assured it. Tomorrow, you'll be in Heaven, with bread and cakes, omelettes and salads, burgers and hotdogs…

What? I am talking about the restaurant, of course!

"Should we tell her she is drooling?" Max's voice interrupted my sweet reverie, yanking me back to the hot dog-less reality.

No. I am the hot dog in this reality.

"I am probably going to die tomorrow, but all I can think about is food," I confessed, wiping a bit of drool off my pullover.

"Not Steve?"

My boyfriend's face flashed in my mind, but my stomach growled, and an image of a hot dog – with an oversized Frankfurter, crispy fried onions and a swirl of mayo – took its place. I swallowed hard and shook my head.

"I can't help it. The hunger is bigger than me."

"Sounds like we are not that different from those folks outside." Dan smiled.

Max nodded. "Sometimes I think about Edsie… You know…"

"He is big," I agreed, "but full of shit."

"Chewy." Dan snickered.

"I still don't get why you are always so pissed off with him, Anna. He is an interesting character, but—"

I patted Max on the shoulder.

Dan spoke for me, "Trust me, it's not a story for an empty stomach."

Never in my life I would admit out loud that it wasn't Steve who appeared every night in my hungry dreams; it was Edsie, looking a lot like a stuffed turkey with apples shining from all the right places.

Don't ask.

"Aren't you thinking of Lesley?" I asked Dan.

"If Lesley is what you call a pool full of barbeque chicken wings, then absolutely."

It was hard not to laugh.

"Why are you guys so cynical? Where is your romantic side?" Max asked, amused. "These are your loved ones, aren't they?"

Dan raised an eyebrow. "You mean the chicken wings, right?"

Max gave him a playful punch in the side, and I handed him the bottle. It was nearly empty, but if I finished it, I would have to give up my cosy place to pick up another.

"The romantic side, young man, tends to wear out over the years… What remains is pure love," said Dan.

I stared at him wide-eyed, not quite believing what I heard. Dan caught my stare.

"I'm kidding," he explained and got up to fetch an extra bottle.

We don't have to worry about running out of alcohol. Before we took over the beamline, Dan and Edsie dashed to the Carrefour down the road and brought back a whole crate of wine to make their long, boring night shifts more entertaining. That's not even counting the leftovers from the previous team – the world will end before we run out of wine.

Sorry, ignore that last bit.

"I guess what this cold-hearted macho is trying to say," I said, "is that the romantic fluff peels off after a few years. It happened to Steve and me, and we've been together for what… mere seven years? These guys," I pointed at Dan, "have done seventeen."

Max snickered. "Sounds like a prison sentence."

"Sounds like our Max is in love." Dan handed him the full bottle. "And his love is as fresh as a morning dew."

Max's face turned red, but he stayed silent.

"And?" I nudged him.

"I met her at one of the all-staff meetings. I saw her and thought that she looked like sunshine. I can't explain it, but… there is something warm and glowing about her. Genny is like a hazelnut and caramel hot chocolate."

His smile turned dreamy.

"Look at him, Anna." Dan grinned. "And this man had a nerve to talk about my chicken wings…"

I'd never been a praying kind. Even when the Zombie Apocalypse hit, I didn't need to start to – Kay managed to do it sixfold for all of us. But this time, it was different. Tomorrow, I'd probably die, and although dying didn't feel as scary with Dan and Max by my side, this wasn't how I'd planned my life to end. In my plan, there was a lot about Steve, a small house on the beach and visiting grandkids, but nothing about monsters and spleens.

As I lay in my makeshift bed later that night, tossing and turning, a prayer appeared in my head out of nowhere, and I offered it to whoever was listening:

If I can't die of old age next to the man I love, then at least, please, don't let me die hungry.

4.

Kay, too brisk for the doomsday morning, woke me up with a smile from ear to ear.

"I had a vision," she proclaimed while dragging me from under the table. "An angel gave me three lab coats and blessed them with a cross."

Struggling to open my eyes, I stared at her through narrow slits, half expecting her to grow wings, horns, tails, whatever.

"The lab coats will protect you from scratches and bites," Kay explained, handing me my lab coat.

It wasn't a bad idea, no matter if it was God-sent or alcohol-induced. Our real-life lab coats were nowhere near as gleaming white as they show in Hollywood movies but soaked in hazardous solutions, making them yellow-brown, armour-solid and capable of withstanding tears, cuts and concentrated acid spills.

Soon, it turned out that Kay's angel had a problem with maths – or he simply didn't like tall people – but we found only two lab coats, Tanya's and mine. The rest of the team never intended to join us in the wet lab, so they'd left their coats at home.

"Maybe, that's a sign for you to stay, Max?" asked Kay.

He waved her off.

Dan couldn't squeeze into Tanya's coat, so I gave him mine. His feet stuck out a couple of inches, and the fabric cracked and gave in the shoulders.

"It's like pulling on a condom three sizes too small," he moaned.

Tanya's coat felt tight on me, too, but I couldn't provide any condom-related feedback. We "proofed" every weak spot with a double layer of silver insulating tape for enhanced protection. That included taping around our socks up to the knees and securing the cuffs around the wrists. Needless to say, Dan – the lucky owner of very hairy legs – had some reservations about the tape.

"Nobody's died from a little waxing," Edsie said, adding an extra layer of tape.

We were about to walk out the door when Tanya crawled from underneath the table, red-eyed and wobbly, like a groundhog on the second of February. She took a moment to study our outfits, then pulled me in for a goodbye hug.

"Thank you," she said and then pointed at the axe in my hand, "just pretend that each of them is Eds."

That counted as a blessing, I suppose.

***

We were not prepared for what we saw.

Nobody could be. They teach you maths and music at school, but not how to navigate a post-apocalyptic reality because – what are the chances of living through one?

Walking through the Ring was like playing a survival-horror video game – bodies hanging from the scaffolding, blood smudged on the concrete walls, shattered glass everywhere. Carefully stepping over the shards, I spotted a few rats crunching on the leftovers in the shadows and wondered how long we had until a rat nibbled on an electrical wire and sent our bunker into darkness.

I tried hard to think of something pleasant. Steve. Our little house back in Birmingham. I am in bed, and this nightmare will end with the early sunshine. I will wake up next to Steve. He will rub his nose on mine, kiss under my ear and say, "Ania, it's pancake day." We will crawl out of bed in an hour or two, and

Steve will start making pancakes. It is our Sunday tradition. When we have kids, we will make pancakes for them every Sunday. But why wait?

The thought of golden pancakes consumed me; I zoned out, lost my balance, my axe slipped from my grasp, and landed with a thud in the gooey substance.

Red.

Smelling of metal.

Blood, all over my hands. I gritted my teeth not to scream.

The source of the blood sprawled on the floor next to me – a man, his stomach torn open, his guts missing. I could see the shreds of muscle and bone gleaming through the hole where they used to be. I clenched my teeth even harder, suppressing the retching. Nothing would come out anyway. I hadn't eaten for a century.

Something grabbed me from behind, pulling me upwards. I was about to kick and smash when I realised it was Dan.

"Man, Anna, watch where you are going!"

I stared at the corpse I'd almost trodden on. It was a young man, no older than me, his eyes wide open in horror and his mouth twisted in a forever cry. The lanyard on his chest was facing away, and I flipped it over, leaving thick, bloody smudges over the photo. I needed to see his name.

"It is Ben Stenton. He worked in the commissioning team. I met him a couple of times." Max's voice was hoarse with tears.

"It's not too late to turn around, man. We can get to the Central Building on our own."

He shook his head and moved on ahead. Dan and I exchanged understanding looks, Dan's words from the last night echoing in my head. *Max is in love.*

Oh well, let's hope the wings of love will carry him unscarred to his hazelnut hot chocolate girl.

My stomach grumbled in response to my thoughts. I wiped my bloody hands all over the lab coat, picked the axe from the puddle of blood and wiped it, too.

As we moved further into the Ring, the smell grew stronger, and we encountered more bodies, most of them at some level of decomposition, maybe a week or so old. I didn't stop to check their names, but I wished I could pray like Kay for each of them to get rid of the growing guilt. What an ignorant bunch of folks we were, hiding in our comfy and cosy bunker! We heard the news and witnessed a few deaths but couldn't even imagine the sheer number of casualties.

Bullshit!

They were not casualties! They were people; they had families, friends, kids, mortgages, lives!

They were all dead now.

I had a life, too. I was going to get engaged and live my happily ever after with Steve. Eat my bloody pancakes every Sunday! Go to see the Blues on Saturday!

"Are you okay?" Dan squeezed my shoulder. "Breathe, Anna!"

In the eighteenth century, people used corncobs instead of toilet paper.

The Eiffel Tower grows up to six inches in summer because of heat.

The Eiffel Tower brought me back to reality. Next to me, Max was crying, tears streaming freely down his cheeks as he whispered the names. Ben. Yvette. Gregoire. Tasha. Bilal.

The Ring was quiet as if the pack of monsters had cleared the area and fled to the new feeding grounds, like locusts that kept going until nothing alive remained.

We got to ID29, five beamlines from our bunker, when Dan, walking at the front, signalled us to stop. We tiptoed over to him and peered around the corner. Twenty or so spleen-eaters crowded around the next beamline, agitated by something or someone inside the control room. They were not trying to break through the doors, so I guessed they had been there for a while and started losing interest.

Indifferent to the commotion near the beamline, two spleen-eaters sat on the floor next to a fresh body, scooping the contents of its stomach out and smudging it over the floor without eating it.

This time, I didn't retch but stared, unable to explain what I saw. The scene made me uncomfortable, but there was something else besides the obvious gore and carnage.

That's it. They were *taking turns*. One scoop at a time.

Dan pulled me by my sleeve. Not a good time for scientific observations, Anna.

We fell all the way back to ID28.

"Skylight is a no-go?" Dan whispered.

Max nodded. "The best way is through the car park. We'll have to go back to ID27, then through the outer hall. It is quite spacious, but there are forklifts and tons of shipping containers all over the place. They've been building new beamlines out there, so it won't be too busy."

Our walk through the outer hall was boring, if one could be considered bored while having a heartbeat of 200 bpm. I tried to establish control over my heartbeat and wandering mind, making sure I was present in the moment and ready to run, but it kept drifting back to the two spleen-eaters near ID29.

Were they really taking turns, or did I imagine it?

I'd seen a crowd of spleen-eaters attack a single prey. They ripped into it like frenzied sharks – no hierarchy, no waiting for their turn. How many of them were mauled by their peers in the middle of the carnage?

But what if, when the hunger was satisfied, they made time to… Play? Were those two spleen-eaters playing with their food leftovers?

Holy Odin!

Nah. Impossible.

We all agreed that they were animals driven by their hunger. But didn't animals have other instincts? Instinct for shelter? For belonging to a group? Didn't they have social behaviours? Wasn't playing one of them?

Before I made any hypothesis, Dan stopped again. We arrived at the doors that led from the experimental hall to the offices in the outer part of the Ring. I pressed my ear to listen in but heard nothing. I signalled Dan an "all clear".

Dan waved his card in front of the card lock. The lock clicked, the red light turned green, and Dan opened the door for Max and me. We got through the door when I realised the hall on the other side was quiet but not empty.

Too late.

The closest monster turned to the buzz of the door and met me face to face. I froze, staring. Its face was caked in drying blood, its eyes draped with a white cloak, but I felt it could still see me and immediately knew I was not like it; I was prey. Twenty other monsters perked up behind it, waking up from their half-slumber. I think I screamed – or was it one of them?

Max yanked me by my sleeve, snapping me out of the shock and into a run. We barged into the toilets opposite the door, pulled Dan in, and locked the door behind us. A nanosecond later, one of the monsters smashed its full weight into it, and its nails scratched the wood with a sickening sound.

Another bash. Then more. Under the push of the whole crowd, the door squealed, and the lock jerked in the door frame. Max drew us to the windows. They were solid glass and frame – no locks, no handles.

"We'd have to break them," I said.

Max pointed at the emergency axe in my hand.

I hesitated. "The sound will attract all the bloody freaks in the area."

The door behind us squealed again. It was a death squeal, the last warning. I smashed my axe into the frosted window. The glass shards rained on my lab coat, and the blinding sunlight blasted into the toilet through the opening. Without delay, I squeezed into the window and dropped over the ledge straight into the thorny bush.

My hands hurt as if the sandpaper scraped through raw skin, but I scrambled to my feet, grabbed Dan and jerked him out of the window, face down into the bush. He screamed and swore. Behind Max, the toilet door smashed open with a loud bang and the first spleen-eaters jumped in.

Dan dragged Max through the window frame. Max was almost out when something tugged him back in. Dan barely held onto him.

"The fuckers have my feet!" Max shouted.

I shoved the axe through the small space between Max and the window and hacked at the monster's hands. It shrieked in pain and dropped its hold. Max's feet free, he swung over the window ledge and fell on top of Dan.

"Come on, guys! Hurry up!"

More than a dozen monsters were closing in on us from every side, drawn by the noise of our struggle, while their friends squeezed through the window behind us.

We ran through the car park. A few abandoned cars remained, some joined with each other in a fatal kiss, doors wide open, mutilated bodies in the seats. Broken glass was everywhere – I focused on the ground under my feet.

In front of me, Dan whacked one of the spleen-eaters out of his way with his lab wrench and ran up the stairs to the central building. The glass door was wide open, but would it hold?

Dan dived into the dark halls, followed by Max. I was almost inside when I felt a swift movement behind me and, without thinking, swung my axe backwards into the face of the spleen-eater. It met the bones with a loud crack and split the monster's head in two, blood and brain splashing onto the side of my face. Dan dragged me in through the door and shut it behind us.

Another monster threw itself on the glass, trampling on the warm body of its fellow, screeching, scratching, its white eyes looking straight at me. Its pals jumped on it and squashed it into the glass. The door rattled but didn't give in.

I dropped my axe on the floor and curled up in the corner.

"It's okay, Anna!" Dan patted me on the shoulder. "That was a good hit!"

I will never forget the image of that skull cracking in two. I had been fighting for my life, but no one's brain deserved such a brutal dealing. That monster, more animal than human, had still been alive, in a way. And I made it *dead*.

I'd killed it.

If I survive, I will have to live with it.

The spleen-eaters bashed into the door, harder with every new monster joining in. The glass door seemed solid, but it wouldn't hold for long.

Max pulled me aside. "Let's get out of their view. They will stop bashing soon if they can't see us."

"They can't see us, can they?" I whisper.

"I wouldn't be so sure," said Dan. At his words, the monster closest to the door lifted its head and growled. The others around it echoed, their hunting song reverberating with chills in my spine.

We moved away from the glass and looked around. The floor was littered with paper, and the furniture was scattered upside-down over the place, but otherwise, it was clean, bloodless, and empty, dust slowly settling down in the sunlight.

"Looks like they were trying to light a bonfire," said Max.

"Or barricade?" said Dan.

"There's no blood," I said. "Whatever they did to defend might have been successful."

Dan muttered something about a hungry horde lying in wait in a poorly lit corridor. Max walked around a massive cupboard lying on its side in the centre of the entrance hall. "Guys, have a look!"

He cleared the paper and glass shards off an octagonal table. Under the debris, we found a paper model of the campus, all its buildings reproduced and positioned around the Ring with neat precision. I spotted the Central Building and the restaurant. Next to me, Dan sighed. Clearly, we'd made the same conclusion.

"We can't go back the way we came," he said. "We can't get out at all. Not with that welcome party outside."

"We will have to try the skylight bridge. By that time, the folks at ID29 might get bored and scatter away."

"What about the restaurant? Please tell me there is a secret passage from this building to the kitchen!"

Max sighed. That counted as a response.

"Genny's office is on the first floor. There's a staff kitchen next to it; we should check it out!"

He led the way, navigating around the makeshift barricades towards a wide staircase covered by paper and a layer of dust so thick that we left fresh footprints as we walked up the stairs.

The first-floor corridor passing through the landing was clear as far as we could see from where we stopped – no barricades, no bodies. Max pointed to the left – the office we needed was down that way. The light from the large window didn't reach the end of the corridor, harbouring a coil of thick, impenetrable shadows. Lined with offices on both sides, it could be a death trap if the monsters hid behind any of those doors.

Dan weighed the wrench in his hand and moved to the front of the party. The fittest of us all, he was relying on his speed and reaction, but what could his fitness do against the monsters' hunger and rage in this narrow passage?

I followed at the end, making sure no one crept on us from behind. To be honest, the spleen-eaters weren't very familiar with the concept of creeping, but at least I felt useful, not merely scared.

We were almost halfway down the corridor when I heard a muffled buzz. It was barely audible but unmistakable as if coming from a nearby beehive. I touched Dan on the shoulder to get him to stop and listen. If something was coming, we would hear the footsteps.

Nothing.

Dan moved again and then stopped and nodded to me. Whatever it was, it was getting closer.

Dan peered around the corner and jerked back, pushing himself into the wall. I lifted my eyebrow and opened my fist twice – how many?

He put his finger to his temple and twitched his head. Too many.

We started turning back, but Max pointed at the door on the other side of the corridor. Office 112. Two nameplates screwed on the wall read: Genevieve Dujardin and Lucien Oreille.

Dan shook his head and moved his finger across his throat. I pointed at the floor. How about we crawl?

"Are you insane?" Dan mouthed to me.

I peered over Dan's shoulder. Around thirty monsters crowded in front of the "Conference suite" door, making a weird noise between a groan and a purr like an odd choir with a bad cold.

A man sat propped up to the wall, his eyes closed in his sleep, but then I realised that the dark slush on his knees was not a spilled tomato soup.

I backed off, feeling sick again.

Dan gestured to drop back. Quietly, we returned to the stairs where the monsters couldn't hear us.

"We can't pass," I whispered. "They're too awake. One wrong move, and they'll be on us."

"They are after something behind that door, aren't they?"

I nodded.

"Live people?"

Fresh spleens. Nothing else would attract them.

"We can distract them," said Max.

"How? Throw a ball and hope that the monsters will chase it?"

"*I* will get them to chase *me*," said Max.

Dan and I stared at him. Did he get the Suicide Squad idea literally?

"I can't go back with you," he said, pointing at his left leg.

A neat, clean wound shone through the thin cut in his jeans. The claw went through the fabric, skin and flesh to the bone. It wasn't bleeding much besides a few tiny drops glistening on the edges.

"One of them got to me in that toilet. I am going to turn soon."

"It's a tiny cut, Max!" I shook my head. "You can't expect all cuts to be from them!"

"You hide in one of the offices. Wait for a few minutes. I will try to lure them away from the skylight. Then I'll lock myself in a room… and wait."

"Are you not listening?" I raised my voice, and Dan pressed his hand over my mouth. I bit his finger, and he let go. "Look at your bloody eyes. They are fine. You are fine!"

"I *am* done, Anna; I feel the virus inside me."

"You are not done until you are one of them. You are not one of them yet!"

"Yet. What will you do with me when I turn? Have you got a spare spleen?"

The sound of the skull cracking in two under my axe filled my head. I squeezed my temples to stop it, push it out of my memory. Max's face blurred in front of me as if behind a window splashed with rain.

I was crying.

"But what about your hazelnut girl, Max? What would she say?"

"I *am* thinking of her. And I'm thinking about Tanya. Tanya's medicine is in that office; there's no other way to get this crowd out of your way!"

"Don't you bring Tanya into it! There should be another way to get to that door!" I turned to Dan. "Why don't you tell him? Why the fuck don't *you* tell him?"

Dan patted my shoulder.

"It was great to work with you, guys." Max smiled. "Even though you bickered half the time. I don't think I've ever met a team so weird. If you run into Genny, take good care of my girl."

"Fuck, man!" said Dan. "It's been an honour to know you. Try not to get your spleen eaten, Max."

Max gave me an awkward hug, but I pushed him away. I was not going to say goodbyes; goodbyes were for the dead, and he was fine, stupid man.

Dan pushed me into the nearest office and locked us in it. The last thing I heard from Max was his cheerful "Yippie, bastards!" as he danced in front of our door, attracting the monsters' attention. In a second, a crowd of growling monsters stomped past, chasing him.

I sat on the floor and let the tears out. Dan landed next to me, and although I hated him for letting Max go, for not telling him it was just a scratch, I was grateful for him being there, again, like he was when I stared at the empty coffin at my parents' funeral, when I stumbled through my first conference presentation, thinking I would die from a heart attack. He splashed champagne into my face when I walked out of the thesis defence room titled a "Doctor".

Will he be there when I turn into a monster and crave his spleen? Will he smash my brains with that wrench?

No, I couldn't think of Max as a monster. I hadn't known him for long, but we could become great friends if we lived through this nightmare. If only we got to live…

Wait a sec.

"Not dead." I turned to Dan, my tears immediately dry. "Max is not dead."

"Of course not. He… what do you mean?"

"If he's not dead, it means he's alive."

"Genius, Anna."

I started pacing the room. There wasn't much space, with enough room to fit a small round table for two, maximum, three people, so I made circles around it, suddenly very excited.

"We didn't see it, Dan! In the movies, zombies are always dead, right? But our zombies – no, our spleen-eaters – they are alive. The virus doesn't kill them, so we can... cure them. Right?"

"We? As if, in us, the five chemists? Since when does a doctor in your title involve treating monsters back into people?"

I shrugged and pulled the chair from under the table to sit on it. My hands were shaking.

"That's detail. In theory, we can. Look, finding a cure is science, right? Is there any better place for science than the Ring? And we are scientists, in the end. Well, apart from Edsie! He is just a jerk."

Dan sighed. "Yeah, but we are not *the* scientists. It is a job for biologists, virologists, immunologists..."

"You've seen the shit inside the Ring. The world outside doesn't look much better. What's the chance that any of those "gists" are still alive?"

"You are crazy." He gave up. "But I knew that. Let's grab Tanya's meds and get back to the others. Then, we can figure it out together, okay?"

We peeked out to scan the horizon. It looked like Max's plan had worked – the monsters were gone. We walked down the corridor and, before going into office 112, knocked on the door of the conference suite. Silence. I tried the handle, but it was locked, as expected.

Maybe, they'd escaped ages ago, died from starvation, or turned into monsters and forgot to tell their hungry friends outside to stop waiting for them.

Or they didn't want to do anything with us.

Unlike the card-locked doors and beamlines at the Ring, the doors in this building had old-fashioned key locks. I pushed the handle, and the door of the Office 112 uttered a tiny squeak, opening. I peeked in, squeezed through the narrow gap and pulled Dan inside.

The office was tiny, with two bookcases and two desks crammed, leaving no space for anything else besides a dying palm near the door. The window desk was spartan-clean: an Acer laptop in the centre and neatly arranged paper in the corner. The other desk was an epitome of personality – two pictures in bright blue frames, a jar of fuchsia nail polish, and a splatter of pink Post-it notes over all available surfaces, horizontal and vertical.

Dan started rifling through the drawers of the pink desk while I lingered by one of the frames. Max and a golden-haired girl smiled at me from the photo, holding a massive melting ice-cream between them. The ice-cream was dripping through their fingers, but they didn't seem to care. I could almost picture them licking their fingers clean after, a sea breeze touching their lips with a salty aftertaste.

Max was right. Genny was pure sunshine, magically trapped in a human form. Her hair, warm eyes, the scatter of dazzling freckles on her nose…

"Bingo!" Dan shouted. "Look, Anna, eighty-four tablets!"

I noticed a handwritten note on the top of the paperwork.

Max, I am fine, Luc and I, we are going to my parents in Saint-Aupre up D49. Find me there, my love. Genny

"Saint-Aupre?" I asked Dan's back. "Where do you think it is?"

"Saint-Aupre?" Dan paused, disturbed by the bitter tones in my voice, and turned to me. "Why?"

I handed him the note. He scanned it in a moment, then raised his eyes at me. I'd been his friend for years, so it wasn't hard to read the answer to my unspoken question in his eyes before he turned back to the bookcase, his shoulders slumped in sadness.

Genny would be waiting for Max in Saint-Aupre, never finding out what happened to him. How long would it take her to accept that he wasn't coming? A year? Two years? Ten?

Doesn't true love measure in eternities?

I looked into the window at the grey February backdrop of naked trees and the river Isère carrying its dark, frothing water down south and thought of Steve. Maybe, our story wasn't that different. Steve might have been dead, and I wouldn't know, hoping to reunite with him one beautiful summer day.

No, I told myself, my heart would know, like all hearts do, through their cosmic connections that span lifetimes and universes. I would feel his last breath on my lips and would hear his last heartbeat...

Who can say that our love would not continue after that?

I imagined Genny walking barefoot on the sandy beach, her golden hair dancing in the wind. Max runs to her, sweeping her in his arms and spinning her in the air. I hear their laughter through the cries of seagulls. They walk into the sunset, hand in hand, heart to heart, never to part again. The gentle tide rolls over their footprints and washes them away, taking away the pain and the sadness. Far away, a small white yacht drifts into the horizon.

Wherever it is, Saint-Aupre knows no pain. Only love.

5.

The staff kitchen next to Genny's office was bright and airy, with dust fairies twirling in the sun rays entering through the window. Chairs lay scattered upside-down on the floor covered with broken glass and ceramics, but there was no blood or bodies. Dan rummaged through the cupboards while I checked a large cupboard box in the corner.

"Oh, hello!"

Instant noodles. Chicken flavour.

I ripped one packet open and plunged my teeth into the dry delicacy, moaning from pleasure; Dan looked at me absently.

"Lesley hates instant noodles."

I handed him a noodle packet. "I'm sure she wouldn't judge you now."

We ate a packet each – a small perk for almost dying a few times today – and packed the rest into our backpacks, alongside two tins of mackerel pate (expiration date three months ago), a bottle of absinthe and a half-full bag of stodgy potato crisps that Dan found in the cupboard.

The corridors were empty and eerie – not a sound, breath, or even a sign of the crowd roaming here half an hour ago. We tiptoed to the skylight passage on the other side of the building without meeting anyone. Despite its rather poetic name, the skylight was yet another long, narrow corridor with white walls and ceiling, brightly lit with LED lamps, blank and sterile, like an elongated operating room.

"What if the monsters are still around ID29? What are we going to do?" I whispered, hesitating at the entrance to the skylight.

I felt claustrophobic, a weird idea, considering I'd spent nearly two weeks confined in a concrete bunker the size of a removal van. Something didn't feel right, and that was a weird idea, too, because hell, when was anything right at all?

Dan shrugged. He looked pale in this spaceship light, and his arm muscles strained as he tightened the grip on his wrench.

It was too quiet, too still in that corridor. I felt watched, not by Dan, but by something else. Walking down the skylight, I checked the walls for hidden cameras – what if we were in a survival reality show and a merry cameraman would jump at me from behind the exit door?

I weighed the axe in my hand. Whatever was behind, I was going to strike first. Dan pushed the door open. Nothing jumped.

We walked out onto a narrow concrete ledge spread over the inner hall of the Ring. What a view it offered! I could see the long bending line of the synchrotron circle and the blocks of beamlines coming out of it like rays. The pipework, the wiring, and the ladders entwined the hutches and rooms like the guts and blood vessels of a gigantic futuristic organism. Right below us, next to the ID29 beamline, a dead body marked the spot where the crowd of spleen-eaters had blocked our way at the beginning of our journey. Now, the monsters were gone, exactly like Max predicted; the hutch door to ID29 stood wide open, and a puddle of fresh blood glistened in the dim lights. I stepped forward, wondering what'd happened inside the ID29, slipped on something soft and grabbed the railing for balance.

A hand on the floor.

The body to which it was attached groaned. A bubble of blood came out of its lips. I jumped back, swinging the axe at it before registering that it was dying. Something grabbed me from behind, plunging sharp nails into my lab coat. A foul smell reached my nose as I felt the spleen-eater's warm breath on my neck. I heard a whack, and the grasp on my lab coat was released.

I swirled around. Dan kept bashing the monster on its head with his wrench. The monster's front teeth were gone, and I could see the tongue tossing from side to side in its jaw. Its right eye had fallen out of the socket, popping merrily on its bloodied face with every whack. In a twisted way, it was funny, so I turned away and threw up all over the dying man.

"What a waste of food, Anna. I hoped you'd help instead of puking over this fella."

The monster slumped down next to me, still twitching in its last spasms, its brain dead, but its body still holding on to life. Following a sudden urge, I grabbed its hand, *his* hand, and squeezed his fingers between mine. It was a human-to-human touch, and I felt the sadness of a human for a human. He used to be a person, a husband or a father; he laughed and cried…

"I'd be careful touching them, Anna. One scratch, and you're done!"

One scratch.

I let go of the dead hand and ripped the duct tape off my wrists. As if the tape had grown into my skin, it felt like flaying rather than waxing. Under Dan's stare, I tossed the rest of the tape on the floor, pulled my lab coat off, lifted my pullover and turned to him with my bare back.

"He scratched me, Dan. I might be already infected."

I tried to sound calm, but my heartbeat went through the roof while Dan examined my skin. Maybe, this is how it ends – Dan smashes my brains with his wrench so that I don't come after his spleen.

That's alright, I don't think I'd make a good spleen-eater. I'm not a big fan of blood and guts, anyway.

"There is nothing, Anna. But you stink."

He pulled my pullover down and leant to pick up my axe from the floor, but I grabbed his hand and forced him to look me in the eyes. I had to be sure.

He shook his head. "Look, this is not something I'd lie about, Anna. Not if you can go all spleens on me. Maybe, don't tell Edsie about it; you know how paranoid he can get."

I put my coat on and grabbed the axe. The dead spleen-eater had stopped twitching and now looked like a cheap Halloween decoration thrown on the lawn on Halloween – not a human, not a monster, but a bag of muscles and bones.

If we had a cure, he might have had a chance. But death left him with nothing.

Well, that's not true.

"Let's grab him," I said.

Dan gawked at me, probably wondering if I'd gone mad because of today's stress. Yep! The whole world had; being insane was mainstream now.

"What? He's dead, and he's one of them. We can study him and find the cure. For Max... and all others."

"I thought you were joking."

"I'm dead serious, Dan! It doesn't matter that we are chemists. Even if we were the bloody Royal family, we'd have to do it. I don't know who's left out there. We might well be the last! If we don't do it, who will?"

He opened his mouth to protest, but I shook my head. "Look, if we don't try, we've fucked up. We've honestly fucked it up for everyone we love. What if Lesley is one of them now? Would you go to her and say, "Sorry, darling, I'm just a fucking chemist"?"

He glared at me, his face flashing with red spots. Expecting an angry response, I thought of other arguments I could throw at him to convince him. Instead of an answer, Dan grabbed the dead spleen-eater by the hands and dragged him down the stairs.

As we passed by ID29, I suppressed a desire to peek inside – I'd sleep better that way – but noted the leftovers of the body that the two spleen-eaters were playing with. I'll think about it later when I'm safe at ID26 and my stomach is full.

We took turns to drag the body back to ID26. Huffing, sweating, and cursing – the bony bastard turned out to be heavier than a floodbag, we were lucky not to encounter anything or anyone on our way. If I believed in god, I'd say that god had shown us some mercy, but from what I'd seen recently, mercy was not within god's remit.

"Did you get the meds? Where is Max?" Kay asked when she opened the door. Great. Instead of letting us in, she did the counting. Very scientific. Check the incoming data before you do anything with it.

"He was scratched. He chose to stay behind."

I might sound cynical – when don't I – but the rest was standard.

Kay prayed and cried.

Tanya took her meds first, then cried.

Edsie also had a wet eye. "He was a hero," he pronounced the pathetic bullshit so typical of him to say.

Dan poured us all a drink. I watched others drink but didn't touch mine.

Then, they turned their attention to Ali.

It was Dan's idea to name him Ali, a racist one, too. Why can't a guy with very dark skin, a black beard, and a Sikh turban on his head be Peter? Out of internal protest, I would prefer him to be Peter, but I must admit that Ali sounded more appropriate.

"What is this?" Edsie asked, prodding Ali with the toe of his shoe. "This isn't dinner, is it?"

It would be ironic for us to snack on Ali, considering that he wanted to snack on me in the last moment of his life.

"We have instant noodles," I reminded him.

Twenty-two packets, chicken flavour. And the shit pate, although the package said mackerel.

"That was Anna's idea," said Dan. "But I've dragged him around."

"I thought we could, you know… test him. The spleen-eaters are not dead; they are not like standard movie zombies. They are alive but a little… sick. So we can try to find a cure. That's what Ali is for."

Okay. That was not the best pitch, and I wish I prepared better. Made some slides. Rehearsed.

There was a tangible silence in the room while they gawked. Some of them might have thought that losing Max hit me too hard. Like a sledgehammer hard.

"If the idea is to stick him into the machine, he won't fit," said Edsie.

"Look," I said. "This might sound crazy, but we're sitting here doing nothing anyway, so why don't we do a bit of science? Try to figure out how we can stop this virus?"

"Is this what it is? A test sample?" asked Tanya, forgetting about crying for a moment. Yes! She could sometimes be a little emotional, but her scientific curiosity came first.

"I think more like a few samples." Dan snickered.

Kay cast him a disapproving look.

"Folks! Max might be dead by now, but more likely, he's one of them. Edsie, think of your wife. Kay, think of Sandy and the kids. Of all the people out there whom you love. We don't know what happened to them. I don't know what else we can do to help them. We can sit and wait for someone to rescue us, but if no one's coming, will we wait forever?"

I thought of the distance between Steve and me, endless miles of land and water that I couldn't cross. Was there anyone who could? Anyone or anything who could stand their ground against the millions of monsters?

And I thought about Max, the beamline engineer who loved a girl with golden hair called Genny. Max, who would reunite with her in Saint-Aupre.

If love was such an omnipotent thing, would it be able to pass my message to them, the man I loved and the man I only met two weeks ago?

Whatever I did, I did it for them.

Chapter 2. Ali

1.

Day 14, 18th of February, Sun, midnight

Steve and I sat at the table in a posh restaurant I'd never been to. The place was lit by candles and so cluttered with artificial roses that there was barely room for a few tables. Steve took a sip of beer, and when the relaxing classical music stopped halfway through the piece, he got down on one knee and asked me to marry him. It looked perfectly romantic – roses and candlelight – but something felt off, unnatural, like those roses or the candles that turned out to be plastic with LED flames.

Don't be boring, Anna, I told myself. Health and safety wouldn't allow real candles in a place like this. And what's wrong with you, anyway? Haven't you waited for this moment your whole life? Isn't Steve the One?

I shook off the unease and said yes to everyone's cheer and the pop of champagne. We kissed, and Steve slipped the ring on my finger. It was a gorgeous band of white metal, with a square amethyst shining in the candlelight. Steve knew I wasn't a fan of diamonds, and the purple gem was truly spectacular. I brought it up to admire the flickers of light in the gem.

"Do you like it? It's made of palladium, your favourite!"

I woke up, thrown out of the sparkly dream into the cold reality of my winter coat and the alcohol breath accumulated in the air. I was shivering, but that wasn't from the cold.

Palladium was the main reason we ended up so far from the people we loved.

Favourite, my arse!

You see, palladium does more than make shiny rings (half a thousand pounds in the high street shop!), it's also a perfect catalyst. Sometimes. The other times, it goes on vacation, chilling in the reaction vessel. The strong synchrotron X-rays could shed light on what made palladium so unreliable.

Did you like the pun?

The experiment wouldn't be easy. I'd bet the Ring bosses allowed us to come because they looked at our experimental plan and said, "Seriously? Let's have a look at those idiots!"

Since our chances of getting everything working were slim, we spent more than six months planning and preparing for all types of unexpected situations.

If our equipment didn't arrive on time, I carried an extra set of sensors in my suitcase. If our chemistry played up, we ordered an extra kilo of expensive palladium catalysts. If one of us died on the way, we had a team of five people instead of three advised.

That was supposed to be a joke, by the way.

Haha. Keep laughing.

Our contingency plan included a lot of things, except for this one. We've forgotten to prepare for a zombie parade!

Problems started as soon as we arrived at the Ring, but luckily, we had planned for these. Our chemical reaction went wrong straight away, and as an act of ultimate self-sacrifice, I moved into the wet chemistry lab, a few beamlines away from ID26, to supervise our potion 24/7. I saw little daylight and almost no people over the first two days, crawling out to the toilet or to get a quick snack from the vending machines. Every few hours, someone dropped in to update me on the latest news.

Kay was the first to mention the rumours about sick people attacking each other somewhere in South America. She shared her theory that it was a side-effect of some new drug the narco-cartels had cooked. After she left, I thought I dreamt the whole conversation in my half-zombie state.

On the second day, the previous team moved out of the beamline, and we took over the hutch with our equipment.

Our idea of a grand experiment was to turn the hutch into a gas chamber. Literally. Bubble carbon monoxide and air through methanol. Add a palladium catalyst. Pray. If it doesn't explode, you get ~~to live~~ fancy reaction products. An array of sensors continuously monitors the bubbling and brewing, which is maintained by chillers at a constant temperature and scanned with x-rays every five seconds.

Gas was our main problem. Carbon monoxide is lethal in high doses, and high doses is our middle name. The ventilation in the hutch was not designed for managing lots of gas, so we had to figure out how to do our experiment without pissing off the health and safety folks and dying from gas poisoning. That would make the health and safety folks unhappy, anyway.

Oh, let me mention those guys, I love them!

We'd met at least three different H&S officers, increasing in ranks until they reached the top of the top, and on the second day, the Boss of the Level came to check on us.

"What's the problème?" He asked. One of his minions blabbered back in French. I can't guarantee he didn't say something like "those stupid English suicidoes".

My French sucks.

The Boss walked around our set-up, poked at our gas cylinders, and looked at us, especially at Kay, who was at the "sign it off, or I'll bite your head off" stage.

"What's the problème?" He repeated. "The gas is in the hutch, and these guys are in the control room. Do not open the doors until the gas goes."

He signed off our installation, warned us about the gas alarms that would drive us crazy and disappeared into the Ring.

I met him again the next day. He was after my spleen.

We'd lost a lot of time at the health and safety level, but by the next day, I had conquered the chemistry, and we moved our reaction vessel to the hutch to start the experiment. Closer to dinner time, we got our first signal from the palladium, and the team sent me off with fireworks and fanfare as the hero of the day. I headed straight to the restaurant. I was about to have a steak.

You know the rest.

It's a sad story, isn't it?

And ironic – we have kilos of expensive palladium catalysts in our coffers, but today, they are worth a cat's bum. I'd happily swap all that palladium for a steak.

Isn't it odd how my thoughts always drift towards food? Automatically, I check the stash of instant noodles on the table. They'll last us a few days. After that, we'll call the Post-it notes to action again. Who will we lose this time?

We paid our tributes to Max last night. We didn't know him as much as we would have liked, but we shared a few stories about our days together, which felt right – the humans honour and remember their fallen.

It was a good word to describe what happened to Max. Not dead. Fallen.

Inspired by this idea, I wiped now-useless science gibberish from the large whiteboard and drew a long line through the middle, dividing the board into two parts. I wrote 'Dead' on the left and' Fallen' on the right. Then I scribbled the names in the left column: Andy, Ben, Ali. I didn't know the name of the woman whom I'd killed at the Central Building, but it wasn't right to leave her out, so I called her Emily.

"Who is that?" Edsie asked, pointing at the name.

I told them what happened to Emily, but I couldn't explain how much it haunted me, the sound and the vision of the poor woman's skull cracking in two, brains—

"Why don't we start keeping scores, then? Wouldn't it be fun?" said Edsie.

I turned back to the board, wiped the middle line, drew two more lines at a distance from each other, and wrote "Next" in the new middle column. Then I added "Edsie" to it.

Dan laughed.

"What does that mean?" asked Edsie.

"Exactly what it says. If you don't shut up, you're next!" Kay said.

"What's the problem? Haven't you seen zombie movies? They all do it!"

"Our spleen-eaters are not zombies, Edsie. They are not dead. Potentially, they can be cured. You don't kill people with Ebola, do you?"

Edsie didn't respond because even his little brain could process the "rhetorical question". But I could see from his face that it wasn't off the books for him.

You might wonder why I am so picky about Edsie. Trust me, it took me months of therapy and anger management sessions to be able to stay in the same building without trying to scratch his eyes out.

I was half a year into my PhD, with Edsie as my PhD supervisor. He barely turned up in the office or responded to my emails. I was struggling with lab work without guidance and advice, feeling like a failure every time my chemistry didn't work, which was pretty much *every time*. And still, after six months, I'd made something useful. 4 grams of powder! One more reaction left to do, an easy one I'd done a few times. It had never failed, so I charged all 4 grams of my powder into a flask, added the reagents, sealed it, and put it into the hot water bath to boil.

Then I left for lunch.

Forty minutes later, I was walking back to the lab, full and content, when the shriek of the fire alarm ran through the corridor.

"Blah," I thought, "didn't we already have one drill this week?"

The lab was full of smoke; the hot bath and the workstation were on fire. A man I didn't recognise attempted to start the fire extinguisher, but his hands shook so badly that he almost dropped it. Edsie was waving the smoke away from the smoke detector with one hand while brandishing my reaction flask in the other.

Why the hell did he take it out of the bath?

I snatched the extinguisher from the man, pulled the seals off and dozed the workstation with white foam until the smoke stopped coming out.

"What's happened here?" I shouted to Edsie over the alarm.

"We… we were… looking," he said, burped, and dropped the flask. The glass shattered, and the contents splashed all over the floor.

Edsie was drunk to shits.

I lost it.

I pointed the fire extinguisher at Edsie and dozed him in foam from head to toe so that only his twat nose was sticking out of it. Then I handed the extinguisher to Dan – where did he come from? – and jumped on Edsie with a banshee scream, pulling his hair out and scratching his face to get to his eyes under the layer of foam. Dan tore me off Edsie and dragged me out of the lab.

Six months of hard work. What would you do?

They had to stitch Edsie's face up, but after a conversation with the University seniors, he didn't press charges – the investigation found him guilty of serious health and safety misconduct. Firstly, he took a visitor – as drunk as Edsie himself – around the labs. Secondly, he switched off the extraction fans, removed my reaction flask from the water bath, and opened the seal. Even a big sign 'DO NOT OPEN! FIRE HAZARD!' did not stop him.

He set the six months of my hard work on fire because he was wasted. Befuddled. Laced. Plastered. Whatever you call it. Twats like Edsie are the reason why the English language has so many words for "drunk".

Dan took me in as a new supervisor after the Head of School made me go through anger management sessions: "A few people here would like to scratch Edsie's eyes out, and I don't really blame you. But I'm worried about your mental trauma, Anna."

Dan's and Edsie's labs were adjacent, so I couldn't avoid Edsie forever, even if he ran away screaming every time he saw me.

"He's a special character, but he isn't going away… you have to learn to live with him," said Dan.

"Like with a wart?" I asked.

Over the next few years, I'd learnt to co-habit with Edsie, too: I stopped noticing him, and he stopped shitting his pants at my name. We'd established an unannounced truce that lasted until I graduated and moved to Glasgow, hoping to never see his twat nose again.

Isn't it ironic?

But now, lying in the dark, unable to sleep because of my memories, thoughts, and his snoring, annoying and reassuring at the same time, I ask myself – would I get upset if the spleen-eaters got him? Kay says love should embrace all human beings, but I don't think my love can stretch as big as Edsie.

And still…

I might miss him.

2.

Sunday.

What a holy day for our unholy undertakings!

Do I sound more optimistic to you? That's because I've had a full meal for the first time in many days. My death from starvation is postponed, and my brain can focus on things unrelated to food.

With that in mind, the Ali thing was a bit rushed.

What on Earth will four chemists (and Edsie) do with a human body? To start with, none of us has the slightest idea of what a spleen looks like.

Before we even get to the spleens, our biggest problem is the samples.

There is a massive difference between Ali, a dead body of a spleen-eater, and *samples* of Ali. Somehow, we had to convert Ali from one whole into a few smaller bits. Now, who is comfortable with this kind of "conversion"?

Even though poor Ali tried to eat me, I held no grudge. He used to be a human being, after all, one of us. He got infected and hunted people for their spleens – we fought back and killed him. That was a natural sequence of life.

Being cut into *samples* is not natural at all.

Dan and Edsie dragged Ali onto the hutch workshop table, and we gathered around it. The view of the dead body wasn't shocking anymore – compared to the horrors of the Ring, Ali looked almost peaceful in his death.

If not for one thing.

"What's happened to his face?" asked Edsie.

"And where is his eye?" echoed Tanya.

Dan shrugged. We brought what we had, not that the menu was vast.

"We have to undress him first," Kay announced what we were all thinking.

Nobody moved.

"He won't rise and eat us!" Kay tried to convince herself.

I winced. "It's not that. It's... wrong."

As if I would try to undress Edsie while he was sleeping... Yikes!

Unexpectedly, this thought helped. Ali was nowhere near as disgusting as Edsie.

I stepped forward and grabbed Ali's shoes. It made sense to start from the feet. Feet are not awkward. Men have feet. Women have feet. Everybody has feet. I hoped that by the time I got to the part that *not* everybody had, someone would come for help.

And they all did, fully undressing Ali within a minute, apart from his knickers and turban. Dan swept away the shreds of his pullover, shirt, and trousers.

"Do we need to do that?" Tanya pointed at the underwear.

"I don't think his spleen is in his groin," said Dan.

We all exhaled with relief.

Ali was a man of unimpressive muscularity; his legs looked like bony hairy sticks. His torso's skin was slightly darker than mine but all covered with bushy black hair. Calling him Ali was a bit premature – obviously a Sikh, his nationality or descent was not so clear-cut anymore.

Dead, stripped of the dignity that clothes give, observed like a museum exhibit, he was not far from becoming a sample, but I struggled to stop thinking of him as human. I couldn't do it...

Nobody looked keen. I was about to suggest Post-it notes when Kay pointed at Tanya.

"Didn't you use to work at the butcher's, Tanya? Isn't it sort of the same?"

What?

Butcher's?

I didn't know what was more shocking – the idea of Tanya, fragile and tiny, working at the butcher's (as who? as a mincer technician?), the overall comparison of the two very unrelated activities, or the way Kay so blatantly "volunteered" Tanya for the task.

Dan picked his jaws from the floor. "Ehm, Post-it notes?"

"Yeah, great idea!" I cheered through the awkwardness of the moment.

Let's rewind the last thirty seconds of this bizarre conversation and pretend they never happened.

"I did work at the butcher's," Tanya said in a voice so grave that you could bury people in it. "I guess I'll do it, then."

She picked up the scalpel with a shaking hand and stepped towards Ali, her face the same colour as his. You don't have to, I wanted to shout. Kay can't tell you what to do, especially if she doesn't have the guts to do it herself.

Ah, screw it!

I snatched the scalpel out of Tanya's hand, nearly cutting my thumb off, gritted my teeth, and pushed the blade under Ali's ribs.

Shit, I wasn't trained for this! I am a chemist; if postmortem exams ever made it to my bucket list, they would be somewhere between drinking methanol and staging a coup d'etat in North Korea.

It shouldn't be a big deal, right? Pathologists, med students, CSI folks – they do it all the time and would consider themselves lucky to work on such a nice body – *almost* no injuries, no decomposition, but a sweet, slightly nauseating smell.

Ali was an exemplary cadaver in all senses.

Maybe, drinking methanol was not such a bad idea?

It's a body, Anna. And it's dead. No complains. No wiggling.

I completed a circle around Ali's belly with the scalpel and peeled the skin off to reveal a small layer of fat underneath. Something resembling a sack of muscle tissue was protecting the internal organs. I cut it off and tossed it in the bucket.

Edsie ran out of the hutch, unable to watch; Kay and Tanya followed him in a minute. Dan's face turned green and yellow, and his jaw muscle strained in a funny but uncomfortable expression.

"You don't have to be here," I told him. "I will call if I need help."

He shook his head. "I killed him. I owe him at least that."

While I took out and separated Ali's organs from each other, I thought of how easy it would be for any of us to become a body on the table. One bite. One hit with an axe. The distance between a researcher and a test subject suddenly became intangible.

Would my colleagues cut me into pieces, too?

Would I care by then?

***

"I think that's all," I put away the scalpel and examined the results of my work. Carefully separated from blood vessels, the organs were laid on the other workshop table. They stank a bit rotten and looked unappetising, but I counted it a success for a first-time job.

"What's next?" I asked nonchalantly as if I'd been butchering dead bodies daily straight after brushing my teeth. If I could pry my fingers off the scalpel before anyone noticed the telltale tremor locking them in place.

"Don't we need to label them?" asked Kay, walking back into the hutch.

This is where the real problems began.

If you studied biology at school, which I hope you did, you would have an approximate idea of where things are in the human body. Stomach, liver, kidneys, heart, lungs.

But.

For obvious reasons, high school biology doesn't include looking at the real-life organs. Their cartoon representation in the textbooks is schematic at best and doesn't convey the organs' actual shape or colour. When they are out of the body, you no longer have a clue about their original position. That is why forensic pathologists take photos at every examination stage, something we didn't think about until it was too late.

With high school biology being a distant memory, we managed to identify the heart, the lungs, and the kidneys. We also had a plausible candidate for stomach – with higher uncertainty.

"This should be it." Dan pointed at the small organ 5 inches long.

"I am sure this is liver," said Edsie. "Missus had surgery on her liver, and they told her that the left lobe was intact."

Indeed, the organ looked like it had two parts to it.

"What about this squishy thing?"

"Don't touch anything! You don't know if he is still infectious!"

"The squishy thing should be it."

"Or this one?"

"I thought the spleen wasn't very big."

"Yeah, but I thought that stomach was like a massive sack, and this one is tiny."

"This might not be stomach at all."

"Aren't you supposed to find the food remains in the stomach?"

"Wanna have a look?"

"Can you please stop picking the… uh, samples from the table, guys?"

"Can we focus? What are our options? Can anyone remember what else is in that area?"

"If he ate someone's spleen before he died, will we find it in his stomach?"

"But that would be a healthy spleen; we need one with a virus."

"Edsie, just admit you are *dying* to peek into this poor guy's stomach for whatever reason!"

"Pancreas?"

Everyone turned to me.

"I've completely forgotten about the pancreas," admitted Kay. Everyone nodded.

"God knows what else we forgot about," said Edsie. "We need more information, more knowledge."

Internet. That's called the internet.

"We still have electricity, so why not the network?" said Edsie.

"We've tried before," Kay reminded.

I walked to the laptop and powered it on. "Still dead."

"There was a power cut the day after the shitfall; there's a good chance that killed the Wifi, but not the fibre," said Dan. "Maybe, the only thing we need to do is restart the modem somewhere in the EHO office."

"What, turn it off and back on again?" said Kay.

The EHO office, or the Experimental Hall Operators' office, is like the NASA flight control room, where the engineers run the synchrotron, the beamlines, and everything attached to it. If there was an ON/OFF switch for anything in the synchrotron, it would be there.

No, no, no. Wait a second!

It's on the other bloody side of the Ring!

"EHO office? If you forgot, there are hundreds of monsters out there. You saw them yourself, Dan. There's no way we can get past them."

"I'd hope they all moved to the toilets now. Or climbed after us through the window," Dan muttered.

A few did. The others are still there, waiting for fresh spleens.

"This time, we go all together," said Kay. "Grab more weapons. Cover each other's backs."

No. No way. The more people go, the more we'll lose.

"We don't even know why the internet is down," I said.

"Anna, you can stay if you want. We'll be back soon." Kay patted my shoulder.

I looked around and sighed. The prospect of facing the hungry beasts didn't enthuse me, but even less than that, I fancied staying in this concrete bunker on my own. What if something happens to all of them? I'll be the last, slowly going insane from solitude, like a ghost stuck in this miserable world forever.

No, thank you.

With these positive thoughts, let's go.

Sample Date	18/02/2024
Sample Name	ALI-001
Category	~~Fuck knows~~ pending
Source	Ali, ~~zombie, spleen-eater~~, *infected, last stage (this means he turned)*, male, ca. 45 years old
Notes	Frozen at 16.43
Sampled by	Anna Evans-Bond
Notes by	Dan Torren
Corrections by	*Kay Newmann*

3.

Has the idea of turning the modem off and on again seemed unscientific to you? There could be a million reasons why the network was down – from a broken signal mast to power supply issues. From that perspective, our venture was like sticking a finger into the air.

Science is all about sticking fingers into the air. Or into things you probably shouldn't touch.

Ali comes to mind.

The start of our journey was sombre, but prepared this time, I was less disturbed by the view of carnage and destruction. The others were shaken. Tanya and Kay threw up in unison at the sight of the first mauled body. Who could blame them – that was my first reaction, too.

We entered the outer hall opposite ID27 and soon passed the first door leading to the offices. Last time, a crowd of monsters waited for us on the other side, so we walked past it to the next door, two beamlines up the Ring. It greeted us with a welcome present – three fresh bodies lying in a pool of blood. It hadn't dried yet, glistening festively on the ripped skin and shreds of muscle. I saw the muscles twitch and flinched away, my heartbeat skyrocketing.

Cockroaches can live without their heads for up to a week.

This door had a glass panel, offering a full view of what awaited us on the other side. Spleen-eaters. Nothing new.

Black humour or not, now Dan calls them test subjects.

"On the positive side, the EHO office is through this door to our right. On the negative side, I see two problems," I said, peeking through the glass.

"Two? There are at least thirty of them!"

"That's *one* problem. The EHO office has restricted card access. Anyone happens to have a pass?"

That was a rhetorical question. Only the synchrotron engineers were allowed into this sacred temple of X-ray science.

"How about those folks? Some of them might be locals." Edsie pointed at the spleen-eaters on the other side of the glass panel.

Indeed, some monsters had white EHO cards dangling on their chests. Stumbling around with nowhere to go in the limited space of the corridor and unable to use their passes to get through the doors, they seemed to be sleepwalking, but I knew how quickly the spleen-eaters snapped into action.

"You're not suggesting we jump on them to grab the pass?" asked Dan.

Yeah, it would be easier to take a collar off a rabid dog in the middle of the rabid dog pack.

"We need to distract them," Edsie said.

I had two things to tell him. One: we'd already lost Max because of these "distracting manoeuvres". Two: he'd chosen a broken chair leg as his weapon against a horde of zombies! How could I even trust his judgment?

"Here's the idea," Edsie continued. "This corridor goes parallel to the Ring, so there should be another entrance further. From there, we'll loop back to the EHO office. Then we will lure one of them around the corner, hit it on the head, and take the card."

"What about the rest of them who will follow?" I asked.

"What if the *lured* guy does not have a card?"

"Yes, how many will we have to hit until the guys with a pass turn up?"

"What do we do with the guys between us and the office, even if we have a card?"

"Okay, okay," said Edsie, "I didn't say it's gonna be a Nobel Prize winner."

Still, it had juice. If this door was a no-go, the next one could do better. We continued up the Ring, Dan taking the lead as he always did, Edsie and Kay following close behind, and Tanya and I trailing at the end.

"Where do you think these monsters went?" she whispered, pointing at the two bodies at the door. "I have an awful feeling about it."

I felt the hairs rising on my arms and rubbed my skin through the lab coat fabric. If it were Edsie preaching the doomsday coming, I wouldn't give a shit, but Tanya had a supernatural sense for dodgy things about to happen. Countless times, she appeared out of nowhere to fix our vacuum pump a minute before it imploded! Or that once, when she dropped into the lab on her day off and found Arina passed out on the floor – a broken carbon monoxide detector would cost Arina her life.

Even without a sixth sense, it was clear chances for a happy ever after were slim. The further we moved up the Ring, the worse the devastation became. The carnage around ID29 was heartstopping, but this was a new level of horror. In places, bodies piled up into macabre barricades: guts torn out, blood splashed on the floor, fingers, eyes and noses missing, chewed away by the rats. Blood stains and smudges covered the walls like art straight from the depths of a psychopath's mind. There were a few spleen-eaters' bodies, too, distinguishable by the milky gauze over their forever-open eyes.

At least someone had evened the score.

I didn't look at the faces or check their badges anymore. With every face and name added to my memory, soon, there would be too many to co-exist peacefully; they would start fighting for limited space in my poor brain, and I would go crazy. I hadn't killed them, so why did I feel so guilty?

My thoughts drifted back to Steve. Was he still human, or was he after the spleens? No, no way. He was strong, fast-thinking and resourceful; he would know how to survive.

Who was I trying to fool? Survival was a lottery that had nothing to do with smartness or thinking; otherwise, how would this citadel of science fall so quickly?

"Hush," Dan stopped. "I can hear something."

I stumbled into Kay's back. Scared, she dropped her hammer on the floor with a loud bang. We froze. Everything remained still. I slowly breathed out and leant to pick up the hammer just as a lone spleen-eater strolled from behind BM01.

It's like love at first sight. There's always that ever-lasting nanosecond when they look at you and know that you are destined to make a tasty dinner. They can't *see* with those milky eyes, but they *know*.

"Run." I pushed Kay.

She didn't move. Two more spleen-eaters followed from around the corner and dashed across the corridor without hesitation.

I pulled Kay's hand and raised the axe, ready to smash. But then I recognised the spleen-eater.

"This is Mary Tighe. I didn't know she was at the Ring!"

"Anna, smash her!" Dan shouted.

What was he talking about? It would be like running into Lady Gaga at the records store and then trying to cut her throat with a vinyl! Mary Tighe was the godmother of palladium! I thought she had retired, but there she was, right in front of me—

Until Dan's wrench went through the side of Mary's head, and her brain splashed out on the wall behind.

"Anna, what the fuck, that's a bloody monster! Run!"

A switch flipped inside of me, and I bolted.

I ran as fast as I could until my lungs burnt so much that little black flies appeared in front of my eyes. Dying for air, I slammed into the wall. Right beside me, the door to the disabled toilet stood open like an invitation. I stumbled inside, shut the door and locked it behind me, leaning against it as my pulse thudded in my ears.

The silence hit me.

I was alone.

Seriously?

While I ran forward, where we planned to go, everyone else ran who knows where and now, I am here, in this disabled toilet, all by myself, like a little girl lost in an international airport.

Just me.

On my own.

Mommy!

4.

It might sound weird, but I've never felt lonely in my life.

As a single child, sometimes I wished for a playmate, but such wishes were fleeting. When I was five, I saw a camel spit at the zookeeper. I decided it would be awesome to have one in our back garden so that the next time Mr Mason, our grumpy neighbour, complained about my football in his flowers, I'd bring the camel out and make it spit. I wanted a sibling as much as I wanted that camel – for five minutes or so.

My Mom and Dad loved me more than the world; their love wrapped me like Mom's old shawl that, after all these years, still smelled of her perfume. They encouraged me to fly solo and free, and knowing that they were always there for me, I never felt scared or lonely. I had them, and after I'd learnt to open cupboards and unscrew lids, I had my chemistry to keep me company.

Over the weekends, I spent hours on my own mixing potions from baking soda, vinegar, and lentils, watching the bubbles of released gas push the lentils up in a mesmerising dance. Sometimes, I added food colourants and glitter or swapped vinegar for water and added the powders from the bath bomb-making kit I got for Christmas.

One day, I ran out of baking powder and decided to try flour instead. When the bubbles didn't come, I cried in front of Dad, but he barely lifted his head from the fantasy book he was reading.

"Now spit in it!" he told me, providing the first insight into catalysis. "Like a camel!"

The image of Dad, snuggled on the sofa with a book, cat snoring next to him, would always be stored in my mind's library of happy moments, no matter where I went or who I was with.

Even when Mom and Dad vanished in the middle of the ocean, I felt their presence as if they were still holding my hand. It was hard to grasp the idea that they wouldn't be coming home – why not if their love was still there and I could wear it like armour.

So, what the hell was so fucking special about this disabled cubicle that I felt so scared, whining like a trapped rat? Mom and Dad didn't raise me a sissy. Frustrated with myself, I smashed the plastic bin with my axe, almost chopping it into two. The contents fell out on the floor, stained, stinky, gooey, and I flinched away from the smell.

That's what self-pity looks like, Anna. We keep going.

I peeked out of the disabled toilet and scanned the surrounding area. The door to the office corridor was a mere five feet away. I tiptoed out of my "self-pity cabin" and listened for sounds on the other side. It seemed quiet. I pressed my pass to the card reader, and after the light turned green, squeezed through a little gap and slowly – a millimetre at a time – pulled the door to close. Despite my efforts, it shut behind me with a loud thump. I froze, listening for the slightest change in the air vibrations.

Nothing. Breathe.

When I breathed out, a monster appeared from around the corner. I'd never seen such big spleen-eaters before – shaped like a globe, rather than a human, he consisted of two hemispheres: the Northern hemisphere was made up of chin and eyes; the Southern one must have had legs under the fat. This semi-human construction was steadily approaching me, growling.

How the hell had he survived? With that fitness level, he was destined to be a meal, not a hunter.

Two spleen-eaters followed him out of the corridor. I touched my pass on the card reader. It beeped, and the light turned red.

Oh, dear. Let's try again.

Beep. Red.

Oh, fuck.

I turned to face the incoming monsters, prepared to swing it for my life. One of them pushed the globe-man out of the way and lunged at me, driving my back into the door. I screamed, swinging my axe in the air, but the monster was too close, and the axe couldn't get it.

Instead, I hit the alarm button.

"Attention, this is not a training alarm. Please proceed to the nearest exit! Attention, ce n'est pas une formation! Veuillez vous diriger vers la sortie la plus proche!"

It was a sound from hell. The shrieking voice that couldn't be human stabbed me in the right ear, drilled through my brain and escaped through my left eye, leaving an explosion of headache in its wake. I looked around, hoping to find a black hole to crawl into, a magical place devoid of sounds.

Then I realised that the monsters didn't eat me.

They were writhing on the floor in pain, trying to twist into embryo positions and hide their heads between their knees. Blood was trickling from their ears through their fingers.

Ouch. They don't like loud noises!

Neither did I enjoy the sound of the alarm, but soon my ears adjusted to the inhumane voice, and I started discerning other sounds – screams, hustling, moaning. Unexpectedly fast for his complexion, the globe-man had compacted his blob body into the corner, obtaining a cube shape instead. I ran past him and peeked into the corridor. Dozens of monsters, disoriented and covered in blood, were running around looking for shelter, colliding with each other and crashing into the walls and doors, unable to open them.

I walked through the chaos like Moses through the parted sea – okay, a bit faster than that – straight to the EHO office. Two dead bodies sprawled near the door happened to have their passes on them. One was fully covered in dried blood, so I picked up the cleaner one, carefully pulling the lanyard over the man's head.

"Jean Villeparillon, Experimental Hall Control Officer."

Merci, Jean. Rest in peace.

I touched the card onto the card reader. The red light on the lock switched to green, making me exhale in relief. I snuck into the office and shut the door behind me.

Phew.

The EHO office was empty and quiet, the ungodly shrieking of the fire alarm half-swallowed by the silence inside. Sixteen desks were arranged in four neat rows, like in a classroom, but instead of a whiteboard, a large screen displayed signals from the beamlines – all reading "OFF". The big red LED display for the storage ring energy showed 0.0 GeV. The Ring was dead.

I scanned the room. All desks had name tags, except one in the right corner, with a "Shift control" sticker. A panel of switches and dials labelled in good old English took over half of the wall next to the shift control desk. I found the "Fire alarm" switch, flipped it and tadam!

The resulting silence whacked me on the head.

"Test," I pronounced aloud, checking my ears were still functioning. "Pal-la-di-um."

My trained eye located a Snickers bar hidden behind an open laptop with the sticker "JV". Look at that! Unless there was another JV, Jean kept providing, even in his death!

Inspired by this find, I rummaged through the rest of desks and drawers, piling up all edible goodies on Jean's desk. The pile was astonishing, although high in carbs. Had the control engineers been unconsciously preparing for an apocalypse? Because with this amount of food, I could last a few weeks on my own.

It would be very bad if I had to last on my own.

I would also develop diabetes.

I started thinking more productively while chewing the Snickers bar. There wasn't much I could do for my friends apart from praying, and considering I was a non-believer, it probably would make no sense. I had always been an applied type, so now that I had some energy, I could apply it to—

Internet.

I hoped to find the "Internet" switch right next to the "Fire Alarm", but that would be too good and, of course, didn't happen. There could be something worthwhile inside all the computers, but...

God bless the guys who stick their passwords to their screens!

I powered up the desktop to the right from Jean's, logged in using the details provided by 'gmarchant' [password Grego1974ry], waited for the screen to load, and clicked straight on the globe icon. The error message was the same as in the ID26 desktop computer ID26. "Le réseau n'est pas disponible. Réessayez plus tard".

While I was considering the next steps, the screen rolled out a Windows-95-style interface with numerous small black and white squares, each with a number and a time stamp.

CCTV!

Not the network I hoped for, but in a way, even better!

Every hutch had a camera that sent a picture to the beamline desktop and the EHO office – in case someone got stuck in the hutch while the X-rays were on. I'd never paid attention to the cameras outside the beamline, but they were directed almost at every room, lab, or workshop.

I clicked the camera under "ID26, main"; there it was, our shelter, our home. With a warm, even nostalgic feeling, I found the coffee cups left on the computer table. Six of them, but now we used Max's to store the tea bags for reuse.

I was crying. What if I never see them again?

What if they are all dead now?

Holy Odin or Jesus, whoever you are, I promise I will not pick on Edsie ever again; please, don't let anything happen to them!

I sobbed, flicking through the camera views.

Camera ID15 AB, pan. A massive horde of the spleen-eaters. So many that they didn't fit in the view.

Camera ID16 and ID13, pan – same.

Camera ID16, hutch – four people, moving. Alive?

Camera BM07, a few spleen-eaters.

Camera ID03, hutch – one person. No movement.

I was about to turn the cameras off when the fire alarm rang again. I jumped on my chair, wondering if I'd accidentally pressed something on the computer. But no, it wasn't me.

A real fire alarm two minutes after a fake one? What are the chances?

It's a glitch, I told myself. I was about to switch it off when it hit me – if we had a real fire inside the Ring, we were screwed with nowhere to evacuate. With that thought, I turned on the view from the "main entrance" camera.

Hundreds of spleen-eaters had gathered around the Ring, and more were coming from all directions. The fire alarm outside the Ring wasn't loud enough to harm the monsters, so instead, it invited them for dinner!

Great job, Anna! And what are we going to do with this zombie party outside? This is the end of our restaurant hopes unless we build a helicopter from scraps and wires and fly away, Hollywood-style, uplifting music playing into the credits.

A loud bash at the door interrupted the works of my imagination. The door handle twitched. I grabbed the axe and dashed to the door, preparing to mince anything that dared to enter.

Nothing did. The handle didn't give in.

Breathe, Anna, breathe. The room is card-locked, and the monsters haven't yet learnt to use their passes. I leant on the door, chuckling at myself. Then I heard a familiar click, and the door started opening. I stepped aside, staring at the widening gap like a bunny at a python.

If it's a spleen-eater coming to eat me, it's a genius one, first of a kind, and maybe, in this case, Anna, you shouldn't be too upset to meet your end.

"Anna, it's us!" Dan shouted into the gap before he squeezed into the room, followed by Edsie and Tanya. Kay got inside last, shut the door behind her and leant on it, breathless.

I dashed to the control panel and flipped the alarm switch. The silence that dropped over the room was so thick that I could slice it for sandwiches. Four red and sweaty faces stared at me as if I were an exotic animal for a limited sale at John Lewis.

"What?" I asked. "I am not dead."

Kay jabbed me with her finger, and I flinched at her razor-sharp nail. She threw her arms around me in a fierce bear hug, squeezing the air out of my lungs. While I gasped for breath, I caught a glimpse of Edsie, his hands inching towards my chocolate stash.

"I told them you had a thing about fire drills!" he said.

After I wiggled out of Kay's arms, Dan told me what happened when we separated. They brought down the two monsters (rest in peace, Sweet Mary of Palladium!) and then hid inside the ID02 beamline until they were sure nothing was following them.

"We searched for food, too," explained Kay. "And look what we've got!"

Tanya held a medium-sized pot with a plant about twenty inches tall. It had familiar leaves, shaped almost like feathers, covered in tiny green hairs. I squinted as if it would help me identify it.

"It's a tomato!" Tanya beamed.

I blinked and stared at her.

"We gonna have tomatoes!" she explained, with less radiance this time. "Vitamins."

There wasn't a single flower on the green stem, and I wondered if Tanya was familiar with the timelines of tomato harvesting. If she was, was she pessimistic or, on the contrary, too optimistic about our survival chances?

I turned to Dan for explanations. He shrugged.

"We thought we'd lost you so... Tanya's cried out half of her body weight in tears. If not for this silly plant, this place would be a swimming pool. Let her have it."

Hm. Should I be grateful that I was missed so much or annoyed that my value as a human being was equal to that of a tomato plant?

As long as she doesn't call it after me.

"We left ID02 when the fire alarm rang," Dan said. "The monsters popped out of everywhere like fucking ants, completely yahoo, running around like mental, smashing into each other, fighting, blood gushing out of their ears! And they paid us nada attention as if we were ghosts. But when the alarm suddenly stopped, they all were coming back around quickly. So, we hid in the toilets, made a plan, and here we go. One of the folks outside this office landed us his pass."

Reunited with my friends again, I realised I was silly to think I'd lost them forever. I'd even promised not to pick on Edsie ever again, but when he grabbed the second chocolate from my goodies stash, I decided that promises made in a state of temporary disorientation were not supposed to be kept.

With five of us present again, the stash no longer looked that impressive.

Having company is great, but rationing sucks.

While they were snacking, I recounted how I discovered the amazing effects of the fire alarm and showed them the cameras. After the fire alarm stopped, the spleen-eaters regained their stance and flocked back to their favourite places. The crowd at ID15 looked even bigger than before.

"What's attracting them so much to that room?" Kay asked.

I kicked myself for not noticing it before. The spleen-eaters around ID15 were very determined, fixed on something inside the hutch, like those monsters outside the conference suite in the Central Building.

"As if there's a telly they all want to watch," said Dan.

"A football match," snickered Edsie.

We all thought of the EURO 2024 that was supposed to happen this summer. No chance of that anymore unless team ID26 finds a cure while chomping Ali into bits.

Sorry, I know I sound bitter. Steve and I had talked a lot about having a family. All these years into the relationship, we knew we were ready for our happily ever after. Steve had bought tickets for the final match. He was going to propose during the break.

I'd never considered myself romantic; I'd always preferred the order of practicality to the whim of emotion. But I wanted my engagement to be different, probably a little old-fashioned. I was waiting for Steve to do the knee and ring thing as they showed in the movies.

Why not? My engagement, my rules.

He's been waiting for a perfect moment.

I might never see him again.

I wiped off an unwanted teardrop and turned back to the others.

"So, we are all here, but what's the point? I haven't found anything to do with the Internet. Lots of funky switches, but all useless."

To strengthen my point, I kicked the glass covering the switch panel.

"Ah, don't worry about that. We've turned it back on. There is a main switchboard right outside. How come you didn't notice it?"

While I was gawking, bedazzled, Dan pushed me away from the computer, typed in "zombie apocalypse" in the browser address line and turned the screen to the others. Photos, articles, tweets, and video previews jumped at my face, flashing such gruesome details that I choked.

"Your phone should have automatically connected, too," he said, smiling.

I pulled my phone out of my jeans pocket. Steve's face, dark chocolate from suntan, winked at me from the screensaver before transferring me to the main screen. I hit the Wetherspoons app twice before I finally touched the green WhatsApp icon next to it and found Steve's name at the top of the conversations list.

"Last seen today at 10.46".

5.

My first call to Steve went unanswered, returning the dialling beeps, each like a stab through my bleeding heart. What if WhatsApp was wrong? What if Steve was already dead? What if he'd never pick it up? I handed the phone to Kay and coiled in the corner, shivering from adrenaline, while my friends reconnected with their loved ones.

Dan cooed with Lesley in the opposite corner, laughing over something only two of them understood. Dan's face lit up with love and joy, and I thought with a bit of jealousy that I hadn't seen him glow like that in a very long time. Would I see the same glow on Steve's face? Would I see Steve at all?

Kay also reached her family sheltered in her in-laws' sheep farm on the border between Scotland and Northumbria. The virus hadn't even landed in the UK, and only scarce reports popped up on the internet, when Kay's husband Sandy and their two children packed their suitcases and left Glasgow.

It saved their lives. Or maybe it was Kay's prayers?

Nobody was prepared when the COVID-19 outbreak set the world on fire in 2020. No, it didn't come as an utter surprise – a pandemic wiping out half of the world population was the first of the possible "end of the world scenarios", but nobody took it seriously until that Chinese guy made a wrong choice for dinner.

According to Tanya, that was the official version.

A couple of years after we'd dealt with COVID-19, the UN, WHO, and other important people got together to prepare the world for the next outbreak. Their plan, called "Lock and Block", prescribed establishing a total area lockdown within 24 hours. Isolate the area, move in the military, fence off the perimeter, and shoot anyone who tries to escape.

The last one's a joke. Sort of.

The plan outlined how the isolated area would go around its everyday life so that the uninfected would not get infected and those with a virus would get the necessary treatment.

But.

The plan didn't expect the infected to be so active in spreading the virus. The Lock and Block quarantine was developed for people wanting their lives back, not their friends' spleens.

When the first infected appeared in Grenoble, I was stuck in the lab with little connection to the real world and didn't know something had gone wrong. Even if they tried to implement quarantine here, it didn't look like it worked. In Glasgow, they successfully Locked and Blocked everyone inside the city.

And then, they dropped the bomb.

The spleen-eaters, the evacuating people, the refugees from the neighbouring towns that flooded into the city expecting order and protection – thousands of people wiped off the face of the Earth… Not by the virus but by the cowardly people who had no better idea.

"I won't be able to sleep, ever," said Dan.

He'd finished his call with Lesley, and we sat scrolling through the photos of what was left of Glasgow. The injured trying to escape the streets a few hours after the bombing while the dust was still settling over the dead bodies. Mothers desperately calling their children's names. An old man crying over the body of a dead dog.

"I don't know anything about God. But I believe in some sort of Universal justice. I will pray for those who did it to burn in hell," Tanya said, her voice unusually stern.

"This is not how it works," said Kay, her voice shaking with tears.

She'd hung up and now stood behind us, watching. I could not imagine how it felt – to see her home wiped off the face of the Earth. Not even her faith could stand strong against those images.

"Is this, then?" Dan pointed at the screen.

She didn't answer.

When Kay finished, I offered my phone to Tanya, but she declined, saying she had no family left. Edsie wasn't too keen on phoning Stefania, his wife, and I wondered if the rumours that Edsie was on the brink of divorce were true.

I tried Steve again in an hour. The second time lucky, he picked up after two dials. When his face appeared on my screen, I froze, speechless, dubmbstruck, the unspoken longing inside me so intense that I couldn't breathe.

I saw new wrinkles and dark circles under his blue eyes. They made him look older and gloomier, and he was almost unrecognisable with a newly-grown ginger beard. No, it was still the man I loved and would marry one day – we had a chance for a happy ever after. After I crawl out of this shithole with a c—

Focus, Anna. He's talking to you!

What is he saying?

"I was helping to fix the fence at Mom and Dad's house. Dad invited me to stay for dinner, but Mom rushed home early from work and asked us to pack as fast as we could. She talked about Lock and Block, but we thought it was a joke. There was nothing on TV besides an odd mention of the patients' attacks on the A and E personnel. But her face, you should have seen it! She was dead serious. She ran upstairs to her room to throw things into a suitcase… I asked her where she would go if they locked us down. She looked at me as if I was insane and said, "You can't lock down everyone." She wanted me to start packing Dad's clothes; they would fit me, and there was no time to return to our house. We had to leave the city now, get away from the people… I went to call Dad in from the garden. I didn't know Mom had been scratched."

They locked my future mother-in-law, or the thing she turned into, in the basement.

"It was too late to get out of the city anyway, and where would we go? I thought of Carol's farm, but we wouldn't reach the first junction on the motorway. The streets were a choker. So, we went out, stashed plenty of food from the supermarket, and then returned to Dad's house. We've been camping out here from day one."

I listened to him but didn't hear much, sending every word into a separate drawer in the depths of my mind. I'd revisit it later when I could think straight. When I could think at all.

The flood of love I felt was bigger than the world. If I were standing, it would throw me off my feet and send me into a whirlpool of emotions. I was breaking into atoms and rebonding again in an unstoppable chain reaction, as if I had fallen in love at first sight, like in one of the romantic novels Mom loved reading before bed.

I had never experienced anything like that until now. In reality, my love for Steve came dressed as a friendship and didn't reveal its true nature for a while. It made sense. I'd never been a "strike of lightning" kind of girl or believed in the "spark passed between them".

Seeing him alive felt like that spark!

But, after the initial excitement gradually went flat, something else crept in, something dark and confusing.

I found myself awkward and out of place as if I ran out into a crowd undressed. I wanted to be home, fighting monsters alongside the man I loved; to keep watch in the same shift and fall asleep in his arms when someone else took over; to go on food raids with him, knowing that we worked and thought as one and would never run in the opposite directions.

I was in the wrong place.

"We've established a zombie-free zone, clear from the virus; at first, a few houses in the perimeter. But survivors kept coming in, and we spread over the whole street, from the main road to the park. We blocked it with the large HGVs on both sides. We have people on watch 24 hours, patrols walking the streets, and two police officers from the Bournville station. They brought some good ammo and guns."

The discrepancy between my memory of Steve and this guy on the screen became hard to ignore. This Steve looked rough, had a fresh, deep scar on his cheek, and spoke of the things I could never imagine my Steve to speak. He said, "clearing of the routes", "patrols", "zombie-free zone", "ammo", and "watch". My soft-hearted and gentle boyfriend had turned into a warrior.

The thought made me uncomfortable. While Steve and his ex-army dad worked hard to clear the area from the spleen-eaters and protect the vulnerable neighbours and refugees, what was I doing? They created barricades and went on food raids, picking up supplies and bringing uninfected survivors. They worked to establish medical help and quarantine wards for newcomers. They sent out rescue missions. Barely two weeks had passed since the Apocalypse started, and they had done so much already! What was I doing apart from hiding in the bunker? Apart from surviving?

It seemed that surviving was not enough.

"We have a good range of weapons, but most of the time, keeping it quiet works. Recently, we brought in a group of survivors, among them three nurses and a doctor. Marla is an ophthalmic surgeon but is great with basic injuries. She stitched Dad after an accident with one of our border trucks. They are now working on setting up a treatment centre in the West Heath Hospital. Or what's left of it. We must establish a safety perimeter around it – that's our next major move."

"What do you do if people get scratched or bitten?" I asked.

He shrugged. "They turn too quickly. Of course, we try not to shoot without an emergency, but…"

How many stories can one single word hold?

But.

When I met Steve at a freshers' party, he was a first-year veterinary student, and I was about to start my chemistry degree. We instantly connected with each other. Steve told me funny stories about his part-time job as a vet assistant. His care for all his patients, were they beloved pets or rabid foxes brought to be put down, was the first reason I gave him my heart.

Who was I to judge him now? My memory reminded me of the axe smashing through the skull, a crackling sound, a face split in two and a brain splashing out – a fast but horrible death.

When my turn came, I told him of our survival struggles – the hunger, Tanya's condition, Max's death, Ali's organs stored in the fridge. At the mention of Ali, his face lit up in awe as if I told a six-year-old Steve that Santa's sleigh had parked around the corner.

"Are you really trying to create a cure? At the synchrotron?"

The same childish disbelief was mixed with excitement in his voice.

"Well, why not? We aren't very busy with anything else, and now that we have internet, we can figure out which one of them is spleen and start—"

"Spleen? Why spleen?"

I felt like a fresher PhD student bombarded with questions at an international conference.

"If we isolate the virus from the spleen, we can study it and figure out how to eliminate it," I explained.

The excitement on his face deflated as if he walked around the corner to find Santa's sleigh smashed into the side of the house and the reindeer apprehended by the animal control services.

"And you don't even know what the spleen looks like?"

I could lie to him like parents lie to their six-year-olds. I could say that now that we had internet finding the cure would be straightforward with five scientists on the roll. We would cleanse the planet from the plague in a couple of months or so.

"Look, I don't know if we can do it," I told him instead. "Science hasn't had much luck with viruses. There are drugs against HIV, but they won't really cure you; they'd help you live better and longer. Or flu, on the other hand —"

Like a kid who realised that the man dressed in Santa's red coat was his drunk neighbour, Steve wasn't listening to me anymore, the awe and hope gone from his face. I felt ashamed, as if I destroyed his childhood dream by telling the truth.

"Sorry, Anna," he interrupted me. "We are sending a convoy down to Asda in a few minutes. I will call you back later in a few hours. Will you still be there?"

Of course, I smiled bitterly into the camera as he turned off. Where would I run from this freak show of cursing elves and rabid reindeer if the drunken Santa was me?

6.

Steve didn't call back. After I'd checked my phone for the millionth time, Kay patted me on the shoulder and took my phone away for safekeeping. I guess she meant my poor heart, not the phone.

"I heard that's called ghosting," Edsie told me.

"I heard that's called tone-deaf, Edsie," Kay bit back on my behalf.

Some say there are no heart wounds that a bucket of ice-cream cannot heal. How about treating those with instant noodles?

No?

Our noodle supplies are running dry, and even the chocolate bars we've hauled through the Ring back to ID26 won't last us more than a day or two.

On a positive note, we've progressed on the spleen front.

After consulting Google Images, we agreed that the blob we initially identified as the pancreas was the spleen, the key to transforming people into blood-thirsty monsters.

We wrote and attached new labels.

"What do we do with the rest of it?" Tanya asked after we put the spleen aside and packed the other Ali's organs into plastic sample boxes.

"Bin it. We've got the spleen," said Dan.

"I'll throw it into the biological waste," Tanya said, loading the boxes onto a small trolley.

She was going to wheel Ali's remains back to the wet lab. We could officially rename that wet lab into "Spleen-eaters' Mortuary". As one of them, Ali belonged there, too.

"I'll help you," said Edsie. "What if you have another seizure?"

Kay, Dan and I stared at them in confused silence while Edsie grabbed the trolley and rolled it out of the hutch. Tanya picked up the hammer and followed him.

Okay. What have I missed?

Since Tanya started taking her meds again, she seemed to be back to her usual self, no issues with her whatsoever, apart from this unexpected feat of helpfulness from Edsie. Had *he* been bitten?

"What now?" Kay asked after the door closed behind them.

"I don't know. That's weird. I've never heard him offer help before," I said.

"No. What do we do with that?" Kay pointed at the chunk of flesh on the workshop table. It smelled rancid and unhealthy. Was it a typical smell of a slowly rotting spleen, or did the presence of the virus make it foul?

"If the virus is in his cells, we should find and isolate it," I said.

"No shit," said Dan.

"Microscope?" I suggested.

"We have to cut it very thin for a microscope," said Kay.

"Not with a knife, I suppose."

"It's not a piece of meat, Anna, of course not with a knife. With a microtome. I even know where we can find one," said Kay.

"Ehm?" Dan and I said simultaneously. That meant "out of all things, microtome? That is not our daily instrument".

Kay pointed at the wall. "While Anna worked on our chemistry, I made friends at BM25. They recently installed a new microtome to cut some tissue samples. It looked ace."

"Looked ace? Have you ever used one?" asked Dan.

Microtome, a device to make very thin slices of anything that needed to be scientifically (and not snack-type) thin, was mostly used by biologists – in nature, samples didn't come in thin layers prepped for the microscope. In our chemical labs, if you wanted thin samples, you deposited them as thin as you wanted.

She shook her head. "I watched them do it. Didn't look like a mindbreaker at all. I am sure I can do it."

"Guys, guys! I don't want to interrupt the fun, but have you forgotten what's happened to the BM25 folks? They are still there."

The whole Team BM25 turned at the same time, apart from one guy who became breakfast for his four colleagues when he tried to get out. We watched the carnage through our control room window, and it was enough for anyone to question the existence of the Father, Son and Holy Spirit.

We called the plan to deal with a gang of spleen-eaters at BM25 "Operation Splendour". For obvious reasons, "they perished in the Operation Splendour" sounded much better than "Monsters ate them". We used the fire alarm to distract the monsters, and this time, nobody got eaten or turned into a spleen-eater. I even managed to pinch some of their food supply on the way. My spleen-eating colleagues won't complain. They don't have much use for chocolate anymore.

It's frustrating that most food I come across has an extortionate sugar content. Why did all these top-class researchers stash on chocolate bars and not on cheese and sausages?

Where was I? Ah, the microtome.

We were a little sceptical about Kay's ability to use it. In our defence, most of the equipment in our lab requires more training than watching someone use it for five minutes. But in less than half an hour, Kay deposited a row of thinly sliced spleen samples on the microscope slides. Impressed, Edsie even attempted to microtome a Snicker's bar.

Our beamline didn't have a microscope – the strong and focused ID26 beam of X-rays was designed for much harder things (e.g., palladium) and would damage the organic tissue. But there was one in the workshop across the corridor, not the world's poshest device, but desktop-operated. That was a pretty good reason to consider it high-tech.

Kay said that when she was doing her PhD in Yugoslavia, a crack-free magnifying glass was considered a high-tech microscope.

How lovely. Good old times.

I mounted the glass slides onto the microscope stage and adjusted the focus in the high-magnification lens. At first, the image on the desktop screen was a blur of dark grey, but when I found a soft spot, the light flooded the tissue sample, and an image of the cells appeared on the screen.

At least, that was supposed to be cells.

My colleagues studied the image on the screen.

"Is that it?" Edsie asked after a few minutes.

"Looks like it," I said.

The wow effect didn't happen. I felt oddly disappointed.

"It does look like cells, doesn't it?" asked Tanya, squinting at the image at a ninety-degree angle.

"Does it look like spleen cells?"

"Why is it red?" asked Edsie.

"Let's google it."

Oh, the day and age when even your microscope has internet access. The image on our microscope screen – purple and pink connected dots, with white splurges and air bubbles where the tissue came off the glass slide – was similar to the images of spleen Kay found on Google.

Way too similar for our liking.

"It doesn't look like there is any virus in it," I sighed.

"Virus is small; it would be stupid to expect to find it with a microscope anyway," said Edsie.

Oh, look who is an expert in stupid!

"It wasn't the virus we were looking for, Edsie. We were looking for viral damage, signs of disease... dead cells? Blood clots? But this looks clean as if Ali was never infected."

"I don't think comparing this spleen to Google Images is a good idea. We need to find a healthy spleen from a healthy person," said Dan.

In deepening silence, a lone spleen-eater shuffled past the workshop, interestless and aimless, while we held our breath and stood still. A few minutes after the spleen-eater disappeared further into the Ring, we risked breathing out.

And turned back to Dan.

"I didn't mean I'm volunteering," he clarified.

"A healthy person with a healthy spleen is not going to share, Dan. Unless dead," said Kay.

"The competition for healthy spleens is fierce these days," said Edsie.

"But in general, the idea is not bad," I added.

Don't forget to point out the good things when criticising – for maintaining balance and a positive working environment. We really needed a positive working environment.

A positive anything.

"We need another plan," said Kay, echoing my thoughts.

"Staining," said Edsie.

I was not alone in being sceptical of Edsie's thinking abilities. On this rare occasion that he said something useful, we stared at him in shock as if he had pulled his skin off to show the tentacles underneath.

If he showed tentacles, I wouldn't be so surprised.

"In one of our papers, we delivered nanoparticles into the HeLa cells and stained them for fluorescent microscopy to see nanoparticles. You can also stain different bits within the cell, like the nucleus. I don't see why we can't stain the virus."

"We did" means his postdoc. The last time Edsie turned up in the lab was during a fire drill (haha, ironic) – he ran in to tell his postdoc he was going to the pub.

"Nick said staining cells was a nightmare," I said. "They kept dying for no reason."

"Well, we don't have this problem. Our cells are dead anyway."

"And you have to have a specific dye," I continued. "Like extremely specific. And there are thousands of different ones. How would we know which one is suitable?"

"Not that we have any at all," said Dan. "To remind you, all we have is palladium."

"The labs in the Science building would have some," said Tanya.

Oh.

Great news. Tanya is right. If there are dyes anywhere on campus, they would be in the Science Building, which houses chemistry and biology labs that are open only to the ESRF research teams.

I don't know why this particular building is called "Science" – as if the rest of the ESRF campus is a bakery.

Even better news. We brought so much palladium that our beamline fridge was not enough to safely store everything. It is a catalyst, right? You never know what it might catalyse if it gets bored in the open air. Max's friends allowed us to put our palladium in y their fridge in lab 404 on the condition that we would clean after ourselves and wouldn't steal any other – more expensive – reagents they kept in that fridge.

Now, the bad news. The Science building connects with the Ring via one of those creepy skylight passages. The last time we checked CCTV, the passage and the areas around it were infested with hungry spleen-eaters.

It sounds like a suicide mission.

Exactly our type.

7.

I'm calling it a woolly hat paradox.

One day, when the world knows us as the creators of the anti-spleen-eating cure, they will build a museum to commemorate us. The woolly hat will become the most important exhibit in its collection. Today, Life and Death are balanced inside this hat. On the Life side of the balance, there are three blank Post-it notes. On the other side – two "X"'s. Each is a potential death.

For now, they are only an invitation.

I've known I'm not the luckiest ever, but today luck has literally shat on me. For the second time in a row, my Post-it note has an X. But it's not the worst.

Edsie has the other one.

"No way!" We step away from each other like duelling gunslingers, ready to shoot.

"I am not going anywhere with this crazy bitch!" squeals Edsie.

I nod. Same here.

"She will feed me to the zombies as soon as we walk out!"

At once, Edsie has an excellent idea.

"I am sure Anna will behave," says Kay, but then she looks at my face and shuts up.

I cannot guarantee that in the blind rage of the fight, my axe will not slip and smash into Edsie instead. This can happen to anyone, but Edsie's chances are higher because I will attempt that deliberately.

"I'll go with Anna!" says Dan. "We are a team, aren't we?"

"What? Are you drunk?"

I sniff him. He doesn't smell alcohol, but I cannot be sure that my sense of smell is still working. Considering that personal hygiene has been low on our priorities list, I wouldn't be surprised if my nose refused to process the unholy stench of our dirty bodies and other smells around me.

"I'm coming with you."

He avoids looking me in the eye.

I hear Edsie's relieved sigh behind me, but I don't care about that loser. I'm worried about Dan and his suicidal urges. Aren't they counter-intuitive? Now that he knows that Lesley is safe, it's high time to triple the survival efforts. Running straight into fire doesn't count as survival.

"I'm not trying to get killed," he says as if in response to my thoughts. "And I'm coming with you, full stop."

If you consider the law of minimal damage, Tanya and I should go. We have no children to take care of and no official families. Ghosting boyfriends don't count.

On the other hand, my chances of survival next to Tanya are slim. She is as physically fit as a handkerchief, and I doubt she can smash the axe through anyone's brains.

Now, think as a spleen-eater. Who would you choose: an airy, almost transparent creature of 5 feet or a juicy, meaty Anna? I've counted my odds. They suck, so I should be thrilled that it's Dan and not Tanya, Kay, or Edsie. Talisman, right?

Then why do I feel like it's the worst idea ever?

***

Cuddled next to Steve under a woolly throw, I looked into the fire curling in the fireplace, aware that this warmth and cosiness was nothing but a dream, a brief moment of light before I woke up in my winter coat bed to the thundering tunes of Edsie's snore, wondering how come the monsters with their excellent hearing hadn't surrounded us yet.

The dream brought me back to the chalet in France. It was our first vacation together, just Steve and me, not attending a family wedding, not getting wasted with friends in Alicante. Snuggled in front of the crackling fireplace, we talked about our future for the first time, sharing dreams of a family and three kids. The windows trembled in the panes, and the wooden door was creaking under the blows of the wind, but for us, it was the warmest place in the world.

When we booked this chalet in the middle of French nowhere, we didn't expect the blizzard to snow-lock us in for days. We intended to go for long walks across the valley and drive around small villages, tasting their local dishes, Hairy Bikers style. But the snow and the strong winds, unusual for this time of the year, herded us inside the cottage, where we had to survive on the vast supplies of cheese, crackers, and wine.

The electricity died on day two, so we moved the food from the fridge into the snowdrift growing around the house and, from time to time, popped out to dig some cheese out of the snow. It was fun until the snow was so high that we couldn't find the cheese anymore.

After that, it was just crackers.

Now I know that the Universe (or whoever is running this horror show) was training me to ration and enjoy what little I had.

But I didn't have little at all. I had Steve, and that was all I needed.

If only he were here with me. He'd love to visit Grenoble…

Well, probably not on this occasion.

Without electricity, we lost access to the internet and Netflix, but the chalet had an extensive collection of board games. We didn't even notice when the blizzard died. A grumpy French man who knocked at our door in the middle of the Monopoly game found us not ready to leave and not willing to.

That made him even grumpier.

"I didn't go up la montagne to deal with children," he said in broken English.

He loaded us and our backpacks into the cabin of his snowplough and drove down the hill to the village hotel. When we were leaving the chalet, I turned around for a last look and for a moment, I saw two silhouettes hugging each other in the dark window of the house.

I don't know if multiple realities exist, but if they do, in one of them, Anna and Steve are still in that chalet, snow-locked by the blizzard. In that reality, the snowplough never came, and the cheese and wine supplies were never exhausted. Anna and Steve didn't need to go back to rainy Birmingham.

It is a magical reality where happiness has seized the moment.

Is it impossible?

What do we know of parallel realities and what laws they follow? There might be no laws, physics, or time, but endless, overpowering happiness.

Maybe, at that point, I got split into two parts. One part of me did not get onto the snowplough and is still there, with the part of Steve that stayed.

They say that parallel realities never cross. If they do, it will create a time paradox which will wipe out all of them and end the world. But that is what happened in my dream. Two of my realities crossed for a second to reunite me with myself.

When I woke up, I still could taste the cheese and the wine in my mouth and feel the warmth of Steve hugging me. I savoured the moment until the two realities split again, and each went its separate way. *This* reality was grim, but it was soothing to know that at least a small part of me remained in a place where happiness was the only law.

When my eyes got used to the meagre light of the control room, I saw Dan sitting at the table alone, staring into a half-full glass of red wine. I picked up my mobile phone. Two thirty in the morning.

Steve was online two hours ago. Still no call.

I climbed out of bed and plonked myself on the chair next to Dan. It didn't look like he went to sleep – so deep were the circles under his eyes. He picked up the glass with a shivering hand but barely drank from it.

"You are not sleeping," I said.

He shook his head. "Edsie is snoring like a rocket. I can't sleep."

I cast a glance in the direction of the hutch door, where unusually quiet Edsie was sleeping next to Tanya.

"Ever since you spoke to Lesley, you don't look yourself, Dan. You said she was all right, but was she?"

"You were talking about cheese in your sleep."

"Yeah? And you are not answering my question."

Dan reached out for the bottle to fill the glass, but I moved the bottle out of his reach and took away his glass. He'd had enough by now.

"Lesley is pregnant," he said.

I looked at him attentively. "Okay."

"Okay?" he laughed. "Is that it, Anna? Are you not going to say anything else? How about congratulations?"

"You are not celebrating."

"Look, I am! Wine and all!"

He reached for the glass again. I pushed him away.

"This is not how people celebrate, Dan. They cheer, and they look happy. You don't look happy. Is that because you didn't want kids? Didn't you decide you were child-free? What's happened?"

"We wanted this baby so bad, Anna! My brothers all have kids, and they've worn on us so much. We've changed our minds, and we want to have children, *our* babies. We started working on it almost a whole year ago, and... and... a couple of days ago, Lesley had a positive test, Anna. She's five weeks pregnant."

Okay, now he looked more excited than sunken. This way, we might get to celebrating!

"I was so happy when she told me. Lesley will be such a great mom… but after I hung up, I started thinking… How am I going to be a daddy? I am stuck in this God-forsaken shithole. What am I going to do? I need to be there with her now, and when the baby comes, I need to take care of them, but how the fuck if I'm here?"

"Is that why you were so keen on coming with me to the Science building? Even though it's a suicide mission?" Although he tried to avoid my look, I peered into his eyes. I didn't need to be a mind-reader to understand what was written across his face in bold, large letters – G, U, I, L and T. "You were going to leave me there, weren't you? Continue out of campus by yourself? You filthy arse!"

"I can't sit here and do nothing, Anna. Not when Lesley needs me."

"Yeah, but I'm sure she needs you *alive*. Dead, you're kinda no use, you know, can't change nappies or do night feeds. Dead daddy is bad daddy!"

Weren't I a boss of prep talk? Every word reflected with pain in his eyes – good job, Anna – but I needed one final blow.

"How are you even going to get there? It's like a thousand miles between us. And what about the Channel? Can you swim? Can you sail? Or maybe fly? If so, why the hell are we all still here? Let's go! Bring out your helicopter!"

He clenched his fists as if he was going to hit me. Good. If he chose to, he could hate me for being unsympathetic – I could live with it. But I wouldn't be able to live knowing that I could have stopped him but preferred to feed his self-pity.

"Look, you said she was staying with her friend, safe and looked after. She's not alone. You need to trust her to take care of herself and your child."

He sighed, shaking his head. "Promise me you won't tell the others. I don't want them to know. I only told you—"

I squeezed his hand, digging my nails deep into his skin so that the physical pain made him pay attention to what I would say next.

"Promise me you won't run away to Lesley without me. If we go, we go together."

For a moment, it looked like he was going to continue his useless objecting, but he sighed and said, "I promise."

So did I.

Chapter 3. Science Building

1.

Day 19, later, 23rd of February, Fri

The walk through the Ring was awful but this time, for different reasons. We had grown immune to the sights of carnage – the bodies were just bodies now, like dead squirrels squashed into the road by the traffic. We didn't meet any monsters, either, so instead of running and smashing, fuelled by adrenaline, we dragged on in sorrow and self-pity. Dan was radiating such unhealthy misery that it echoed in my head with headache and guilt.

Still nothing from Steve.

I was stupid when I complained about him not calling back! I got the message, you, bitchy Universe; now give me back my Steve to tell him I love him. Let me talk to him again, you, ironic little—

Dan stopped, interrupting my plea. Before leaving the EHO office, we checked the CCTV to identify the areas with the biggest infestation. The stretch of the Ring from ID09 to ID12 looked like a MonsterCon – a hundred of them, no less. It was unlikely that in the last few days, they'd dissipated.

Upon Dan's sign, we stopped behind ID09, from where we could observe the small space between the beamlines and the corridor to the lift.

Goodness! It was one thing to look at this crowd through the camera lens, but seeing them so close, feeling their stench, when all of them could attack any moment, woken up by a careless sound... They were everywhere, swarming around the beamlines like bees in a hive – restless in their half-slumber. Some of them had injuries that would put any human into a hospital bed; some had wounds still bleeding, but they didn't seem bothered. Their eyes, now entirely white, as if they never had pupils or irises, were glowing in the shadows.

What were they guarding so fiercely? The cameras at ID11 had been offline, so the best we could do was guess. Maybe, there were live people. Or maybe, like bees, the monsters had a queen, and that was her nesting spot.

Dan patted my shoulder – time to get on with the plan.

Past the hive, then right, I repeated in my head for the millionth time. *Down the corridor. The lifts are straight around the corner. If one of us goes down, the other does not stop. Run.*

"Are you ready?" Dan mouthed.

I shook my head.

Dan hit the alarm button.

Chaos descended on the Ring. Brutally awoken, the spleen-eaters went into a blind frenzy, bashing into each other while trying to get out of the alarm's reach. They screamed in agony and frustration and clawed their faces. A few spleen-eaters found an open door to the ID10 control room and rushed inside, trampled over by the tide of following monsters.

We dashed for the lifts. One of the spleen-eaters pushed me out of the way before I even lifted my axe. I ignored the growing pain in my shoulder and jumped into the lift straight after Dan. He pressed 3. There was a chance that the lift was disabled during the fire alarm, but the doors closed, and the lift started moving.

When it stopped, I readied my axe. The door opened into the skylight passage, a twin of the passage in the Central Building – empty and hollow, squeaky-clean white laminate, cold LED lights. But it smelled much worse of rotting flesh and sewage.

"I don't like this at all," Dan echoed my thoughts, taking the phone out of his pocket.

The passage took us to the staircase on the third floor, where I remembered lab 404 to be. I pressed my ear to the door, mostly out of habit, not expecting anything to hear – the newer Science Building had heavy fire doors and much better soundproofing.

"Right or left?" I asked.

"Right. And don't start unless they come after you", said Dan.

I gave him a dirty look, slowly pulled the door onto myself and peered into the hall. No monsters, as far as I could see. White and white.

I pulled the door wider. Dan stepped in first.

"Clear," he said. "Look out for the alarm buttons but try not to walk into anything."

He pointed at the floor covered with scattered glass bits as if someone drove into a shop window. I moved forward, carefully stepping around the large debris and scanning the walls ahead of me for the alarm buttons. There weren't any, as far as I could see. Not great, but we anticipated this: the newer building was equipped with an intricate system of carbon monoxide and heat sensors that would trigger the alarm automatically rather than rely on a human to spot and call the fire.

"Keep away from the doors," Dan whispered further instructions. "And whatever happens, don't run back to the lifts. Run!"

They appeared out of nowhere, no, from everywhere at the same time, endless monsters flowing into the small hall like ghosts seeping through the walls. One grabbed my shoulder, but I swayed him away with the blunt side of the axe. More came into his place as I fumbled with my phone, trying to press the "play" button with one hand.

"Now!" Dan shouted, kicking one of the spleen-eaters from his way.

I pressed. The sound of the alarm filled the hall. It was loud but nowhere near as loud as the real one. The closest monsters winced and backed off, but the guys behind them immediately pushed forward.

"Why isn't it working?" Dan shouted.

I grabbed him by his sleeve and dragged him into the nearest lab a second before one impatient bugger jumped on us from the crowd. He missed by an inch, his claws scratching the wooden door I shut in front of its face. I turned the lock and pushed the first heavy thing that I found to barricade the door.

It was a mini fridge with a half-peeled sticker on the front.

Lab 404.

2.

Doesn't the Universe have a sweet sense of humour? Sometimes, it's black like a rotten banana, but oh well, what will you do? The Customer Service is on holiday for the next thirty million years, and the Chief Complaints Officer is still dealing with the dinosaurs.

HOW IS IT? Kay texted while I was installing the next barricade. The cupboard or the gas cylinder? Which one matches the colour pallet?

The gas cylinder turned out to be heavier, so Dan helped me move it to the barricade. The door shook and creaked under the pressure of the spleen-eaters. It wouldn't last.

Neither would we. The lab had no side doors, so we were trapped, and without ninja training, fighting was out of the question. Even if we were trained, how would we take on the whole blood-thirsty crowd? We were not in a Hollywood movie; although Dan was bald, he was not Bruce Willis.

I sat on the floor next to the chemicals cupboard and stared at the door creaking under the pressure. This was not how I planned to die. I was going to grow old next to Steve, get a Nobel Prize when I turned eighty – chemistry academics are long-lasting species – and die peacefully in a holiday house in Cornwall.

I've never been to Cornwall. I don't know where that came from.

"There is a house in New Orleans, they call the Rising Sun. And it's been a ruin of a many boys," I started singing. In the movies, dramatic music plays when the main character dies. Without better candidates, I was this movie's main character.

Without a grand soundtrack, my singing would have to pass for, well, singing.

The monsters didn't enjoy it, and the banging and bashing intensified. The first cracks appeared along the door frame.

Dan landed next to me and handed me a small box. "Dyes. I found them in the fridge labelled 'dyes'."

I nodded. "Exemplary organisation! A rare place where you find the specified under the label "shit"."

"I wish our lab was as ordered."

"It doesn't matter anymore," I said, sounding whimpering instead of tragic.

Dan kicked my leg. "Hey, we are not dead yet! Let's get going."

He jumped up and went on rummaging through the drawers, making such an awful noise that the guys behind the door doubled their efforts. The hinges started to yield. The cracks in the door frame deepened.

I put the dyes in my backpack and watched Dan with mild interest.

"Aha!" Dan pulled out a roll of silicon tubing.

"Not the best time for synthesis, Dan."

He unrolled the tubing and tied it around a sink stand soldered solid into the floor. It didn't hold at first, coiling around in knots, but I joined to help, and we managed to fix it together.

The door behind us squeaked and cracked, and a large piece of wood chipped. One of the monsters pushed through the gap but got stuck.

I pointed at the tubing. "What's this for?"

"Do you know how to rappel?"

"Rappel? Are you kidding me?"

Dan grabbed a hotplate from the bench and threw it at the window. An angry roar of the monsters echoed the smashing of the glass.

"Of course, I can't rappel. Was it a part of the academic induction!"

"It's only three floors, Anna. It's not that high!"

"Are you fucking kidding me? What is 'high'?"

"I will do it, and you hold on to me!"

The first spleen-eater finally pushed himself free through the hole in the door and past the barricades, tumbled into the room, and sprinted at us.

"Ah, who cares!" I tossed the end of the tubing to Dan.

Near the window, he twisted the end of the tubing around his waist, tying two knots to fix it in place. I prepared to face the spleen-eater coming at me. It was a tall, bulky woman, flat-chested, short-haired, and furious as if I pinched the dinner from under her nose. She knew I was dinner about to be served.

Not today, darling.

I stepped forward to meet her and smacked her with the axe. It got her shoulder, dug into the flesh, drawing blood and chipping the bone. She flinched from pain and dropped back, pulling the axe out of my hand.

I tumbled forward after it, but Dan grabbed my hand, threw me onto his back like a sack of potatoes and jumped out of the window.

"Fuck you!" I screamed, grabbing his neck so tight that I could almost feel his spine column under my fingers. "I thought you said rappel, not jump."

I will never forget those few meters of free fall, clutching Dan's neck, smothering him, and praying to all gods I believed in or not. The tubing jerked us up, stopping our fall below the second-floor windows. Following the inertia, we swung into the wall. The collapse was inevitable, but Dan bounced us off the wall with his legs. We swung away and then back into the wall, softer this time. We stopped swinging and hung up in the air, twenty feet above the ground.

The spleen-eaters in lab 404 stuck their heads into the window, licking their lips in anticipation, but none jumped after us. Below, a spleen-eater climbed through the bush, undisturbed by the scratching thorns, and headed in our direction.

"What now?"

Dan wheezed, breathless, and I shifted to free his neck. "Where... is... your ... axe? I can't... untie..."

"I don't have it anymore."

"Oh... crap!"

Indeed.

"You can... get off," he said.

I pointed at the first spleen-eater arriving at our would-be crash site.

"Fuck," he said.

Indeed.

"Maybe, we could use the wall to climb up?" I suggested, having no idea how I would implement it.

Then, something awesome happened. The tubing around Dan's waist strained, and we started to go up, pulled by an invisible force. Right on time because the first monster jumped up, reaching for our feet.

"Gosh, he's human!" Dan choked, looking at something above us. I followed his gaze.

A man was pulling the tubing with us still attached to it through the second-floor window, the blue veins webbing from strain through the pale skin on his massive hands. Before I uttered an unnecessary comment about Edsie no longer being the most steroidal man on campus, I noted that the guy's eyes were clear blue, and his clothes were clean.

Soon, we reached the window level, and I grabbed the window ledge and climbed inside. Dan followed in, tumbling onto the lab floor. While he caught his breath, I untied the tubing from his waist and turned to the man.

"Thank you for saving our poor arses! I'm Anna, and this bloody rapellist... rapellent... rappeler is Dan."

"Michael, my pleasure. It's been dead quiet for more than a week, not a face in sight, and then all the screaming and breaking glass. You guys have kicked up a storm upstairs."

An angry growl echoed his words, and I peered down the window. The fan crowd outside had grown even bigger but looked lost – our smell lingered in the air.

"But I am glad you did. Otherwise, I'd still think I am the last man standing."

He laughed, but his laughter sounded a bit unnatural, maybe because of his accent. He spoke deep, coated English, typical for an American from the South, with a tiny speckle of … Scandinavian? Yeah, I suppose he could pass for a Swede with that bleached hair, transparent eyelashes, and blue eyes.

"Have you been all alone here this whole time, man?" asked Dan, shaking Michael's hand.

I looked around. This lab was larger than lab 404 and of non-chemical research. There were no extraction fans, fume hoods, rotary evaporators, or glassware – only a line of fridges, worktops, and four gloveboxes.

Biochemistry? Biology?

I felt uncomfortable. Biologists weren't a very welcoming folk. The last time I needed something from a biology lab, their technician fended me off with a mop.

"Is this your lab?" I asked Michael.

"I shared it with some other guys, but yeah! Great lab, isn't it?"

It was a weird thing to say. Like "Look at this office where I spend eight hours of my day staring at the screen – isn't it amazing?" or "Look at this bus that I drive daily; how beautiful it is!"

She. They think the buses are girls.

"So, where are you guys coming from? I don't think I've met you before."

Dan explained to him how we ended up in the Science Building searching for dyes. I walked further into the lab, admiring its cleanliness, longing for my *home* lab, where every stain had a name and a story. This place was untouched by slaughter and destruction, but something felt off, something I couldn't correctly place.

Tanya and her shit-radar could be handy.

Walking deeper into the lab while the two men chatted, I wondered where Michael had set up his bunking spot. The control room in ID26 looked like an old, lived-in house of a crazy family – our things scattered all over the floor, empty bottles lining the wall, chocolate wraps spilling out of the recycling bin. Edsie believes that recycling will somehow survive the apocalypse, even if we don't, and won't let us put them into any other bin.

A barely audible sound caught my attention, a muffled whine of a scared dog.

Come on, Anna, there are no dogs here.

Oh, there it was again. Louder, closer.

Michael and Dan were still absorbed in their conversation, and I moved on to find the source of the sound, sniffing around the lab like a filthy spy. It didn't feel right, not after Michael had saved our lives, and I was about to turn around when I heard the whine again.

I approached a large yellow metal cabinet and listened in. For a few seconds, no sound came. Then the cupboard shook as if something shifted inside. Another whine came from inside.

A dog? Seriously?

What if there's a monster?

I scratched the cupboard door to see if I got an intelligent response. Nothing came back at first, and then the cupboard shook again.

A spleen-eater, I thought. Michael had locked a monster in his cupboard. The images of Will Smith playing golf in the ruins of New York crept into my head. I pushed them away and turned around to leave when another sound from the cupboard made me change my mind.

Muffled bangs. Something wrapped in fabric was hitting the metal of the cupboard. It was not the sound itself that put me on guard but its rhythmic periodicity, which, I knew by now, the spleen-eaters were incapable of.

A dog?

I could spend an eternity standing in front of the cupboard, guessing what the hell was inside. Not having an eternity, I turned the locking handle, pulled the door open by an inch, peered inside and closed it again, making minimal noise. I put the locking handle into a "closed" position and walked away from the cupboard as if I had never even come close to it.

What the fuck?

3.

When I made it far enough from the damn cupboard, I picked up an automatic pipette from its stand and stared at it like I'd never seen one before, with a corner of my eye watching Michael and Dan. The two were laughing at some joke, having forgotten all about me.

Good. I need a minute to think.

The dog in the cupboard. Not a dog, a woman, around Kay's age, although it was hard to judge in the shadowed, confined space of the cupboard. A deep blue, yellowing bruise under her right eye might have added age, too, but without a doubt, it was an uninfected human woman, locked up in the chemicals cupboard with her hands tied up in front of her and a purple fabric stuck into her mouth.

Is that how you treat a colleague these days? Or was she a health and safety officer?

I didn't want to think badly of Michael. He'd saved our pitiful lives. He would have an explanation. I'm sure there were hundreds of good reasons to shove someone into the cupboard...

Only I struggled to think of any.

I sent Dan a WhatsApp message, MICHAEL KEEPS A WOMAN LOCKED UP IN THE CUPBOARD, and headed back to them.

"...They don't seem to like acid at all, especially if you spray them in the eyes," Michael was telling Dan when I came back after my 'lab tour'.

"I don't like acid in my eyes, either." Dan laughed.

Michael fist-bumped him on the shoulder, "Well, it is great that we have plenty of this stuff here, man!"

What a sweet bonding moment!

"You have a very clean lab," I said.

Michael flinched, looking uncomfortable with my interruption. I'd heard that smiling people were more likely to be perceived as friends, so I smiled at him as wide as I could. Let's not piss off the guys who lock women in the cupboards. Dan cast me a weird look. Okay, maybe that was a little too wide.

"Michael was telling me how he sprayed the monsters with acid and finished them with the stand." Dan pointed at one of the metal stands with a row of attached clamps. A great weapon, indeed – long sharp metal pole if you like stabbing monsters and a heavy flat stand on the other end if you're into smashing them on the head.

"I don't like being sprayed with acid, too." I nodded.

"Ha, that's exactly what I said." Dan laughed.

Michael didn't smile.

My phone went off, vibrating in my pocket. Shit, the last text I'd sent Kay was about us preparing to die in lab 404. With everything going on, we'd forgotten to let them know our dying had been postponed.

"Hi Kay, how are you doing, guys?"

"What the hell do you mean, a woman in the cupboard?" Kay shouted into my ear, the strong dynamic of the phone splashing her shrill, worried voice all over the place. "Anna, what's going on there? Who is Michael?"

Oh, well. I'd sent the message to the wrong chat.

I swallowed and looked at Michael. Now's a good time for explanations.

"What the hell?" Dan asked, his eyes darting between Michael and me.

Before I could answer, Michael jumped at me and grabbed me by my neck.

Wheezing in his grip, I dropped my phone screen down, cutting Kay's panicking voice off. Michael shifted his grip, not to let me breathe in but to pull something out of his lab coat pocket. Something sharp scraped against my lab coat and rested next to my thigh. My eyes almost popped out of their orbits while I tried to see what it was. A syringe filled with liquid, the touch of the bare needle stinging through my jeans.

Then, a sweet, easily recognisable smell reached my nose.

Methanol. In a syringe.

What? Who keeps a syringe with methanol in their pocket?

"Oh, crap," said Dan. "What the hell, mate?"

"Don't do anything rash, Dan," Michael said. "And I won't hurt your friend."

Anna. My name is Anna, douchebag.

"A woman in the cupboard? What kind of shit is that? Do you really have someone in the cupboard?"

"Of course I do."

He said it as if nothing could be more natural than keeping people in the cupboard. Totally mainstream. Like twerk. Or TikTok videos. Yeah. When the Apocalypse happened, everyone received a set of survival instructions, and the first thing on the list was to get a nice cupboard.

Everyone's got to go locking!

"A healthy spleen will keep you from turning into one of them," Michael said.

"I have a healthy spleen, mate. I don't think it helped lots of people anyway!"

"What kind of scientist are you that you don't know?" Michael waved the syringe in the air, letting a few drops of liquid out. "You won't get infected if you eat healthy spleen after they bite you! You should keep taking clean spleen until the virus leaves your body."

Eh.

"What kind of scientist are you?" Dan screamed. "This is mental! Do you have someone in the cupboard to eat their spleen? Are you going to fry it up, aren't you, crazy lunatic?"

I rolled my eyes at Dan, signalling him to please shut up and stop supplying Michael with cooking recipes. Yes, the spleen shit sounds bonkers, but I'm in grave danger! I don't want a methanol injection!

"Listen, man, this is insane. Nothing will help you if they bite you, man. Let Anna go. We can sort it all out. You've saved our lives, man; you can't be serious about that shit!"

Dan's words seemed to trigger a reaction, but not the one we both wanted – Michael moved the syringe to my neck and shouted, "You're an idiot if you think you can survive this. But it's okay; your spleen will do, too, although I'd prefer hers."

I wasn't into advantages of my spleen over Dan's, even if it meant that Michael would leave the best for last and throw me into the cupboard to marinate. I wiggled in his arms, and he pointed the methanol syringe at my face.

The first thing they teach you in any chemistry class is Health and Safety Rule Number One: never stick your nose into bottles!

The smell of the solvent, so sweet and familiar, tickled inside my nose. I sneezed.

Sneezing, a natural reaction to a strong smell, ripped through my whole body, causing a twitch. The syringe scratched my skin and, having nothing to push against, came loose in Michael's hand and dropped on the floor. Michael released his grip on my neck. I lurched forward, grabbed the metal stand from the bench, and, without looking twice, swung the metal base behind me where his face was supposed to be.

There was a thump, a muffled squeal, then silence. Nobody grabbed me from behind and looking at Dan's face, nobody would. I turned around. Michael lay on the floor, face down, a small trickle of blood crawling from under his head.

"Oh, goodness, did I kill him?" I kicked Michael in the ribs with the toe of my shoe. What if I didn't, and he would lunge at me with that syringe?

Dan kneeled over Michael and placed his fingers on the neck under his chin. "I think I feel the pulse. Guess he's only KO'ed. You didn't say you played baseball," Dan said.

Zombie training, that's all.

"I sort of hoped to smash his head," I said. "Where is that syringe?"

"Under?"

"Uhm." I wasn't ready to put the lab stand away. "Let's tie him up first."

It didn't take long to fix Michael's hands behind his back with three zip ties and a few layers of sticky tape. While fixing him up, I realised what seemed so odd about him – his vast chest was bulging through the clasped buttons of the lab coat, too narrow in the shoulders and not reaching the knees. Three-four sizes off, it couldn't be his lab coat.

But no. His name was sewn over the chest pocket, "Michael Levits, PhD."

What had they been cooking in this lab? Maybe, he tested his lab's products on himself to end up like Hulk, but human colour?

Never trust the biologists. They always play with things they shouldn't touch.

I picked up my phone from the floor. The screen, shattered right in the middle as if hit by a bullet, was lifeless and didn't come to life after I pressed the "ON" button for a minute.

Shit.

I should have killed that dickhead Michael!

There are ten times more bacteria in humans than human cells. Turtles breathe through their bums.

"Can you text Kay?" I asked Dan, pulling the sim card out of my useless phone. "I'll check on the woman. She should know what's going on in this place."

I left Dan to watch over Michael but took the lab stand in case the woman in the cupboard followed other dodgy diets. I unlocked and opened the door with caution, inch by inch, almost expecting her to jump on me with a banshee yell. As soon as the gap was enough for the bright lab light to squeeze into the cupboard, my eyes met hers, grey and clear.

She did not rush to get out, so I opened the door a little wider and stepped aside, giving her space. She didn't move, with cold attention watching the lab stand, still covered in Michael's blood.

"I can't put it away. What if you jump on me?" I explained to her and pulled the end of the purple cloth to free her mouth.

"I am not going to jump on you. I am not one of them," she said in English with such a thick French accent that I could smudge it on a croissant.

"Yeah," I nodded, "Michael was not one of them, either."

Her eyes widened. "Michael?"

Yet, she didn't rush out.

I decided to give her time and walked back to Dan. He managed to roll Michael over and recover the syringe from under his body. The wound on Michael's head looked deep, the blood still oozing but not gushing. Good. In the end, I didn't want to kill him; I wanted to make sure he didn't kill me.

"This looks bad."

I turned around to meet the cupboard woman face to face. In the bright lab light, she looked a little younger than Kay but more fragile and cute, like someone you'd want to cuddle and protect. This desire passed within a second because her grey eyes watched like the lens of a CCTV camera, without warmth, emotion, or worry that such a stare would make you uncomfortable, which, of course, made me uncomfortable straight away.

"Louise," she said.

I told her my name and was about to shake her hand. She still had the cable tie around her wrists. I rummaged through the drawers next to the sink – the common storage place for random bits and bobs – and found an old-style cutthroat razor. That did the job.

She leaned over Michael and pressed her fingers onto his neck. She shook her head. My heart sank.

"I wish he bled to death, but this cr-razy bastar-rd will live."

She put little emotion into the word "bastard" for someone who dodged an opportunity to get eaten for zombie virus prophylaxis. Her accent, so overpowering at first, now sounded tamer, only breaking through with the unrestrained roll of the "r"s.

"Thank you." She turned to me.

I shrugged. "You see, I'm attached to my spleen, and Michael, he had this crazy idea—"

"I know," she interrupted, "but this is not Michael."

Dan cast me a warning look. I checked Louise once again. She didn't look weird, apart from the black eye, and my gut feeling – a weak dupe of Tanya's shit-radar – was silent. Michael also didn't look weird, but my gut feeling was screaming danger. I promised myself that next time, I'd listen to the guts.

"He said otherwise," I said.

"This guy is not Michael!" she snarled.

Her accent was razor-sharp again as she pointed at Michael, or whoever he was. I stepped back and tightened my grip on the lab stand.

"This is not Michael!" she repeated, calmer this time. "The r-real Michael is dead! This guy is fr-rom the comms department. I think his name is Gr-reg. Yes, Greg Machado."

"But the lab coat?"

"Not his! Look at his size!" she said.

As she spoke, one of the clasps on the lab coat popped open, revealing the blue fabric underneath. Michael's breathing became deeper. He would be back up again in no time.

Should I hit him again?

I wasn't ready to deal with this shit.

"Why would he say he's Michael if he's Greg?" asked Dan.

"Why do men say they are single when they are married?" Louise asked back. Dan didn't answer – it sounded like a rhetorical question anyway. "Michael, real Michael, was my PhD supervisor. He was eighty and getting too old to run the big team. When they opened these labs a couple of years ago, he invited me to help. He was a great man, nothing to do with this scumbag."

"Has he turned?"

She shook her head but didn't elaborate. Everyone had a sad story by now, but not all were eager to share it with the world. They say that happiness likes silence, but what about the pain? It's not shouting, either.

A blood-curdling shriek pierced the air in contrast to my thoughts. Dozens of hellish voices joined into one demonic choir, were so loud that the flasks wobbled in the cupboards, and the glass shivered in the windowpanes. Then the shriek started to fade, cutting the choir down one by one.

"What was that?" Dan whispered, peering out of the window. The crowd of spleen-eaters directly under our window had dissipated, and in the evening shadows, we couldn't see any other monsters.

"It is them," said Louise. "This is their 'goodnight' song! They do not seem to be very active in the dark."

"I've never heard anything like it."

She nodded. "Only the ones outside do it. They sense the light levels decreasing at sunset and tell the others about it. Then they all go into semi-slumber, semi-sleepwalking. Michael called it a swan song... Very unique; no other species are known to have it."

"How do you know all of this?" I asked.

She sighed, "I am a biologist. Observing living organisms is my job."

Wow.

Dan sent me a brief, meaningful look. I nodded. Yesterday, I'd pop open a champagne to celebrate such an amazing coincidence, but today had brought so many twists that I felt nothing would ever be able to surprise me again.

Louise is a biologist. She might help us find a cure.

Right. Give her a gold medal, and two chocolate ones to Anna and Dan for timely pulling her out of the cupboard. Now fireworks, everybody dances.

At the thought of chocolate, my stomach rumbled. I reached for my backpack but remembered that I'd stuffed the last Snickers bar while preparing to die in lab 404. Couldn't leave food to rot next to my dead body.

"We have food in the office," Louise said.

Did I say nothing was going to surprise me ever again?

Watch this!

Louise opened the lab door and stepped outside as she was – no weapon, no protective suit, not even checking the horizon in case spleen-eaters roamed around. While Dan and I gawked, she disappeared into the corridor.

Just like that.

4.

Michael, sorry, Greg did not lie when he said this floor was now clear from monsters, but he forgot to mention that it was the actual Michael, a semi-retired professor, Louise and their two postdocs Priti and Quinchang, who did the "cleaning" job.

"When we witnessed the first attack, we decided it was safer to stay here. Most of our colleagues left to take care of their families, but the four of us stayed," recounted Louise. "We did not get out for the first five days, and it was hard not to know what was going on without phones or internet connection. Priti hoped the rescue would come soon, an orderly evacuation, and we would miss it if we continued to hide.

"When nobody came, we grew desperate and started arguing. We could not stay in anymore, not without information. None of us was combat material, so we needed weapons that worked at a distance without direct contact. Michael suggested spraying them with strong acid." Louise pointed at the squirty wash bottles on the shelf.

We were sitting in Louise's office, chewing on the protein bars from her supplies. It was a small space that felt claustrophobic after the vastness and brightness of the lab but similarly sterile. No papers scattered on the table, no posters or certificates lining the walls, no cacti or other vegetation.

Okay, they might have eaten it by now. Not cacti – the other vegetation.

The books on the shelves were primarily manuals, monographs, and theses as fat as the Bible. The order on the shelves suggested Louise was an OCD maniac, but the keyboard and the desktop were covered with a thin, visible layer of dust. She ran her finger across it and didn't bother wiping it off.

"For some reason, they react like that only to sulfuric acid. Any other strong acid burns them but does not stop them from attacking."

I didn't ask how they'd figure that out. I counted – they started with two postdocs, and now there was nil.

"We packed the bodies into bin sacks and threw them out of the window. After we had cleared out the floor, we started to collect food. We found Greg during one of the raids a couple of days ago, more or less. He was hiding in the cafe of the Langevin Institute, that large building to the right. We lost Shayne in that raid, and Michael got injured. Greg and I carried him while Priti covered our retreat. He was not infected, but the bleeding was so bad I did not think he would make it back here. I left Greg and Priti to set Michael up in his office and ran to the staff room to get a first aid kit…"

"I didn't know there was a cafe at Langevin," I said, filling in a long, painful pause. "Should we drop in, too?"

Louise shook her head. "We had barely made it out last time. They were hosting a conference when all hell broke loose, so there might be nearly a thousand people instead of a hundred. But do not worry, we have got enough food here."

Louise pointed at the large box full of fusilli packs, tins of pasta sauce, tuna cans and a lonely packet of prawn crackers like a cherry on top. I tried to remember the taste of pasta with tomato sauce, but my memory responded with a chaos of flavours – sweet, sour, and salty at the same time, and I gave up. A scrumptious dinner will have to wait until the whole Team ID26 can enjoy it.

"What's happened to Priti?"

"I do not know. When Greg attacked me, she was in the toilet. She walked in on him strapping me to the chair. She managed to escape… I hope so. He went after her but came back alone."

Why didn't Priti come back to rescue Louise?

She could have been too scared. I was more terrified of Michael than of the spleen-eaters outside lab 404. Those folks were very down-to-earth, with simple motives. Michael was full-throttle kooky.

It was the first time I met face-to-face with insanity. [Apart from that paper in *Acta Materialia* – the authors used sodium oxide to extract proteins after the solid phase synthesis. That was sick!]

"What are we going to do with Michael?" I asked.

"Gr-r-r-reg!" Louise growled.

"Should we ask the others?"

"The others?" Louise stared at us, a half-eaten protein bar in her hand. The wrapper said it was chocolate-flavoured, but it stank like it was made from rotten blood. Believe me, I know how rotten blood smells.

"Wait a sec. What are the alternatives? We can't let him go. He knows where we live. What if the bugger creeps up on us while we sleep?"

"We lock the doors," said Dan.

"You know what I mean. He will come after us."

"After you."

"And you. He didn't mind whose spleen he got."

"We can't leave him tied up like that," Dan insisted.

I wondered if Kay's preaching sprouted roots in Dan's brain. She talked of love and respect for all living things, and on some occasions – take today as a prime example – that would annoy the shit out of me. I'd like to see how much love she would have for Michael.

Greg, for shit's sake!

"If we untie him, he will be free to go," said Louise.

"Thank you, Dr Obvious!" Dan bit back.

"He will be able to follow us, too." Louise ignored the bite.

"If we don't untie him, the monsters will get to him, or he will starve to death," Dan said.

"Go untie him, then! I bet the bugger can't wait to have your spleen for dinner!" I shouted. "He tried to kill me! He wanted to eat Louise's spleen! He is not better than any of those monsters! He is a monster! I wish I killed the bastard then so I wouldn't have to do it now!"

I grabbed the lab stand and stormed out of the office. I had to end the problem of Greg or Michael or whoever the fuck he was… and one thing I was sure of.

I would not spend the rest of my life scared he would come after me.

Maybe, Kay was right, and God's love somehow extended to all living beings, although I'd seen enough evidence that it was bullshit. Maybe, Michael-shit-Greg was deserving of that love and forgiveness, yada, yada… only because he qualified as a living being.

That's fine. I also brought love and forgiveness. In the form of a heavy lab stand.

Don't think I wasn't ready or capable. I was going to finish him off.

But the lab was empty.

***

I was shaking in the dark, sweating like mad, until something cold and comforting landed in my hand. My fingers intertwined with the metal of the lab stand pole. Louise's pale face hovered over me in the darkness.

"Bad dream," she said, not asking.

I rubbed my eyes with a sweaty hand. Coiled on a hip of lab coats, Dan was snoring in his sleep, a peaceful smile touching his lips as if the scares of the real life did not follow him into his dreams, a much better world where he and Lesley were together again and their baby was chasing butterflies.

"I dreamt of M… Greg," I told Louise. "Of what would be if I killed him, then and there."

She stared at me, her face eery in the scarce moonlight. "Do you feel sorry that you did not?"

"I was worried I'd killed him when I saw him lying on the floor. There was so much blood. I didn't know how to live knowing I was a murderer. But now, I'm not that sure. I dreamt I killed him, and it felt… okay."

I don't know why I'd decided to share it with Louise, out of all people.

"I have spent the last two days imagining what I will do to Michael when I get a chance. I have gone through millions of ways of murdering him, and you know what? I had an opportunity, and now I feel sick because I did not do anything. Did not stab, did not strangle, did not drown him. While I was in the cupboard, the only thing I desired was giving him a hundred painful deaths."

"You still can do it. I'm sure he'll be back." I patted her on the shoulder.

Fresh livers are hard to come by, so he'll pass by ID26, if the spleen-eaters don't get to him first. That would be nice of them.

We gave the rest of Team ID26 a full coverage of yesterday's events. "This is sick" was a general agreement. Kay volunteered to pray for Greg's soul because "that is the outgoings of a diseased mind. In normal circumstances, the poor guy could receive treatment and turn for the better."

I opened my mouth to comment on that statement, but Dan kicked me in the leg. I said, "Amen," and got another kick.

"Why did he pretend to be someone else?" Tanya asked aloud the question that bothered me even more than how Greg came across the idea of a spleen remedy.

"Why? That's easy," mumbled Edsie, "the bugger knows the rules of the game. If you can't be bothered to do anything yourself, make someone else do it and steal it. Pretend that you did it all. He claimed to have cleared this whole floor from zombies because he wanted to be in the spotlight. How much of that do you get in the comms department if there are Nobel winners next door?"

These rules are shitty and unethical, and the players are often egotistic, narcissistic sociopaths that feed on the young and naive, lured into the system by sweet promises of making a difference. It's not a game I want to play.

"Edsie sometimes provides surprising insights," Dan broke the silence. "Surprising insights" is not what I would call it, and I could see from Kay's and Tanya's faces that they had a lot to say on the subject. But nobody did because Edsie was one of us, and we wanted "us" to remain for as long as possible.

And yet, I couldn't stop thinking of Greg and his adopted personality. Believing that someone's spleen would prevent him from turning into a zombie was one level of insanity. Pretending to be someone else, someone you killed…

This was a shit from a horror movie.

After stirring for another half hour, I decided to share with Louise, who also wasn't asleep. "I've seen a lot of Hollywood movies, you know. All psychopaths are always, you know, monodirectional? Focused? Is that a good word? I mean, they are insane in one way, but Greg… He is worse than the spleen-eaters."

"The virus has reduced the infected to an animal state. What they are doing is normal from the point of view of basic instinct. They are hunting to feed. They are not insane. Mental disorders are very uncommon in nature," Louise said. "In the wild, deviating from the norm does not lead to a long and happy life. Sick brains do not help with hunting and breeding, so natural selection takes care of those out of the norm."

That's when it hit me. The sick brain!

We'd been looking in the wrong place!

The virus attacked the brain, not the spleen, and altered the monsters' behaviour so they wouldn't know their mom from their hunger!

I was about to call Kay and Tanya and tell them to dig out Ali's brain and slice it up, but then I remembered that Ali's head, with all of its valuable contents, went to the bin. Even if we managed to find his head, the brain had rotten into a slurry by now.

So wasteful. So stupid of us.

We'd have to get ourselves a new brain.

I settled back into bed, thinking of what it meant. Another spleen-eater would have to die.

No, that was wrong. Spleen-eaters didn't die by themselves, even if we asked them nicely. They required serious argumentation, generally in the form of a wrench. We would have to kill another spleen-eater. That is correct.

We would have to kill.

5.

The morning sunshine, so rare in this part of France at the end of winter, was basking us in warmth, making the night shadows a distant memory. I sat at the window, working out my vitamin D factory. If I had the equipment to do it, I would be photosynthesising!

The sunshine was a reminder that the world didn't stop existing. Humans are selfish; we think the Universe rotates around us, and once we are gone, everything will be gone. Bullshit! Our civilisation has crumbled, but the sun still rises every morning, the birds dart through the skies, and even the spleen-eaters, lethargically stomping the lawns around the Science building, fit perfectly into this circle of life.

Humans are not the top predators anymore. Now we are prey. But does it matter to the world? The ashes go back to ashes, the organics go back into the soil, and the balance of matter and energy remains unshaken.

This might sound scary for some: you matter very little in this grand scheme of things. But for me, knowing that the fundamentals still worked was soothing – if you, like all good scientists, rely on fundamental laws of Nature, you need an occasional reassurance that those laws are still sound.

Louise insisted we had a proper breakfast before moving out. As a Professor of Biology, she knew what was best for the human body, so who was I to argue? I had pasta with tomato and mascarpone sauce, with real mascarpone and tomato in it, unlike the chicken noodles we'd been eating for the last few days – despite the name, there were only noodles.

While eating breakfast, I briefed Dan on my late-night revelations and explained our science project to Louise.

"We need a fresh brain, then," said Dan.

He was not too keen on smashing and axing, understandably so. The virus had done great for wiping out the Earth's population; no need for our contribution.

"Can we go back a little bit first?" said Louise. "You killed a zombie, or as you call them, a spleen-eater, named it Ali and then cut it into samples, right?"

I nodded.

"And you named him before you cut him?"

"Why does it matter?"

Louise sighed. "We do not give names to the samples. Only numbers."

"Who – we? Why?" Dan and I asked at the same time.

I could see she was about to answer, and that answer would be significant, almost life-changing. We stared at her, ready to hear and ingest the wisdom, but she sighed again – were we that frustrating? Even after we pulled her out of the cupboard? – and nodded.

"Yes, the brain makes sense. It would explain the behavioural and sensory changes. The eyes, too. I would expect the eyes to have the largest virus pool – they go first. We can look at your brain samples and the eyes. They are easier to stain, too."

I cast Dan a warning look. If she didn't like how we named our samples, what would she say about the way we managed them?

Also, the eyes… were not all there.

Louise didn't need to know.

With Louise's food supplies, we could have gone straight to ID26 – if there were a direct way back, but the third floor that led to the skylight passage was infested with monsters.

Instead, we decided to visit the café in the Langevin building. According to Louise, it was full of food, so it would be a shame to miss the opportunity to grab some extras, even if food was not the only thing the Langevin building had in abundance.

"There are hundr-r-reds of them, confer-r-rence, r-remember? It is not possiblé!" Louise said, her French accent seeping back into the "possible".

Ha. We are the gurus of impossible and impossibles-in-chief!

Dan said he had an idea and disappeared into the lab before I could remind him that it was because of his inflammation of ideas ("Can you rappel?") that we ended up in this godforsaken place.

When he returned, Dan held four wine bottles. I didn't ask where the bottles came from – they grow like mould in France – but Louise stared at them suspiciously and stepped away from Dan.

"What is that?"

"Molotovs!" Dan said, handing me one bottle.

I grabbed it without thinking. My nose caught the familiar smell of benzene, and I almost tossed the bottle away, which – ironically! – it was intended for in the first place.

"What? Is this from your gang time?"

"Gang time? Is it because he is bald?" muttered Louise.

"Yes, I was in a street gang," Dan dropped. "But how do you imagine gangs, Anna? We don't walk dropping Molotovs around town."

"How would I know what's within a gang's job description? As if I applied. Why then?"

"I am a chemist, Anna. They are not so difficult to make. You need something flammable and a bottle."

"A street gang?" mused Louise.

I gave up. Obviously, not all chemists were made equal, and as a young and inexperienced chemist, I had a lot to learn.

About Dan, too.

"Do you know how to make Semtex?" I asked, just in case. You never know.

"Is it going to help?"

"So, you *do* know!"

Now, he would tell us that he used to be in the Secret Service and could fight the zombies with his left eyebrow. Or that he was a number one international assassin. Or that he *is* an assassin, and the academic career is an elaborate cover...

Wait a second!

"Is this for the spleen-eaters? But didn't we talk about it earlier? Each of them could be cured! We can't blow them up!"

"These are Molotovs, not dynamite, Anna!"

"Still, weapons of mass destruction!"

"Call the UN! I need to get back to Lesley alive!"

"How? Exterminating them like rats? There are not enough flammables in the world to get you to Birmingham!"

"What's wrong with you, Anna? The one thing I want is to make it through and get back to my family!" he roared.

I closed my eyes. Dan was right. Who cared about filthy spleen-eaters, whether people or zombies, if you couldn't hug those you loved? Who was I to judge the price he was willing to pay? Wouldn't I do the same?

I was jealous. A thousand miles away, like a lighthouse, like a guiding star for his ship, Lesley was waiting for him. I hadn't heard anything from Steve for almost three days, and now that my phone was destroyed, I wouldn't hear for much longer.

"I'm sorry, Dan," I said. "I wish there was something I could do."

Dan walked to me and hugged me. This hug made me feel even worse, so I blinked the tears back before the tap opened and the flood drowned us all.

"Maybe, this can help?" he whispered into my ear, sliding something flat and heavy into my lab coat pocket, like a drug dealer passing over a stash. "I don't know who it belonged to, but I'm sure they won't need it soon."

Louise grabbed the squirty bottles, Dan packed away the grenades, and I picked up the lab stand. We were about to head out when Dan's phone chirped an incoming WhatsApp.

"Kay's wishing us to break a leg," he snickered.

The image of Dan, myself, and statue-rigid Louise dancing can-can – in France, it had to be can-can – in front of the monster crowd made me snicker, too. Maybe, Dan's pyrotechnics would make our audience more sympathetic to our limited dancing skills, and they'd applaud before eating us.

The last to leave the lab, I turned the lights off and locked the door behind me. Then, I pulled the flat object from the coat pocket.

It was a mobile phone.

6.

When Kay wished us to break a leg, I'm sure she didn't mean it literally, but the Universe, a humorous bitch, took this request to heart.

The start of our journey was promising. The lift took our heavy-duty trolley to the ground floor. We readied our weapons, but like Louise said, there were no monsters in the vast foyer of the Science building. I wished she'd mentioned the sheer number of dead bodies all over the floor – people mauled by monsters, monsters with their brains smashed out, all mixed up in a macabre display of Apocalypse, no clear patch to step on.

And the stench!

We couldn't roll our trolley through this cemetery. In the lead, Dan picked up the front wheel, and I grabbed the back of the trolley. Treading forward, I focused on each step, avoiding the heads and faces as much as possible while the small bones cracked and broke under my feet.

The exit was so close.

Then Dan slipped, landing awkwardly onto his right foot, dropped his end of the trolley, and plonked face forward into a heap of bodies. I ditched the trolley and rushed over to pull him up on his feet. He groaned and pushed me away.

"I think I broke my ankle."

He sat on someone's back, rolled up his jeans, took his shoe off, and stared at the foot. It was red and swelling rapidly but didn't look broken to me. Hell, I was no expert – how many broken ankles had I seen in my life?

"Can you walk?" asked Louise from above. "I can hear the footsteps. We need to get out of here!"

I helped Dan up, letting him lean on me and distribute more weight towards his left foot, but his face turned red, and he dropped to his knees with another groan. "Get out of here and leave me!"

Leave him? Oops, he's hit his head, too!

I heard the footsteps, too, coming from the depth of the corridor. Perfect timing, bastards!

"Louise, help me with the trolley. Dan, get on it and let's go!"

Once we dragged the trolley over the bodies to the clear patch at the doors, I dragged Dan on top of the trolley and pointed at the food box. "Guard it with your life, or I'll get to you before those buggers do!"

"I know that is not ideal," said Louise. "But those Molotovs might come in handy now."

Before I could protest, the spleen-eaters ran from around the corner.

Oh yes! Get the grenades out!

They were a throng, and as soon as they located us, they sped up, undisturbed by the bodies that they trampled on their way.

"Louise, cover our backs. Dan, get the Molotovs out!"

I could make a great army general – if my army were fully disposable.

We rolled out of the Science building straight onto the grass slope, and the heavy-duty trolley immediately gained momentum, continuing down the hill, with little control from me, past the Langevin building.

Change of plans!

Dressed in suits, with ties waving merrily behind them, dozens of spleen-eaters flocked out of the Langevin building as we passed. Oh hello! How was the conference?

"Dan, it is time for the Molotovs!" shouted Louise.

The trolley sped up on the slope, making me run so fast that my lungs were bursting out of my chest. I focused on the path ahead – if I tripped the trolley, we were cooked.

Dan took one of his deadly bottles out and fiddled with a lighter.

Louise screamed.

"Fire in the hole!" shouted Dan.

I expected a kaboom, but nothing happened. I turned around and saw a monster kicking the bottle out of his way, the flame on the bottle dying.

"Abort mission!" shouted Louise. "Get inside!"

Heavy with supplies, plus the weight of Dan's fat arse, the trolley jumped on a bump and went wild across the lawn, almost tipping over. With an enormous effort, I forced it straight, trying to steer the trolley into the open doors of the restaurant, but the stupid trolley went too much to the right.

At our speed, there would be no braking.

"We gonna go in full!" I shouted to Dan. "Brace yourself!"

Dan took a "brace-brace" position, protecting all the vital body parts, I ducked my head, and we throttled at full speed into the restaurant hall through the glass wall.

The ringing of the broken glass filled my ears, and the stinging shards rained all over my head and shoulders. The trolley dragged me on, my feet ploughing the floor. With a final effort, I steered the trolley towards the kitchen. The kitchen doors swung open under the weight of the trolley, and we finally stopped.

Louise hopped in a second later and locked the door behind.

"Barricade!" I screamed, pushing a massive deep fryer, still full of cold, thick oil, to the door a second before the first wave of the monsters smashed into the door.

The door cracked but didn't give in. Louise pushed a fridge to the door while I looked around for an alarm button. We really needed a weapon of mass destruction!

Or a fire.

"Dan, I need one of your babies!"

Dan lit up another bottle and handed it to me.

"Louise, get Dan to the back!"

She carted the trolley away, and I turned to the door. I had one go at it; if it didn't work, the hungry buggers would have a good go at me.

I broke the small window in the kitchen door with my lab stand and tossed the bottle through the hole. The bottle smashed into pieces, spitting out fire flames. The closest monsters lit up and, trying to shake it off, threw themselves onto their fellas. In less than a second, almost all spleen-eaters I could see were ablaze. They screamed, scratching and thrashing to get the burning clothes off, their screams attracting more monsters. Those who came caught the fire, too. The smell of fried meat filled my nostrils.

The water sprinkler system clicked on and started pouring water onto the monsters, drowning their moans in the noise, but the fire alarm still didn't ring.

I decided that if I survived, I'd log a maintenance complaint with the Health and Safety. Or not. I just saw one of them turn into a torch. He wouldn't be accepting complaints this week.

An inhuman shriek from the back of the kitchen brought me back into reality, and I ran, praying that we hadn't carted ourselves into a trap while setting on fire our only exit.

There was barely any light in the back room. Dan stood on his left foot, holding onto the kitchen worktop, staring widely at something – someone – in the shaded corner. I prepared to swing my lab stand hard, when the zombie with purple hair jumped on me from the shadow and… gave me a bear hug.

"Max?"

"I should have known it was you guys. So much noi—"

"MAX!"

Louise lowered her squirty bottle.

"This is Max," I told her when he let me out. "He is alive."

It was Max, for real, alive, not his ghost. He looked awful, though, his face gaunt and grey, with massive blues under his eyes, his cheeks sunken, his collarbone showing through his dirty pullover.

It was our fault. We'd left Max to die, and now he looked as if he had, was buried, and then scraped himself out of the grave.

"But how…?" I asked.

Max rolled up the leg of his trousers, showing a thick scab instead of a nasty wound. "I had a few rough days outside but managed to make it here. It could be worse, I suppose."

He pointed at the freezers and shelves around him. The storeroom was full of food pallets, with batteries of cans and jars lining the shelves. An empty tin of beef ragout lay tipped over on the rug in the corner next to two freshly killed spleen-eaters.

"Here I am, chilling with my dinner. Then, bang, the sky's going down on me. The doors slammed open in my face, and Dan almost fell into my arms. And those guys with him."

Max pointed at Louise, "This lady here drove one over with a trolley."

"It is nice to meet you, Max," said Louise, "but there are more of 'those guys', and they will break in through the door any minute. Is there any other exit out of here?"

"They are not coming," I told her, "I've used one of Dan's cocktails."

"Cocktails?" asked Max.

"Anna has toasted some spleen-eaters!" Dan cheered with a kiddy joy in his voice. I cast him a look of grown-up disapproval.

"Let's get out before we are toast, too!" said Louise, swiping the tins off the shelves into the box on the trolley.

"Why is there no fire alarm, then?" Dan turned serious.

"There is no electricity in the building," said Max. "If the alarm is wired to the mains, it won't work."

"I don't think there will be an alarm," I nodded. "But the sprinklers have gone off, so we won't get toasted."

We shoved the cans and tins from the shelves into the box on the trolley and some more into our backpacks. Then I helped Dan to climb on. Max led the way out of the storeroom and, via secret eleven passages, to the other side of the restaurant.

This area was dry and quiet, with no trace of anyone or anything alive, as if we were in a Stephen King's novel, and our plane had landed in the past, in the middle of the break between lunch and dinner time. The air had a thin veil of smoke and smelled pleasantly of a well-done steak.

And no Langoshmangers, or whatever they were called.

The restaurant was full of voices and laughter what seemed like yesterday. We sat around the corner table, strategically located next to the wine cabinet, and argued how much palladium we needed for the reference samples while sticking our forks into a creamy fish parmentier.

That world didn't exist anymore. Restaurants. Take-out coffees. Food delivery. Langoshmangers ate it all.

Instead of leading us out of the building, Max opened an internal door and helped me roll the trolley into a dark room. Dan turned the torch on his phone.

The room was a large, windowless meeting space with an oval table in the middle and a flat-screen TV on the wall. It smelled dry and stale, as if it hadn't been used for months, apart from the message drawn in the thick layer of dust. "Les temps de merde".

Shitty times...

That should be fresh.

"We can hide here until dark and then walk to the ring. Crossing the campus in the daylight is sheer madness; no offence, guys. The zombies are slower at night, so we will have a better chance."

"I guess their circadian rhythms are similar to those of humans. They do not sleep but need some downtime," Louise nodded.

"That's a great way to put it." Max studied Louise's face in the scarce light from Dan's phone. "Do you work on campus? I think I've met you before."

"New labs in the Science Building, Cellular biology, mostly BM16".

"Do you know Michael Levits? He looks after the new labs."

"He is dead," Louise said. "He was my boss."

I sat on the floor next to Max. I had much to tell him about Genny and Saint-Aupre, Ali and dyes, the internet and our search for a cure. But most of all, I wanted to say "sorry" and "I told you so" because – didn't I tell him it was nothing but a scratch?

I looked at his face, and the words didn't come out.

I was so excited to see him alive and uninfected in the kitchen storeroom that I forgot to… see. A rookie error.

No, don't get me wrong, my eyes did the watching, and my brain processed the image – Max looked terrible – which made sense because, hell, he had to survive the shitshow on his own.

But now I *saw*, with my heart. As if someone flicked a switch inside Max, his eyes no longer had the light in them. It's weird how you start noticing this kind of woolly things when the times turn dark. Kay might have a good word for it, something from the Bible, but I've never believed in things that can't be plonked on the scales or detected with a good blast of X-rays.

Kay says that a longing heart always finds God, one way or another.

I think she's a bit yahoo. We all are.

One way or another.

"Anna! Anna? She's spaced out!"

"Does it often happen lately?"

I shook the thoughts off and stared at Louise, hovering over me with a first-aid kit. "Your face is bleeding."

She dropped a pack of plasters on my lap and walked over to Dan, who lay stretched on the trolley. Even without pulling his sock down, I could see how swollen his ankle was. Louise grabbed his foot and poked the ankle with her fingers. Dan echoed her touches with a muffled moaning.

"What is pain if not an electrochemical reaction?" Louise's soft voice spread around the room. "The tissues in the injured area release chemicals, pain mediators, that react with the receptors on the nerves. Those receptors change shape or oxidation state, creating an electric impulse that travels from one cell to another and straight towards the brain, reaching the parietal lobe. There, the neurons connect with the other parts of the brain and process the information about 'what', ' where' and 'how much'."

Then she found a soft spot, grasped it tight, and pulled. Something cracked. Dan meowed out a "fuck you" and dropped dead on the trolley.

Oh. Wow. She's killed him.

7.

"...I made it to the Technopole but couldn't keep going further. There were more and more monsters closer to the city centre, and I was scared of what I would see."

Max's voice penetrated through my sleep, and I opened my eyes. The torch on Dan's phone drew a bright circle of light on the ceiling, sending shadows creeping across the room. Max's face looked ghostly in this light as if he didn't belong to the world of living anymore, but then he scratched his side, and that ordinary human gesture reminded me he was of flesh and blood.

Dan was propped up next to me, his ankle – sprained and not broken – fixed in a sophisticated ballpoint pen and elastic bandage construction. Louise huddled near the door, her eyes closed, her hand grasping a squirt bottle.

I stretched, and my body responded with pins and needles.

"I think I fell asleep," I said. "What time is it now?"

"We all dozed off," said Louise. "But it is past six, so it should be dark outside. Perfect time to get going."

Nobody moved.

Dan didn't want to move at all – even despite the painkillers that Louise fed him, every movement still hurt. Max also didn't look very excited about going back to ID26. Okay, living in the restaurant had certain advantages over our cramped control room, but what about the added appeal of the crew?

"Have you been to the city, Max?" I asked.

He nodded.

I'd never pluck up the courage to venture outside campus. The Ring was a depressing jungle of concrete and metal, spiced up with Edsie's snoring, but it was also a safe zone, a comforting "known" in our crumbling reality.

Walking out of the electric-fenced campus was beyond my imagination. With cold winds sweeping from the Isère and tall grey buildings overshadowing the streets like giant gargoyles, Grenoble was not a welcoming place even in its pre-zombie times. A beautiful city, in its own way – if you found beauty in grey, cold, and miserable – but now it lay barren, ruined, and full of predators. Why would I go anyway?

"I walked along the Avenue des Martyrs but didn't see a single human, but a few spleen-eaters. There was a bed sheet hanging from a balcony with an SOS written over it, but when I got to the apartment, there were six dead bodies. Rotting. Might be a week off. Not eaten, shot, but I didn't find a gun or anything. I don't think it was a suicide."

That is what I've learnt from Hollywood's take on the post-apocalypses. Rule number 1: if you think you are a sole survivor, you are wrong. Rule number 2: if you think the other survivors are friendly, you are wrong. Rule number 3: if you can avoid meeting other survivors, do that.

Max rubbed his eyes and continued. "Cars are everywhere, all abandoned, some with bodies in them. A derailed train over the lines, burnt almost to the strips. The only way to get out of the city is by boat. Or by foot."

"Can you get to Saint-Aupre by boat?"

Max looked up at me, a heartache splashing in his brown eyes.

"I saw the message," he said. "Genny's one of them now. She's never made it out of the building."

I could have told him we would find a cure and bring Genny back, but I didn't. The more time had passed, the less hope I had left for myself. The cure seemed like a dream rather than a guaranteed reality.

Only heartbreak was guaranteed.

I recalled how Max insisted on joining our mission. He was never going to return to ID26 with us – all he wanted was to find Genny. Was the scratch a ruse? Did he know he wasn't infected?

Dan stared at Max, too, an angry wrinkle forming on his forehead. Before he opened his mouth, I forced out a cough, two, three, until he turned to me. Luckily, we'd known each other for long enough that I could communicate a "shut up, not now" in a single, very intense look.

Wasn't Dan the one going to run away to find Lesley? He would have to run much further than Saint-Aupre.

"We should get going," Louise suddenly stood up. "It should be dark enough."

While I helped Dan back onto the trolley, Max stopped by the table and wrote on its dusty surface with a permanent marker: "Anna. Louise. Dan. Max. 24.02.2024".

I chuckled. Soon, vandalising things could become mainstream. Why don't you draw on the table if you can't sit down for a meal anymore? Why don't you paint a skull on the car no one will ever drive? The world turned into a canvas for the self-expression of the few remaining.

A grim realisation hit me then. That was no art.

That was a tombstone.

Within the few hours we spent in the meeting room, the weather outside had changed – the sunshine turned into a blizzard, unleashing the rage of heaven and hell. We stopped by the exit, peering through the wall of rain, sleet, and smashing wind, straining to see a single glimpse of light. It was quiet inside the restaurant, like in a derelict cinema, and I couldn't force myself to open the front door. The raging elements suddenly scared me more than the monsters, no doubt waiting for us behind this wall of rain.

"Can't see shit," said Dan.

"Fantastique!" Louise nodded.

Then, in her regular straightforward manner, she pushed the door open and walked off into the waterfall as if the waters parted for her, like for Moses. Well, even if they did, we wouldn't see shit.

Max stared at me. I shrugged.

"Yes, she is one of those, very strong-minded," I said. "I guess sitting in the cupboard can do that to you."

"Cupboard? What the…? Does she even know where she is going?"

"That way" would be the best answer, but I couldn't even say which way that was in this darkness. Louise simply vanished behind the wall of water, and even if I called her to come back, she wouldn't hear me.

She wouldn't see me, hear me, or know I was next to her, and neither would the spleen-eaters. For once, Mother Nature was on our side!

I pushed the trolley into the elements, hoping that Dan would hold on to the boxes of supplies. The freezing wind almost swept me off my feet, but I grabbed the trolley tight. Pushing it against the wind seemed impossible at first. Then, the wheels started moving slowly, as if they were square.

One foot at a time. Another foot. Boiling sweat trickled down my neck. The wind smacked my face, twisted and tangled my hair, sticking it onto my wet cheeks. The rain stung my eyes with water every time I opened them, so I squeezed them shut and kept moving forward, wherever this "forward" took me and my hobbling trolley.

It could lead me to the other side of campus or sweep me like Dorothy into the Emerald City, but I trusted it; I felt that nature was with me. I was in the middle of the hurricane, and I felt free.

There could be hordes of blood-thirsty zombies parading around me in the rain – I didn't care. I dropped the trolley and ran into the rain, raising my hands into the skies in a cathartic dance.

The world was still there – with its sunshine or blizzard. The mountains stood, and the tides came and went. Was the Universe itself telling us that not all was lost? That there was a chance to rebuild if we held on?

"Can you hear me?" I called out to the Universe. "Am I your child?"

There was no sign from the open skies, no lightning to say someone up there heard me. Max gently patted me on my shoulder. I grabbed the trolley again, and we moved ahead, where Louise's lab coat briefly glimpsed white through the darkness.

The walls of the Ring rose in front of us. I expected hundreds of spleen-eaters around it, but there was not a being in sight, which meant a distance of a couple of inches in this pouring rain.

"Where are the buggers?" Dan shouted to me from the trolley.

"All animals are taking shelter in such weather," Louise's voice cut through the howling storm. "Come. I will get us in through the service door."

She stopped at the Ring outer wall, waved her pass in front of the solid concrete, and a secret door opened like in an Arabic fairy tale, letting us into the warm and dry building. I cast a questioning glance at Max, but he shrugged.

The cosmic bond inside me snapped when the door shut behind us, cutting off the noise and elementals outside. But I felt it again before it was gone.

Hope.

8.

Dan said that we couldn't take every spleen-eater we'd killed with us. He was right – not all dead spleen-eaters made good samples. Take Veemal and Christian; we had to leave them for good. Christian, the cleaner, fell after a close encounter with Louise's squirt bottle. Veemal, a visiting researcher from ID31, met Max's butcher knife "face to face". We discarded what was left of his brain as unsuitable for sampling.

"Please do not aim at their heads next time," Louise asked Max. "We have wasted pretty good brain samples."

He shrugged. "If I don't, they'll keep coming after me."

"How did you know they would make good samples?"

Have I told you about Louise's proprietary stare? Here it was, telling me all I needed to know about my level of intelligence.

"Good brain samples are the ones that you do not need to scrape off the floor," she explained, in case the stare was not sufficient.

From this point of view, the campus was full of samples. The problem was that they were attached to the bodies wanting to eat our spleens. For the rest of it, they were ace.

This time, coming back was different – with WhatsApp running, we'd informed the remaining ID26 crew of our progress, exchanging "Shit, we are going to die", "Who the hell is Greg?", and of course, the infamous wish of breaking the leg from Kay.

But for one thing.

"What the— " said Kay when Max entered the control room. She turned to me – why me? – and asked, "Was it some kind of a prank?"

"Yeah, man," said Edsie, "not funny. We kinda buried you and all."

He pointed at the whiteboard with the expanding "Fallen" list.

"Sweet. And I expected champagne and fireworks!" Max chuckled.

"Come on, folks, it's Max! He is not a spleen-eater, and he is not dead! Isn't it a reason for celebration?" I nudged them.

Kay grabbed her cross and started muttering.

What's next? Exorcism?

"What the hell is wrong with you all?" I shouted. "This is Max! He's back! Get your act together!"

Did the fact that he died (although not for real) and came back alive make him an actual zombie? Ironically, that would make him the first proper zombie in this stupid "Evil Dead" carnival.

Kay must have received a ping back from "the Top" that Max was valid because she stopped muttering into her cross and hugged him. Finally!

After that, we fell into an established routine: Tanya snivelled, Kay handed her tissues, and Edsie demanded a recap, interrupting with stupid questions ("Squirt bottles? What are those?"). While Tanya and Kay cooked dinner from the food we delivered, fiddling with the kettle to cook spaghetti in it, and Louise tended to Dan's foot, I pushed my sim card into the new phone and put it on charging. The screen lit up within a few minutes, and I reset WhatsApp to my account.

Not expecting any response, I sent a message to Steve. But in less than ten minutes, he replied, CALL NOW?

I retreated into the hutch and dialled, my hands shaking in anticipation. This time, I promised myself, I'd spend every second telling Steve how much I loved him. Who knew how much we had left? He had to know. He had to know that nothing had changed, and I still loved him, now even stronger than ever.

But when his face appeared on the screen, I choked on my words of love.

Steve was not alone. Four other people sat beside him around a small table, staring at me through the screen, like in a Zoom job interview, with their notepads and pens ready to take notes and score my performance.

Confused, I scanned the faces but recognised one – Steve's dad, my almost father-in-law-to-be.

"Are you there, Anna?"

And you, hello. I nodded, not sure what to say. Was I in the correct meeting, and why didn't anyone send me an agenda in advance?

"Last time we talked, you mentioned that you were working on a vaccine. Have you made any progress? Can you tell us more?"

I froze, feeling ashamed for some reason, as if I'd lied on my CV and got ousted. But I didn't do anything wrong! I told him about our research efforts because I wanted to share what had been happening in my life, not to get a job interview.

"I was expecting to talk to you, Steve." I was getting angry.

What was this show about? I had been worried sick that he died or turned into a monster because he didn't bother to call or respond to my messages, and all this time, he was busy getting an interview panel together. Is this Asian lady to his right a part of the Equality and Diversity team?

"I am sorry, Anna," said Steve, at least making himself sound sorry. "I… it's been quite tough in here. We've lost many people in under two days, and all the monsters in the city seem to be coming after us. If there is anything that can help, we need it asap."

He almost begged, and my anger flipped into guilt. Stupid baby Anna whining about not getting love letters while Steve was doing the adult things – leading people, taking care of refugees, bringing supplies.

Couldn't his super-military dad or another one of those panellists do it and leave my Steve to text me from time to time that he was alive?

I sighed.

"We don't have much. We know that the virus attacks the brain," I said.

That was a lie, scientifically speaking, because we *thought* differed from *knew for sure*. The latter required testing, data collection, analysis, and the brains that we didn't have.

Monster brains, I mean.

A muffled rumbling sounded from Steve's side as the people around the table turned to each other. I couldn't hear what they were saying but could see from their faces – it wasn't enough.

I wasn't enough.

I hadn't realised how advanced the modern technology was until this moment. It transferred the disappointment – through wires and satellites – and splashed it into my face.

Yikes. It hurt.

"Do you have anything else, Anna?"

I shook my head. "Normally, our test samples wouldn't be trying to eat us—"

Steve smiled, and my heart flapped from my chest, dropped to the floor, and broke into pieces.

"When you know more, can you drop me another message? I'll talk to you later," Steve said. "Alone," he added.

I nodded. He hung up.

I sat there, staring at the screen absent-mindedly, trying to focus on the positive things. I'm back to ID26. I haven't died today. I'm about to have a proper meal that doesn't involve noodles. I'll talk to Steve later. Alone. I'll tell him that I love him.

It will be fine, won't it?

When I returned to the control room, the guys had already finished dinner. Tanya handed me a bowl of cold spaghetti with tomato and tuna sauce, and I tucked in, my mind going through the details of my interview. Should I have shared Greg's ideas with the interview panel? How many of them would take it seriously?

"You did the right thing," Kay patted my shoulder sitting down next to me. "Crazy or evil, he's one of us."

"Who?" I asked, still thinking of Steve.

"Greg. It's good that you didn't kill him."

There was a lot I could have told her about my ideas of "good", but she would label those as "sin" and then waste her whole life praying for me.

"How have things been here?" I asked instead. "Has Edsie managed to get hold of his wife?"

Kay shook her head and whispered. "I've heard that he wasn't really into that marriage anyway. I've met Stefania once, and I'll tell you, she's more like an icebreaker than a human woman. Hardcore lady!"

She checked that Edsie wasn't listening and added, looking pointedly at Tanya, "Anyway, it looks like some other parallel lines have crossed."

Was there a sin of gossip? Was it my turn to pray for Kay?

While I stared, Tanya put the last spoonful of her tuna pasta into Edsie's plate. He picked it up, without noticing where it came from, and shoved it in his mouth while talking to Max. She took his empty plate to the sink to wash it.

Oh, for crying out loud. Edsie, of all people!

"You were looking in the wrong place," Louise's voice interrupted my internal speculations, and at first, I thought she meant Tanya and Edsie.

Louise held a microscope glass slide with Ali's name scribbled on it. Straight after dinner, she disappeared into the lab to look at the samples of Ali's spleen. Now, she came to confirm what I suspected earlier.

"To cause such behavioural damage, the biggest colonies of the virus would inhabit the brain, not the spleen. Of course, we cannot exclude any molecular damage on the cellular level, but the spleen looks intact."

"So, all this dye was for nothing?" Kay asked.

"No, why? Have you got any brain slices? Those will need staining."

"Ehm," I sighed, "we kinda don't. We binned them."

"No, we didn't!" said Tanya from behind Edsie's shoulder.

We all peered at her.

"I packed Ali into the fridge. Didn't feel right to throw him in the bin."

Louise turned to me.

"When you said you named him Ali, I thought you were joking!"

I pointed at the labelled glass slides in her hand, "What did you think Ali stood for? Advanced laser image?"

"We don't know his name, but he had a turban… you know, a Sikh hair thingy," Kay explained.

"It's called a burka."

"You are a burka, Edsie! Burka is for women!"

Imagine an early years teacher watching their students write their first word, but it's a "C" word scribbled on the wooden desk with a penknife. That is how Louise looked at us, and I felt ashamed and confused at the same time.

"Have you guys never heard about ethics in research?"

"The sort of don't plagiarise and don't fake the data?" asked Edsie.

"She means the whole "living thing" ethics," said Tanya.

Louise smiled at Tanya. Oh, look who's on a good list!

"You see," Dan explained, "normally, our test subjects aren't very *living*, so we don't have much training in that direction."

"None at all," Kay clarified.

"None at all," agreed Dan. "We are all chemists. The only living thing in my lab is me. Or rather, Anna. Okay, most of the time, it's Anna. I don't know about Anna, but our samples don't usually complain about unethical treatment. Anyway, Ali can't complain, either. He is not very living at the moment."

We could have had an interesting discussion about what or who was considered living – generally and for the purpose of this exercise, but from the little time I'd known Louise, I knew that she chose her battles wisely.

"Fine," she said. "Let's look at Ali, then."

Sample Date	26/02/2024
Sample Name	ALI-013-BR
Category	Brain
Source	Ali, infected, last stage, male, ca. 45 years old
Notes	Frozen at 16.43 on 18/02/2024
Sampled by	Louise Aurelienne
Notes by	Louise Aurelienne
Observations	Confusing

Chapter 4. Max

1.

Day 22, 26th of February, Mon

To our relief, Louise took over the scientific agenda. When Tanya brought the brain back from the freezer, Louise sliced it with the microtome onto twenty glass slides and coded them as ALI-013-BR.

Then she taught Kay and me how to stain and prepare the samples.

Meanwhile, "the boys" decided to refurb the hutch. Those massive chillers, now useless, would serve a better purpose outside of the beamline as a first circle of protection against the monsters.

"And we could turn the hutch into a proper bedroom for all of us," Dan added, jumping around on one healthy foot and mainly giving orders.

The idea of barricading was a good one. The concept of shared sleeping quarters – so-so. Not with Edsie already nesting there. We would have to kick him out to make it inhabitable for everyone else.

Except for Tanya.

Tanya had moved her makeshift bed to the hutch next to Edsie. I hoped that was because Edsie was big and radiated lots of heat, not wanting to admit that the more I looked at them, the better I saw that Gossip Kay was right. But goodness, who in his sane mind would pick Edsie? He was twenty years older, brainless, mannerless, and full of... Edsie!

But then, what did I know about Tanya?

Quiet, withdrawn, highly introverted, very professional. Born to Vietnamese parents who moved to England when she was around ten, she had been working with Kay since her first day at the University. No boyfriend, no family.

That's not much at all. I didn't even know Tanya had epilepsy!

Is that why she wasn't very outgoing?

When we went out as a group – in the academic community, those outings were critical for maintaining the desire to live among constantly depressed staff and students – Tanya would suffer through a tiny glass of wine by the time we finished our third bottle and would sneak out unnoticed.

Not everyone's a party animal, I know. At work, she's always been irreplaceable. As a senior technician tasked to look after the lab and equipment, she had a supernatural sense for any glitches before they turned into disasters, leading to shutdowns for days.

We'd never had shutdowns.

One day, she turned up in the lab, barely standing on her feet, shivering from fever.

"I have a bad feeling, Anna," she said, almost fainting.

I called her a taxi and promised to check everything twice before locking the lab for the night. When I was about to leave, I heard a hissing sound – one of our gas cylinders was leaky. If I weren't there to turn on the extraction and retighten the valves, the lab would become a gas chamber overnight. One spark of static and we would be a sweet memory!

Now, if Tanya's shit-radar was so sensitive, wouldn't she know better than to mingle with Edsie? Or had the radar been broken during the Apocalypse?

No, the option where I was wrong about Edsie did not exist.

I needed a brain recharge. No better place for that than the toilet, where I could stay alone without people asking me what was wrong with my face.

For other purposes besides thinking, the need for the toilet as a facility is overrated, at least in our situation. See for yourself. An average human being needs to pee 6-8 times per day, beer unaccounted for. If you are situated within a hand-reach from the toilet, those 6-8 times do not matter, but if you have to leave the safety of the beamline, those 6-8 times are a lot. One time could kill you.

Luckily, humanity has a well-tested solution to this problem – a potty.

For hygienic reasons, we'd installed our version – the cleaners' bucket – in the small chemistry room at the end of our beamline and emptied the "potty" one or two times per day. That was my excuse to get out of the hutch.

Shadows were dancing around the toilet; the last lightbulb had burnt out a few days ago. Dark circles under my eyes had grown since I last saw myself in the mirror. I tipped the bucket contents into the toilet bowl, closed the cubicle door, and put the toilet lid down.

Sit. Think.

The door to the toilet opened with a bang. In the following second, my brain went through a million ideas of using the bucket as a weapon and settled on the "prepare to die" strategy.

"Anna?" Louise's voice. "I know you are there."

"Gosh, Louise! You've scared the shit out of me. Are the girls going in pairs again?"

I unlocked the door and peered out of the cubicle.

"No," Louise shook her head. "There is something I wanted to ask you. Your fr-riend, Max… Have you noticed how he scr-r-ratches his side?"

Her French accent perked up again.

"Max? What about him?"

And why are we discussing him in the toilet?

"Watch him. I do not think he even notices, but he scr-ratches his left side all the time in the same spot as if he has an itch there."

"What if so?"

"He might have got scr-ratched in that stor-rage room."

"And what?"

"He got scr-r-r-ratched, Anná!" she shouted. "I think qu'il est infecté! Bientôt... soon he will tur-rn!"

I pulled a chunk from the toilet roll and crumpled in my hands.

"Bullshit! Didn't you say that the incubation period takes around twelve hours? It has been almost a day! He would be already one of them!"

She sighed.

"Listen, I do not know. He is young and physically fit, so his immune system might be fighting the virus. But if I am right, soon it will start to show, his eyes and all... I do not know how much time we will have after that."

"Then we should tell him," I turned to the door and hesitated, wondering how exactly I would put it down.

Hey, Max, how is it? Rate my spleen on a scale from one to ten.

"No, wait! It might sound crazy, but I think we should not."

"What?"

She hesitated. "Look, it is sort of... final. Once you are infected, there are not many options. And not much time... Would you prefer to know you have just a few hours?"

"I think so."

"It is not that, Anna. It is about what happens to him *after*."

I caught my reflection in the toilet mirror – wide eyes, pale face, the vein beating through the skin on my neck. I began to understand.

"You *want* him to turn! You want him for samples!"

She nodded.

"No way, Louise. Weren't you the one about ethics? We can't do it to Max; he is one of us. It's not some random dead bugger out there."

"When he turns, we will not be one of us. He will be *them*."

I covered my ears with my hands – kids do this when they want to block off the outside world, searching for comfort from pain. The mere idea of having Max as a lab rat, infected or not, made me sick. There was a massive difference between Ali, an unknown spleen-eater we killed in self-defence, and Max. Ali was merely a dead body, but Max was a friend. He'd saved Dan's life. How can I even discuss this with Louise – a stranger all in all? What does she know?

I ordered myself to focus. Emotions were a plague of good science.

Even if she was right, Max had been scratched, and the virus took over him in a few hours; he still wouldn't be dead. We would need to convert a spleen-eater Max into a Max-set-of-samples.

What Louise was proposing was beyond human. But it was a very scientific approach.

"What do you suggest?" I sighed.

"Watch him, and if… when his eyes start going, we lock him in the hutch. When he turns completely, we can take samples."

"You missed one bit," I pointed out.

She shrugged. Her scientific approach didn't offer suitable solutions to killing the elephant in the room.

"I need to talk to the others about it. And no, I am not avoiding responsibility."

"I know," she nodded. "That is why I came to you."

I walked out of the toilet, unsure what to do next. Maybe, I should have let Louise start the conversation. Wasn't she our expert in unusual side-scratching?

The guys were finishing arranging the chillers around the control room door into some sort of a wall with gaps that reminded me of arrow slits. I immediately noticed Max scratching his T-shirt on the left, right under the ribs. Now that a lab coat didn't cover it, I saw a thin cut in the fabric.

It didn't mean anything at all.

"Can I have some quick help, Dan?"

He turned around and eyed the empty bucket in my hand.

"With that?"

I nodded.

"Now?"

I grabbed his hand and dragged him into the small room at the end of the beamline. Behind the closed door – which, of course, didn't look suspicious at all – I told Dan about Louise's speculations.

"Yes, I've noticed it, too," said Dan.

"What do you think?"

He shrugged. "We just wait and see."

"What about the incubation period?"

"What about it?"

"It's been over twelve hours since he could have been scratched. It can't be the virus, then."

I didn't want to wait and see; I needed reassurance.

"Look, nobody did proper tests. We don't know anything about the incubation times. They might vary with ages or gender or whatever else."

"You are not helping, Dan!"

"Louise might be overreacting. No need to do it, too. Relax, Anna."

I wouldn't consider Louise a hysterical type, but sitting locked in the cupboard could affect even the most resilient psychic. On the other hand, she did not imagine it – Max was scratching – but suspecting something as sinister behind something as innocent?

Wait and see.

I hate it.

I went back to the control room, hoping to find something to distract myself with, and found Tanya sitting alone at the table, staring at our whiteboard absent-mindedly. Yesterday, Edsie had scraped Max's name off the Fallen list. Would we have to add it back?

"You all right?" I asked.

Tanya perked up and turned at me. For a minute, it looked like she didn't want to open up, but then she said:

"Do you remember, once you told me I was like a lab fairy? With a special sense for things that could go wrong?"

I nodded. No need to tell her that I'd moved from the fairy theory and now called it a shit-radar.

"You laughed then. You are not a fairy believer," I smiled.

"Are you?"

I chuckled.

"Sometimes, I have this funny feeling that something is not right. Something very close to me. That could harm me. It's not a gut feeling, as you call it; it's some sort of a warning... that there's a glitch and—"

There was fear in Tanya's grey eyes.

"Are you having it now?"

"You see, I didn't have a safe childhood... so I've learnt to trust my feelings. When they say "run", I run; when they say "danger", I'm ready. The problem is that I don't know what has gone wrong this time. This is not my lab. A million bad things could happen, and I wouldn't even know!"

She was pale and trembling, a drop of sweat trickling down her temple. I reached out to hug her, wondering how the hell I was supposed to talk to her about Max when she was already scared shitless.

"I'm sorry you are so worried, Tanya. But look, whatever it is this time, we will deal with it. We have managed so far, and we will manage again. Right?"

She relaxed in my embrace in a few minutes and moved away her face, now wet with tears. She smiled, got up and ran away, ashamed, like most people do after a public breakdown even though they did nothing wrong.

So... I didn't tell her. How would I put it? "I know how it feels to be out of control. By the way, it looks like Max is going to turn into a monster, and we'll have no control whatsoever. He might not, and we have no control over that. We're totally control-less. Now freak out. Oh, no, wait. Louise wants to chop Max into samples when he turns. What does your shit-radar say about that?"

***

"You have that face again," Kay patted my shoulder.

I looked at the clock on the wall. Unless I fell asleep, I'd spent the last twenty minutes staring at the whiteboard, like Tanya before me. Talk about being helpful. At least Tanya was monitoring the environment for potential hazards with her shit-radar.

"Where would I go?" I chuckled.

"Oh, I go away all the time," Kay said. "In my mind, I've been to the distant planets inhabited by unimaginable creatures."

"Bullshit."

She laughed. "True, most of the time, I go back to my family. I am blessed because they are still around. There are people who will protect them. And God is always guarding me – and them."

"What would your god say if one of us was infected?"

The smile dropped from her face as she scanned the room.

"Max," she said sadly.

Was Kay getting tip-offs through her top-level channels? I wasn't surprised she guessed straight away. It seemed like everyone had figured it out one way or another but me.

"Louise thinks he's been scratched."

"God will take care of him as He has taken care of us," Kay responded with her usual chant, but I heard doubt in her voice. A tiny grain, but as a scientist, I knew how much damage a tiny grain could do to an experiment. So many good samples had been wasted because of a speck of dust on the otherwise smooth surface.

How long will Kay's faith last?
We will wait and see.

2.

We locked Max in the hutch thirty minutes ago. He is smashing his head into the hutch door, his blood-covered face with milky eyes beastly and almost unrecognisable through a tiny window in the door.

Max didn't take long to turn. I was talking to Kay when he dropped the boxes he carried out of the hutch, complaining that he had something itchy in his eye. Tanya gave him her pocket mirror. He studied his face for a minute and tossed the mirror into the wall.

"Max?" Tanya eyed him in worry. "Are you okay?"

"I am done!" He shouted at her. "Can't you see I'm done? They got me, too!"

Tanya reached out to hug him – like I hugged her half an hour ago. "Hey, Max, everything is okay, everything is fine!"

"Get away fr-r-rom him!" Louise screamed. "He is infected!"

I hopped off the chair and reached for the lab stand, unsure who to hit – screaming Louise or sobbing Max.

Max turned to her. His right eye was now fully covered with a white veil. "You knew, you fucking hell knew it!"

He lunged at her, but Edsie caught him by the hand and jerked away from Louise. Max stumbled over the boxes and fell to his knees. Dan pressed him down to the floor, holding his hands while Edsie grabbed his thrashing feet. Twisting and wiggling, Max was lashing out at the men, saliva dripping from his mouth, but Dan and Edsie held him tight, dragged him into the hutch and locked him in it.

"Are you okay?" I asked Louise. She slipped down the wall, speechless, and nodded. I turned to Kay and Tanya. "You? Has he touched you?"

Both shook their heads. Tanya turned to Louise. "Is that right? You knew that he was infected?"

"I have noticed him scratching his side. I told Anna."

Tanya looked me in the eyes, and I knew from her face I'd better stand still and not blink. Keep eye contact. That's what the fighting cats do. If you blink, you'll get attacked.

"So, you knew, too?" she hissed.

My eyes started to dry out, but I kept staring.

"I told you I felt something was wrong, and you lied into my face. You knew all this time that Max was infected!"

"I didn't lie, strictly speaking. I just… didn't elaborate on silly suspicions. You seemed already disturbed, so I didn't want to make you more unhappy, especially if it all turned out to be nothing!" I finally blinked.

"Me? Unhappy? Let me show you fucking unhappy!"

She pounced, skipping the part where the cats puff up to look bigger and scarier. Her long, sharp nails snapped a millimetre away from my face. I caught her hands, pushing her away, but she kicked me in the belly. I let go and bent over, trying to catch my breath. Freed, her hands immediately grabbed and pulled my hair. I yelled. Even the monsters didn't use this dirty trick.

"Tanya, let go!" Edsie's voice sounded somewhere above us.

That's not Tanya, I wanted to shout, but only a wheeze came out. Tanya is a gentle, kind, if not slightly over-submissive soul. This is a bloody monster; check her eyes out!

Slowly, Edsie pulled Tanya away from me, and I crawled under the table like a cat licking his wounds after a fight.

"Are you okay, Anna?" Kay leant down to check on me.

"My hair," I moaned.

"Still there, well, most of it."

Oh, great. A large chunk of my hair was stuck between Tanya's fingers, tightly clenched into a fist. Most of it? Was there any left on my head?

I recall the times when I used to take a piss out of Dan because he was bald, you know, the aggressive type of bald that often went with race crime and drug dealing. It would make him the first-ever academic denied promotion because he didn't have enough hair.

At some point, Dan tried wearing glasses – blue filter plastic without actual lenses – to look more like a respectable academic but lost them in a student piss-up a few days later.

Respectable, heh.

Gosh, what was I thinking? The world was spiralling down, and I was worried about my hair. Was it a female thing?

Tanya seemed to calm down in her corner of the ring. Edsie brought her a glass of water and her epilepsy pills and, while she drank, untangled my hair from her grasp.

"Here, maybe you could stick it on or something," he muttered, handing it to me, his eyes avoiding mine.

I sighed. In the absence of hair salons, Tanya could keep it as a war trophy.

She put the empty glass away and scanned the room. If you didn't count the muffled screaming sounding from behind the hutch door, the silence in the control room was full of shame, guilt, and sadness, a perfect combination to start an AA club.

"You all knew. Why didn't you tell him?"

Louise shrugged. "What would it change?"

I recalled the first time I met Max. We were unloading our equipment – dozens of boxes piling up on the floor of his beamline, wires snaking around, ready to trample you over if you didn't pay attention to where you stepped. He danced around the obstacles to the corner where I attached the flow meters to the gas cylinders.

"Did you say Health and Safety let you in?" he asked. "How much have you bribed them?"

Kay chuckled. "It's all for the sake of science!"

"That means at least a few thousand," he nodded understandingly.

Kay tossed a ball of crumpled paper wrap at him and ordered him to get out of his hutch while we were wiring the gas cylinders.

"Dangerous," I explained.

"You or your gas?"

I would suspect him flirting with me, but he talked to everyone on the scene, including Edsie, in that merry, playful tone.

"I bite," I said then. "Gas doesn't."

Now look who bites.

"I would like to know," Tanya sighed. "If I got infected, I mean. It's like a malignant tumour. You'd prefer to know, although you can't do much about it."

"Cancer always gives you a chance, a hope, to the last minute," said Edsie. His sister had died from cancer four months ago.

"I felt like I had to tell him, but then there was a chance that he wasn't infected at all, and I'd look paranoid. I wanted to be paranoid. I didn't want him to know I was paranoid about him," I said.

"Now that he has turned, is it what we will do? Take his brain?" asked Kay. "Even though it's Max?"

"He is in our hutch," I said, not suggesting anything specific.

"And he has a brain," said Dan.

"All of them have a brain," I noted.

"They are not going to share."

"Is Max going?"

We stared at each other, confused about whether we were arguing or agreeing.

"Are we even discussing it for real?" Tanya rose from her chair. "Are we talking about chopping Max?"

"Yes," said Louise.

Tanya cast her an angry look. "Who the hell are you? You don't even know him! He's nothing to you but another bloody sample!"

"I know him," said Kay, clenching her cross in her trembling hand. "And we need to make a decision. We can't leave him like this. God will help us, Tanya. He will guide us through light and darkness."

Gosh, that sounded lame!

In the bright light of the control room, I saw Tanya's grey eyes turn black, pupils dilate, and before I could warn Kay, Tanya lunged, snatched the cross out of her hand and shoved it across the room. With a metallic cling, it hit the hutch door, and Max, attracted by the new sound, bumped into the hutch door from the other side, his howling reaching a new high.

"Fuck your God, Kay!" Tanya screamed. "Fuck your shitty little god! He gives no shit about you or anyone at all! Fuck him, then!"

Edsie dragged her back to the corner and forced her to sit down. Unable to pounce again, Tanya grabbed one of the glass slides from the table – with Ali's brain spread on it – and hurled it at Kay. It scratched Kay's shoulder, smashed into the whiteboard behind her and shattered into tiny pieces on the floor.

"Is this what you want to do with Max? Chop his brain? Put him on a glass slide?"

This was too much.

"Stop it, Tanya!" I climbed from under the table and grabbed my lab stand. "This is enough! Edsie, if you don't calm her down, I will chop Tanya for samples! And you, too!"

She screamed, kicking Edsie away, but he grabbed her tight, threw her over his shoulder, and carried her out of the control room. Next to me, Kay gasped and breathed out with relief.

"Are you okay?" I asked Kay.

She nodded, shaking, her eyes wide in shock. A heart-wrenching howl sounded from the hutch, reminding me to deal with real monsters first. Thrashing in the hutch was a beast, not Max we all knew, not the person in love with Genny from Saint-

Aupre. Max we knew was dead. We could put a full stop right there.

What about the cure?

We couldn't keep him locked in the hutch until we had a treatment. We would have to transfer him somewhere else; the further, the better. How would we feed him? What?

We couldn't let him loose. If he didn't come back to ID26, drawn by the flickers of memories, instinct or pure luck, one day, he would encounter another survivor who would fight for his life and cross Max out of the equation.

Or, if we were looking at pessimistic scenarios, he would starve to death when no more prey was left.

We couldn't let him go. We couldn't keep him.

As if he was a pet that we took in and were forever responsible for. A rabid one.

You put the rabid animals down.

But not the sick humans. We don't shoot sick people. We cure them.

What was different about Max that we would choose to kill him and not cure him?

One thing – he was locked in the hutch.

What would Max prefer to do?

A few days back, before he ventured outside and found out that his Genny had turned into a monster, I knew the answer – he wanted to live.

But now... I saw his eyes. This person we found in the restaurant was as much Max as this new, berserk Tanya was the lab fairy we knew.

But even if I didn't know him personally? If it was a random, unfamiliar spleen-eater locked up in the hutch? Who was I to decide on his life and death? Did the title "doctor", attached to my surname, make all the difference?

This was not a one-person decision. It was a decision of all humanity; without better candidates, the six of us would do.

"We vote," I said.

3.

People who say there is no choice but an illusion of choice are not ready to accept responsibility for their actions. Full stop.

I think of the spleen-eater that I killed on our first mission out – a woman slightly younger than Tanya with matted hair that used to be blond; I called her Emily because she deserved to have a name. Every human deserves a name, even if it's only for a postmortem tick on our whiteboard list.

I made a choice to kill Emily, and please shoot me if I ever say that I didn't have any. Oh, I did!

I could have let her eat me. I could have let her eat me and then eat Dan and Max. Or, maybe she would bite me a little, and we'd go around biting people, hand in hand, like an odd same-sex couple.

Here is to the vastness of choices!

I keep asking myself what Mom and Dad would say. Adjusted for the Apocalypse, would they say I sustained their values and made them proud? They taught me love, compassion, and hope, but what could I build from those things when everything had collapsed? What were they worth in the "kill or get killed" world?

Even hope is fleeting, flickering in the darkness like a dying star before turning into Nothing. There's not long left before it's gone, so what will remain?

We will, I remind myself. We'll still be here – hopeless, loveless, broken-hearted people and the choices we've made.

The door to the lab opened to let Dan sneak in.

"Louise told me you kicked her out of here."

I shrugged. With Edsie and Tanya occupying the toilets – in a rather unfriendly and militaristic manner – I needed to find another place to think in peace. The microscopy lab seemed suitable, even though I had to throw Louise out of her new den. She'd already Louisified it, which meant the lab looked as clean as if nobody had ever set foot in it.

"I needed to think."

"About Max?"

I turned to him. "You see, when Max was gone the first time, I imagined him and Genny in Saint-Aupre, on a stunning beach, full of sunshine... We'd let Max down, but this vision kept me hopeful, believing that something out there – God, the Universe, karma – would restore justice in the Afterlife. But now..."

"You don't believe in Afterlife for zombies?"

"I don't believe in Afterlife for samples, Dan."

God, repentance, Afterlife – that was all Kay's department, where not many scientists tended to drop in, whether because they didn't believe or couldn't admit their faith for fear of being ridiculed. And now, for the first time ever, I wondered how lonely it should have been for her.

No, I still didn't believe in God, but after seeing all the pain and heartbreak bestowed on humanity in the last few weeks, I wanted to believe in some sort of justice, a payback for the suffering and loss...

Balance. I wanted to know that the sadness would be balanced with love, if not in this lifetime, then the one that runs parallel.

There is a Universe where Anna and Steve play board games in a snowed-in chalet.

Max holds Genny's hand as they walk into the sunset.

Mom and Dad send postcards from all over the world.

And people don't get chopped into samples.

"Weirdly, I see what you mean," Dan said. "But if you keep focusing on 'could be-would be', you won't be able to keep going. And that's all that you need right now. Keep moving. Keep working. Now that we have Louise, I honestly feel we have a chance."

"So, have you made a decision, then? You want to kill Max?"

I didn't say "make samples" or "test Max" because all that was secondary. The decision was about killing or letting live. Dan looked me in the eyes, perfectly aware of the sub-text within my question, and then nodded.

"It doesn't matter if our decision is right or wrong... Is it wrong to kill one to save humanity? Is it wrong to let Max live and kill another spleen-eater instead, just because that spleen-eater isn't our friend? Or is it wrong to not kill anyone at all and give up any hope of a cure? What is wrong and right in the end? And if there are so many wrongs, is there a right at all?"

He made a point. In the absence of rights, who will judge me for picking one wrong out of dozens of wrongs? Is there a lesser wrong? Who decided on it?

I knew all he thought of was Lesly, but I suddenly felt angry. It came too easy to him, a quick decision – chop it, move on. By far, he wasn't the first one waving family like a flag, thinking it could justify any atrocity.

"I'm doing it for the people I love", and you are automatically allowed to kill. Humanity has done so many cruel things for love! Isn't it time to make decisions for humanity itself, especially if there's a grand possibility we are what's left of it?

When it comes to project management, the experts recommend "do nothing" as the first possible option when dealing with a problem or opportunity. Maybe, that's what we should do instead of deciding. Wait. Let Fate or Destiny figure it out. Do Nothing.

That might work. Until Nothing comes after us.

I looked at Dan, who seemed so easy about his decision. I recalled Tanya's anger and bitterness. I wondered what difficult conversation Kay was having with her God... and her conscience. I thought of Ali's brains neatly sliced onto a microscope slide and ready to view. I listened to my heart, knowing perfectly well how unreasonable, unreliable, and stupidly naïve it could be.

Then I made my decision.

4.

We voted four against two to make the samples out of Max.

In the whole picture of the Universe, each vote didn't matter – the majority decided, and this time, it was not in Max's favour. That's just life, someone would say, and believe me, this someone has not been on the fucked-up side.

In the whole picture of the Universe, small things rarely matter. The Universe has much bigger concerns than Max or me. I don't think even the whole of humanity – whatever is left – would be enough for the Universe to reconsider its normal flow of things.

The Universe gives no shit at all.

It's a relief of some sort. No one will prosecute us for making a wrong decision, only ourselves. The trick is that no matter how correct and reasoned the decision is, we will prosecute – we didn't simply say "yes"; we put our conscience and morale on the balance of life and death. The four of us will have to live with it.

I will live with it.

Every day I survive, I'll ask myself if I did the right thing. I took on the burden of responsibility, and although it might look like I shared it with the other three people, it's not true.

You can't share it with anyone.

It's not about samples or science. It is about the life and death of a person, and I hereby confirm that I have chosen death.

Isn't it ironic? We are probably the last representatives of humanity, and the four of us voted to kill.

No, that is not correct. Didn't I claim that the spleen-eaters were humans, too?

As the last intelligent representatives of humanity…

No, also not correct. That would include Greg-slash-Michael.

As the last sane representatives of humanity…

Haha, very funny; look at us.

Whatever. We are the last – quite likely – and as the last, we've made the decision on behalf.

What does it say about humanity in general?

My decision hasn't come easily. I've listened to all sides – my heart, mind, and conscience. It was not a compromise. A choice between life and death is always black-and-white; no greys allowed.

It was harder for Kay.

I picked up Kay's cross from the floor and returned it to her. She clenched it in her fist, muttering the soothing words of prayer, and then – tossed it in the bin. No intermediaries – imaginary or not – were allowed into the conversations with someone's conscience.

While Kay was not watching, I pulled the cross out of the bin and shoved it in my pocket. She would need it later.

With the votes cast, Tanya stormed out of the control room back to the toilet, which the opposition party of anti-samplers had made its headquarters. Edsie's vote was the same as Tanya's, but he decided to hang around. I couldn't blame him for it – Tanya's fits had started to piss everyone off.

After the votes were cast, it was nothing but business, and business was a heartless bitch.

"How do we do it? It's not like anybody will volunteer to go in there, right?" said Dan.

"Gas," Kay suggested.

While Dan and I nodded in approval, Louise looked a bit lost.

"We have cylinders full of carbon monoxide ready for the experiment. We will gas him down," Dan explained.

"We have pressure regulators on ten mil per minute," I reminded him. "This won't be enough. We made sure that the extraction in the hutch could deal with that flow."

"We'll blow them out. Fire the cylinders to full; the tubing is wide enough for a pressure build-up. We'll blast out the connectors on the regulators at full power."

"How do you know the connectors will blow, not the cylinders outside?" Louise was sceptical, a biologist in her uncomfortable playing with lethal gases. The chemists in the room were not that fussy – our samples had never minded a little gas.

"For the cases of the pressure build-up, the connectors on the regulators were made the lousy part. They will go first like a fuse."

She didn't look convinced but decided to give it a try.

"Well, I guess getting blown up is not the worst that can happen in the given circumstances."

"I'll go fire the cylinders then," I volunteered, "Louise, if you want him fresh, you better get ready for… your part."

5.

Good news – the gas had worked! The regulators went out. The room got filled with CO. Max-the-spleen-eater died a horrible death. Kay prayed for him. Louise put us on the black list on behalf of the ethical approvals board.

All within the scope of this project.

Bad news – we forgot about the gas alarm. As soon as the gas levels reached lethal, the alarm in the control room went off, just like the Health and Safety boss warned us. The thick walls of the beamline contained the sound inside, but unfortunately, *we* were stuck with it, too. The original ID26 crew was used to it by now, but Louise became agitated and restless, showing signs of mild claustrophobia.

Sitting in the cupboard did not affect her, but the beeping alarm did! Just as I started wondering if she was a human or an emotionless android.

"It will stop when the gas drops to healthy levels," Dan assured her.

It took the room almost six hours to get cleared of the gas. If we had done the calculations – as we should have – we would be ready for the wait. We knew that the extraction in the hutch struggled even with 10 ml per minute of gas, turning the hutch into a gas chamber in an hour of constant bubbling. For Max, we hit the hutch with 150 ml per minute – we didn't want a gas-drunk throwing-up zombie with a bad headache and breathing difficulties. By the time Max was dead, the gas levels hit almost 2,000 ppm.

To get the gas out, we opened the door between the Ring corridor and the hutch. The alarm became louder outside, and if the spleen-eaters were wandering nearby, they would come to check us out. But we had no other option – with the door closed, Max's body would decompose by the time the extraction took the gas out of the hutch.

It was working for the first few hours – the gas making the Brownian motion, slowly leaving the room. When the concentration dropped to less fatal but still very unpleasant 85 ppm, a spleen-eater walked straight into the hutch – doors open wide; welcome home, darling.

That was an unplanned disruption! Tanya and her shit-radar could have warned us, but since she reappeared from the toilet, her head up high and her majesty not crushed, Tanya hurled up in the corner, refusing to talk to anyone, including Edsie.

Or, probably, on her chart of shit events, a stray spleen-eater was not worth mentioning.

Now he is there, feeling drowsy and unwell but very much alive.

We have two test subjects now, but it will be another hour before Louise can move in with her tools. In this hour, we must figure out how to bring down test subject number two.

We've run out of gas.

6.

While we were considering the next steps, test subject two had nibbled a finger off test subject one. Finding it fascinating, Louise made me write a note about "the first observation of the cannibalistic/scavenging behaviour in humans infected with V-2024".

I didn't know the virus had a name.

Whether we wanted to or not, we had to deal with subject two, and quickly.

"The best way is to get the head," said Kay, offering her emergency axe for the job. "That's what they show in the movies – a hit and immediate death."

"No heads, please," Louise reminded. "We need it for samples."

"Anywhere else will not kill it," I said.

"Hey guys, I'm not going in there to *not kill it*. Because then it'll kill me," Edsie said.

There was no woolly hat this time. Only a man was suitable for the job because we were a sexist bunch of weak and scared women, wink-wink. I'd choose Dan for any mission, but he had his sprained ankle as an excuse. That left only Edsie.

I handed him the axe.

Tanya looked like she wasn't happy, but she said nothing, and I wondered – without challenging her out loud – if her monster-loving tendencies now embraced everyone outside ID26. You know, like treehuggers seemed to be in love with the whole forest and not a specific —

"Hit it on the legs," said Dan. "Straight through the knee. It won't be able to jump on you. Then, hit it through the heart. We want it dead, not vivisected!"

Reluctantly, Edsie took the axe. According to Louise, time was ticking fast for Max's brain and in a bit, the brain death would be complete. I could hardly imagine how much more dead anyone could be after that CO chamber.

"Do you trust him to do it?" Louise whispered into my ear as Edsie walked out of the control room.

Did I trust? I wouldn't trust Edsie to hold my beer. On the other hand, what could go wrong with such a detailed operating protocol? Through the knees, then through the heart. Done.

He snuck into the hutch through the same door the spleen-eater entered. Kay banged on the hutch window to attract the monster's attention. I switched the hutch camera on. At a closer look, the spleen-eater turned out to be a woman. Her pixie haircut had lost shape, and with dirt and blood covering it, it was difficult to say the colour. Her face was swollen and dirty and looked scrawny. She moved uneasily in the cramped space of the hutch, and her ragged pullover sleeves caught on the hooks and wires, slowing her down.

Attracted by the noise, she threw herself on the hutch door, not noticing Edsie sneak up on her from behind. He bent down and struck her so hard that the axe almost cut her left leg in two. Blood splashed on his feet and jeans. The woman screamed in pain and dropped down on the floor like a ragged doll, but twisted around and lunged at Edsie, barring her teeth.

"Through the heart now! We want it dead, not crawling around," I shouted, turning away to fight sudden nausea.

"Where the fuck is he going?" muttered Louise, her French accent thick in every word.

Oh no, that's no good.

Edsie, all covered in blood under his waist, barged in through the control room door, breathing heavily. A broken wail sounded from outside. It carried such unholy pain that I wanted to plug my ears with concrete and never hear anything in my life again. I locked the door behind Edsie so that nothing from outside would follow him in.

"What the hell?"

"The bitch is coming after me!"

"Comment peut-elle venir si tu lui as coupé les jambes en deux?" Louise screamed. "You were supposed to kill her!"

"It jumped on me, it jumped on me!" Edsie whined.

"It is a she, imbécile!" shouted Louise.

She pushed Edsie out of her way and stormed out of the control room, weaponless. I grabbed the lab stand and ran after her, unsure what she would do. In the hutch, I almost stepped on the body of the female spleen-eater. She was screaming in agony, her left leg barely attached to her body with a tiny piece of a shredded muscle. She kept crawling forward while a thick trail of blood started clotting behind her.

"Oh shit!"

She heard me, lifted her head and turned her face to me. I stared at her, unable to look away as if hypnotised by the milky, unseeing eyes.

The spleen-eater was crying. Her wail subsided to a quiet whine; she stopped crawling. She was barely holding her head, but when she looked at me, I knew she could see me, and I started crying, too.

Whoever she was, she deserved a dignified death, not a fucking butchering!

Louise picked up the axe that Edsie dropped on his way out, swung it high in the air and landed it precisely between the woman's shoulder blades. The bones cracked, a short whine echoed, and the body dropped to the floor with a quiet thump.

Silence.

"Twat!" said Louise. "Je vais le tuer!"

She leant over the body, pulled out the axe, wiped the blade clean with her sleeve and stormed out of the hutch.

Uh-oh.

Sample Date	27/02/2024
Sample Name	-
Category	A whole infected stage 3, female, ca. 30 yo
Source	--
Notes	--
Sampled by	
Notes by	Louise Aurelienne, recorded by Anna
Observations	The first ever observation of an infected biting another infected. Could be cannibalistic behaviour but it only chewed off a little flesh and snuffed the rest.

7.

In all honesty, we should have let Louise kill Edsie. One less mouth to feed and even less bullshit to listen to.

Dan moved out of the way when Louise headed to Edsie with the axe ready to strike. Edsie cast him "and you, Brutus" look and screamed, "Get that bitch away from me!"

Tanya bravely stepped in front of Louise.

I sighed, "Right now, the only bitch here is you, Edsie! Calm down and shut up!"

"She's going to kill me!" he continued screaming.

"If you don't shut up, I am going to kill you myself, Edsie!" said Dan, giving Louise enough space to manoeuvre the axe.

Edsie shrieked and coiled in the corner, covering his head from the blow.

It didn't come. For a moment, I considered grabbing the axe from Louise and finishing the job. Then, Greg's face came into my memory. Edsie was a twat but, in general, pretty harmless.

Louise put the axe on the computer desk and, without saying anything, turned around and went to open the door to the hutch.

"I like her," Kay said after a few silent minutes. "She doesn't look like a softy type of thing."

"You mean slimy, like Edsie!" said Dan.

She nodded.

"Hey guys, what's up with all of you? The bitch just tried to kill me, and you are on her side? She is not even one of us! We don't even know her."

"What is "one of us", Edsie?" asked Tanya. "To remind you, Max was one of us. And they gassed him! They killed him, Edsie! They will also kill you, too. Why would it be a problem? Max was a better person than you, and they still killed him. Now the crazy bitch will chop him up."

Tanya started crying. The colour drained from Edsie's face.

One day – it can be today – I will get scratched and gassed like Max. Would I care? It's a better destiny than hunting like an animal or rotting away like the leftovers of someone's dinner. But what if they come up with a cure and manage to cure everyone but me?

You can't cure the dead…

Tanya's tears felt like daggers, ripping through the skin, going straight through the heart. Her kicking and screaming felt okay, and even the hair-pulling was acceptable… in a way. She made a stand for what she thought was right. But now we had two bodies in the hutch, and Tanya's tears ran down in defeat.

Not hers. Mine. Ours.

Nobody won in this shit game. We all lost. Max lost his life; I lost hope, and Kay tossed away her faith.

"Let's go back to work," Dan said. "Louise could do with some help. Edsie, you'd better clean yourself."

Edsie nodded, still scared to speak. I patted Tanya on the shoulder, but she shook my hand off.

"If I get infected, can you promise she won't touch me? Gas me if you want, but I don't want to be a body on the table, Anna. Don't let her touch me!"

"Why me?"

She looked me straight in the eyes, anger glittering in her tears.

"Why you? Aren't you fine with all of this? You think it's right. You're doing something for humanity… You will chop your friend into pieces; how is it good for humanity? You've made friends with that psycho woman who thinks of people as samples… I don't want to be "samples" after I turn. I don't believe all that stuff about the dead people rising again, but I prefer to be burnt rather than chopped and microscoped."

She was about to walk away when I grabbed her hand. I heard you – now you listen to me.

"You think I am enjoying the 'chopping' as you call it? That it's a hobby I've dreamt of? Then listen to this – I wish I could be doing many things right now. I wish I weren't locked up in the bunker with a bunch of twats and shitheads who can't think besides themselves. I wish I didn't have to go on raids for those twats, risking my life and not knowing if I'm going to become samples or not. I wish I didn't have to kill. Or gas. Or smash. I'm very peaceful at heart. But I'll continue doing what's right, even when I wish I didn't have to. And if it means you, Tanya, have to become samples after you turn, I'll do it. I promise you. I will do it myself."

I let go of her shoulder and walked to the hutch. I knew she was staring at my back in horror, like the rest of the crew, but it didn't matter anymore.

I said what I meant.

I'd do it myself.

***

If you look at it properly, "myself" is a very harsh and lonely commitment. After putting my self-confidence stamp on it, I realised it might have been rushed, and I did need help after all, at least in the form of moral support.

So, I called Steve.

While the dials went on, I struggled to recall the last time I relied on him for comfort and assurance – let's agree that our last meeting was more formal than comforting – but when his face appeared on the screen, I discarded the doubts. His familiar face was tired and distant, and I felt like I hadn't seen him for ages, although barely a day had passed since I failed my panel interview. He looked much older than his twenty-eight; with bags under his eyes and a greying unshaved beard, he was a striking copy of his retired dad.

"Anna? I was worried for you; what's happened? What does the SOS mean? Are you hurt?"

Was it the first time he asked if I were okay? I didn't want to seem paranoid, but to me, our recent calls felt one-sided, so I started wondering about things I didn't want to wonder. Our things.

Our thing.

Understandable. The world had become fragile in the last few weeks, and things could break too easily.

My memory carried me back to our house in Birmingham – a small two-bedroom semi with a tiny back garden. After the death of my parents, I was unable to sell their house, my childhood home, stupidly hoping that if they had a place to come back, one day they would. But I used some of their leftover savings to put a deposit for a house together with Steve.

Our tiny house was enough for two of us, a little cosy spot in a cold Universe, almost a paradise if not for the crazy couple next door. They were always fighting with each other, shouting, dropping furniture, and keeping both of us awake into the witching hour. When Steve struggled to sleep through the noise, he would coil in bed, put his face on my chest, and I stroked his neck until he started snoring.

His sleep was often light, uneasy. He got hot, threw off his duvet, and pushed me away. Sometimes, he would jump up in the bed, jerking my hand.

"Are you okay, Ania? I thought you were falling off the bed," he said.

"Go to sleep, Steve; I'm turning around, that's it."

Then he drifted off. I would spend a few minutes listening to his calm breathing, making sure he was finally deep asleep before drifting off myself.

Was he sleeping at all these days?

I heard shouting and commotion in the background, and he turned over his shoulder to check it out. As he looked, the wrinkles around his eyes grew deeper.

"Is it a bad time?" I asked.

"We've brought in a large group of survivors. They were homing at Aston Villa stadium. About a hundred people were already starving, but it seems—" he paused to nod to someone off the screen. "Seems like nobody taught our new friends to wait for their turn. We have food for years to come, especially with people still turning, but some of our new guys got too excited about it. Stashing away the communal supplies is prohibited, and we warned them about it."

"Probably you shouldn't have rescued them?"

Steve looked at me intently.

"Every life counts, Anna, especially here. Every man's a soldier, and every woman's a healer."

"Sexist!" I chuckled.

"No, listen, there are fantastic women here who fight better than men! I wanted to say that everybody needs to have a role if we want to rebuild our community."

What am I? What is my role in this community? Do I have one?

"By the way, some of them are scientists. They say they were studying the virus before their lab at the QE hospital got overrun. Even got some details of its shape."

"I wish they had a vaccine," I sighed.

His face remained sad despite the short smile. "No such thing, not even close. And I don't think we will get there any time soon. All labs in the city have been overrun, some destroyed to the ground. Oh, what again? Do you mind hanging on for a minute?"

He got off his chair and left the room. Looking at the crates towering in the background, I imagined myself in that makeshift warehouse, full of supplies or ammunition, people dressed in khaki overalls running errands around me – a picture of a perfect military base from the Hollywood movies I used to watch.

I didn't fit into this picture.

I wasn't a fantastic woman who could fight, but a girl on the other side of the screen, a lab rat scratching her way through a maze of samples.

The shouting in the background stopped, and the room was quiet until Steve returned, "Sorry, Anna, we have an urgent issue here. Can we chat tomorrow at the same time?"

He disconnected.

I put the computer into sleep mode and sat before the black screen, thinking.

If I were honest about the facts, my latest data didn't support my starting hypothesis. I could scrap the new data as corrupted and pretend the signs weren't there, but that would be bad science.

Bad science meant a lie.

He said he was worried, but in all the time of his worry, he barely texted me or asked me how I was doing. I could be lying dead, chopped into samples, and he wouldn't know. Not like Dan, who texted Lesley every waking hour, even if the only text he got from her was, "Leave me to brush my teeth!"

I guess it was time to admit the truth – I was chasing the bus that pulled off a bus stop and kept speeding up, intent to leave me behind, together with the promises of love, marriage and a happy retirement in Cornwall.

It was too late.

I decided to cry because that was how you celebrated heartbreak. Before I squeezed the first celebratory tear out of my eye, a hand lay on my shoulder, almost sending me into a terror coma.

No, not a spleen-eater. Just Louise.

"Anna. I have got something to show you."

8.

"When you said you're going to show me something interesting, I was expecting, you know, something. What is this?"

"Nothing!"

She was so excited that her signature French "rrrr" sounded even in the words that didn't have any Rs. The other ID26 members looked like they gathered in the lab for a show, which unexpectedly turned out to be a success. Even Tanya, who swore never to touch any "samples" a few hours ago, perked up in the corner of the microscopy lab, her eyes glistening in the shadows.

Excitement or alcohol?

The organs extracted from Max and the unknown woman lay on the workbench next to the microtome, packed into transparent Ziplock bags. Unlike Ali's organs, Louise's samples boasted ultra-smooth surfaces and fine cuts, and I felt thankful that she'd done a good job. The last favour we could offer Max after gassing him down was to leave the butchering to the professional.

Amen.

"You wanted to show me nothing," I sighed and turned away from the screen with two almost identical images of poorly contrasted spleen cells.

"Precisely!"

It'd been a long, sleepless night, and instead of going for a snooze for a few hours or crying over my crumbling relationship with Steve, I had to deal with these idiots. Before the zombie party, they were considered respectable specialists in their scientific areas. What's happened since then? Had we overlooked a brain-sucking virus in this mess?

Louise clicked the mouse, and two other microscopy images appeared on the screen next to each other, different from those I saw a minute ago. With better colours and contrast, I discerned separate cells, some garnished with bright purple and pink dots.

"We used Fluora Ardent Twelve stain for the spleen cells as it usually works for viruses. The staining did not work," she brought the original dark images to the screen. "Look, not a single fluorescent particle in the whole field! For both samples!"

"Bad stain?"

Louise nodded. "That is what we thought at first, but then we decided to test the other hypothesis, that the virus was not in the spleen but in the brain. We stained the brain slices, et voilá!"

The brightly dotted cells came up on the screen once again. I studied the images closely. There were more dots on the right image, resembling a splodge of fireworks in the dark sky.

"BEL-002." I read out loud. "What is that?"

The red colour of shame washed over Louise's face for a second. When I blinked, her cheeks were pale again, and her expression impenetrable.

"Bella," Dan spoke instead. "We gave her a name. We thought, you know... Bella. Beautiful in Italian."

Oh, I see. Louise's ethical ideas were tested with real-life challenges, and not all survived. That's okay. The least we could do to the unknown woman to honour her contribution to modern science was to give her a name.

"Bella's a bit more sparkly, isn't she? Does it mean she had more virus?"

"Well, it does. Max has only been infected, and she has been there for a while," said Kay.

"I am not sure it is about when they got infected. Something else is going on," Louise said.

The shocked silence was disturbed only by the sound of the wheels on Tanya's lab chair slowly rolling towards the microscope.

"While Kay and Dan were working on the Bel and Max samples, I added the leftovers of Ali's brain into the staining incubator. His spleen was virus-free, like everyone else's, but his brain—"

She opened another image next to the previous two.

No doubt Ali was infected when he died – he'd tried to eat me, hadn't he? But in Louise's pictures, his brain looked as squeaky clean as his spleen. I hovered the mouse over the image, zoomed in on an area and counted a single bright dot.

"Is this an artefact?"

Louise shook her head and added a few more images onto the screen. Some had two or three dots, but they all were like starless nights compared to MAX and BEL samples. Dark and scary.

"What does this mean?" Kay wondered. "Ali didn't have any virus? But that's bullshit!"

She cast me and Dan a nervous look anyway. Dan chuckled, "Yeah, if Ali wasn't infected, then I am the Queen of England."

"Ali was infected… just not as much."

Louise sounded unsure.

"Yeah, but he attacked me anyway. The same way that Max attacked Louise. There should be some other explanation why he has so little virus in his brain." I looked at Louise for assurance. "Right?"

Louise sighed. "There are too many factors, but we can exclude gender."

"And age. Bella was closer to Ali than to Max."

"I am not racist, but…"

"Shut up, Edsie!" We all said simultaneously.

"His physical condition? There's no way we could get his medical records."

"Like brain damage?" I asked.

Louise shrugged. "It can be anything."

"No, wait! Brain damage! We are looking at it from the wrong point," Kay started pacing around the microscopy table.

"Let's go back to the basics. We know that the virus caused aggressive behaviour in all infected, right? Louise suggested that it was a result of brain damage. So, we know that all three were aggressive from brain damage. Correct?"

We all nodded.

"So," Kay continued, "we'd expect to find the virus in all of them. Unless between now and then, something happened that made them different."

"I still don't get where you're going with it, but yes, they all died," said Dan.

Kay pointed her forefinger at the ceiling. "Can it be about how they died?"

"You can't imagine a better variety. Smashed brain, gas chamber and an axe through the heart," I said. "We didn't think much of statistics when we killed them."

"It is not "how", it is "when"," said Louise.

From her voice and a spark in her eyes, we got that she stumbled across the Big Idea. We kept quiet while she was digesting it for a few very long, intriguing minutes.

"Okay," she said.

We looked at her.

"It might sound bizarre."

She sighed, unsure if she should continue. "And very far-fetched."

"Spill it out, Frankenstein," said Edsie.

We pretended not to notice the new nickname.

"Ali died a few days ago, and Max and Bella – today. I think the virus only lives in a live person's brain, and as soon as they die, it clears out."

The dumbstruck silence confirmed that I was not the only person who had a problem with this theory.

"Pardon me," I ventured, "isn't it like a normal thing? The host dies, so it is no longer useful. Bye-bye, see ya?"

She shook her head, "It is not that straightforward. If a virus kills someone, you can find it during the autopsy and identify the cause of death. Of course, it was not the virus that killed him in this case."

"Not directly," Dan pointed out.

"Even if you're right, what does it give us?" Edsie voiced from the corner, still reluctant to come closer to Louise. Well, who could blame him for having an instinct of self-preservation? "The virus dies in the dead zombies, so let's kill the fuckers?"

"I have an idea," said Louise, "but first, I need to make sure my hypothesis is correct. We stain more brain samples in a day or two, and if I am right, the virus will be gone."

"And if you are not?"

"Then we are screwed."

Sample Date	27/02/2024
Sample Name	**MAX-001-SPL**
Category	spleen
Source	Max, human, infected, time between infection and death – 25 hours, ca. 29 yo
Notes	Time of sampling after death – 8 hours, microtomed from frozen (not cryo)
Observations	Samples stained by Fluora Ardent Twelve (see Orlov et al, 2012), no virus detected
Sampled by	Louise Aurelienne
Notes by	Anna Evans-Bond

Sample Date	27/02/2024
Sample Name	**BEL-001-SPL**
Category	spleen
Source	Bella (real name unknown), human, infected, time between infection and death – unknown, ca. 45 years old, female
Notes	Time of sampling after death – 30 min
Observations	Samples stained by Fluora Ardent Twelve (see Orlov et al, 2012), no virus detected
Sampled by	Louise Aurelienne
Notes by	Anna Evans-Bond

Sample Date	27/02/2024
Sample Name	**BEL-002-BR**
Category	brain
Source	Bella (real name unknown), human, infected, time between infection and death – unknown, ca. 45 years old, female
Notes	Time of sampling after death – 30 min
Observations	Samples stained by Fluora Ardent Twelve (see Orlov et al, 2012), staining successful, possibly V-2024 detected
Sampled by	Kay Newmann
Notes by	Anna Evans-Bond

9.

I was tossing in my makeshift bed, Edsie's snoring keeping me awake late at night, when my ear discerned a quiet rustling sound to my left. It was pitch-black since Louise insisted on turning the lights off at night to maintain "healthy circadian cycles". A shit idea, I realised, cursing Louise and her stupid cycles as something brushed past me in the darkness.

I grabbed the lab stand, but before I brought it up and smashed the cycles out of the nighttime creeper, I caught a glimpse of light reflecting from a smooth, pale surface.

"Dan?" I whispered, squinting at his bald head through the dark.

He didn't hear me or preferred to ignore me because he opened the control room door, letting in a faint smudge of light from outside, and walked out into the Ring with a backpack on his back.

I slipped out after him. "Where are you going?"

He held the scream in, uttering a cough instead. I patted him on the back.

"Gosh, Anna, why aren't you sleeping?"

I shrugged. "Missing my goodnight kisses. Without them, only stirring."

"I need to go, Anna. I need to be with Lesley."

"But you've promised me!"

Didn't I know that it was only a moment of respite before my seal of reason wore off, and he tried to flee. But I didn't expect it to happen so soon; otherwise, I'd chain myself to him every night.

"You won't survive there on your own. Especially with that," I pointed at the fixing bandage on his ankle.

"I can walk," he said.

True. The limping was almost gone.

"To survive, you'd need to run."

"You've survived," he reminded me of my little adventure on the way to the controls office. "And your running sucks."

"It was only for half an hour, if at all! I suppose you'd like to make it all the way home?"

Stubbornly, he kept on walking. As we went further up the Ring, I felt increasingly exposed. I'd left my lab stand in the control room and hadn't even put my shoes on! If something walked out on us in search of a late-night dinner, I'd have to fight it off with only my charisma.

Zero chance, then.

"I need to make sure she's okay. I can't just hang around, slicing brains, while my wife—"

His voice trailed into tears. I grabbed his hand and turned him to face me.

"What's happened, Dan? You aren't telling me everything. Has something happened to Lesley?"

"She hasn't been online for almost a day, Anna!"

"Online? Is her internet down?"

"How the fuck would I know? Wouldn't she try to get to me another way?"

"Not if she's smart. Getting out of the house is a suicide mission!"

Venturing into the world was risky for people of Edsie's strength and complexion, not to mention vulnerable pregnant women.

I thought of Lesley. Pregnant – yes, vulnerable – not really, although if you've never met her, you could make up a somewhat erroneous image – a lead violinist in the Birmingham Symphonic Orchestra, an ex-national polo champion, Lesley knows the difference between Monet and Manet and owns a 12-bedroom mansion and stables with real horses because Lesley's grandmother is a baroness of some sort, and you have to curtsey when introduced.

No kidding.

Have you pictured an ethereal, dreamy-eyed creature with a sticking-out pinky? Wrong. Real-life Lesley looks more like a Mother of Valkyries riding a lightning – tall, loud, unstoppable, the only kind of woman who could demonstrate to Dan all the advantages of choosing science over crime with one click of her mighty fingers.

No, women like Lesley don't perish in silence, bitten by an opportunistic zombie. They go down in flames with a large kaboom. I'm sure we would hear something from Steve in case of a kaboom.

"You need to think straight, Dan. Your chance to get to Lesley as you are now, with your ankle and all, is tiny. The best thing you can do for her and your baby is to survive. Do it here! This is the best place!"

He didn't seem to hear me at all.

"If something happened to Lesley, I must be there with her, Anna. I've overstayed already."

"Overstayed? This is not a vacation, man! You can't go anywhere by yourself! You'll get done before you even leave the Ring. What will I tell Lesley when I see her? Huh? Sorry, I have a feeling your husband got eaten somewhere in Paris? Or maybe, in London?"

"What's the use of me sitting here like a scared piece of shit? My wife might be rotting away somewhere in the streets!" he whined.

This conversation had started to annoy me.

"Your brain's rotting! If she's dead, that's it! Done! You can't un-die her! But if she's one of them, you can bring her a cure. You need to stick your fucking sentiments back where the light doesn't shine and hold on for a second! You are not Superman; you are a scientist! So, turn around and go back to do what you do best! And I'll ask Steve to go and find her. He has guns and all that stuff. Or I can ask Ben. It's his dad. He used to be navy seals back in the day or whatever."

Dan stopped and turned to me. "Would he do it?"

I nodded. I didn't even need to ask Steve. Of course, he'd do it, not for me, but because of me. Like the Blind Lady, I was holding the balance of justice in my hands, and if Steve couldn't put love on it anymore, he'd have to provide me with something else, no less valuable. In this case, Lesley, even if he'd have to fight against armies of spleen-eating monsters.

A bleeding heart has a right to be bitter.

I grabbed Dan's hands and pulled him back toward our beamline. "I know how much it hurts not to know, not be able to do anything. But it's not true. You can help here. And when we're done and have the cure in our hands, we'll all go home together. Even though I'd very much leave Edsie behind."

As we walked back, I wondered how long he'd waited for the best moment to sneak out and run back home through the wastelands. We'd watched the videos on YouTube. Crater in the centre of Berlin. La Tour Eiffel on fire. Smashed glass of the Louvre pyramid. The gardens of Versailles burned to dust. Endless crowds of zombies roaming the ruins, hungry, desperate for a meal.

How strong was his love for Lesley that miles and monsters did not matter? And if this was love, then —

"Why don't *you* want to go home, Anna? Isn't Steve waiting for you there?"

"No."

No other word encompassed so much pain in only two letters. I spoke it into the world, and it felt like a knife that kept my heart numb and frozen was pulled out. Blood gushed out with every beat, but my heart was beating again. One day, it could heal.

I loved Steve more than the world, but the virus burnt that world down.

Tears rolled down my face, and Dan reached out and hugged me. I hid my face on his chest and sobbed until I ran out of salt, and the tears ran dry.

Pain. There was so much pain that we could build a whole new world on it. In the absence of clay and wood, it would suffice.

Chapter 5. The Machine

1.

Day 27, 2nd of March, Sat

I was late for the Big Reveal.

No one to blame but me. Kay's nose caught something wrong about the beans when she opened the tin. She stuck it under my nose to confirm, but I let my inner stinginess win instead of confirming her suspicions.

"It's absolutely fine, Kay. They are not supposed to smell of bacon!"

She trusted me, and that was a mistake we all paid for.

We'd spent three days doing a toilet rota, bucket routine forgotten. Supplies of toilet paper dwindling. Air freshener prices hiked up. Bulk-buying. Panic at the tills…

Our food incident came with the positives. It was hard to wield war while sharing the same toilet woe, so we'd established a thin peace between the majority and the opposition party.

When the atmosphere in the ID26 improved, Louise called Kay and Dan into service, and together, they stained another batch of Max and Bella's brain slices.

When I arrived at the microscopy lab, the moods were upbeat – a welcome change after the days of gloom. The images on the computer screen were dark, and even when I got closer, I couldn't find any coloured dots.

"What's the latest in Bunker Communications?"

"Clear as moonlight!" said Edsie, beaming. "Our Frankenstein is a genius!"

Louise sighed but didn't say anything. This was the highest praise she would get out of Edsie, anyway.

"The virus is totally gone from MAX and BEL samples," Kay confirmed.

"Maybe, now, you can let us into your theory?"

"It is just speculations. Some parasitic bacteria can live in an animal organism for a while. But if an animal gets sick, say, with diabetes or an adrenal tumour, the bacteria trigger a suicide mechanism, fully eliminating itself within a few hours. I guess that something similar happens in this case. The only difference is that it is not a disease but a full death of the organism that triggers the clear out."

"Life is a fatal disease. Its only positive is that it's sexually transmitted," issued Edsie.

"The bacteria in animals left not because of the disease itself but because of the high level of hormones. They recognised the increased level of steroids in the bloodstream," explained Louise.

"What are the hormones associated with death?"

"Not hormones. When you die, the cells start breaking down and release a lot of, let's call them, "death molecules". They alert the other cells in the body that time is up."

"I thought it was the brain."

"The bigger commands, yes. But even the most powerful electric impulses from the brain would not be enough to coordinate the total shutdown in such a short time. Say you are shot in the stomach, slowly bleeding. Your brain might not even know that the wound is fatal, but your death molecules are already sending the signals to the rest of the cells that your time is over. That makes your heart stop beating, your stomach – stop digesting, your kidneys – stop filtering urine…"

She'd drawn such a vivid image of the death molecules claiming the body that silence fell over the lab. I wondered if everyone else was imagining their body closing shop – muscles relaxing, eyes closing, the heart slowing down. Beat. Another. Finished. From now on, you are the property of Chop Inc., the leading supplier of top-quality spleen and brain samples.

"Ace!" Dan woke up from the reverie. "Is that the plan? Prick the spleen-eaters with death molecules?"

"Wait a sec. If they are death molecules, aren't we going to kill the zombies in the process?" asked Edsie.

Hm. Did I hear the voice of reason, or was it the sound of the wind in the willows?

"Potentially," admitted Louise. "We do not know the correct concentration to make the virus leave but not kill the host."

"I think we can deal with that," I said, recalling my master's studies. "If the virus reacts to a specific molecule, it has a recognition mechanism on its surface. Sort of a lock and key situation. If we identify which key fits the lock, we can create one that's similar enough and will trigger the virus death but won't kill its hosts."

"There are hundreds of death molecules. How do we know which one's the key? We have neither the time nor the molecules to test them all."

"Look at it from the bright side. Test subjects are in abundance!"

"Edsie!"

"What?"

Trying to defend ourselves, we killed spleen-eaters alright, but intentionally going out for them? I imagined us rounding up a batch of monsters, witch-hunt style, with pitchforks and torches.

"They have to be alive, of course," added Louise.

Hilarious, I hadn't noticed that Louise had a sense of humour.

Dan shook his head, "Let me summarise, guys. We need a few hundred spleen-eaters, alive and kicking, to test some molecules we don't yet have. Why don't we start with the easy bit? What are those molecules, and where do we get them from?"

Louise shrugged. "No idea. It would still be impossible if we had a chemicals supermarket next door. When I say molecules, I mostly mean macromolecules. Not typically on sale."

"Proteins?"

"Sugars, fatty acids, anything and everything."

"Great!"

"We can do it *in silico*," I suggested.

In the world "before", the major challenge of creating drugs for diseases was the problem of targets, not drugs themselves. Chemists cooked new molecules daily, but most of those molecules never made it to the drugs cohort. Why? Well, if you have a bunch of keys but no locks – what are the odds of opening the right lock with the right key?

It's not all misery, don't get me wrong. Science keeps digging deeper into the secrets of our body mechanisms, discovering answers and providing solutions. We know that overreacting adrenaline receptors cause high blood pressure, so we block them using small molecules. They are called beta-blockers. We know what pregnancy looks like from a chemical point of view, so we give the body the hormones to fool it into thinking it's already pregnant instead of getting pregnant for real.

But some conditions are more complex. Those usually are the ones that affect the brain. We still don't know which chemical processes cause autism or dementia. Millions of chemical reactions occur in the brain every second – which one would you target? Or which two? Or three?

Once you find suitable targets, a computer simulation (or so-called in silico drug design) is a cheap and quick way to identify the correct keys. The interactions between drugs and targets in the body are very intimate and tight. Only a computer can estimate how well the two match and where the matching could be improved, reducing the number of potential keys from twenty million to only a couple.

Then, the humans take over to do the dirty work of testing those in a flask and then in a rat.

Rats, I shivered; let's not get there yet.

"What would you need?" asked Louise.

"Death molecule structures shouldn't be a problem. The Internet would know them all. How about the virus? I don't think anyone posted a picture on Facebook?"

"Facebook is down," Dan mumbled.

"Can't you use that thing?" Edsie pointed at the microscope. Louise sighed.

"I have bad news for you. To get the structure of the virus, we would need to grow it, crystalise it, and then fix it. And we will not even see it in this microscope. The virus is too small."

"What does that mean?" asked Kay.

"We are all fucked," explained Edsie. "And our science is fucked."

I looked at Louise, hoping for a correction to Edsie's statement, but she nodded.

Oh yes.

If Edsie is right,

we are definitely fucked.

2.

No one would mail us the virus for scanning, so we had to do everything ourselves.

What, have you thought we'd give up because the task seems impossible? Hold my beer! We are not the giving-up type of folks. "Perseverance" is our second and third name.

Now that I've given you the prep talk, here's the truth: none of us, including Louise, knows how to cultivate viruses.

"Why are you looking at me like that? Yes, I did it in my first year of uni. That was a century ago."

Whoah! She doesn't even look fifty!

If Louise, with all her biological training, can't do it, we are screwed. We knew that already.

Would our luck stretch as far as stumbling over a trained virologist if we went on another scavenging trip? Looked through the cupboards?

I messaged Steve. HAVE YOU GOT ANY TRAINED VIROLOGISTS IN YOUR ARMY?

I didn't expect him to reply, but an hour later, he wrote back. ARE THEY PREGNANT, TOO?

I scratched my head, NO, WE NEED TO FIND ONE. WE NEED EXPERT ADVICE.

WHAT ABOUT LESLEY? DO I STILL NEED TO GET HER?

I sighed. Looked like Steve's brain processor could only work through one request at a time. It never used to be like this. I'd heard the Army affected people, but that was way too quick!

No worries. I knew how to play this game.

LESLEY IS A PRIORITY ASSET. URGENT EXTRACTION REQUESTED.

I added a kissing emoji. That was my boyfriend, for Christ's sake!

I expected a ROGER THAT or something along those lines, but nothing came. I could only hope my instructions from a few days ago (plus Lesley's photo and address) were enough.

Another hour later, Steve sent me a new message. I'VE GOT A COVID-TRAINED NURSE. IS THAT OK?

I replied with a sad emoji.

"There should be other people alive out there, right?" asked Dan. "But how do we reach them? Facebook is not working, so we can't post online."

"Maybe, we should try Tiktok?" Edsie suggested.

"What's that?"

"Or maybe not."

"Have you heard of the six handshakes rule?" asked Kay.

"Yep. I don't have six alive people on my WhatsApp," Dan said.

Edsie shook his head.

Same here. I've managed to get hold of only four of my friends. Not too bad, considering that not all places held onto their internet connection. The best part of Moscow was destroyed by rockets, and although some people evacuated to the surrounding forests, none of my Russian friends reappeared online. China had never been good with WhatsApp anyway, so I only heard from my friend in Taiwan. Plus, my former PhD classmate in the Netherlands and a brief acquaintance from Saudi Arabia.

None of them was a virologist.

I messaged them one by one and asked them to spread the word, picking up their surviving connections. Everyone else did the same. Between us, we'd send messages to twenty-two people, with Edsie providing most contacts. One of them was his barber. What were the chances that a barber from Kenilworth would have a virologist friend?

It was a test, and we all understood its true meaning. It was not about how many people still had access to WhatsApp or the internet; it was about how many people were still there to hear our call, not for a funny picture repost, but a genuine call for help, for humanity.

And help came.

When her phone beeped, Louise was online, scanning through lab protocols and making notes about cultivating and harvesting the virus. The message was for her – we asked any people who could help to add her as a contact and drop a couple of lines.

It was more than a couple of lines.

"Dear Dr Louise Aurelienne,

The people of the People's Republic of China have heard your call. After coordinating with the Leadership, the decision has been made to allocate human resources to your project. Dr Yuin Biao has been identified as the most suitable resource. Upon completing the necessary preliminary checks, he will contact you directly through a video call using this number. Please confirm your identity by providing us with a photo of yourself dated this day, with the date written on a blank piece of paper you are holding. With our best wishes and the interests of all people at heart, always.

Allegra Qiang."

We mused over it.

"A photo with a date? Is this a new thing in recruitment?" asked Kay.

"Allegra Quiang? How legit is that?" asked Dan.

"Our Chinese students quite often take on European names so that we can pronounce them easier. It could be fully legit. I don't see any problem," said Edsie.

"Apart from, who calls herself Allegra… Or is it a guy?"

Louise opened a webpage on her phone. "I have checked Dr Yuin Biao through Google Scholar. He is a virologist from Tsinghua University. Has lots of papers on covid and Zika virus. Got medals and all."

"Who cares? If he's alive, he's good enough."

"Then let's do it. Are you okay with a mugshot, Louise?"

"No."

Tanya said it so quietly that any other word would slip unnoticed in our blabber, but this "No" had an unexpected weight, a determination that exploded in the control room like a small grenade.

We all turned to her.

"They can't be trusted," she whispered.

"Ehm? Is that because of… what?" asked Dan.

"Doesn't it bother you that somebody out there," Tanya said, louder this time, "*made a decision to allocate resources to our project*? It means they've managed to organise things, resources, and even people somewhere in China. Someone *is making decisions*, and that scares me."

We all fell quiet, reconsidering our options.

"You think *they* are responsible?"

I couldn't get my head around the idea that someone had deliberately turned most of the Earth's population into spleen-eating monsters. As if she heard my doubts, Tanya continued:

"We don't know where the virus came from or how it affected different nations. What if it's only around Europe? Have you seen many pictures of ruin in China? What if they fabricated and released the virus to eliminate all of us here? Do you remember where COVID came from? Did you really believe it was an accident? That's bullshit! The Chinese government is responsible! They've managed to get away with COVID, but we all know they developed it as a weapon. It's not a coincidence that the Americans had the biggest number of deaths from COVID, isn't it?"

I've heard this theory before: COVID-19 was a runaway from one of the government labs in China tasked with developing new types of biological weapons. If so, the weapon had turned against the Chinese before they came up with a cure. Just like it happened to the Umbrella Corporation.

Only the Umbrella Corporation was not real.

Or was it?

What if Umbrella existed and all those movies were a distraction, an elaborate but efficient way to throw us off the trail while the real Umbrella developed a new zombie virus in 2024?

Come on, Anna, don't let this conspiracy bullshit get into your head…

"Did you see what happened to China? They had like two million people sick with Covid!" said Dan.

"Ha! Two million? Out of how many? They have more than a billion population, Dan. Do you think they care about a couple of millions of their own? Not really. Do you know what those two million were for them? They were *resources,* test subjects, just like Max. They were locked, monitored, and then chopped into samples! Covid was just a start. It was a test to see what we would do. This virus is a real weapon!" Tanya continued. "They are all killers!"

"Even if they created this virus and accidentally let it lose, they are the people who know the most about it. They should be able to help!" I said.

"Really?" Tanya hissed. "You think they will want you to help stop it? Is that what you think they want? They want to find *you* and stop *you*! Now they know where and what we're doing; they're coming after us!"

There was so much power in her quiet voice that my brain had conjured an image of the men in full combat ammunition, with guns and grenades, raiding the Ring to round up and eradicate a bunch of unsuspecting scientists. Or would they send us a bye-bye rocket? That would make less fuss and more sense.

I shook the images off.

"They wouldn't contact us then, would they? Why alert us and tell us the name of their virologist?"

"What if they want to ensure we are serious, legitimate scientists and not some kids playing with expensive equipment? Otherwise, why waste resources on us?" asked Kay.

Goodness! The conspiracy virus had gotten into her head, too!

"Then let's have a chat. They will see we are absolutely harmless," Louise muttered. "Kids playing with expensive equipment is a pretty good description."

"We're not harmless. We'll make it work with a virus doctor or without," said Dan.

I patted him on the shoulder, acknowledging his determination.

"We need help, Tanya. No matter how smart and hard-working we are, we won't manage alone. Let's take that photo and send it back."

Louise tore a blank page out of the beamline shift logbook and scribbled the date and time on it.

"No! You shouldn't do it!" Tanya snatched the paper from her hand, crumpled it, and tossed it in the paper bin. "You can't work with them! They're all killers, and if they find us, they'll kill us, too!" she shouted, shaking.

Then it hit me. It was not about the Chinese people responsible for releasing COVID-19 or this new virus. It was about Chinese people responsible for something personal to Tanya.

"Who did they kill, Tanya?" I asked straight.

Before Tanya could answer, Edsie, who'd been sitting out the argument in the corner, munching away on our last Snickers bar, called out. "Wait, wait, wait! I'm not getting what the problem is. Aren't you Chinese, Tanya?"

A bull in a china shop? Here's a bulldozer.

Now – duck!

"She's not Chinese," Kay swiftly pushed herself between Edsie and Tanya, whose face was glowing red like a fuse about to go off. "And not Vietnamese," Kay cast me an apologetic look. "She is Uyghur!"

"Yogurt? What's that?" Edsie asked.

I couldn't deny his consistency. Being consistently ignorant is a rare ability in our world, satiated with news and newspaper titles. He read the titles, didn't he?

We decided to ignore him, waiting for Tanya to elaborate. She sighed.

"When I was ten, the Han Chinese army occupied our region. They scared me to death; I've heard of people dying in bombings and fights. I started having nightmares and a spiking fever, and then I fell very sick. My mother tried to take me to a bigger town to show me to the doctor, but the army people turned her around. She was scared for my life, so she decided to smuggle me over the border to get help from the Soviets. My mother paid everything that our family had for the safe passage over the mountains. We'd escaped China just before the Uyghur cleanse, leaving everyone else behind, including my dad, my little brother and the rest of the family. There were riots against Han Chinese, so our village near Barin was completely destroyed in retaliation, and everyone was declared missing. You might have seen the human rights reports all over the news – women sent for sterilisation and then to the workhouses, equal to slave labour; children in the orphanages, growing up without mothers and forgetting their language and origins. In horrible conditions, women died in thousands. Men were sent to a 'health monitoring facility', a cover-up for a laboratory developing new drugs and bioweapons. They were used as test subjects. There were names in those reports, but none of my family. I still don't know what happened to them. As if they vanished from the face of the Earth…"

"Did you know about all that?" I asked Kay.

She twisted a string between her fingers, her hands missing the familiar touch of her cross chain, and nodded.

"When Tanya told me about her background, I decided not to work with Chinese researchers - for Tanya's sake and the sake of my own conscience. It's hard, I won't lie, they have a lot of funding and capabilities, but we are a team…"

"And epilepsy? Is that from childhood trauma?"

For the first time since we gassed Max, Tanya looked at me as if I was a human being, not a brick wall.

As a proper child of the new millennium, I contracted infectious ignorance fuelled by the mass flow of information, whether useless or not. I read the news on the internet and might have even seen photos accompanied by a trigger warning, and because of that, I thought I knew what happened to people in different parts of the world.

But did I?

What did I see?

The photos edited so they wouldn't hurt the feelings of people reading the news over their morning latte. The information polished squeaky clean to convey the right level of truth, not too much – otherwise, someone would demand real action; not too little – otherwise, you'll be blamed for silencing the truth.

I consumed the reality cooked for me, believing that the bad things that happened elsewhere were not so bad. Now, listening to Tanya's story, I felt scared and ashamed – of the world, of the people who lived in it and did horrible things to each other. The wars and the genocides were never a thing of the past; they just took place further away from me.

But they were still there.

Was this world worth saving at all? What if it didn't need a cure but to burn down to be reborn clean again? If this virus was not an invention of a crazy scientist but Nature's final shot against humanity, we should let the Universe dust us out. Enough. Humanity had its chance.

Nobody will cry over us.

It would be easy to step down, turn off the microscopes, and throw away the samples. Give Ali, Bella, and Max a well-deserved funeral. Turn the lights off in the control room and go home.

Go home.

We could leave this godforsaken place and hike back to England, free from these concrete walls that destroy hope and endless questions that don't have good answers.

We could stop. Stop being scientists and be humans instead. Let Nature consume us. I'd make a lovely apple tree. Or a raspberry bush.

I tried to think of what Mom and Dad would say and do, but their images had turned into bleak shadows of memories, their faces blurred. I'd held onto them for so many years, but now I was letting them go as if I was letting go of hope and strength. Maybe, that was for the best – my lovely parents had no place in the world of splattering blood and guts. They belonged to the sunshine, aquamarine waves, and golden beaches.

They belonged to Saint-Aupre, a place with no pain.

And where did that leave me? I closed my eyes, imagining the tender breeze blowing in my hair, my feet sinking into the warm sand, and the seagulls echoing the sound of the rolling tide. I could give up and go there, fuck going home, fuck Steve and his army friends, fuck science and samples.

Just me and the waves.

I opened my eyes. The concrete walls were closing in, suffocating me. Who was I kidding? There was nowhere to run. When we got the internet back up and running, I'd googled it. Saint-Aupre was almost two hundred miles away from the nearest beach.

"I guess that means Allegra fella is out of the question. Any more virus folks we know?" said Edsie, opening a beer bottle.

I didn't know what surprised me more – the magical appearance of the beer bottle out of thin air or the fact that, once in his useless life, Edsie had thought of someone else's feelings and acknowledged them in his twisted manner.

Whoah.

"No way!" Dan stood up. "We needed a virologist; we have one. What else is there?"

"The moral?" asked Louise.

Everyone stared at her as if she declared herself a cousin of Cthulhu. Although Louise was a devotee of the Church for Ethical Treatment of Samples, she had never expressed concern about the *morality* of our research. She was set to chop Max into samples before he had even turned!

Ah no, look at her face; that was a rhetorical question.

Dan laughed bitterly. "Moral? We'd run out of it when we gassed Max in the hutch."

"But working with the Chinese? Knowing what they've done to all those people?" asked Edsie. "Isn't it like working with Nazis?"

Yeah, and it was Cthulhu who put Max through a gas chamber.

"To be fair, the German research, backed up by their leaders, including Adolf Hitler, was the first to demonstrate the link between asbestos and the development of ca—"

"Shut up, Louise!"

Jeez, that woman is... different.

Look for yourself: Dan's dedication to our science undertaking was bordering insane lately, and it didn't help that Louise – 100% somewhere on the sociopathic spectrum – was feeding into his insanity. We'd started our experiments sober-minded and clear-headed, perfectly aware of our limitations as people and scientists, but the way Louise handled everything in the lab was more than science – it was religion.

The more I knew her, the more often I asked myself how the hell Michael/Greg had managed to get her calculating, analytical, cold-hearted ass into that cupboard.

Dan turned to Edsie. "It's unlikely that Yuang, or whatever his name is, was personally responsible for what's happened to Tanya's people. Looking at his photos, he might not have been born then. His government had done all those atrocities. But wasn't our government responsible for the colonisation? Slavery? We need to get on with it... We can't ditch our perfect chance only because some Chinese people suffered!"

"But it's Tanya's family," muttered Edsie.

"And what about it? Since when are you bothered about anyone's family? You didn't seem to give much shit about yours!"

That was harsh and not like Dan at all. Tanya started crying. Edsie put his beer aside and rose from his chair, towering his bulk over Dan to demonstrate his intentions. It would be impressive if not for the last weeks of rationing and a low-protein diet. Edsie's T-shirt, which used to cling tight to his bulging biceps, now hung loose and sad.

"Sit down and shut up!" barked Kay. I opened my mouth, but she added, "All of you! There won't be any more fights! We will vote. Like the intelligent species we are supposed to be."

A vote? Not again.

I did a quick calculation – the odds weren't clear: Edsie sided with Tanya physically and mentally, and Kay had already made her choice many years ago.

On the other hand, Louise didn't care about where her science came from, and Dan would do anything for Lesley and their baby.

What about me?

My decisions made on behalf of humanity didn't make humanity look good. Maybe, it was time to make a decision on behalf of myself.

"I vote to engage," said Louise.

"No." Tanya shook her head.

"No," echoed Edsie.

"I vote for, too," I said. "Max has died in vain if we don't do it."

"For," said Dan. "Lesley is pregnant. If something goes wrong, I need a cure for her and the baby!"

What a great timing for his big reveal! Kay patted his shoulder with a quiet "congratulations". Tanya turned to Edsie and whispered something into his ear.

"Stefania is dead, anyway. My sister-in-law has found her," announced Edsie. "I don't give a shit about your cure!"

"Oh, I see," snarled Dan. "How quickly you've found another bed-warmer! Isn't it time to start thinking about someone else but yourself?"

"Bastard!" Edsie jumped off his chair.

"ENOUGH!" yelled Kay.

What a shit show! Here's a recap of today's episode: Edsie's wife is dead; Tanya is – sort of – Chinese; Dan reveals his big secret; and the best and final – Kay can yell! She is not an all-accepting Christian daughter and is probably asking herself how on Earth the Father, Son, and Holy Spirit allowed our bunch of freaks to end up in the same room.

Edsie plonked back into the chair, Dan retreated behind the table, and we all stared at Kay. What now? With three votes against three, our fragile peace won't last.

I grabbed the lab stand. If I go down, I'll go in a fight, and then the Valkyries will take me straight up to Valhalla, where I will eat until I explode.

Not bad.

"Yes," Kay said. "Let's do it."

Oh hello.

3.

At least Kay got to keep her hair.

The door shut behind Edsie and Tanya with a clang, and we all exhaled at once. A roaring hurricane had rolled over our control room, leaving only debris, smashed glass, and broken hearts behind it.

Is it why they named the storms and hurricanes after women?

Ours was called Tanya.

I'd never expected this fragile woman to have so much destructive power. It looked like she had stored it for decades, compressing the pain and fear inside her petite body until there was no more space inside. The tight string snipped, and even Edsie didn't dare to climb from underneath the table while Hurricane Tanya crushed everything on her way until there was nothing left to break.

Then they left.

While Dan was swiping up the glass debris, Louise took a selfie with a dated paper and sent it to Allegra Qiang. The only person with no chores assigned, I sat beside Kay to provide PTSD therapy,

"Are you okay?"

She nodded. Her face was dead white, ghostly, her hands shaking, and she kept twisting her fingers, wrenching them out of the joints without noticing.

"You heard her. She thinks I've betrayed her. This is what hurts. I've known her for so long that I can't stand that she's so upset with me."

"What could you do? You've made your decision. It's not against her. She only thinks it's against her. But she's wrong, just like she's wrong about other things. You definitely aren't a fat skunk!"

I pretended to sniff her, and she chuckled. Humour, just like hugs, had remarkable healing properties.

If only we could inject our zombie friends with a bit of Bill Connolly!

"Will they be okay there?" she pointed at the door.

Sweet motherly instinct! Even after being called names, the nicest of which was, indeed, a skunk, Kay still cared that the big bad zombies didn't eat her little Tanya.

"Don't worry about them! Edsie will drive Tanya up the wall soon, and she'll run back to us. She might smash a microscope or two, though," I said.

"Don't we need it for work?"

I shrugged. "I'm sure we'll find another one... If you don't mind me asking, why did you change your mind?"

"Change my mind?"

"Why did you say yes?"

She sighed, "I am with Dan on that. This is the only way I can help my family from where I am. Nazis, Chinese or Klingons, does it matter? Science always comes at a high cost, and we'd agreed to the highest bidding when we gassed Max. There's no way back. Giving it up now because Tanya's family suffered, among millions of others, would be the betrayal of the living. That's the price I can't pay."

I wondered what her God would say about it, but she hadn't spoken to Him for days, as if she had given up on her faith when she voted to make samples out of Max.

I pulled her cross out of my jeans pocket and pushed it into her open palm. Her fingers immediately entwined around it in a familiar gesture, and her hand stopped shaking.

"You need this," I said. "Pray if it helps. There is no shame in having faith."

She smiled sadly. "I know what you all think. That I'm some sort of a religious freak, harmless but annoying, praying all the time, preaching. Maybe, you aren't wrong, but I've been in such bad places, back then, in Yugoslavia… I didn't know if I would live the next day. I found God then, and I held on to Him. I prayed, and the prayer was like music… But now, it's just words, and this is just a piece of metal," she let the cross slip out of her fingers on the floor, "and I am out of faith."

"It's okay; I saw some in that cupboard," I pointed at the drawer in which Edsie and Dan kept the stash of strong alcohol. Kay laughed.

"You can never be serious, can you?"

"Not when it's life-threatening," I picked the cross up from the floor and hung it over my neck instead of shoving it back into my pocket. "I'll keep it safe for you. One day, you'll want it back. Praying's like bike riding. The skill's always with you."

She shook her head, but I could see that her own decision haunted her.

Before I could offer more Bill Connolly-type remedy, Dan and Louise called us from the workstation.

"The Chinese are ready."

***

At first, I saw the board, then the man behind it. The man was Asian-looking, in massive round glasses, and, unusually for Chinese, bald. The rest of him was hidden behind a large whiteboard.

IT WASN'T US.

We lined up behind Louise – three of us against one man and his board. We stared at him in silence, unsure how to proceed. Such a weird conversation starter demanded an adequate answer.

Or sufficiently inadequate.

No one moved.

The silence stretched out.

Surely, it was a test. But of what and for whom?

Finally, Dan grabbed the logbook from the table, scribbled two large letters with a blue marker and showed it to the camera.

OK.

The man on the screen relaxed, put away his board and stepped closer to the camera. He seemed to be in his early fifties, around Kay's age, with deep wrinkles around his eyes, amplified by the glasses that made his round face look like a perfect circle.

"My name is Yuin. I was told you are working towards a treatment and need a virologist."

Uh-oh. We talked about treatment between ourselves, but for the rest of the world, we were "researching the nature of the virus". They'd rigged the ESRF with bugs and been listening to us all along!

Gosh, this conspiracy bullshit is inside of me! Get it out!

"Can we please address the whole "It's not us" thing first?" said Dan.

Yuin sighed; his wrinkles deepened and darkened.

"After the covid outbreak, we have implemented swift reaction protocols which allowed us to lock the borders and stop all transport within a couple of hours. I know other countries had such protocols, too, but we had done more than the rest. One of the first actions was an immediate move of the priority labs into several military-run underground facilities, this facility," he pointed somewhere behind him, "included. This is my virology laboratory. Or rather, its poor reminiscence. I only have half the staff; the army people are continuously watching me; most equipment has not been calibrated since the COVID outbreak when this lab was installed… and no TikTok."

We all nodded in astonished silence. TikTok?

"I am joking, of course! It's not the best lab in the world, but there aren't many labs left in the world at all. I was surprised to hear about you doing science in a zombie-infested synchrotron!."

"We don't call them zombies," said Kay.

"And doing science is not our main activity. We're mainly surviving." I reminded him of the harsh reality of "doing science" when a man in full ammo wasn't standing behind us to guard our backs. It was only our gut instincts, lab wrenches, and squirt bottles.

"I am sorry," he said, serious and sincere. "We've lost almost half of my team during the initial evacuation, but we've become very complacent after all these months. We are doing what we can to find the cure and stop this zom… virus apocalypse!"

"And it wasn't you," I reminded him again.

"No," he shook his head, and I did believe him because he sounded like *he* believed in it. "The pandemic spread did not seem to follow man-made patterns. Our epidemiologists traced its origins to a remote village in Argentina. One of the locals celebrated his wedding to a British woman, inviting many of her friends and relatives from all over Europe. The first reported cases of the virus were the residents of the neighbouring villages who attended the wedding. By the time the reports reached the authorities, the international guests carried the virus all over the world."

"Did they serve bats?"

"Unlikely. People in that area have conservative food habits. But it's not even that. We've studied the genetic trace of the virus and believe it has components that are thousands of years old. It's not a new strain. Those villages in Argentina were recently flooded, caused by the melting of their local glacier high in the mountains. This makes us think the virus has thawed from the ice."

"You said you studied the genetic trace. What else have you looked at?" asked Dan.

Yuin chuckled. "In no conference have I ever felt under so much pressure. Should we get introduced, then?"

"Dan, polymer chemistry lecturer, Birmingham University."

"Kay, chemical engineering lecturer, Glasgow."

"Anna, polymer chemistry postdoc, shared."

"Louise. Local."

"Polymer chemistry and engineering? A weird line-up for virus studies," Yuin looked disappointed. Yes, man, I also wished I was trained in guns and judo, not flasks and palladium.

"It's our last gig, no reunions," said Dan.

Yuin scratched his cleanly shaven cheek. "We've done quite a lot. We are only a few weeks away from our vaccine trials. But with almost ninety-five per cent of the human population infected, what's the use of it? We need a c—"

"What did you say? Ninety-five per cent?"

He nodded. "That's an optimistic forecast... I must admit that our evacuation protocols didn't exactly plan for the treatment scenario. After COVID-19, we were so concerned about vaccines that we didn't expect the virus to take over the world in two weeks. Our facilities aren't designed for deep science research. Your facilities—"

There are more of *them*, I wanted to say. The facilities are more *theirs* than ours.

"Have you got a structure of the virus?"

He sighed. "We have high-res electron microscopy images, an idea of genetic make-up and the family the virus belongs to. Genetic tracing is common for older Flaviviruses. West Nile virus is the modern version – you can find some information on the internet, but it's well-known for affecting the brain and causing encephalitis."

"Just like our little friend."

"Yes. Our TEM images confirm that the shape is characteristic of *Flaviviridae*. But we don't have the right tools for the proper structure model. Nothing we operate here can give enough structural detail even to attempt a decent model."

"We do."

Dan was talking about the Machine, the sleeping beast in the heart of the Ring.

But *she* was dead.

I turned to Dan. "We can't operate it. The only person in the team who could is now samples," I muttered through my closed teeth. "Or do you think our Chinese colleagues have a synchrotron expert in their team?"

"We can make it run. The power's still on, so technically, the only problem is to fire the linear accelerator. We can reach stable energies if there are no structural damages to the booster or the accelerator itself," Dan told me and then turned back to the camera. "We can try to get the Machine to work. But what's the point? I don't expect you to send us some virus in a vial."

"Have you got any z... infected people around you?" asked Yuin.

"Too many for our liking", Kay chuckled. "But we call them spleen-eaters."

"I can teach you to grow and harvest the virus while my scientists develop the crystallisation conditions on our material. Who of you is going to be the lead on this project?"

We exchanged confused looks – we'd never considered assigning all the responsibility for our scientific fail... efforts to one person.

"Louise will," said Dan. Louise nodded as if she had expected it. "Anna and I will pack our stuff. Time to get those X-rays going."

4.

"It's not Mordor we're going into."

Even the Fellowship wasn't sent off with as much crying. I wondered if we should have brought Kay along to avoid the flooding of the Ring.

And leave Louise on her own with Edsie and Tanya?

Hmm. Was I worried about Louise or the others?

Dan appeared from the control room, all packed, and Kay finally let me out. "I'm sorry for all the crying. I have a bad feeling this time."

Great! Another one with a shit-radar.

"We'll be fine. I'm more worried about you staying here. I sense a lack of friendliness within our ranks."

Edsie and Tanya didn't even come out to say byes.

"We'll be fine," echoed Kay. "Work will keep us busy. I'm one hundred per cent sure Edsie and Tanya will come out to help. Tanya's not a bad person; she's just struggling with what happened to her family and now Max. She doesn't know how to deal with this pain. Not that we do it, you know, every day."

I knew. We voted for peaceful gas.

I hadn't known Tanya for as long as Kay did – only for under two years – but I felt that Kay was right. There was something corrosive about spiteful and vengeful people, an invisible smoke that polluted the air around them, making it hard to breathe.

There was nothing hard to breathe about Tanya. Even in combination with Edsie, who was borderline toxic, Tanya did not seem harmful. Only hurt.

I didn't want to admit it, but I also had this nagging that something wasn't right, and it became harder to ignore after Kay mentioned her "bad feeling". The tension that settled in after we decided to engage with Yuin had destroyed something vital in our group, creating cracks in the fabric that could lead to nasty things seeping through uninvited.

It made me think of Greg, a surprising, fleeting thought I immediately tossed in the bin.

More importantly, what if Tanya's shit-radar was infectious? What if ominous premonitions were a symptom of another virus, one that cooked our brain into a slurry instead of making us go after spleens? First, the virus got Tanya, then Kay.

Now it's my turn.

The main problem of co-existing in the closed space was too much socialisation. Everything became shared, even insanity, and shared, it grew out of control...

Dan gave Kay a brief hug and set off without looking back. I trotted behind him, imagining we were going on a hike, almost like a vacation, away from the crazy family.

Louise popped out to say goodbye when we passed the microscopy lab. But instead of a hug, she opened the lab door and pushed us in.

"You should see this."

The word "trashed" was a very gentle understatement. No woman-named hurricane could achieve such destruction: not a piece of equipment intact and debris covering the floor in such a thick layer that I couldn't see the tiles underneath.

"Sweet. I thought it would be just the microscope," I muttered.

"I have found the computer," Louise pointed at the pile of mangled metal. "I do not think we can get any of our data out of it."

"Wow. I didn't expect Tanya to go that wild."

"I'm sure Edsie helped," Dan looked at the ceiling.

Three out of four tube lamps hung loose from above, the light of the remaining lamp casting ugly shadows on the walls smudged with blue and purple. The smudges looked like blood in the slasher movies.

"Tanya says it was not them."

"Yeah, alright."

"She says they have not been to this lab at all. They were hiding in the toilet all the time."

"And you believe her?" I asked.

For the first time, I saw Louise at a loss. "I… I do not know… They looked genuinely surprised."

Great! In addition to Tanya's shit-radar, it was time to get a bullshit-radar.

"So, it was an unfriendly ghost! Are we seriously talking about someone else destroying the lab but not Tanya?" asked Dan.

"What do you mean, *someone*? Who else is out here?" I looked around just in case I was missing someone.

"Exactly my point!"

"The microscopy lab is never locked. Anyone could walk in here," said Louise.

"Who? It's only us! Or are you trying to say that our Chinese friends are not friends at all? That they have snuck into the Ring to find and stop us, just like Tanya says?"

"Anna, calm down! Of course, it was Tanya and Edsie! I don't understand why they don't admit it, and we all move on!"

The dark thoughts crept back into my head, scary, disturbing. I felt them tossing and turning in my brain, and a sudden chill spread down my spine.

"Should we better stay until we sort it out?"

Louise shook her head. "No, you should go. But I will be keeping a close eye on our conspiracy friends. No idea what kind of game they have started, but I do not see why I cannot play along."

I don't know what was scarier – her sudden smile or the dark excitement in her voice. I saw a glimpse of insanity, and Greg appeared in my head again.

Was it insane that I suspected insanity in everyone and everything around me? If I thought everyone was crazy, probably the crazy one was *me.*

On the other hand, what is insanity, if not a different opinion about reality?

Just look around me. Bodies, blood, guts and bones – does this look like a reality you want to hold on to or pursue? Wouldn't it be better to go crazy and see pink unicorns everywhere?

We walked down the Ring, heading towards ID17, where we would get outside the central Ring and towards the smaller booster ring through a fire exit. The shady corridors greeted us with the familiar views of dried blood and rotting bodies, the decay process slowed down by the dry, motionless air inside the building. I had to admit that the gore had stopped bothering me by now. The bodies were nothing else but dead flesh and bone, no matter if I knew them when they were alive. There was enough shit with the living to waste emotions on the dead.

There was always a possibility that we, all of the ID26 crew, had inhaled too much carbon monoxide methanol and drifted off into a new reality, sharing a joint nightmare, while the real world – with Tiktok, World Football Cup, and climate change – went on its merry usual way.

There was another, scarier possibility that the nightmare was only for me, and I was in a coma while my brain sent me here, a place where the science must go on at any cost, even if it's only in my mind.

Does it mean that I'll wake up when I find the cure?

"Do you think we're all insane here?" I asked Dan.

While I was absorbed in my inner debate, dragging my feet behind him, Dan was trotting forward, way too brisk for someone with a sprained ankle. The swelling had died down, and, according to Dan, it didn't hurt anymore, but an experienced eye could notice a slight limp as he walked. He didn't seem to care, excited with our new mission, which didn't require gassing or chopping anyone for a change.

"Are you thinking we're all sharing a weird dream while lying in a coma?"

I chuckled. "I'm glad you think it's shared. I've started to wonder if the fun was only mine."

"I'm not sure I want to be a part of anyone's nightmare. Everybody deserves their own story."

"Nobody deserves *this* story," I pointed.

Just opposite the ID20 beamline, Dan stopped to consult the evacuation plan on the wall. I was about to issue a valuable statement about needing directions *inside a circle* when the hutch door opened, and a dozen spleen-eaters spilled out to greet us.

As if they had been lying in wait.

Haha! No way! It would be properly insane! The spleen-eaters can't open doors, and they can't wait. They smash through the doors as soon as they sense the prey.

Yes, Anna, great thinking, now tell them all about it.

"Shit! Run!" I grabbed Dan by his hand and dashed forward.

A far cry from Usain Bolt, and with Dan leaning onto me, I was gasping for air within a minute. The distance between us and the fan club started to shorten.

We had to hide, barricade, lock up, and pray something would distract them. I peeked back. A lanky spleen-eater with long hair waving behind had broken out of the crowd and gained upon us.

Oh gosh, he could be an Olympic athlete or even a rock star, but instead, he ended up eating spleens!

In a minute, he'd be eating mine.

I readied the lab stand, trying to balance Dan, who was now fully leaning on my shoulder.

"Leave me," he hissed into my ear.

I choked on my laughter.

"Sure. Who's going to start the Machine, then? That guy?" I nodded towards the hairy spleen-eater. I could almost feel his stinking breath on my neck, a horrible mixture of rotting flesh and wet iron, when I noticed a fire alarm button in a glass box only a few feet from me. I shook Dan off my arm and lunged for the button, smashing into the glass with a naked fist. My brain registered the pain as the glass sliced through my skin and stuck in my knuckles, but I also heard the heavenly song of the fire alarm.

Behind Dan, the hairy rockstar dropped to his knees and bashed his head into the concrete floor like an ostrich trying to dig into the sand. The crowd of spleen-eaters scattered in a panicked disarray, colliding with each other and into walls.

"Attention! Attention! This is not a…"

"Door, Anna!" Dan wheezed, trying to get up.

I also saw a small door well hidden behind the ID17 beamline container. If only it were open…

"Quick, we need to find an access card!"

Dan dropped onto his knees and started checking the bodies, four of them lying next to the door in various states of mangling and decay. None of them had a pass.

Neither did we.

The spleen-eaters behind us started regaining consciousness – the loud alarm sounds didn't seem to be working as well as they used to. We might have used it too much and made them immune.

The rockstar rose up from the floor and, after a quick scan of the room with his milky eyes, stared right at me.

Oh, look who's got a pass!

I weighed the lab stand in my hand and squinted back at him.

Jingle bells rock, mister!

But before I made my first step toward him, something smashed into my side at full speed, driving me into the wall. I dropped my lab stand and hit my head on the concrete. Through the sparkles in my eyes, a bloodied jaw clicked in front of my face in anticipation. The spleen-eater on top of me was heavy, squashing me breathless. I grabbed his hands a second before he touched my face, but while I was fluttering under him, unable to scream, his teeth got too close to my neck.

And I'd just had a perfect one-liner!

Instead of biting straight into my flesh, the spleen-eater... looked at me. Don't tell me he couldn't see me with those hazed eyes! Trust me, you know when someone's staring at you!

He looked. He watched. He saw.

Then Dan smashed his brains with his lab wrench.

He tore off a yellow booster ring pass from the spleen-eater's neck, scanned it at the card reader, and pushed me outside when the door clicked open. I fell tumbling on the gravelled path and rolled to a complete stop.

The stars in my eyes set off on a wild dance, twirling and leaping until Dan's face appeared before me. I tried to blink the stars away, and while some of them disappeared, the others turned out to be the real stars in the galaxies far, far away.

"W-what was t-t-that?"

"That was a "thank you, Dan, for saving my life"! What are you, mental for real? Why did you stare at that guy? Do you know him? Was he your long-lost love from the nursery?"

There was no immediate danger if he found this moment appropriate to mock. I pushed him away and got up on my feet. Everything hurt as if I went through a tumble drier on a few cycles.

"Have you seen that? He was looking at me."

"Yes, with eyes full of adoration, deciding what part of you to serve first!"

"Stop it! He was looking at me, Dan. Looking, like... meaningfully."

"Yeps. Thinking, 'Anna... that means dinner in my zombie language.' What's come on you? Were you just going to stare at him while he ate you?"

I sighed. How could I even attempt to describe that feeling?

All this time, we've been sure that the spleen-eaters couldn't see with their eyes, not in the usual sense, when the light falls onto the retina, and the photocells convert it into electrical signals. No way the light could penetrate through their milky haze!

Louise hypothesised that they distinguished the heat patterns and didn't attack each other because the heat patterns in infected differed from those in healthy people.

"We only need a thermal camera to confirm it," she said.

"Yeah, and a big puddle of mud," added Edsie.

Even if they could "see" the heat, this guy was different. He stopped because he saw and he was….

Thinking. He looked like he was thinking, if only for a second.

But that wasn't possible. The virus turned their brains into mash, leaving only basic instincts, which didn't include thinking about prey, especially when it was a bite away. Zombies were monodirectional. They were hungry. They hunted. They ate.

Wait a sec…

"They were waiting for us!"

Dan had already crossed the lawn to the booster ring door and was about to click it open with the yellow access card. He stopped.

"What?"

"They were sitting inside the hutch, waiting for us. Not us, anyone. Then we appeared, and phew, here they come all at once through that door."

"That's impossible!" Dan rubbed his bald head.

"Is it?

Under my stare, Dan rubbed his head again, activating the thinking neurons inside his skull.

"They are evolving," he sighed.

I nodded.

"It makes sense," he added after musing it over, "in the beginning, the prey was practically unlimited, and they didn't have to be creative. But now the prey is scarce, and they devise new ways to get it."

"By prey, you mean us. *We* are scarce," I pointed out.

He sighed.

Even if biology was not our field of expertise, we found observing the spleen-eaters curious. They were developing, like any other respectful species, and I had to admit that, in a weird sense, I was proud of them.

Only that was way too quick.

Louise said that the evolution of new behaviours in a species usually involved a few, if not many, generations. These guys were evolving at an enormous and very concerning speed. A few weeks ago, the spleen-eaters did not exist. A few days ago, they wandered like lost souls, hoping to bump into prey. Today, they've learnt to hunt.

Two options from here. Option one: in a couple of months, they'll elect a president and start selling each other weapons of mass destruction, as all "developed" civilisations do. Option two: they'll go extinct because no prey will be left. As a representative of prey, I don't find the second option attractive.

Time for us to evolve, too.

5.

Day 32, 7th of March, Thur

I didn't realise what time it was. The shadows, early harbingers of sunset, crept into the room and waltzed around me when I lifted my head from the microscope. I blinked to refocus my eyes and checked my phone.

Oh no! I'm late!

I'd planned to leave earlier and walk, but now, even if I took a taxi, I wouldn't make it on time. Steve would have to wait for me at the train station. Again.

Not that he'd ever complained. During the week, I always stayed in the lab late, working long hours deep into the night, not keen to return to my rented accommodation. So far from Steve, I couldn't call it home.

On weekends, I would travel down south, or Steve would come to see me, only to split up again on Sunday evening. We both knew this twisted arrangement couldn't last forever, even though it benefitted my career. Why bother if it would kill my relationship with Steve? It was only a matter of time.

Tonight, I would tell him I've decided to quit and will hand my notice on Monday. After this synchrotron trip – my last ever – I'll move back to Birmingham and find a lab manager job in a chemicals company, with nice 9 to 5 hours and a yearly bonus. No more late-night shifts before the submission deadline, no more tears over unfunded research proposals, and no more celebrating birthdays over Zoom on the different sides of the planet because of the conference schedules.

I was about to leave the lab when I heard Steve's voice calling me from the gas cupboard. We never locked this small cubicle where we stored our helium cylinders. If people came to steal, helium would be very low on their "wanted" list, somewhere between the mop and the washing-up sponge.

"Steve?" I called. "Are you already here? How come you're so early?"

The correct question would be, 'What the hell are you doing in the gas cupboard, Steve?' because he could only end up inside it if he'd learnt to teleport, but I didn't think much of it.

Steve responded with a sigh.

The shadows around me got darker, and the bright ceiling lamp blinked and went out, like in a cheap horror movie. The light from the windows was still enough to see, and I made myself a mental note to file a request to the estates for a new lightbulb.

I opened the cupboard door and peered inside, straining my eyes to see the figure in the shadows.

It wasn't Steve. Steve was slender and petite compared to that bulky man. I couldn't see the face, but the hair was darker and straighter than Steve's.

"Hello," I said. "What are you doing here?"

Then, the figure stepped out of the dark.

"You!" I said and woke up.

At first, I couldn't remember where I was. Then, the humming of fans and Dan's snoring reminded me that we were banking for the night in the booster ring control room. I climbed out of the makeshift bed and checked the numbers on the master station. 200 MeV. Better, but not enough. I made some adjustments in the accelerator parameters and climbed back to my bed, wondering why, out of all the days stored in my memory, my brain had picked up the day that never happened.

And placed Greg into it.

I'd never told Steve I was going to quit. In reality, when I got up from my chair, ready to call the taxi to the train station, I saw a WhatsApp message he'd sent almost two hours ago. His mom had gone into hospital with appendicitis, and he hopped off in

Crewe to take the train back. He was back in Birmingham by the time I saw his text.

I didn't see him that weekend. By the following weekend, other things took over my attention, and I postponed this conversation until I came back from ESRF.

And now I'm here, half-asleep, half-imagining what would be if I told him then and there that I was finished with science and would be coming home for good.

I used to think that science was as vital for me as breathing, but it wasn't true. Being next to him was like breathing. Science was, well, all I could do. Perhaps if he knew that, things would go differently between us. Maybe, there would still be an "us".

It made sense that my mind was using dreams to work through the issues with Steve, but I didn't get why Greg was involved, appearing in my mind and memory like an annoying pop-up notification.

The hum of the master station fan grew louder. I wrapped myself in a puff coat that served as a blanket and went to check why the computer was straining so much.

The energy levels had dropped again, this time by order of magnitude. There should have been some beam leak in the Machine, making the poor computer recalculate the reflection angles and magnet parameters in an endless cycle. The buzz of the fan grew even louder, to no effect, and after a slight rise, the energy values dropped again.

I debated waking Dan up but then gave up on the idea. He had only slept a few hours since we arrived at the booster ring control room two days ago. There were manuals for different occasions, including an emergency machine stop/start, so we'd managed to kick the Machine off by firing the electrons from the electron gun into the linear accelerator. Leaving the accelerator at 200MeV, they were supposed to speed up to 6GeV after a few cycles through the booster ring, but for some unknown reasons, they didn't.

Annoying little shits.

We spent our first day uncasing the accelerator and the transfer lines and doing visual and computer-run checks on the equipment. Nothing looked broken, shattered or badly misaligned. We didn't touch any electronics or optics, hoping that if there was no damage, the computer would refocus and re-parameterise the electronics. But the energy remained unchanged in the best case. The optics somewhere in the booster ring were causing losses.

I rolled the numbers back to their previous values and leaned back in the chair.

"I can't sleep, man. Any advice?" I asked Francesco.

He didn't respond. It made me feel even more lonely as if I expected him to say something. Francesco had been dead for a long time when we met him – in the continuously vented air of the control room, he was sort of mummified. We rolled his chair to the other end of the workstation and cleaned his dried-up blood off the floor. Now, he looked like a regular synchrotron scientist, watching the energy numbers on his screen, only without the toilet breaks.

We could have done the usual thing and packed him into a black bin sack, storing him away in a quiet room. You might even wonder why we didn't.

I don't know.

His badge said his name was Francesco, and he was a senior booster ring engineer. He could have been anyone; I'd lost any trust for badges by now. We pretended he was a part of the crew and that we could revert to his expertise if needed.

Dodgy? You bet.

From time to time, Dan talked to him, asking what parameters to choose or for explanations for the unclear descriptions in the SOPs. Francesco stared into the screen, and Dan muttered, "Yes, you are right."

They made a great team.

I guessed a part of Francesco's charm was that he was not an ordinary victim of the spleen-eaters. He wasn't eaten or even bitten – he preferred to kill himself, well, *himself.* Before we rolled him aside, I pulled his pullover sleeves down to cover the gaping wounds in his wrists and patted him on the shoulder. It's okay, man. No judgement there.

Sanity? Who's that?

The screen in front of me brightened, and the pop-up window notified me that the rollback was performed successfully. The energy climbed back to 200 MeV. I checked that the numbers on all electrodes were correct and that the chambers showed a deep vacuum.

Everything seemed right.

But something wasn't.

I'd ask Francesco, but he's busy.

My phone pinged me with a WhatsApp message from Steve, the sixth in the last two days. After making all his way across Birmingham, he found Lesley's friend's house empty but neat, with no traces of fighting or blood. I asked him to check the closest fuel stations and shops in case Lesley had found shelter nearby. Since then, Steve wouldn't stop spamming me with pictures of women, all blonde.

And dead.

I didn't ask whether they were pregnant – *that* didn't matter anymore.

IT'S NOT HER, I texted back and pushed the phone back into my pocket,

Was I bitter?

Apart from the photos, some of them gory even for the current circumstances, I didn't get any other messages from Steve. Are you telling me about bitter?

I decided to walk along the booster ring to vent out the nasty thought. It was an oasis of peace – the barely audible humming of the machinery, my steps loud and echoing in the corridor, and not a trace of monsters. The Machine didn't know anything about our human struggles. She worked restlessly when there was someone to push her buttons. She slumbered when people forgot about her. She had an ultimate performance and work ethic, untroubled by pandemics, personal relationships, or emotional breakdowns. Above all, she didn't have to make difficult choices between Life and Death.

But she couldn't make a cure. The humans were necessary for that – fragile, emotional, lazy, unethical, varyingly intelligent, and unreliable.

The red enamel on the vacuum chamber casing was cracking at the joints from wear. I traced the cold metal with my hand, feeling a slight tingling in my fingers.

The human brain was so fragile. Wasn't my brain playing tricks on me, sticking the impostor bastard into my dreams where Steve should have been? Greg appeared in the least expected places, stalking me from the shadows, always there, always watching. He could have been a monster from the nightmares, but I wasn't scared of him in the slightest. On the contrary, it felt like he belonged. I knew he'd come after me one day, whether as a human or a spleen-eater. He'd come to get even, but that didn't bother me.

I wanted him to come. He bore the print of absolute insanity, deep and unnatural, and I craved to understand it. It could give me a definite answer to the question that *did* bother me.

Was *I* going crazy?

I stopped by one of the vacuum chambers and peered behind it, trying to see the wall through the tubes, wires, and equipment. I imagined Greg hiding behind the transfer lines, waiting for a chance to jump on me, laughing like a villain from a children's cartoon.

I found an untouched spot in the vacuum chamber casing and traced a large "Fuck you" in the thick layer of dust.

The tingling in my finger turned into a sharp prickling.

Houston, we've got a problem!

6.

Day 33, 8th of March, Fri

"Grounding," repeated Kay. "I am no expert, but wouldn't it sort of show in one of your parameters?"

I shrugged. I was no expert either, but when I woke Dan up and told him we had an electricity leak, he immediately understood the essence of the problem. I felt like this ability to translate "electricity leak" into "grounding issues" was a sacred knowledge passed from father to son, carefully avoiding females.

"Dan's fixed the loose earthing connection, so now he's running the tests before we put the machine casing back and try again."

"Fingers crossed."

I hurried to shift the conversation from my side to hers. "How are our naughty little friends?"

I meant the virus. Not Edsie and Tanya.

"Very healthy, considering that our conditions are far from sterile. Yuin said we could try to make our first inoculations in the wet lab, but we would need specialist equipment for proper harvesting. It looks like we'll have to move."

"Where?"

She sighed. "The science building is the only place on campus with all the facilities. Louise has already started packing."

"I bet she's not very happy about it."

I doubted if even Louise had enough courage to return to that place. Greg, the man of my dreams, might still be there.

"I'm surprised how quickly she's made best friends with the Chinese guy. He's friendly with everyone, even with Edsie, who sometimes calls him a Chink; God bless him. But he has a true

The Synchrotron | 239

connection with Louise. The other night, I caught them chatting about pizza!"

I chuckled. Since when has chatting about pizza become suspicious?

Oh, wait... the apocalypse!

"You think she's made *that type* of friend?"

I laughed. No way our cold-hearted, calculating—

Well, she's human.

Or is she?

Initially, I assumed every humanoid creature not chasing my spleen to be human, but lately, the word has become less black-and-white and more 3D.

"Are you serious about moving?" I asked Kay. "Like, permanently?"

For a second, her face showed fear. "I don't know how permanently. We can't finish the virus harvesting here, and we'll need different equipment for crystallisation. Louise said that a part of the Science building is completely monster-free, so I shouldn't worry about it. But it's not what I worry about," she leant closer to the camera to whisper. I almost expected her to say Greg's name, but she surprised me. "I haven't left the beamline much, Anna. I feel like I'll never be ready to come out. Even if this whole thing's over, I feel like... I've rooted into it. I'm scared to get out."

"That's not true. You got out when we went to the controls office. You get out every day to work in the lab with Louise!"

"It's not the same," she said, her voice shaking, "I don't know what I'll do outside. I don't know if outside still exists at all. What if everything outside has disappeared, and I live in a loop? What if all this is just my imagination? What if I'm lying in a coma, and it's all a dream?"

I smiled. Even if all of us were going crazy, it was nice to see us going in the same direction.

"It's more likely that we are in a simulation, and a secret government agency is testing the zombie apocalypse scenario on us," I told her with a serious face.

Kay cast me a disgusted look, and I laughed out loud. Great! Tanya's ideas weren't that infectious after all.

"If you are sleeping, you will wake up," I reassured her. "And there'll be your old world around you."

Kay hadn't been outside for many weeks, hadn't seen the sun or felt the rain on her face – all those things that reminded me that the Earth was still moving and that there was hope.

"By the way, we've noticed that the spleen-eaters are evolving."

I told her what happened two days ago.

"It doesn't sound good at all, Anna. If they become increasingly intelligent, soon they'll be as smart as we are."

"Maybe, as Edsie."

"I'll tell the others, but I suggest we don't jump to conclusions. It might be that this particular batch... pack was different from the start."

"What, bitten by a local genius?"

She nodded. "I think that the behaviour of one group can't serve as a reflection of the whole population. We need to observe such behaviour multiple times in several independent groups before making solid conclusions."

"You sound just like Louise," I sighed, not meaning it as a compliment.

She decided not to insist. "We are leaving in the evening. Tanya and Edsie are coming with us."

That was a surprise.

Or not really, if one of them (or both) was planning to trash the lab every time we made a step forward.

Kay read my mind.

"We haven't had any more... episodes. Tanya's been quiet, but she's not through it yet. Edsie put down a lone walker the other night, and Tanya went berserk, insisting we didn't chop the bugger. The spleen-eater, not Edsie. She even made Edsie drag the body away so we couldn't get to it. Louise found it hilarious. You should have heard her laugh." Kay rolled her eyes. "At least Tanya's stopped crying. She still doesn't talk to us much, but at least she cooks... every little helps."

"Is she still denying the first, hm, incident?"

Kay shrugged, looking around. She was in the microscopy lab, and what I could see in the background was a drastic contrast to what it looked like the last time we stopped by. It was tidy and organised; even the tube lamps were back in their places and on full brightness.

"They swear it wasn't them. Does it matter in the end? Edsie helped tidy up; we didn't even have to ask."

"As long as Louise is happy...."

"She only cares about her viruses. She doesn't yet call them "my babies", but she's getting there... don't get me wrong, this is Louise we are talking about. She backs everything up twice. She's even running two virus colonies in two separate fume hoods. And I don't think she's worried about anything in particular; it's just her normal way of working. She's very pedantic... Which poses a question."

"Of how she's ended up in a cupboard?"

Kay laughed. "There's one thing... She's wrangled out all the cupboard locks, so they no longer work. She tried to do the same with the toilets, but I caught her before she broke anything!"

Okay. Locks weren't the worst that could happen.

"When we're done here, we'll come to help you," I assured Kay.

Something heavy smashed into the door behind me and dropped onto the floor with a shattering sound. Kay winced and looked at me with sympathy. "Dan?"

I sighed, counting how many working screens we had left. I'd begged Dan not to touch the master station computer, but I wasn't sure he heard me, not in his current state of mind.

"How did you know?"

She shrugged. "Last time you called… he didn't look that good."

"None of us looks good anymore."

"You look fine."

I smiled, but it was a pained smile.

"That bad?"

"Worse, Kay. And I don't have any good news for him. It's been a few days since I've heard from Steve, and with every minute, there is less Dan and more of… I don't know what that is, but it scares me." I pointed at the door behind me. A thud reverberated through the door as if on cue, ending with a metallic clang. "Must be his lab wrench. I'd better make sure he leaves me at least one working computer."

I pushed myself to my feet, casting an unenthusiastic glance at the closed door.

"Be careful, Anna," Kay said and ended the call.

I suppressed an urge to call Steve, Louise, or maybe even Edsie – anyone – to postpone the inevitable. I couldn't spend the rest of my life in this cleaning cupboard, even though I preferred the company of mops and buckets to the thing outside. Yes, that thing used to be Dan. No, he hasn't bitten.

Since we arrived at the booster ring, Dan had been working non-stop to restart the Machine, stealing an hour of sleep here and there. I had to replace his computer mouse with snack bars and sandwiches, and he put them into his mouth automatically, his eyes glued to the screen that showed minimal energy levels.

His face turned darker and darker, and I knew that the exhaustion of the last few days would soon creep up on him. I saw a glimpse of hope on his face when we sorted the grounding issue – the energy levels started rising for the first time…

Then they dropped again.

And Dan did, too.

Instead of my friend, something else reared its head. Something frightening that I'd never encountered before, a beast with Dan's face, Dan's bald head, and even his voice.

Dan it wasn't.

My phone went first, its only fault that it didn't have any positive news about Lesley from Steve. Shoved into the master monitor – the red energy numbers low at 0.45 meV – it didn't do any damage but crash-landed on the floor. The phone screen shattered, and the back cover cracked open to reveal the electronics inside. I pulled the SIM card out of the dead phone while Dan grabbed Francesco's desktop screen and sent it flying across the room. I crawled under the table, sheltering from the next bomb. A keyboard cannoned into the table above my head, and I crawled towards Francesco's chair, hoping to grab his phone before this beast with Dan's face ripped the whole control room apart. Francesco had an old Samsung, its screen webbing in the corner, but it was still working and would take my charger.

The beast continued hurling things around, shattering glass and smashing plastic. It was not a hurricane but a hurting animal that did not know how to help itself. I almost plucked the courage to get from under the table and approach him to offer comfort when he tossed a wooden chair at me. I jerked away, and the chair leg grazed my thigh before crashing into Francesco's chair and toppling him on the floor. I darted to the cleaning cupboard and hid there, rethinking my life choices, until Kay called for updates.

I had to come out no matter how scared I was. It was my fault that Dan had turned into this – I should have forced him to rest and distracted him instead of letting him brew in the hot pot of hopelessness, worry, anger, and pain. I should have danced, sung, and fired stand-up jokes, but never left him like that.

What kind of friend was I?

A pragmatic one, I decided, grabbing a heavy metal-base mop, and opened the closet door.

"Not the master computer, Dan!"

I tossed the mop at him just as he reached for the desktop. It didn't hit him but halted him enough that I dashed forward, pulled the computer out of his hands, and stepped back, putting the desktop between him and me.

Eh, not my most strategic move.

"What are you doing, Dan? Stop, it won't help!" I shouted, hoping that the sound of my voice – shrill, panting – would wake him up.

Red-eyed, he didn't seem to even recognise me. He stepped forward about to hit me, so I hit him first straight into the right tibia so hard that even Francesco twitched in his seat. Dan squealed, bent over, and dropped to his knees.

I returned the desktop to its place and stood over Dan, waiting for common sense to creep back into his head. He stayed on the floor, hiding his face from me behind a waterfall of tears. I sat down next to him and squeezed his hand, digging my nails deep into his skin and flesh.

"I know what you're thinking, but it won't work, Dan. This is just a machine… It doesn't know any better."

He wept, and I hugged him, wishing his pain and worry would flow away with the tears. I don't know who said that men don't cry. They do, and they should, and maybe I should have cried with him. But my eyes were dry, and my heart was numb inside, and instead of my own pain, I felt the echoes of his.

"I don't know… I don't know how I can live without her," Dan whispered.

I looked around the control room, searching for a clue, a wording to comfort his soul, but my eyes met only the cold blinking of the indicators and the large red numbers on the master monitor. 0.42 meV. Yes, the Machine didn't know any better.

But I knew.

"Do you remember what you said when my parents died? You told me to get up and pack my stuff. It hurt like hell, but I did and moved on. I don't know if Lesley is dead, but even if she is, I want you to get up and move on, no matter how much it hurts. Even if it feels impossible, she would want you to get up and go."

My speech was a far cry from the heartfelt inspirational speeches they showed in the movies, capable of jerking people out of their black holes and straight into the dazzling light of the day. But Dan looked at me and nodded.

"For Lesley?"

"For yourself." I put the screwdriver into his palm. Four bleeding crescents from my nails were imprinted on his pale skin.

Chapter 6. V-24

1.

Day 36, 11ᵗʰ of March, Mon

I am happy to announce that after a brief hiatus caused by a temporary breakdown of the leading cast member, the freak show "ID26" is back on the road! Someone runs behind me with an "Applause" sign, and the audience cheers, complaining quietly that they still haven't gotten the refund for the cancelled shows.

In the meantime, three things have happened.

Number 1. We've managed to get the Machine up and running. All credit goes to Dan for giving it a healthy reviving kick in the bol… vacuum systems. It took us almost a week, but it's okay because—

Number 2. Louise and Kay needed this time to grow and isolate the virus in workable amounts.

But then—

Number 3. Dan and I made it all the way to the Science building, lab 213, to see our friends. Right on time for the virus funeral.

Please don't ask me how the journey went. It's sufficient to say that, although we both made it through alive, I'd do it again only if they threatened me with a gun. On a positive note (no, not really), we've confirmed our initial hypothesis – the spleen-eaters are getting smarter and will be ready for the next University Challenge.

Jeez, our evolution is broken!

When we turned up, Kay was in the middle of the freezer clean-out, crying over the dead virus colonies as she sent the inoculation tubes into a yellow sack labelled Biological Waste. Okay, it's hard to be sure if she was crying in that respirator mask, but she didn't look happy at all.

Maybe, because of the stench.

Edsie and Tanya, wearing identical filter masks like some cheap astronauts, were venting the labs, running all extraction fans and opening windows to encourage at least a gulp of fresh air to come in. It was good to see them cooperating, although I'd prefer it happened in a less stinky atmosphere.

"What's this shite?" I asked Louise, trying not to breathe through my nose. She was standing next to the fridge, in the epicentre of the stench, without a mask, examining the fridge door as if she were a fridge door expert.

"The fridge broke overnight, and our virus thawed."

"What, all dead?"

She nodded gloomily.

"An accident?"

She looked at me with *that look* but didn't add anything. I realised she didn't want to bring it up in front of everyone else. But I wanted to bring it up! Whichever shit did this, they had to bloody explain themselves!

I felt sick from the idea that, while Dan and I made circles around the Ring, risking our lives with every step, one of my colleagues, whom I trusted to cover my back when the spleen-eaters attacked, was stabbing me right into that very back. It didn't matter how angry Tanya was with Chinese, Klingons or polar bears; it was bloody time to grow up and stop whining!

This little sabotage wasn't directed at Louise but at all of us who worked our asses off to find the cure.

I wanted to kill, and I would if I could breathe. My lungs rang out of air, and I dashed out of the lab, followed by Dan, his face green, yellow and blue, which, as I suddenly recalled, made up the flag of Gabon, wherever that was.

"Jesus Christ!" he muttered, bending over in a retch.

Was it weird that nothing reverted us to religion as much as that unholy stench?

Kay walked out of the lab without her mask, pulling the nitrile gloves off.

"It stinks, but overall, it's not a big deal. Annoying, of course – we were about to start crystallisation according to Yuin's protocols. On the positive side, we've polished the growing procedure. Now, we can get a new harvest in under fifty hours. The equipment here is fantastic, and Yuin provides support pretty much 25/7. I don't know when he sleeps."

Indeed, lab 213 was impressive, fully equipped with centrifuges, rows of glove boxes for inoculations, massive stations of automatic pipettes, fridges and freezers, incubators and hot plates. Louise looked at home in this vast space, and even her French accent faded for good.

"So, what's the plan?" Dan asked.

Since his breakdown in the controls room, he seemed to calm down to the point that I trusted him to hold things without smashing them into me or the wall. Before we left the booster ring, I handed his lab wrench back and pointed at myself. "Anna – no." Then I clawed the air in front of me with a growl, "Monsters – yes!"

Repeat daily.

"We'll reseed the virus once the labs are inhabitable again. I don't think it'll happen today. What's the forecast, Tanya?" Kay asked when Tanya and Edsie walked out of the lab, pulling off the filter face masks, followed by Louise.

"It won't get better by the evening. We might need to give it a night, too."

"I can work on my own," said Louise.

Nobody seemed to like this idea.

"It's not safe in the lab on your own, Louise," said Kay.

"Yeah, never know what shit walks by. Doctor Frankenstein and her boss have done a good job of driving the zombies out of this part of the building, so we haven't seen any of those buggers. But one loud bang and the whole campus will be here for dinner," said Edsie.

Louise shrugged. "There is no rush. Twelve more hours will not make us an omelette."

"Tell us what we can do. With four extra hands, it'll be much faster!"

"I don't think it'll make a difference," said Kay, looking at Louise for support. "This is a two-person job. The time adds for holding the virus to let it grow."

"Heh, you guys can't help," smirked Edsie, "unless you sing and dance to entertain those stinky little buggers in their incubators."

"Is that your job?" asked Dan.

Edsie's face turned red, but he didn't respond.

"You two should go back to the Machine," said Louise.

Dan and I stared at her, wide-eyed, our jaws dropping to the floor. Haven't we just arrived? We've almost got killed on our way! Three times!

No way. She *will* have to threaten me with a gun!

"You said the energies were not always stable," she added, eyeing me weirdly, her left eye twitching. "Someone should watch the machine so that when we are ready with the samples, we can jump on it straight away."

"The energies weren't great at first, but we've made it work," said Dan. "I don't think anything will happen to the Machine in the next few days."

"Yes, but what if they drop again? Are you going to waste another week winding it up?"

"No, but—"

"Do not you need to top it up?" insisted Louise.

I got it then. It wasn't a question but an order. *"I want you to be somewhere else right now."*

Honestly? I could do with some rest. I could do with twenty-four hours of sleep in a proper bed with fresh linen, or any linen. Dirty would do; just let me have a day off from this endless run in the hamster wheel. I was fed up with walking along the Ring corridors, not knowing if I would make the next turn. I was tired of killing to make sure I lived and was worried that one day, my hand, exhausted from all the hitting and chopping, would not move in time.

I could pretend I didn't get her hidden message.

I sighed. I'd gotten into this shit when I pulled Louise out of the cupboard. It was time to trust her, hoping she knew how to play the game she had started.

"We do," I nodded. "It takes around seventy-two hours for the electrons to reach the booster ring, and every cycle depletes the energy by a third, so we might not find any electrons left when we return."

Dan turned to me. Judging by his face, my science bullshit was spectacular. I felt a sharp pang of guilt as the others, complete non-experts in synchrotron radiation, ate my bullshit and asked for seconds.

"Sorry, guys." Edsie nodded. "It sounds like you should go back and keep the fort until we're ready."

"Yes," said Louise. "Go get those electrons running!"

Half an hour later, Dan and I were packing our squirt bottles and food supplies, only two of us in the room.

"Seventy-two hours to reach the booster ring? What the hell, Anna? Since when are we herding electrons? Where has all this bullshit come from?"

I shrugged. "Louise wants us out of here. I couldn't think of any real reason."

"*She* needs to give us a real reason why we would go out there again," he hissed through his teeth as Edsie came with another pack of instant noodles. I shoved it into my backpack, wondering how long the supplies would last. We'd been quite relaxed about rationing, assuming we'd keep getting more food from the restaurant until someone rescued us or we all turned into the spleen-eaters. But Yuin was clear on our chances – nobody was coming and nobody was going anywhere.

The farewells were warmer this time, and Edsie and Tanya came to say bye. Tanya even hugged me, whispering, "I'm sorry", as I wiggled out of her embrace. She looked genuinely upset that we were leaving again.

Should I check my backpack? Has she packed me a ticking bomb? Her sadness was believable; if the distrust hadn't rooted so deep inside me, I would feel sad to be leaving, too. Instead, I felt annoyed. Did she have the same believable face when she told Kay she didn't trash the microscopy room or break our fridge and kill the virus?

Louise was the last to bid farewells. I didn't expect much from Louise, model X, serial number 012, but out of nowhere, she hugged me, too. While I stood there dumbstruck, amazed at the human warmth radiating from her, she brushed her palm against my side, and I felt something land in my coat pocket. She moved away with a single word.

"Crystal."

With that, we left to herd the electrons.

2.

Of course, the electrons didn't need herding, despite the bullshit we told the others. Once they achieved the correct energy, they could run in circles around the Ring, and the Machine's systems would automatically top-up with fresh electrons. Great, I didn't crave another visit to the trashed booster control room.

Sorry, Francesco, your charm is hard to resist, but I prefer the company of living.

This time, we headed back to the beamlines. Although we both wanted to go *home* to ID26, we figured that the X-ray beam at ID26 would be too strong for the soft organic viruses, so we chose ID30 instead.

Although I tried to imagine myself as a hobbit walking to Mordor with a crystallised virus sample instead of One Ring, in all honesty, the best I could aspire for was a pizza delivery girl. There and back again. And back there again. Enjoy your food, sir. Is it cold? Massive apologies. The orcs attacked us on the way, and the closest I had to a noble swordsman was Dan with his lab wrench.

No, the orcs weren't after the pizza. They were after us.

The only reason why Dan and I had survived so far, touchwood, was that we did our best to avoid direct engagement with our spleen-eating fan club. An occasional smack and a cheeky hit were okay, but facing a whole crowd, Jacky Chan-style?

Twelve spleen-eaters who walked on us from behind ID31 counted as a crowd. Without discussion, we dashed for the beamline. Dan ran to lock the hutch while I locked and barricaded the control room door.

The spleen-eaters hit the reinforced glass. They couldn't break it, but each hit reverberated with fear in my spine. I saw their milky eyes staring at me through the glass, and I knew they saw me. Heat or light, it didn't matter what signals they processed.

I walked into the hutch, out of the spleen-eaters' view, and looked around in terror. A stark contrast to our comfy ID26, ID31 was packed with ragged bodies, half-stripped of flesh and bone, and bone chippings everywhere.

And the rats!

Millions of rats, fussing, shuffling around like oversized maggots, on top, between, and inside the bodies. Dan stepped on a tail snaking from under a chewed thigh, and a big fat rat the size of a badger hurried away, squealing, carrying something that looked a lot like a bone.

I swallowed, retching, and turned away.

"I'm going to say something crazy," Dan said.

I glanced at him, only slightly interested. Nothing could be crazier than the reality we were living in.

And dying, don't forget that.

"One of those guys outside had normal eyes," Dan said.

Now I looked.

"I'm not joking," he said. "Something's caught my eye out there, but only inside it got to me... One of them was human."

"Bullshit."

He sighed, rubbing his eyes. "I guess I'm tired. Whatever you say, we shouldn't have left straight away. I haven't even cleaned up after our last trip."

I looked at his lab coat. Covered in biological liquids and tissues, it had seen better days.

We all had.

"What are we going to do? They won't leave us now."

Dan shrugged. "Let's sit down and think."

We climbed onto two high lab stools – further away from the rats – and pulled out our snack bars. After we finished those in silence, we spent the next few hours kicking away brash rats and pretending to be thinking, which looked a lot like mindless staring at the wall. Surprisingly, the spleen-eaters soon lost interest, their hungry growls getting quieter as they wandered off one by one. When we plucked the courage to peer outside ID31, the last monster slowly shuffled away, following the rest of his flock.

This was new. We'd observed before that a crowd of spleen-eaters was unlikely to dissipate as if held together by a shared gravity, and only a handful of loners could leave its pull in search of prey. The new spleen-eaters travelled around, actively seeking dinner opportunities and devising new ways of hunting.

ID30 was around the corner, straight after the unfinished BM30. We expected it to be quiet and deserted, like most beamlines these days, but when we opened the door, a beamline scientist ran out of the hutch straight into the line of fire. I sprayed him with acid, and Dan finished him with his lab wrench. We pushed the body into a bin sack and left it outside.

This beamline was more like ID26 – no dried blood puddles, no rotting body parts. The hutch was a mess of wires and equipment scattered around the room, but the sampling platform looked fine, with all the bits in place and aligned. Jateendra, our friend in the bin sack, ensured the beamline was ready for the next research team.

Us. We were the research team, the crew of ID26, with an experiment that was never meant to be.

Does it mean we are the ID30 crew now?

I left Dan to deal with the equipment and went back to Jateendra. We couldn't leave him outside our new place to rot, stink, and attract his livelier friends, so I dragged him to ID31. Even post-mortem, when bodies get heavy and limp, Jateendra felt lightweight. The bin sack caught on something and ripped when I was on my way to ID31. I pulled Jateendra by the legs, sweating and swearing. Inside the beamline, I pushed the body into the corner of the hutch, on top of the others, watching with a gloomy indifference the swarm of rats roll past my feet and over the fresh flesh.

If they eat the infected body, would they get infected, too?

No, I reminded myself, we would already have hordes of spleen-eating pests all over the Ring. We wouldn't be able to fight them.

Would they want our spleens, anyway?

I was walking out of ID31 when my phone notified me about a WhatsApp message from Steve.

WE'VE FOUND HER!

Great. He said the same last time, so here comes another dead woman's photo for my serial killer-style collection. Man, I didn't sign up for this macabre WhatsApp subscription! There are a lot of dead women and men here in the Ring!

This would be the last one, I decided. Steve should go home and leave all those women in peace. I'm sure he's got more fun things to do.

My brain readily offered me the memory of the snowed-in chalet in the middle of French nowhere, fire cracking, wind howling outside. I shook it off with a sigh. Thank you, but that's a wrong reality. In this one, I'm packing bodies, and Steve's cataloguing dead women.

And Lesley, of course. What will I do if her dead photo lands in my WhatsApp? How will I tell Dan? What if it's today? What if the only thing between Dan and a smashing heartbreak was a slow internet connection?

I listened in to my shit-radar. Quiet.

Not today.

By the time I got back to ID30, the photo hadn't come. PHOTO? I texted Steve, walking into the hutch.

Dan was shouting at the sampling platform, kicking it.

"Your banner rod!"

The platform shook violently, and the thin film samples left by the previous research group rained on the floor.

"What are you doing, man?"

"The detector is down. The red lights are on, and the system says that the vibrational sensor is faulty, but I don't know how to get the bugger to work! Your banner rod!"

Dead women forgotten, my brain switched to science – a nice, comforting switch.

"There should be another detector. Every beamline has at least two."

"Not sensitive enough. And this one's aligned already."

"If you keep smashing it, the alignment won't stay long. What's that Rod Banner shit?"

"Your banner rod! One of my Russian students used it to restart our lab chiller. No idea what that means. I guess some order for the stuff to work."

"While smashing it? No wonder most Russian labs look like they've been bombed. Now, stop abusing the equipment and let's pinch a detector from someone else. I'm sure no one will complain."

I saw a suitable detector at ID30, only slightly covered with rat shit.

"Even if we find one, connecting it will take a day at its best. We can't waste time. Your banner rod," he kicked it again with doubled force. Something on the sampling platform squeaked and clicked. I'd already ordered a funeral band for the detector when the steady humming of the fan indicated that the camera was back online.

I walked around the platform. The red flashing lights on the camera turned to steady green. I was about to ask what the banner was about, but my phone pinged. The photo arrived.

I briefly glanced at it. In the bad light, I could see that it was a woman, blonde, gaunt, like all of us, so that even if it were Lesley, I wouldn't recognise her. Pregnant? In the photo, she was hugging her belly – pretty flat, in my opinion – and smiling, but with the other half of her face covered by a shadow, it could be Lesley, but as much, she could be any—

Wait a second!

Posing. Smiling.

The woman in the photo was alive.

3.

"We've found them at the fuel station by chance, quite far from the address you gave me. We'll take Lesley and her friend Angela back to the safe zone. We've got doctors and equipment, so she'll be all right; nothing to worry about."

Lesley had lost her phone in a spleen-eater squabble, so Steve's dad gave her his for a minute, which he now clearly regretted. I noticed him in the background and waved. He waved back and yawned, his face reflecting boredom and annoyance. Finally reconnected, the star-crossed lovers Dan and Lesley had been on the phone for almost an hour, their giggling increasingly annoying. I struggled to focus on Steve's words through the loud spurts of laughter, so I kicked Dan out of the hutch and closed the door between us to do the final tests before we fired the X-rays.

"And sorry for all those photos, Anna. I didn't expect to find her, you know...."

"It's all right," I nodded. "There's so much death that you always assume the worst. Like I did when you said you found her. I couldn't imagine that—"

I laughed. "I was expecting yet another photo. To check if it was Lesley. I didn't realise that you didn't need me to confirm this time."

He chuckled. "Yeah, I texted you straight after she told me her name! We were fortunate that we passed that fuel station. We were about to give up, to be honest."

I was about to give up, too, I remembered. One last woman, and then Steve should go home.

Well, he is going home. And Lesley, too.

I propped the phone on the work surface and turned it to face me as I placed the calibration sample into the holder. Since the unknown Rod Banner helped Dan revive the detector, all systems aligned and clicked correctly. It was my turn to set up the sampling platform, the most critical bit in the X-ray experiment. It had to do a full circle turn, smoothly switching between various angles, with high precision and without dropping the alignment.

I sat on the stool in front of my phone, watching the sample platform whizzing about, first on its own, then with the weight of the calibration sample.

A loud, bawling laugh sounded from the control room.

"Is that Dan?" asked Steve. "He should bring the volume down a bit, or all the monsters will be at you in no time."

The sample platform clicked, switching to the next angle with an unhealthy jerk. I leant over to tighten the screw on the right and release one on the left.

"Let him have a breather. He's been down under since Lesley's disappeared. I was really worried for him. He's lucky to have her back."

"And pregnant! What a time to bring a baby into the world!"

Even on the video, Lesley didn't look pregnant, and when I asked her about it, she told me it was too early to show. Was it? Probably. What did I know about babies?

Only one thing – they had no idea about timeliness!

Steve sighed, a dark thought clouding his face.

"What's that, Steve?"

My internal shit-radar popped up the "danger" notification. Steve hesitated, and I stared until he uttered, "Do you think... Do you think if we had a baby...?"

He didn't have the guts to finish the question, but I knew what he wanted to ask. Would we still be a thing if we had a baby – before the Z.A., before the synchrotron? But to finish Steve's unasked question meant acknowledging that *we* weren't a *thing* anymore and didn't have a future together.

Steve had always been a family man, inspired by his parents' long-lasting marriage, dreaming of two children and a peaceful retirement in Cornwall.

Fucking Cornwall again! That's where it came from – it was all Steve's idea.

Last year, Steve's parents celebrated their thirtieth anniversary. "Since the day we married, we've never been apart," his mother said with happy tears in her eyes, and Steve squeezed my hand under the table.

"I don't want to be apart anymore, too," he whispered, "You're everything to me".

Later that evening, while pulling the tie off his neck in front of our bedroom mirror, he asked me, "Why don't we have a baby soon, Ania?"

I choked. Then I laughed. Then I shrugged it off like a silly joke. Steve was in Birmingham, and I was in Glasgow. How would we raise a baby? Online?

In a way, he was right. If we had a baby, I wouldn't be stuck here, finely balancing between my conscience and the greater good. Caring for our child, I would have quit my job, moved back to Birmingham, and put my dream of the Nobel Prize on the shelf, hoping that one day, the family would release me from its loving grip.

Don't get me wrong. Steve would be a great father. But I...

Not all women are made wives or mothers. Some of us are made scientists.

I am where I'm supposed to be.

The sample moving platform whizzed loudly, returning to the starting position – the entire 360 cycle was complete. I clicked the buttons to release the sample from the sample holder and put the calibration unit back into its box.

Time to get the baby out.

Baby... Isn't it ironic? I have a baby in the end, just of a different sort.

I looked back at Steve. He awaited my answer, even though he hadn't pronounced the question. Sad. There were times when he could read my mind, knowing what I wanted from the way I blinked.

"Any idea who Banner Rod is?" I asked.

"What?"

"Your Banner Rod?"

"What's that?" he muttered, confusion in his eyes.

I could still read his mind just fine. He was wondering if I'd gone kooky. That's all right. Not a day had passed that I didn't wonder the same about myself and the world around me. Was there anything sane and reliable left at all?

I thought Steve and I were, but look at us now.

The world was crumbling down, and nothing survived.

Something soft hit me on the back of my head. I turned around. Smiling, Dan was standing at the hutch door with another paper "snowball" ready.

"Yippe-yay! Baby Torren says hi!" he shouted, hopping into the hutch like a cheerful toddler.

Well, no.

Some things remained unchanged.

4.

Day 42, 17th of March, Sun

I was crying.

Hadn't I waited for this moment my whole life? Hadn't I dreamt of a ground-breaking discovery that would put my name next to the names of the other glorified researchers?

I had, and I was crying.

These weren't the tears of happiness, like those shed by Oscar-winners while they wiped the snot with their gold-plates statuettes, but of pain and anger that the discovery came at such an enormous cost, a price paid by so many, delivering me this ironic moment of triumph in the times when nobody in the fucking world gave a shit about science.

"It's okay, Anna." Dan patted my shoulder. "You've done a great job!"

"Have I? If I'm finished, can I go home now? Can I spend my last days next to Steve, whether he loves me or not? No? So, it's not good enough! It will never be good enough! Will it?"

"Look, people take years to get it right, and we've done it in only a few days."

He pointed at the desktop. Rendered in green, yellow and red, the structure of V-24 slowly rotated on the black screen.

It took us one hundred thirty-five hours to do this magic. The Machine did thirty of those. We had to do the rest. The X-rays could only distinguish between heavy and light atoms. But in any protein, there were hundreds of light atoms tightly packed into one square pixel. With such resolution, the Machine produced only a colourful blur, which we cleaned, sorted, and assigned atom after atom in a virus consisting of millions of atoms.

It would be impossible if our predecessors didn't spend decades studying virus structures.

"Looks like a typical Flavivirus," Yuin confirmed when we showed him the first captures of the crystal structure – a hundred and five hours ago. "Our TEM scans have also distinguished those specific surface dimers."

I had no idea how he could distinguish anything in the mess of dots we showed on the screen, but he looked satisfied. That had to do.

"We'll need all known flavivirus structures as separate files," I told him. "We can start rendering as soon as we get them."

"How long will it take?" he asked.

I shrugged. "It depends on how many "dark" spots we have. If this guy here is not the most typical of the Flavi-vavi group, it might take years, and we still wouldn't get anywhere."

Our next job was to take the structures of the known viruses and match them with the dotty chaos on our scans, praying that some pieces would match without leaving too many "dark spots".

"We have genetic data that our scientists converted into the amino acid sequences," Yuin said.

Most of the time, the amino acid sequences coded by the genetic material would make little use in identifying the 3D structures. The proteins in nature do not exist as linear sequences – they fold, bend and bond with each other into elaborate shapes. This so-called tertiary structure is what makes them functional.

However, the sequencing data could be useful if you, like us, have some 3D shapes to play with.

"Throw in some sequencing data from the other flaviviruses if you can access it," I nodded.

That was the last conversation with anyone outside of ID30, a hundred and five hours ago.

I hadn't slept for a hundred and five hours.

I might have closed my eyes for a few minutes until the rendering program alerted me to the end of its cycle with a gentle beep. I checked the parameters, threw in new assumptions for our model, did sanity checks, and re-sent the program into its loop again.

Until we got to the 94.37% match.

No, you can get a hundred per cent match only in cheap Hollywood movies that give the same shit about actual science as they give about narwhal babies. In real life, getting to ninety per cent was a miracle.

Getting to 94.37% was Nobel Prize-worthy.

But it wasn't the number on the screen that made my eyes fill with tears of relief. It was the image that showed no black holes anymore. All atoms looked matched. All energies were plausible. All bonds had appropriate distances. All the dipoles ticked.

I was rechecking the structure for the third time when Dan came to the control room with the dinner ("noodle soup with tuna", as always). He stopped in front of the screen. He stared.

"Yes," I said and started crying.

That's how success looked like after the End of the World.

Like shit.

"I thought I would feel triumphant. I thought we'd be celebrating… but instead, all I have is sadness," I told Dan. "And guilt."

"Nothing of this is your fault. We could have just sat on our arses and hoped that one day a hero would come to save us. Or we chose to be heroes ourselves. Not just you. We all did. Max did, too. Because of who we are. We all have different motivations for science, but do they really matter? We are here, and we have made it work."

"What is yours? Lesley? Baby Torren?"

He chuckled. "Before Lesley, I was a foot away from jail, but she saw something in me that made her hold on to the worst of me to make the best. I'll never stop proving to her that she was right. I thought a fat prize or medal would be good, but if we manage to get a fix for this mess..."

"It will be proof good enough," I finished.

"For me. Lesley does not need proof."

I had a sudden blasphemous thought that Steve was more of an obstacle to my scientific career than a motivation. I'd always felt his support during my PhD studies, which were grinding and challenging even without Edsie's helpful interference with my experiments. But after I moved to Glasgow, his support turned a little impatient. He couldn't wait to have me back and start a proper family, as he used to say, but...

What was a proper family? Did *I* really want it?

Before I had another splash of tears, the phone vibrated in my pocket.

"It's Kay." I accepted the call and propped the phone against the desktop stand so that Dan and I could fit into the screen and announce the discovery of V-24 together.

Kay's red face appeared in the camera, her eyes wide open with fear.

"You need to be here, guys. We had another... well... a fire in the lab. All of our colonies are dead, and the equipment is screwed. Please, you need to come over. I don't know what Louise will do next, but it won't be good."

Dan and I exchanged worried looks.

"We'll take a few hours, Kay."

She nodded. "I really need you here, guys. It'll blow up any minute now, and I don't know how long I can keep her at bay. She's furious. And she has this thing... it looks like a gun!"

"It is called a flame torch." Louise's voice sounded from the distance. "And I know how to use it."

5.

We arrived just in time.

I hoped a little that there would be one casualty by now, but no, I could still see Edsie through the meeting room window, helplessly stuck between Tanya, coiled in the corner, and Louise waving the flame torch at her.

"It wasn't us," he kept saying.

"Should we tell them we're here?" Dan whispered, pushing me away from the window to peek in.

"You kidding me? And miss Louise put Tanya on fire? You saw what Tanya's done to the lab!"

Most of the damage occurred in the corner where Louise seeded and harvested her viruses in a dedicated glovebox. It had burnt to the metal posts; the heat-resistant glass cracked and exploded. The floor, walls and ceiling all over the lab were covered in soot, and the whole room stank of toxic chemicals released by decomposing plastics.

It was not an accidental fire. It was an arson.

"They say it wasn't them." Kay appeared from the room next door, slurping tomato soup from the tin.

"You don't look too bothered. What's happened to the SOS?" Dan asked.

She shrugged and burped. "Sorry. Yeah. They've been like this for a while now. I got bored. If Louise really wanted, she'd torch Tanya by now. Want some soup?"

She waved the half-emptied tin in front of us as if brandishing a goblet of wine at a medieval feast.

"Have you got any popcorn?" Dan asked, turning back to the window.

I pushed Dan away from the door and marched into the room.

"Enough, everyone! Louise, turn this thing down! Tanya, get out of there and tell me what the hell's going on!"

I had never thought I had such a commanding presence! Louise immediately switched off the torch and put it in her pocket. Tanya crawled out of her corner but hid behind Edsie.

"This filthy slime." Louise pointed at Tanya. "Have you seen what she has done to my lab?"

"It's not your lab, Louise!" started Edsie.

"Shut up!" Louise and I shouted.

He backed off, stepping onto Tanya's foot.

"I saw what's happened to the lab," I nodded. "That was arson."

I looked at Edsie.

Edsie looked at me.

My eyes told him, *I remember what you did six years ago. Don't you think I know it was you again?*

"You have been sabotaging our exper-riment from the start. You tr-rashed our micr-roscopy lab. You damaged my fr-ridges and killed my first vir-rus batch. You put acid into my incubation media. And now this! This is your last move!" hissed Louise, her hair standing upright on her head like fur on a cat's back.

"Acid in the incubation media?" Dan walked into the room with tomato soup. "I haven't heard about this one!"

"You have done everything to spol this experiment, you filthy, slithering animals!"

"What are you talking about?" Tanya pushed Edsie out of her way. "We didn't trash your lab! We didn't do fuck all to your fridges. Edsie, tell this mental cow – what the fuck is she talking about? We didn't do shit!"

Oops. Swearing Tanya... The last time she did it, I had a hair-restyling.

"You bitch, do not tell me you do not know!" shouted Louise. "You killed my viruses!"

"Are you high? Nobody killed your viruses; you said it was a power surge!"

"Yes? And what about the fire in the lab? Was it a power surge, too?"

"Didn't you say a faulty electrical connection caused a spark? Isn't that true? How do I know that you aren't bullshitting now? What if it's your fucking solvents exploded, and you are just trying to blame us? Fuck off, Louise, we didn't do anything!"

There was no guarantee that Tanya didn't have hidden Oscar-worthy acting abilities, but she sounded, felt, smelled genuine and a little bit of soot. And if it sounds, smells, and feels genuine, then…

Louise stepped back.

"There are no solvents. It is only water," she muttered, plonking down on the floor in the middle of the room in sudden exhaustion. "But… you were so against our experiment, we thought you were trying to sabotage it. You were so angry, Tanya. We thought you wanted us to stop!"

"Of course, I was angry! You motherfuckers are not much better than Nazis. I wanted you to stop! But not like that, not trashing things or getting anyone in danger. I'm not against science. I'm against the price we had to pay. But it doesn't mean I'll be trying to kill everyone with fire. And what about Edsie? I know I didn't help much, but Edsie did! Do you think he enjoyed seeing his work go fuck up in that fire? He was crying like a baby because his colonies died."

Edsie nodded.

"I loved my little stinky shits. I sang them lullabies."

I wanted to question the idea of Edsie being in love with anyone – at least in the common, sacrificial and all-forgiving sense – but I forced myself to focus on the important bit.

"If it wasn't Tanya and Edsie, who did it? And why?"

In a cut-throat silence, everyone looked at each other, wondering who had the motive and ability. Crossing Dan and me out of the equation left only two of them. Louise and Kay stepped from each other simultaneously.

Something clicked in my brain.

"It was Greg," I said.

"Greg? Louise's cupboard friend?"

"Anna's, too," Dan muttered from behind me. "I'm sure he can't wait to chat to Anna again."

"He'd have to chat to my lab stand first," I said.

Tanya waved her hands, interrupting us. "Wait a second. Do you think that crazy bugger's trying to sabotage the experiment? Because you released Louise from the cupboard?"

"More like because Anna smacked him on the head?"

"Okay, maybe, but why doesn't he face us?"

"All six of us? I doubt he is *that* crazy," Dan muttered.

I turned to him, annoyed. He was drinking the cold tomato soup straight from the tin, the red "moustache" framing his mouth.

"But the experiment?" insisted Tanya.

"He *is* crazy," sighed Louise. "He wanted to be a scientist but never made it to get a scholarship. If he can not do it, he will not let us do it, either."

"Sick." Edsie rolled the word on his tongue in agreement.

"But what do *we* do now?" asked Kay. "The experiment's fucked up anyway. We have no virus and no equipment. We can't even *enter* the lab. And how do we know that we are not next? What if he sets *us* on fire when we're sleeping?"

"Probably, we should start locking the doors," Edsie suggested in his first-ever fit of intelligent thinking.

In our situation, wasn't it a reason for celebration?

And not the only one.

I stepped forward. "The experiment... It didn't exactly fail."

6.

I admit we're very good at this celebration thing.

Maybe, a bit too good.

Kay stares into the screen behind my shoulder, thinking I don't know she's there. Her alcohol-infused, loud breathing has given her away. She tells me that, even if I write "the celebration thing" instead of "got wasted", the ringing in my head and the blurry haze in front of my eyes won't disappear.

Indeed, "got wasted" is a more accurate description of what happened last night, straight after our fight when Edsie and Tanya learnt about our activities behind their backs. They were pissed off right until it dawned what the discovery of the V-24 structure meant.

Team ID26 is back in the game!

The bottles lined up near the glass waste bin are evidence of our celebration skills – six bottles of wine, one whiskey, and one tequila. Though the tequila bottle was already half-empty when we found it.

I like working with French. They always have a helpful stash of spirits in their offices.

Now, I wish one of them had an Alka-Seltzer. Or half of an Alka-Seltzer.

I crawled out of my makeshift bed closer to midday, washed my face, and found Dan staring into the computer, his face hung over and confused.

"What now?" I asked.

"The computer is down. The hard drive has been formatted. All data gone."

"Another little surprise from Greg?"

He shrugged. "As a sabotage attempt, it was a shit one. Louise has been backing up everything like four times."

No, this wasn't proper sabotage, but a mini version.

A nanosabotage?

In a building with more computers than live uninfected people, the murder of one computer was more like a mockery than a real hit. Whoever wanted to undermine our progress would have to reverse time and un-discover the V-24 structure. I spammed every contact in my address book with the virus structure files, even if there was no one on the other side to receive and open them.

"Edsie and Tanya have sourced some laptops so we can all work together," Kay walked into the lab with a glass of water and stopped, waiting for me.

I had to show the rest of the crew how to use the *in silico* software – in the absence of any real experts, I would have to do, a pitiful rookie with limited experience.

Yeah," I sighed, "together sounds great."

The last night's celebration and today's suffering, shared by everyone equally since nobody planned a paracetamol, allowed us to mend some issues so that Tanya and Louise could coexist in the same room without torching each other. It also helped that the computer simulations did not involve chopping or gassing anyone to death. But it's a fragile peace. Tanya smashed her laptop lid closed and stormed out of the room when I dialled Yuin for a debrief. Edsie only stayed because he couldn't climb from under the table. Kay put a laptop and a glass of water on the floor beside him and patted his shoulder.

"You're not going to die," she said.

After the call with Yuin finished, Kay invited Tanya to return to the room. Louise rolled her eyes, and Dan mouthed something abusive. I sent him a warning look. Kids, no bullying in my class!

Now that we have a full quorum, it's time to work. Our Chinese colleagues provided us with every record of "death molecules" they found online, from small molecules to large proteins. Miles away, safely hidden in their military bunker, they'll do the same exercise – order the computer to match the virus structure and those molecules, looking for a perfect "lock-key" fit.

We've uploaded three hundred twenty-three files to the shared folder. Each of those molecules will create endless megabytes of data and eat endless hours of our time. I cringe at the thought. It's an impossible task.

I don't have the heart to tell them the truth.

I recall my last year's BSc project: endless nights in front of the screen, eyes bleeding from the flashing numbers, and my heart always missing a beat before checking out the final values. I had thirty-five weeks, five thousand eight hundred eighty hours, to get one molecule fitted into one protein.

It didn't work. I ran out of time.

7.

Day 45, 20th of March, Wed

Of course, she was kidding us.

But no, she wasn't. She was dead serious.

Gosh, she was serious!

"How else do you imagine we test it?" Louise had been repeating for an hour.

It wasn't the best moment to breach the idea. Molecule number 56 failed the simulations after fourteen hours, sending Edsie's laptop into Valhalla with a blue screen of death. In anger, Dan smashed it into the wall, making me climb under the table in a bout of PTSD.

On top of it, our food supplies were dwindling.

Soon, we would have to go back out there and get more food from the restaurant or anywhere else that still had food. We would have to repeat the procedure until the ESRF campus ran out of food or – we ran out of us.

Dan estimated that the restaurant would have a few months' worth of supplies if nobody else had raided it and our spleen-eating friends didn't switch to less organic, tinned food. Nobody brought up the subject of the hungry crowds standing between us and the food – our moods were dark without any such reminders.

That's when Louise decided to share her cunning idea – a rat lab.

"No problem," said Edsie. "But we don't have any rats."

She looked at him long and straight, and although I couldn't directly enjoy the piercing force of her stare, I realised that we had to hunt and catch those rats ourselves.

She was insane!

"There is no other way we can test it. I do not think any of us is keen to inject ourselves!"

"We don't have anything to test yet," Dan pointed at the black screens, all laptops in sleep mode while running another round of simulations. "And the way it's going, never will!"

"Inject? I thought we would make pills," whispered Tanya.

"None of us is infected anyway," said Dan.

"We're not even sure if rats can get infected. Have you seen any spleen-eating rats?"

"I saw rats feeding on infected bodies. None of them looked, you know, crazy," I recalled the rat infestation at ID30.

Louise shook her head. "Anna is right – we have not seen any infected rats. The virus does not stay in dead bodies, so it is unlikely that rats would pick it up from eating rotten flesh. I also have a feeling that even if they bit a live infected, they would not get it, either."

"You think they can digest it?"

Louise shrugged.

"Then how do we infect them?" asked Edsie. "Lock a zombie and a rat in one room and pray that the zombie will get hungry?"

"We inject the rats with a virus, Edsie!" said Dan.

"Can we please skip this injecting stuff for now?" Tanya pleaded from her corner, turning white.

"I didn't know you were scared of needles," Kay whispered into her ear. At the "n" word, Tanya almost fainted on her chair.

"I'm not hunting for rats," I said out loud. "Full stop."

There was a limit to what I would do to save the world.

"Okay, I can do it," said Edsie. "ID30, you said?"

Oh, here we are. Heroism and stupidity. Or only stupidity?

I stared at Edsie, expecting him to say it was a joke.

"Rats are just rats," he said.

Oh, I see. And I thought they were badgers.

"I'll come, too," Tanya called from her chair. "Better that than the whole needle thing."

She gave Edsie a wink. Gosh, they are like rabbits, constantly snogging in the dark corners.

Yes, why can't we test our drugs on rabbits? They are fluffy and cute, don't pass horrible diseases, and are great in a stew.

"We need at least four rats for a start, and then, the more, the merrier," Louise jumped off the table and started pacing around the room, dictating the details of the mission to Edsie and Tanya. "Make sure they are healthy and not too old; little wounds and bitemarks are okay."

Dan and I exchanged bewildered looks. I imagined Edsie politely enquiring about a rat's age before marking it off as too old. Would it be counted as ageism? Or if they discard rats for missing tales or broken limbs, would it be classed as discrimination against the disabled?

***

They brought six.

These rats were massive, almost double the size of those in ID30, their grey fur shiny in the lamplight, their red eyes staring at me devilishly, with fervent hatred. While I shifted further away from the plastic crate, Louise qualified all rats as acceptable test subjects by a simple visual check. She didn't comment on age, gender or disabilities, although one rat was missing an ear. I could see it from three meters away.

Now, Edsie is drilling holes in the other plastic crates – we've prepared only four for our first batch, not expecting Edsie and Tanya's mission to be so successful. Tanya says they didn't even have to go as far as ID30. The foyer of the science building was covered with dead bodies, and swarms of rats were feasting on the rotting leftovers, scrumming, fussing – easy prey for even inexperienced rat hunters.

Edsie and Tanya planned to go back tomorrow and grab some more rat samples. But after a look at our dwindling food supplies, we decided it was that time of the month again – time to replenish noodles and soup tins.

Kay and Dan have pulled out the "X" Post-it notes. Kay is scared, but Dan is relieved. "I'm fed up with stewing here while the stupid machine can't do shit," he says, his hands shaking from excitement, his eyes reflecting a spark of insane enthusiasm.

Crap!

I can't let him go like this.

I'm about to raise my hand, but Kay's stern look pings me down to my chair. Anna's been qualified as a critical resource. Anna has to sit tight and watch the simulations go in endless loops.

Like a merry-go-round, just not merry.

And then the most unexpected thing happens.

Edsie volunteers to go.

In his sane mind and plain English, he says, absolutely sober, "I am stronger, so I could carry more stuff. I might as well go, too."

I don't know how I feel about it. Surprised that Edsie's not the level of twat I thought he was? Relieved that Dan and Kay will have a helping hand? Worried that he has sinister secret motives?

I'll leave the paranoia to Louise. She's good at it.

8.

They aren't back yet.

Two days since they left, my heart is sick of the radio silence. Not a message from them. Every WhatsApp I send – a hundred by now – comes back with two faint ticks.

Delivered. Not read.

We're packing the squirt bottles; no need for extra discussions on who stays and who goes. I wish Louise stayed with Tanya, especially if our vigilante Greg is lurking around, but Tanya is such a sobbing mess that staying alone with her would kill even the strongest of spirits.

"Please look after the rats," Louise asks Tanya before we leave the meeting room. "We will need them when we come back."

Tanya reaches out and hugs Louise.

"I'm sorry, Louise. Please bring everyone home."

Astonished, I speak no words, walking away with a heavy heart and a tiny spark of hope. For a change, something wonderful has happened in the Kingdom of Denmark. Please, let it be a good omen, a sign of good change.

Please.

***

We loaded into the lift, waved Tanya goodbye and, tactful as always, the first thing Louise asked me after the doors closed was:

"Do you think they are still out there?"

No, she didn't mean our spleen-eating friends. I wondered why she came along if she wasn't sure, but then I remembered it was Louise I was talking to. While I was coming to rescue my friends, she might have had purely scientific purposes: observe the spleen-eaters in their natural environment, make some notes, chop some samples…

The last time we went through the Science Building foyer, it stank ungodly, but this time – goodness! The lift doors opened, and the nauseating wave of foul air smashed into my face. I choked, plugging my nose. Next to me, Louise lifted her squirt bottle, prepared to shoot, totally unshaken by the smell, like some perverted Rambo.

I didn't know whom she was preparing to attack. The last monsters chased us outside to the restaurant, and then I burnt them alive with a Molotov cocktail. Tanya and Edsie confirmed that the place was clear of monsters during their rat-hunting trip.

Edsie gave the names to the rats.

I'll ask him when I see him next time.

When my eyes stopped watering and stinging, I could see the foyer in front of me, lit up by the bright LED lights built into the plastic ceiling. In the relentless electric light contrasting the thick night outside, the macabre presentation in front of us looked like someone had just unloaded the truck full of wax mannequins for a horror museum – cheap wax, cheaply drawn faces, no more than two quid for the entrance ticket.

Then one of them moved!

I froze, ready to scream and run, and then realised it was only a rat scurrying between the legs of a body. God knows what it has been feeding on!

God, I thought angrily while carefully walking around the bodies, whoever and wherever you are, little shit, don't you dare leave Kay. You owe her. You cannot just abandon her because she's had a little glitch of faith. She's looked up to you her whole life; now it's your turn to look after her.

Instinctively, I found Kay's cross on my neck and squeezed it between my fingers. Did it sound like a prayer? At least a little bit?

If I have to pray to bring them home, I'll do it. But bear with me while I find the right words – nobody has taught me this shit.

"Are you praying?"

Louise gave me a brief look and focused on the bodies under her feet. She trod on the arms and legs, carefully avoiding the open guts. We hurried, trying to get out of this horror museum into the fresh air as quickly as possible, and slipped, barely holding our balance.

I couldn't shake the growing feeling that, under the unabating LED light, I was also an exhibit in this museum.

"I think I am," I told her. "I'm not sure if it will work."

She shrugged. "I used to pray. My family were strict Catholics; prayer was like breathing for them. I spent my youth thinking that Holy Mother would be there for me, and since she never turned up, I gave up! I told my parents that hoping that someone, Holy Spirit or Holy Mother, would come and solve all their problems was stupid – and weak!"

I hushed a rat from under my feet – the bugger was chomping on some leftover muscle and didn't even move when I stepped next to it. I tried to imagine little Louise, with her pale, sharp face, kneeling in front of a cross, but all that came up was a picture of Wednesday Addams and her raven pigtails.

Yeah, Louise didn't look like a praying kind to me.

"But I looked at Kay as she prayed and realised how much strength is needed to believe in something that can never be proven. She does not care. Her faith does not need proof. What can be stronger than that?"

Before I could mention a lab wrench, my phone chirruped with an incoming WhatsApp message. Louise's phone followed only a second before the third beep echoed from the centre of the room.

We froze, exchanging confused looks. Then I pulled out my phone.

THERE IS SOMEONE IN THE LAB NEXT DOOR, read the message from Tanya.

Goodness, it hasn't been ten minutes since we left, and she's already in trouble! How come the shit-radar didn't warn her? Did it run out of battery?

"It's in the group chat!" whispered Louise.

What? Is the shit-radar in the group chat?

"Do you think it's Greg?" I asked.

She looked at me as if I was retarded and ran towards the centre of the room, carelessly stepping on faces and spilled guts. "Ran" was a bit of an overstatement because she slipped and fell immediately and then kept crawling forward.

It got to me, then.

I didn't bother running. I dove and landed on a dead body, my hands smudging something stinky and squishy all over while I grasped for anything to hold on to.

"Where did the sound come from?" asked Louise, frantically searching over the bodies closer to her. I pulled my phone out and sent some gibberish back into the chat.

Oh God, please let it be just the phone; let it not be one of them!

The WhatsApp ping sounded very close to where I was.

I dug into the pile of bodies, rolling the closest of them over on its back. Face distorted in fear, a dark-skinned dude in his early twenties, no one I recognised and honestly, no one I cared about. But I saw the phone under the body. The familiar blushing face framed with thick blonde hair smiled at me from the lit-up screen.

"Com'on, Louise, help here! It's Dan's phone!"

I reached to grab it, but it was buried deeply between two bodies – one slender, female and relatively fresh, only slightly chewed by the rats, and one straight underneath it, half-decomposed into gooey liquid. It stank into my face as I tried to pull the phone out.

"Anna."

"Come help, Louise!"

"Anna."

I managed to pinch the corner of the phone case and pull it out when my brain finally processed the signal – not what Louise was saying but how she did it.

She was eerily calm. She wanted me to stay calm, too.

Slowly, I turned around and almost screamed.

The dead were rising.

9.

And I thought I'd seen it all.

But hell, no, hungry flesh-eating monsters weren't enough! Now they *are* fucking zombies, dead and risen! After we've tried so hard not to kill them! We wanted to *cure* them!

I blinked, hoping it was a stench-induced hallucination. Still, the dead bodies around us were slowly getting up onto their feet, their milky eyes fixating on us.

"Seriously?"

I was scared shitless, don't get me wrong. Scared and disappointed, and for once, my disappointment was stronger than fear. We've chopped Max into samples, all for nothing! Science is a powerful shit, but it doesn't have a death cure.

"They are not dead," Louise whispered. "They have been waiting for us."

"What?!"

My voice echoed in my head, *They are learning… to hunt.*

No. *This* was not possible.

I swallowed hard and quickly studied the risen spleen-eaters. Standing behind Louise, there were six monsters, gaunt-faced, covered in scabbing scars and slime, but none of them looked like Hollywood zombies walking around with grey matter spilling out of their skulls.

"Why are they not attacking?"

Louise swallowed. "I think they are waiting… for a command."

"Whose command?"

Louise shook her head.

What now? Are we waiting for a command, too?

"We need an alarm," she said. "And to run."

She didn't move.

"There are no alarms in this building," I said, trying to copy her still, robotic voice. "It's got a smart fire system."

"Makes sense," she said. "Then, we run. But, Anna?"

"Yes?"

"Please, don't look back!"

Louise leapt forward, sprayed the nearest spleen-eater with acid, and, although I anticipated her to do an army rollover, she slipped on the goo, swinging off balance. I pounced and grabbed her under her arms, pulling her upright. Something swung at me from behind, and she dozed it with more acid. We dashed towards the corridor on the left, out of the lights and into the shadows.

I didn't need to look back to know that our movement woke the spleen-eaters up, and now all of them, ten or so, were after us. The head start gave us a bit of an advantage, but we would need more than that – a full-fledged miracle – to get away in these unfamiliar dark corridors.

Away from the foyer, the stench had gotten a bit better, and I allowed myself a big full breath while scanning the surroundings. The bodies at various stages of decomposition lined the walls on both sides, stacked neatly on top of each other in a few rows like a sick brickwork – as if someone had taken time to tidy up and make the corridors passable. Before today, that meant there were live people, but now I saw what the monsters were capable of.

Why would they do the cleaning?

I ran, looking out for any movement in case there were more spleen-eaters disguised as dead bodies. Something gleamed in the dark, drawing my attention, something that wasn't supposed to be there.

A tiny strip of silver insulating tape.

"Wait, Louise!" I shouted and dropped onto my knees in front of the pile of bodies. They all looked fresh, almost untouched, with their guts still intact. What's that? A stash for later?

"Anna, come on, what're you doing?"

I pushed the top two bodies off the top, revealing a foot in a black snicker sealed around the ankle with silver insulating tape.

"Dan!"

I grabbed and pulled the foot to get the body out of the stack. It shook and collapsed, the bodies rolling to my feet as I stared at the bald head buried deep in the pile.

Louise jerked me up by my hand, "Anna, come on!"

"It's Dan!" I shouted, twisting my hand out of her grip. "Can't you see?"

"He is dead, Anna! You ca not help him! Leave him!" She grabbed my hand again and pulled behind her, setting back into a run. I shuffled behind her, aimless, dumbstruck.

I'll go home and think of some way to get him back.

Back from the dead?

If I need to.

As if an invisible force lifted and propelled me forward, I dashed forward, dragging Louise behind me. Soon, she started dropping, slowing down, out of breath. I let her lean on me. I wasn't Bruce Willis, but I was young and strong and had a purpose.

I couldn't let anyone else die.

Not today.

Another group of spleen-eaters ran out straight at us from around the corner. Louise screamed, her shrill voice exploding in my ear like a launching rocket. I jerked to a full stop, freaked out by her voice more than by the zombie parade, dragged both of us into the nearest room and locked the door behind me.

"We. Are. Fucked." Louise looked around.

We found our not-so-glorious end in a tiny windowless kitchenette with a mini-fridge, a rusty kettle, and instant coffee spilled over the work surface. Wonderful! When our guests arrive, we can serve them a coffee.

I opened the fridge. A dried bulb of garlic.

If only the folks outside were vampires…

"Do not tell me you are hungry now," Louise snickered.

The first spleen-eater smashed into the door, almost ripping the hinges out. I pulled the fridge from its place and pushed it to the door.

"How long do we have?" I asked Louise.

"When they break in, there is nowhere to run… or fight, not in this space. I do not think we can use the bottles. We will only blind each other."

"Louise," I spoke slowly because I didn't know how to say it. "How about… I will cover for you while you try to break through? At least one of us could make it!"

She patted my shoulder, her cold, pale face lit by a kind smile never seen in Louise models before. "Call me Lou. And no. We will come up with a better plan."

"Dying together is a better plan?"

At least I won't be alone.

I sighed. Dying alone didn't scare me, but dying without saying goodbye sounded much worse. Should I text Steve?

HELLO. I'M GOING TO DIE IN A MINUTE. SEE YA.

The spleen-eaters kept smashing into the door, their blood-covered faces squeezed against the narrow glass panel, their unseeing eyes wide open and staring. The door creaked under their weight and pressure, uttering a broken swan song. Not long now. A few more minutes…

Then it hit me.

The eyes. One of the faces lingered against the glass panel for a split second before another blood-covered face replaced it, but in that second, I recognised it even though the mask of dried blood, hunger, and fury. The eyes were milky-white, but yesterday, those eyes were hazel.

"Kay?"

Louise nodded. "I asked you not to look back."

I went to sleep in the lab and woke up in a nightmare. A few days ago, we were toasting with wine that soon we would be home again, reunited with the people we loved.

Dan and Kay won't be.

And neither will we.

The door choked on its final squeak and burst out of its frame, wrenching the hinges. Louise and I hopped on our feet, readying our weapons. While the first intruder wrestled with the fridge in his way, I smashed his head with the lab stand, sending him backwards into the crowd. Immediately, they tossed his body out of the way, and two slender spleen-eaters squeezed into the room.

"Fire!" Louise shouted, and we dozed them with streams of acids. They shrieked, scratching their faces with their hands, one monster's eye flowing out of his socket like a broken egg. I finished him with the lab stand and turned to the second one when something tackled my knees, sending both of us tumbling hard on the floor. I hit my head on the floor floor tiles and dropped the lab stand, trying to grab the hands of the spleen-eater on top of me. The spleen-eater was clicking her jaw only a few inches from my face, dripping pink-coloured saliva all over my face.

It's not how I imagined our last meeting.

"Please, Kay, don't you see me? It's Anna, it's me! Kay, wake up, Kay! It's not you! You don't really want to eat me!"

But what if she did? What if, after all those days locked up in this concrete bunker next to me, she *wanted* to eat me – more than anyone else?

"Please, Kay, you're not a monster! You're one of us!"

For a glimpse of a moment, I thought she heard me. She slowed down, stopped, and stared, her milky eyes so close to me that I could see my reflection in the white surface.

Kay bobbed her head to the side as if she recognised me.

No, not me. The cross on my chest.

That moment lasted a lifetime, cocooning Kay and me from the real world. Outside of the cocoon, Louise screamed, smashing zombies with her lab stand and spraying them with acid. An explosion somewhere above me penetrated into the cocoon and stabbed my ears. A vaguely familiar voice roared: "Here we go, zombie bastards!"

It was close, but it didn't matter. Kay and I no longer belonged to this place; only two of us existed and mattered in our private Universe. Like two dazzling cosmic giants, we sought each other through space and time, closer with every second but still millions of years apart.

Don't worry, Kay. I'll wait for you as long as you need. If you hear me, come to me.

She couldn't not hear me – in our joint Nothing, only my voice could reach her, leading her to the place where we would hold on to each other. A place where, in one shared singularity, we would be above her rage and hunger, more than the virus in her head preventing her from seeing what's real.

I'm real, Kay. Hear me. Come to me. See me.

I'm with you.

She was still, her eyes fixated on the cross on my chest, as if she was hypnotised, but I felt something changing inside her. I could reach her. I could lead her into the light.

If only the moment lasted…

"Kay," I called to her. "You're coming home."

"Anna." I heard a bleak echo in my head.

"Kay."

Our joint Universe imploded, ripping apart the weak bond between us. Kay's head twitched, her eyes rolled up, and she slumped onto my chest as the tip of an axe sliced through her left cheek.

"Gotcha!" Edsie's voice roared next to me.

I screamed.

10.

I thought I'd died and went to heaven. An ocean of dazzling light lulled me on its waves, soft as a pink marshmallow, sending me back into sleep. I didn't want to wake up, wishing this warm, cuddly dream didn't end.

In it, my parents and I were building a sandcastle on the beach. Dad was scooping sand into a big bucket; Mom was designing an elaborate tower, and I was picking up shells for windows and decorations. I was happy and at home, but the light grew brighter, seeping into my eyes through closed lids, and squeezed me out of the dream into the world of LEDs and halogens instead of sunlight and breeze.

Then Edsie's smiling face drifted into my field of view. I blinked, and the light disappeared, together with warmth and cuddliness. Edsie did not, his stinky breath touching my cheeks. I moaned, shifting away from him, and my body screamed back with pain. I shut my eyes tight, willing to expel every single pixel of Edsie out of my head.

Lou, Lou, skip to my Lou, suddenly played in my head, a hoarse, patch-dry voice that felt like sandpaper rubbing against my skin. Not angelic at all.

"She's still out," another voice filtered through the singing. "I hate this song, by the way. Where the hell is it coming from?"

"I have asked her to call me Lou."

I'll find another one prettier than you...

"What? I thought we were going to die."

"How's Dan doing?"

Cat's in a cream jar; what do I do?

"Still out. We will not wake him up at all if he does not come around soon. The brain damage might be too much."

"She's waking again."

"Look, she's stopped singing. I don't know how much longer I could bear it." I identified this voice as Edsie's. At least he stopped pushing his face into mine. Thank the Universe for its little gifts.

I opened my eyes, suddenly aware that Edsie didn't fit the picture. In that picture, Kay was about to bite my nose off. That's the last thing I remembered.

No, my brain said, this wasn't the last thing. After that, there was something else which I won't show you just yet because you'll black out again.

Okay, okay.

When the dazzling light left my vision, I tried to focus on my surroundings, blurry but identifiable. Long oval table. Bright ceiling lamps. Tanya staring at me from across the room, bloodshot eyes on her pale face, her head wrapped into a turban.

Turban?

I was slouching back into the black, Tanya's face blurring away into a lump of colours. No, no, no, don't let the turban send me into the overload; think about it later when I've got some processing power again.

I was in the meeting room where we set up our simulation lab.

Before I started to doubt my memories – did I even leave it? Was this all a bad dream? – I turned around to scan the room and met with Dan face-to-face.

He had a turban, too.

Have we all died and gone to heaven where everyone must wear one? I touched my head. Where's mine, then?

"Was it a dream? What's the turban shit about?" I asked.

Dan smiled at me. When I looked closer, I saw a massive bruise on his forehead; the blood had already dried up and sealed the wound. And what I thought was a turban was a neatly crafted head bandage. Tanya had one, too.

"Okay," I said. "What's happened?"

"How much do you remember?" asked Louise walking into the room with two packets of ice. She gave one to Dan and Tanya each.

"I... I'm not sure what's real and what... I've dreamt of."

She grabbed her phone, leaned over, pushed my eyelids open and shone the torch into my right eye. I kicked her away.

"Your reflexes look good. Then, I would guess most of your memories are true."

"Even the unicorns?"

She spun around.

"Sorry, I'm kidding. Does it mean..." I paused, unable to voice it loud. "But how come, Dan—"

Prompted against the wall, he looked deadly pale but not dead!

The puzzle didn't fit.

"Dan was only knocked out, and we dug him out after Edsie saved our sorry arses. Looks like our spleen-loving friends are learning to ration."

"They've left him for dessert!" Edsie beamed as if we were talking about a piece of Victoria sponge, not one of us.

Edsie...

Where on Earth has he come from?

"They've lured us into the same trap," he explained. "Hid among the bodies, then attacked. It was a bad fight. We could manage ten of them, but the buggers kept coming from nowhere. I lost my phone, then."

Edsie choked and started coughing. Louise, the self-appointed nurse of our infirmary, handed him a glass of water.

"We've found Dan's," I said, pulling his phone out of my pocket.

"We decided to split so that Kay and Dan would distract them and let me get to the restaurant. I did, but I got scratched in that fight. I lay low until I knew I wasn't infected. I couldn't return to you all, knowing I'd put you in danger."

"And he didn't want to become samples!" Tanya called from her corner.

"I waited for the night and headed back. When I was at the entrance, I heard the hustle down the corridor, Louise screaming. I ran straight up, and that's how I bumped into you guys."

"Edsie has managed a dozen of them on his own," said Louise.

"The squirt bottle worked ace. And at the restaurant, I found an axe, you know, a biggie. For meat."

"Thank you, Edsie," I said. No, don't get me wrong, he was still a twat, but he saved my life, and on the scale of twats, that deserved him a good downgrade.

Say, to a douchebag.

"Can't we get to the point, everyone? Did you see what they were doing?" Dan said. "They had a plan. Lay low, wait for prey to turn up..."

"How would they know we were coming?"

"They could have clocked Edsie and Tanya when they came for the rats. Or, even worse, they might not have been waiting for us at all."

A dreary thought swirled in my head. How the spleen-eaters applied tricks and tactics differed from how animals hunted. Only humans devised elaborate plans to fool, round up, and trap much bigger prey.

"What's next? Zombies picking up guns?" Tanya snickered and winced from pain at the same time.

"You haven't seen it," said Dan. "They knew what they were doing. They knew there were live people in the building and waited for us to come out. I don't know how they know or how they've learnt it, but those fuckers aren't stupid. We can't go out there anymore. Not before we understand what's going on and how the hell they are learning so fast."

Neither Dan nor I was going anywhere soon. His head wound looked grave, and the bruises under his eyes made him look like a starved panda. According to Louise, he spent almost two days knocked out, entirely unconscious. Even not being a medical professional, I knew what it meant – some processes in his brain were damaged beyond repair. Although his basic cognitive skills and his memory, at least short-term, seemed to be intact, we were yet to discover what part of our Dan was gone.

"What's happened to Tanya?" I pointed at Tanya's head bandage.

"Someone's knocked me out," she growled. "I went to check on the rats, and some bastard out there hit me on the head."

"Greg," suggested Louise.

No one argued.

"While I was out, the bastard trashed our rat lab and our laptops. I caught two rats before they legged it, but that won't be enough for our experiment."

I imagined Tanya grabbing thrashing furry rats with her bare hands. Goodness. She's got balls!

"We are lucky we have not infected the rats yet. Loose spleen-craving rats would be the end of it," Louise pointed out.

"I'll go look for the bastard and when I find him, I'll chop his spleen and feed it to our zombie friends." Edsie rose from his seat brandishing an axe so big that I could see half of me reflected in it.

Wow. Is that to chop the whole cow in two? In one go?

"Not now, Edsie." Tanya moaned from her corner.

"Tanya's right. Besides Greg, we have more urgent problems. We've lost our laptops and rats; we'll have to start it all again. Of course, if we manage to find any more computers."

"Wait." I caught the nagging thought fluttering at the back of my mind. "Where's Kay?"

It's how they looked.

Or rather, how they didn't.

No one looked me in the eyes.

Edsie hid his face in his hands.

"Anna…" Tanya started but didn't finish.

No one tried again.

I strained to recall what'd happened, but my memory, always so helpful with images and words, was hopping chaotically between scenes to avoid answering my own question. But one scene, no, not even a scene, a feeling, stood out from the chaos.

A connection.

The field of gravity between Kay and me, a bond leading her home through the universes, a string reaching from me to her…

She was coming.

And then the axe went through her cheek.

The string snapped.

"She is dead," I said out loud. "Edsie killed her."

"I didn't know it was her," Edsie cried from behind his hands. "I didn't know."

I closed my eyes and probed for the cross still hanging on my neck. It felt warm from the heat of my body. I pulled it off, snapping the thin chain as if it were the connection between Kay and me, and squeezed it in my palm. The sharp edges of the cross bit into my skin, but I didn't feel any pain. I was numb.

There was an ocean of pain around me. I could dive and become a part of it – yet another drop among billions of drops. My name would be forgotten.

My name will be Pain.

"It's not your fault," Tanya assured Edsie.

I nodded. "You saved my life. Thank you."

"And the simulation is not exactly wasted," Tanya added.

We turned to Tanya and gawked at her as if she said Elvis was coming tomorrow to throw us a free gig.

"We had a hit just before I got attacked. I checked the energy report and the docking structures like Anna taught us, and all looked legit. I sent everything over to Yuin straight away."

"We have a match?" asked Dan.

She smiled. "A molecule called ENZ. It looked like a small protein."

"So, we work?" Dan looked at me.

"We work," I said. "But first—"

We say goodbye.

Chapter 7. AZ

1.

Day 50, later, 25th of March, Mon

Once, ages before the virus had put us all in one line a step away from death, Kay told me that she would like to be buried. Ashes to ashes, she said. But without a body, a church, a priest and a coffin, there wasn't much we could do in terms of a funeral, and I wasn't sure she'd be keen on a church, considering her somewhat strained relationship with religion lately.

We were the Witnesses of the Black Sack. It made sense for the spleen-eater bodies – if there was anything left after sampling – but we couldn't do it to Kay. Going back to pick her up only to wrap her in plastic and stash her away in a dark, remote lab would be beyond humane.

In the big picture, we couldn't offer her *any* funeral, apart from what looked like a ritual of black magic. I dug up a small hole in Tanya's tomato pot – yeps, the bugger's still here, but no sign of actual tomatoes – slipped Kay's cross into the hole, and covered it with soil. Tanya lavished the soil with water. Edsie read out a prayer he found on Google, a Catholic one; you could see it was the first prayer in his life, so much he stalled.

Kay wouldn't mind.

When Edsie finished, we stood silently, staring at the tomato.

It would be a good time for uplifting recollections of Kay as she was – generous and kind, a friend and a mother, a mentor… so many different shades of one extraordinary person, now – nothing but memories. No future. No tomorrow.

We couldn't find the words.

"Does anyone know a song?" Louise asked.

My head was blank. I kept staring at the tomato pot, hoping that someone else suggested an appropriate soundtrack to this shitshow we lived in. Next to me, Edsie swallowed and started quietly, his voice a mere whisper so that, at first, I couldn't distinguish the tune or words. But after a few lines, his voice suddenly gained strength, and I recognised the song.

He was singing "Hold On to Memories". His voice was deep, slightly rusty on the higher notes, but comforting and soothing. I was surprised at the choice of the song, not because it was inappropriate – what another song could be more suitable for a funeral! – but because I didn't expect to hear this heartfelt song from Edsie.

At the second verse, Tanya's voice joined, hoarse from the spasm of tears in her throat. The rest of us picked it up in a choir of broken, disconnected voices: not a homage to the fallen, but an anthem for those still standing – shaken, injured and wounded, hearts bleeding and hopes lost. We could well be the last of humanity, and it could well be humanity's last song.

Nobody left but us.

I stepped beside Edsie and took his shivering hand into mine. You aren't to blame, and you aren't alone, I wanted to tell him. He gave me a light squeeze, accepting my offering of peace.

After the funeral, we went back to work.

***

ENZ is an interesting little fella. It sits comfortably in the pockets of the virus as if some time ago it had been its piece and dropped off – for only evolution knows what reasons. It contains thirteen (what a suitable number!) amino acids, but only six of them are critical for bonding and unlocking the virus structure. Hundreds of simulations we'd run on our last surviving laptop confirm that ENZ is a perfect baby.

At the same time, ENZ would kill you, as this is its true purpose. The thirteen-acid sequence tells your brain cells that the drought time has come, and blood supply will be scarce. Time to hit the bucket.

We could not fire ENZ at the unsuspecting brains – it would burn them in seconds. A great way to get rid of the spleen-eating zombies, but not cheap. The axe through the head would do the job just fine and much faster.

We had to turn the ENZ ("End the Nasty Zombies", as Edsie calls it) into a new molecule. Using a computer program, I stripped the ENZ of its atoms, except for those that formed strong low-energy bonds with the virus. Then, I recreated the rest using the smallest structures that would fill the space, keeping only the essential parts. I ran the range of new molecules through the lock and key matching process. None of these new structures matched the virus as well as ENZ itself, so all molecules returned lower matching values. Some lost a lot, and I discarded them. A couple held tight, and I improved them further by adding a chemical group here or there, like designers improving the dress by adding a few sequins.

I shared the resulting four structures with the rest of the team. I didn't expect much input from Louise or Tanya, but, as trained chemists, Edsie and Dan knew the difference between "design a molecule" and "make one".

"Crap," Dan concluded from a quick glance at the results. "Any other options?"

I shrugged. "This is close enough to ENZ structure but not too close to yield non-specific reactions. I tried my best to make it flatter, but you know…"

Dan nodded. Flat molecules are easier to make in the lab – that's how chemistry works; it likes to save space. The problem is that the proteins that viruses are made of are not flat at all. They are 3-bloody-D.

"Our best bet is this one. If we start with a substituted quinoline, could we get there in five steps?"

I sighed. "More like six. If we have all the necessary components."

And all the time in the world. Hundreds of chemists spend years working out multistep synthetic routes, learning to make molecules that will probably never be used. We are only five now, which is, mathematically speaking, far from a hundred, and even our Chinese colleagues have gone quiet on the other side of the WhatsApp connection.

It's only us, and only God knows how much time we have.

2.

Chemical synthesis is like bomb diffusion. Before you touch anything with your dirty little fingers, please have a comprehensive plan of how you'll make it to the end, or you might get to the final wire two seconds before detonation and discover that you don't have the correct wire cutter.

Ka-boom and ca-put!

Before starting the ENZ project, we had to stock up on all necessary bits and bobs, from chemicals to pieces of glassware, from tubes to cleaning brushes and filter papers. Dan, Tanya, and Edsie left for shopping, which, in our case, meant that they would rummage through the labs on this floor. Louise wanted to come, too, but then she looked at the shopping list.

"Two-di-cyclo-hexyl-phos... what the hell? Does this thing not have a normal name?"

"RuPhos." I pointed at the little note next to it. "Or equivalent. I don't mind, although Ruphos would work better."

"Ru-what? How do I know what is an equivalent?"

Edsie glanced at her with noticeable pity. Like a stray animal, she trod into the unfamiliar zone with its laws and rules. Straining her eyes to read the chemical names off the phone, she looked humiliated.

I patted her shoulder. Not everyone's a chemist.

And that's a relief!

"I think you would be more help here, Louise."

While scribbling a large synthesis plan on the whiteboard, with detailed schemes and drawings of lab set-ups, I pulled the glassware and equipment out of the drawers and explained to Louise how to put things together. Even blindfolded, I could assemble a vacuum filtration line or create an inert atmosphere in a reaction flask. But if – when – I'm not here, the scheme could make all the difference in the world. Dan and Edsie haven't done anything in the lab for years, and Tanya, although very good with equipment, was not the best cook.

The whiteboard was a backup. An Anna backup.

"You have been very different since Kay died, Anna. Is something bothering you?"

I stopped in my tracks with a two-neck round-bottom flask in my hand. Was something bothering me?! Louise hadn't been the most people's person, but this was way over the line.

"My friend is dead. Isn't that enough for being bothered?"

"You know I did not mean that. Tanya has known Kay longer than you, but she is not like that. It is how you do things... like you are preparing to die, too."

"Bullshit!"

I put the flask aside and changed the designs on the whiteboard. Two necks won't be enough – make it three. I dropped a WhatsApp message into the group chat, asking for a couple of three-neck flasks, and turned to Louise.

"Since when have you become so people-tuned, anyway? I don't want to sound rude, but you, Louise, have never stricken me as very considerate of other people's emotions!"

She chuckled.

"You know what they used to call me back during my university years? Louise-la télé."

"What?"

"Louise-la télé. Not because of the TV, but because of télésurveillance. You call it CCTV in English. I am very observant, Anna, might be even too observant. But most of the time, I prefer not to act on what I observe. It makes me look cold and emotionless, and honestly, that is what I want because then nobody expects me to give a shit about their shit."

I blinked. This calculated approach to interhuman relationships sounded about right for Louise. This exact woman had spent a few days locked in the cupboard, expecting to part with her spleen without consent, but since we pulled her out, the only thing that slightly unsettled her was the cupboard locks.

"So, tell me, what is bothering you? And do not bullshit me about Kay's death. I know it hurts. It hurts everyone, me included. But there is something else, too."

I shook my head. I didn't know how to explain it, especially to Louise, who never cut it as a spiritual type. Of all the people at ID26, ironically, Kay was probably the best to understand.

"When Kay attacked me, she didn't bite me immediately. She jumped on me, and we went down, but then... she looked at the cross on my chest as if she saw it. And recognised it. I knew if I could look her in the eyes, she would probably see me, too. So, I called for her."

I closed my eyes, reliving the cosmic connection between Kay and me. It was so vivid that I felt like I could touch her again – a mad idea, considering that there was no one on her end to touch. I still felt her, as if she was unavailable... but not gone.

"Did she answer?"

I opened my eyes and looked at Louise, her cold grey eyes fixed on me emotionlessly.

Louise-CCTV.

Just right.

"I think she did. I think I heard her voice before it all went wrong. It felt like she was coming to me as if she was pulled into my orbit, and I thought that if I didn't let go, I would be able to bring her back home."

"You did not let go," she said.

I shook my head and smiled. What was the use of it? Kay was dead, and no matter where she went, no cosmic bond would reach that far.

"You will think me crazy now."

"I wish I could. But we have seen so many crazy things recently that I do not know if anything normal is left... But what you experienced is not impossible at all."

I almost dropped a piece of glass connector I was mindlessly pushing into a small flask in my hand, its neck too narrow to accommodate the connector. I put the glassware away before I cracked or snapped something.

Louise chuckled.

"The neurons in our brain have developed a unique ability to form plastic and complex connections with each other. Our brain is not a static piece of machinery; it constantly changes, creating more neurons and connections. But even in its amazing complexity, a single brain is only a tiny part of what is possible. What if your brain could reach out to the other brains just like those tiny neurons? What if each of us is a tiny neuron in a possible supermind?

"I have seen valid scientific studies on how twins' brains processed pain. It should not be possible for one's brain to feel the pain inflicted on someone else... But I saw those twins, connected only by genetic similarities, cry in unison when one was hurt. They were miles apart. They could not hear or see each other. I know what I saw. It was not magic. It is a science that we have not yet understood."

Science. I could do with that.

Science had a certain endorsement against insanity, and most of all, I was scared to lose my shit now when so much depended on me holding it all together. Unwanted thoughts were creeping into my mind, darker and scarier every time, and I couldn't vouch that my defences were strong enough.

I always thought of myself as a person with a solid direction, an unwavering vector, but since I voted to gas Max, I realised that my vector was no more than a weathervane spun by a raging storm and that I was losing myself, bit by bit. First, a piece that belonged to Steve. Then, a part that was friends with Max. Now, a massive chunk that missed Kay and couldn't stand that I didn't even say goodbye. The pain ate me from inside, a bite at a time, and there was nothing to shush it away.

When the others returned from their shopping trip, the whiteboard was ready. I even wrote a few additional instructions in a notebook – nothing special: how to mix so that nobody died and pour so that nothing exploded.

"We've got you almost everything!"

Edsie was gleaming, unloading the glassware on the workbench, while Tanya and Dan lined up the chemicals in the fume hood.

"Almost?"

This is what I was worried about.

"Hey, I was picking up the glassware! That's a full set. All questions to those powder freaks." He pointed at Tanya and Dan. "They almost had a fight about some black shite."

"It's not black shite, Edsie; it's a ligand. It's very important," muttered Tanya.

I helped Dan and Tanya to unload. They brought back a lot of stuff, some of it a lucky find. They'd found the right protecting groups, the best solvents, even the substituted quinoline – we didn't need to make it ourselves! Minus one synthesis step!

"So, what are we missing?"

Dan shook his head, his bald head missing its usual shine in the LED lamp of the lab. "The catalysts, Anna. I don't think there is a femtogram of palladium in this whole building."

Wasn't it ironic?

We had a kilo of palladium – all shapes and colours – back at ID26. In the *old* times, we could sell it and buy a seaside hotel on the South Coast of France. We could retire, all of us, twenty years earlier. But between us and that palladium stash was an unpassable distance, guarded by hungry, intelligent, and unpredictable monsters. And without it, the magic of chemistry won't hold past midnight.

"We can't go back there," I said. "We won't make it out of the building."

Everyone was silent. Everyone stared at the floor as if it was somehow our fault that the little luck we had left had run dry. It felt like another funeral. Only Edsie didn't sing, and instead of someone we loved, we were burying hope. "Killed by the irony" would be written on its tombstone if lost hopes and broken dreams got their stones.

But I didn't want to bow in defeat! I wanted to scream and trash the lab and turn into a woman hurricane and maybe, for a second, forget how much it hurt. I sat on the lab stool in front of the fumehood full of now useless chemicals (even the substituted quinoline!) and slowly crumpled an instruction to the rotavap in my hand. Hurricane Anna was out of juice.

I tossed the paper ball into the sink in the fume hood. What's the use of it?

What's the use of it all?

A soft hand touched my back. I spun around to see Tanya behind me and suddenly realised how old she looked. She was some ten, twelve years older than me, but working with her in the same lab, I'd never noticed it – now wondering if I'd ever noticed *her*. An equipment fairy, a magical creature with a shit-radar. Now, the age showed on her face with a net of thin, visible lines, and I saw a tired woman who had lost everything.

"Look. I don't know if any of these are useful. They weren't a part of our main experiment, and Kay wanted to X-ray them only if we had time. They didn't have to go into the fridge, so she's always kept them in her backpack. She had a feeling that one day we might need it."

Tanya's hands were cupped around a small tin box, barely the size of a deck of cards. I carefully took it from her and opened it. Six dark glass vials with black powder lay on the plastic liner.

Palladium catalysts. Samples from the ID26 experiment that never happened.

I didn't think that God existed. I didn't believe in Heaven, Hell or any other form of the Afterlife, but the tin box in my hands was warm from Tanya's touch, and I felt the kind and soothing presence next to me, a connection that survived against all laws of physics through distance, darkness, and death.

Kay was still here. She still took care of us.

I told her that I was sorry and that I loved her.

And I knew that she had heard me.

3.

Day 54, 29ᵗʰ of March, Fri

We'd made it through the first two stages of our synthesis when an unknown saboteur (Tanya, who else?) let Edsie sneak into the lab and touch the equipment.

Au revoir, our rotary evaporator.

I'd like to know what he'd done to it and how he'd done it – purely out of forensic interest. The rotavap exploded, or rather imploded, because a vacuum was involved, and the precious contents of the flask ended up in the hot water bath.

Dan has drawn a scheme. I think he's taking the piss.

Tanya has gone berserk because it was the first proper chemical reaction she's done since her uni years. She's chasing Edsie around the lab, threatening to stick the rotavap remains into his... places.

Very romantic.

Lou, Lou, skip to my Lou.

Head trauma talking; I don't know why it can't be Metallica, for crying out loud.

When should I tell her we can still recover everything from the water bath? It will take a day of purification, but not impossible. And since it was Edsie who screwed it up in the first place, we can make him do all the work.

No, probably not. Not Edsie.

The Synchrotron | 307

4.

Four spleen-eaters passed by the labs around midday. Sluggish and not very directed in their trails, they looked starved and somewhat pitiful if we didn't focus on the fact that they were looking for dinner, and dinner was us.

We were lucky that no one ran into them.

"I wonder what the hell they're doing here," said Tanya. "A few loners have drifted by, but four in one go?"

"As if they are scouting," said Dan.

"On a mission," echoed Louise.

Dan nodded.

"Could well be. If they're obtaining new skills, by themselves or from others, and learning to coordinate the group effort, that suggests some hierarchic organisation."

"What?" asked Edsie.

"They should have a boss," explained Louise.

"Should I go after them?" asked Edsie.

"We do not need any more samples, thank you!"

"No," he said. "To make sure they are gone. I promise I won't merk any."

He tiptoed out of the lab, following the four spleen-eaters. We were quiet for the few minutes he was gone and breathed out in relief when he reappeared in one piece.

"Gone." He nodded. "Went downstairs. They do look like they are sniffing out for something."

It was a good thing that they passed undisturbed. What if we killed them and alerted the others to our hiding place? Is it their scouting tactic? To send out disposable units?

Too smart, too human.

But weren't they?…

Too much thinking, Anna. How about we focus on the important stuff?

Our first animal trial.

"I've called them Chip and Dale." Edsie pointed at the ineligible blue marker scribbling on the plastic crate. Squirmish about the rats, I tried not to get too close to the crate, but my natural curiosity won. I wanted to see what the rabid rat looked like twenty-four hours after Louise infected it with the V-24.

I expected it to be thrashing in its makeshift cage, banging into the plastic, its hellish red eyes radiating hate and hunger. Of course, its eyes weren't red but covered with a milky white haze, so characteristic of the V-24 infection. The rat was still, sprawled in the middle of the cage, but when Edsie tapped the plastic, it scurried up to the noise and pushed its furry nose towards Edsie's face.

"That's Chip; he's my favourite."

"These are rats, not chipmunks," said Dan.

"How do we know that they're infected?" I asked Louise. "I can see the eyes, but what if the virus doesn't cause any behavioural changes?"

I couldn't think of any other, more scientific way to ask if the rats developed the appetite for their species' spleens.

"Oh, you should not worry about that, Anna. We injected only one rat with the virus. The other one got it naturally transmitted."

She pointed at the other cage. At first, the rat was hard to find, a heavily breathing lump of fur hiding in the corner. I couldn't see its eyes but didn't miss the wound on the rat's side.

"You let Chip bite Dale?"

"I would like to say it was a controlled bite."

"I couldn't rip him off the poor bugger," said Edsie. "Is that what you call a controlled bite?"

"I cannot instruct them on where exactly to bite and how strong and long it should be, Edsie."

I had to agree that Louise's scientific methods edged towards the unorthodox side, but hey! They were effective, exactly what we needed. We only had two rats left and a total absence of rat-hunting enthusiasm.

"If only we could get them to breed," I mused out loud.

"Yeah, too late for that," said Edsie. "They are zombie rats now."

In any case, we didn't have enough food to sustain a rat army. Although Edsie got a hefty handful of food supplies during his last trip to the restaurant, those were dwindling much faster than we thought. We'd been rationing, but Tanya, tasked with keeping an eye on the supplies, said we had less than a couple of days' worth left. Then, we would have to make harsh decisions.

"They are males, anyway," said Tanya. "I googled, they have, ehm… balls. Both of them."

"Chip and Dale." Edsie nodded with a smirk. "What's this for?"

Dan held out his phone, the camera on, pointing it at the cage. "Video evidence. Louise insisted we film all our animal experiments."

It looked like Edsie had something to say, but he stepped away and let Dan take the front place near the cage. I wondered where this unlikely bond between Edsie and his tailed friends had come from. Then I thought of the even less likely union with Tanya and shook it off.

Strange times, strange alliances.

Speaking of Tanya, I didn't expect her to come in, needles considered, but she stood bravely at some distance from the cage and winced when Louise pulled out the syringe. Edsie opened the cage to grab Chip.

"2.5 ml of AZ," Louise announced into the camera, sticking the syringe needle into the back of the rat's neck.

"AZ?"

"Antizombine." I shrugged. "I've never been good with names."

The rat thrashed in Edsie's hands like mad. Edsie almost dropped it into the cage, and Chip crawled into the corner and froze there, its breathing shallow and fast.

"Looks like it's going to hyperventilate," I said, staring at the rodent and wondering if rats died from stress. It would be problematic for our experiment if the local rats turned out to be a sensitive kind that couldn't stand needles.

Minutes passed. The rat's breathing steadied down into a deeper, more natural rhythm. Its body visibly relaxed.

"Is it asleep?" Tanya whispered.

The rat shuffled in its corner and started shivering as if in response. Its small body reverberated as if the electric current was passed through it non-stop. The poor critter squeezed further into the corner, trying to cover itself in paper shreds. There was nowhere to move, and it started clawing at the plastic surface.

Something was very, very wrong.

"What's going on, Louise?"

"Shock," she said, her eyes never leaving the rat, not even blinking.

"What can we do?"

Louise only shook her head. "Pray."

We watched in terrified silence, Tanya's sobs echoing the sound of little paws scratching the plastic. I tried very hard to think of something comforting that could numb the growing feeling of failure. Nothing worked.

"Look at its eyes," Tanya whispered behind me.

The rat's eyes lost their milky veil and turned dark brown and then deep black, so black that we could see the lab lights reflecting in them. I stared in awe, not daring to hope, while Louise nudged Dan to film closer, to fix the magic on the camera.

And then the moment was gone.

The rat started screeching; blood appeared from its damaged fingers. Deep lines crossed the transparent walls of the crate where it tried to scratch through. Most of all, I wanted to close my eyes and plug my ears, but I kept listening and watching because, in science, you must stay through.

It's the price you pay for the everlasting bond between a researcher and its test subject, even if it makes your heart bleed. The price of Max in the hutch full of gas. The price of the woman we called Bella – she could have been Anna, as well.

It was an agonising view. It felt like hours passed while we stared at the dying rat until its paws scraped the plastic one last time, and it dropped still on the top of the paper pile, its deep black eyes open wide and unblinking. Louise lifted the crate lid and poked the rat's body with the tip of her lab stand. The body slumped to its side.

"Well, that is a negative."

She returned to her notes, typed in the observations, and pushed the lid closed on the laptop.

Sample Date	03/04/2024
Sample Name	CHIP-001
Category	Whole/live subject
Source	Rat, infected, last stage, male (100%)
Treatment	Antizombine 1 mg/ml
Observations	Rapid clearance of the retina, potentially positive, then symptoms of histamine shock, increased heart rate, tremors, uncontrolled shivering, probable cause of death – heart attack
Outcome	Negative
Notes by	Louise Aurelienne

5.

Our Chinese friends were experiencing problems with their internet connection and couldn't take WhatsApp calls anymore, so we reverted to good old texting. Here's the thread.

Yuin

We've got a hypothesis about what's happened to your rat, but first of all, are you sure your dosage was appropriate?

Louise (actually Louise)

I think so. The symptoms were more characteristic of a histamine shock rather than a general overdose.

Yuin

We agree. One of my researchers mentioned that AZ's structure reminded him of something, but we shook it off.

At first, we did.

When you failed, our initial thoughts were about dosage, but then he found out what bothered him. You have an issue with specificity.

Louise (Louise)

Ehm, specificity? In a new drug?

Yuin

Yes. Google the structure of saquinavir.

Louise (me this time because Louise – an untrained chemist – was still comparing two structures on another screen)

Oh shit.

Yuin

Now we call the guy "eagle eye".

Louise (me again)

More like a bloody database guy...

Louise (me, after a pause)

How specific are we talking then? They are not exactly the same thing. This saqui something has a lot more on the end. And we have a fluorine.

Yuin

This part might be the one responsible for saquinavir's side effects. One of them is acute acidosis shock. From the video, it looked like a possible explanation for the seizures. But congratulations, the eyes looked almost pristine!

Louise (Louise this time)

Not good enough if we kill people off while curing them.

Yuin

We will send you the simulation results. We are trying to find any information on the origin of the side effects, but this might take a bit of time.

***

That was the last message from Yuin.

We are pretending that this is what he meant by his last message – he would go away, charge his small army of scientists with searching, and then go radio silent until they found something. They haven't responded because they are still searching. Or their internet connection is gone.

Yes, it's their connection that's gone.

Deep inside, we know the truth. Before we ran the tests on Chip, we'd warned Yuin about how quickly the spleen-eaters were evolving. He didn't look surprised.

"They've been attacking our facility directly for the last few days. One group of monsters tried to break off our satellite antenna. We've pushed them away, but they keep coming. I don't know how long we've got."

Our WhatsApp messages have been undelivered for the last two days. Louise has locked her phone in a drawer, having no one else to message or call. It felt like another funeral, a third one after we buried Chip next to "Kay" in the same tomato pot. There were no tears or songs this time, only a silent determination in Louise's tired eyes.

And no tomatoes yet.

I wonder if our botanical skills are akin to our knowledge of human anatomy, and the tomato plant is not what it seems. Tanya swears it's going to bloom any minute now - high time! Spring has hit even this miserable part of France with glorious sunshine and we can feel it, even locked inside the building. Maybe,

The next step is to design AZ-2 that would be sufficiently different from the other saquinavingy molecule but not too different from AZ so that we didn't have to start the synthesis from scratch. You see, the molecules are flat and straight only on the paper; in reality, the bonds twist and turn to create 3D structures. Adding a tiny functional group here or there might not look much on paper, but in real life, the molecule will take a new 3D shape and won't react with the target.

We've garnished AZ-2 with a tiny amino group on the end of the chain. It's not a "let's just do whatever random crap", more like "this random crap is what we can do with the chemicals we have in the lab". Coincidentally, this random crap created a very convenient hydrogen bonding that changed the part of the molecule responsible for the side effects. Great? Very scientific?

You should know enough about science by now to accept that planning, organisation, and sobriety are not involved.

Or maybe, we are just shit scientists. That's a possibility that I fully accept.

Then I look at Dan, who is busy mixing pure ethanol (99.8%) with water to make up homemade vodka, his eyebrow furrowed, his tongue sticking out in ultimate concentration while he watches the meniscus of liquid rise up in the measuring cylinder. No, I conclude, we are okay.

But we've run out of wine.

6.

It turned out that wine was not the only thing we ran out of.

Our regular mornings used to start with a head count and hygiene procedures, and then someone would dash to the lab to check if it still existed. Then we would gather around the cooking AZ-2 precursors where Edsie would provide his professional opinion – "This smells like shit" – and I would distribute the tasks for the day.

However, the first thing I saw this morning when I unstuck my eyelids open was two bright orange pills in a silver blister pushed right under my nose.

They are inviting me to the Matrix, I cheered and woke up immediately, but it was only Tanya, not Morpheus, and weren't the pills supposed to be of different colours? And out of the packaging?

I stared at Tanya, from the corner of my eye noticing Edsie hanging behind her like an ominous shadow.

"My last ones," Tanya explained.

I shot out of my coat. "But, how? Didn't you have, like, eighty in the pack?"

She shook her head, guilty tears glistening in her eyes. Edsie spoke instead. "After every seizure episode, she had to take a double dose next."

"How many episodes have you had?" I asked.

That was a very idiotic question, and honestly, nobody had to indulge my stupidity and insensitivity. Still, Tanya did, in a quiet voice so uncharacteristic for her newly developed hurricane personality.

"Way too many. But Edsie's been looking after me."

I made a mental note to review Edsie's status on my scale of twats and poked Louise quietly snoring away next to me. She muttered something like "Quiche Lorraine" and rolled over to her right side, kicking Dan in the leg. He stirred and opened his eyes.

Saw Tanya.

Focused on the pills.

Blinked.

"Oh shit."

"There's a doctor's office in Langevin building. That's our best bet. We are leaving after dark," Edsie said.

I preferred to ignore the striking matter of Edsie volunteering for something – or has Tanya blackmailed him into going? – and focused on the "we" part of the plan.

"We?" Dan echoed my thoughts. "You mean you and Tanya?"

"And me," a voice added from behind me.

Louise sat up in her coat, yawning, with an imprint of fabric fold on her cheek. Any other, less Louis-y, person would look cute and vulnerable in the first minutes of awakening, with the sleep leftovers still all over, but Louise looked as shrewd and CCTV-esque as always, if only a little pale.

"I don't think it's very reasonable for Tanya to go on a mission if she can go into a zap any mo—"

"I'll take care of her," said Edsie.

I observed him for a minute. He was the only ID26 teammate who avoided being smacked on the head, punched in the face or killed whatsoever, so why did he suddenly behave as if the aliens had abducted the real Edsie and placed some other person into his skin?

Or could V-24 affect people with alternative brain matter differently?

Shut up, Anna.

"I know what to do, and I will be able to protect her," he reiterated in response to my stare. "I don't think she'll be as safe here."

"I'll come, too!"

It was Dan's turn to taste the gooey sandwich of everyone's pity. Out of all candidates for a food raid, he was in line straight after the mop and the imploded rotavap. The consequences of his head trauma were vast and worthy of a good *Lancet* article and made him an unreliable team member. No idea what'd happened to him – medically, I mean – before we found him under that pile of bodies and how he'd managed to survive for a few days while knocked out. Louise says he could have periods of consciousness because otherwise, his brain damage would be irreparable. Sometimes he faints out of nowhere or forgets where he is, but he recovers quickly, and for now, we find it funny instead of freaking out. Louise assured us it was a sign that his brain's plasticity had been retained and that his brain functions would be restored to normal one day.

As always, we had too many volunteers for food and not enough for chemistry.

"I guess I'll have to babysit the reaction," I sighed.

Edsie patted me on the shoulder. "I trust you, Anna. You are the best. If you can't make it, who can?"

Thanks, Eds, no pressure.

***

"Do you think they'll come back? I mean, all of them?" I asked Dan as we waved Tanya, Louise, and Edsie goodbye, probably forever.

I closed the lab door behind them, silently wishing them good luck again and again, and turned back to the fume hood, where AZ-2 was stirring away in a round-bottom flask.

"Do *you* think they will?"

Did it matter what I thought?

We both knew what we'd sent them to.

War.

It was us against *them*, and, stripped of illusions, we were ready this time, no matter how inhumane it sounded. Every spleen-eater Edsie, Tanya, and Louise encountered on their way would be killed if they could kill it. Total extermination.

We'd equipped them appropriately. Dan and Edsie had crafted flamethrowers from the chemicals we found in the lab. In addition to a full gas canister for the flamethrowers, each carried five Molotovs and a whole arsenal of large, sharp, and deadly tools designed to take out as many spleen-eaters as possible without getting too close to them. No more mercy. No more remorse.

Only death.

It's not revenge for Kay or Yuin. It's only about survival. The fittest and smartest survived, so we had to make sure it was us.

We can't cure the dead, so fuck them! There are at least seven billion more spleen-eaters outside of the Ring. I don't care anymore because all I want is to see Louise, Tanya, and Edsie return human and alive.

I am angry.

Dan says it's because of hunger, but I'm not thinking of food. Lately, eating has been reduced to a simple physiological activity, like sleeping or urinating, nothing more than a calorie intake process devoid of joy or pleasure. And that's okay. We only have quick-cook rice packets left, and I don't recall them ever providing much joy or pleasure.

Or nutrition.

Louise suggested topping up our rice with protein. That sounded good until we realised it would be the *actual protein* – 99.99% purity powder from the chemical cupboard. "I like chemistry, but not like that," said Edsie.

On the other hand, we didn't object to making vodka from ethanol or sweetening our meals with chirally pure glucose from the same chemical cupboard.

If this hasn't created a clear image of how low we fell, here's one more for you: Edsie suggested going down to the basement to hunt some rats.

Yes, for *natural* protein. Have you ever had a juicy chargrilled rat? No? Well, we're getting there. Although I'll go for the lab protein first.

Anyway, here we are, the two of us cooking AZ-2. I ended up babysitting, indeed, not the reaction, but Dan.

When I was a rookie PhD student, staying late, working deep into the night, Dan would drop into the lab to check on me, mainly that I didn't inhale something dodgy and pass out under a bench, much to Health and Safety's discontent. We would have a chat while I weighed, poured, and connected.

Good old days.

Now I'm the one giving him tasks to weigh and pour while watching him from the side, like a PhD supervisor he was once for me. Not that I can't do any of it myself – it's something for his brain to keep busy and shush those horrible thoughts in his head…

The thoughts that we all have.

The question that bothers us all.

When we finally find AZ-2 or AZ-42, how many of us will be here to celebrate?

7.

Pain.

There's only pain but no words. Words are betraying me. I've always had plenty, but I can't squeeze one out now. I don't know how to say it.

Physically, I'm almost untouched. There is a shallow cut on my palm, the wound already healing, and a few bruises on my hands and shoulders. Nothing to die of.

But the pain will kill me.

Louise says that I should write it all down from the start – of the end – because that's what I've been doing since we came to this French Shithole of Doom. Documenting. Reporting. Remembering.

So that someone in the World After knew what happened to us.

So that someone else would *remember*.

Me. Dan. Kay. Max. Yuin. And others, too, whose names I don't know. The dead. The Fallen.

Louise is right.

I should start from the start.

From Steve.

Chapter 8. HUM-001

1.

Doesn't matter

It was the chromatography column. That's what Dan was doing when the idea came into his head. I don't know why we hadn't thought of it before. Maybe, we hoped that Yuin and his army friends would reappear when all hope was gone, by some Hollywood magic, but it was time to admit that hope had gone twice by now, and there was still no sign of Yuin.

"When was the last time you spoke to Steve?" Dan asked from his workstation while swapping the test tubes under the column tip.

If you live in the future when chromatography does not exist – for any reason, not only apocalyptic – you only need to know that it's the most boring lab activity ever, and that's why Dan was doing it, not I.

I was cleaning the test tubes, the second "most boring" activity.

"What do you mean?" I responded from the sink.

"We need to tell people about antizombine. You know, now that Yuin's not there. Tell them how to make it."

I stopped washing and looked at him.

"But we don't know if the new one will work."

"Does it matter? If something happens to us, at least someone will know where we were… someone can finish. Not to mention that if we're successful, we'll need mass production, and we don't have any capacity here."

He made sense, but I hesitated. It was against my professional habit to disclose work that hadn't been finished and peer-reviewed. Yuin knew it was "in progress", but would other people understand?

Plus, the whole Steve thing.

In my mind, I put him away on a distant shelf to pick up when I was ready to deal with the heartache. I longed to see his face but feared *what* I would see in *it*. Because I knew, with any call and message now, he'd finally have the guts to tell me what I didn't want to hear. It'd be a full stop, a total end, but until I heard it from him, I had an illusion to hold on to.

Sometimes I still imagined our future together when all this was over and we were back together again. In my midnight dreams, we would grow old together, bloody Cornwall house included.

Don't get me wrong, I knew the truth. I just couldn't start accepting it.

"You don't want to talk to him, do you?" asked Dan.

Ah, curse the bloody voice of reason. Fine, I'll go and tell Steve about AZ-2. He can decide what to do with all this information – make his military-looking friends happy and throw it in the bin.

I shoved the clean test tubes into my lab coat pocket, picked up the phone from the bench, and retreated to the equipment room. Surrounded by glass walls, like a fishbowl, it offered some privacy, and I could still watch Dan through the glass. I knocked, and Dan showed me his thumbs up.

What was I scared of? I bet Steve wasn't going to pick up.

But he did; his face appeared on the screen almost immediately – bearded, exhausted, but smiling.

"I was going to send you a message, Anna. It's been a long time since we spoke, and I started to worry."

What was it? A few weeks? A few weeks in a zombie-infested facility, and he only started to worry now?

I chuckled and bit my lip.

Salt, that's what the bitterness tasted.

"I missed you," I said because that was a more appropriate greeting for two lovers than "I started to worry" that Steve offered me so generously.

Oh, Steve... I whispered your name every night before going to sleep. I whispered it straight after waking up every morning as if you were a god, and I worshipped you for giving me yet another day. I prayed to you as the ancient prayed to the sun and the blood. I offered you a sacrifice, each and every monster I killed paving my path back home... to you.

"I miss you, too, Anna. I'm sorry I haven't been in touch. Many things happened —"

"Yeah, here, too."

How do I start? By the way, Steve, we have a cure. Or, we think we have a cure.

Should I do small talk first?

Gosh, as if we weren't almost engaged, didn't live together, didn't plan to grow old and die hand-in-hand, surrounded by children, grandchildren, and eight cats.

How awkward can it be to talk to someone you love?

"By the way —"

I started, but I was too late because he said:

"We need to talk."

Oh.

Eight cats, heh?

Don't some people believe that the phrase "we need to talk" is an act of "unmitigated aggression"? I wonder if anyone has ever kept statistics on how many heartbreaks happen straight (or almost straight) after these four words are thrown into the air? They are like a bomb – pain with delayed action.

I looked at his face on the screen.

We need to talk. Lou, Lou, skip to my Lou. I've lost my partner, what should I do?

I didn't deserve this pity in his eyes.

"Are you seeing someone else now?"

No need to drag it on. We are grown-ups.

He nodded.

"It's just—"

"I know," I said. "She's there with you. And I'm here... with this." I pulled the test tubes out of my pocket and brandished them before the screen. My white flag. Full capitulation. "Is she a covid-trained nurse?"

"A covid-trained... what? No, she's a... was a dog groomer. You know, in the world before."

"A dog groomer and a vet. Interesting."

"It's not that, Anna."

The bomb exploded, and the pain was excruciating. It came right from the bottom of my heart, where I already had a small, slightly bleeding wound. It's not that, Anna.

It's not that I didn't know. Do heartbreaks ever come as a surprise? Don't you know they're coming but always hope you're wrong? The death of hope is what brings more ache.

It's not that, Anna.

It is more than *that*. It gave my hand the strength to whack and smash and my mind the hope it needed to keep going. It helped me survive through these weeks of blood and heartbreak. It was my map for finding my way home, now snatched out of my hand.

I'm not going back home, am I? Where would I go?

It's not that, Anna.

I wanted to hit the screen and see his face shatter into pieces, to shriek so loud that the scream would turn my lungs into dust. Instead, I squeezed my fist so hard that the test tubes smashed in my hand.

I looked at the screen and told him it didn't matter anymore.

I disconnected.

Only then did I notice the blood trickling from my palm.

***

I walked out of the room to find Dan setting up the rotavap to remove the solvent from the last batch of the chromatography solution. He poured the contents of the remaining tubes into the rotavap flask, attached the flask to the vacuum, and lowered it into the warm water.

"You look dead," he told me when the flask started spinning. The vacuum popped in a countdown to the final product.

"Stray bullet." I nodded, discarding the debris of the test tube into the sharps waste.

"Straight into the heart?" he asked without smiling.

Another brief nod.

"Oops. How bad?"

Ignoring the question, I ripped a piece of the blue paper towel and wrapped my bleeding palm into it. The towel got soaked with blood within a second, and I tossed it into the bin. The first aid kit had been emptied to treat the head wounds, not even a tiny little plaster left.

I scanned the lab, unsure what to do with my bleeding hand. Dan opened a drawer next to him and pulled out a piece of gauze. He took my hand, wrapped it in gauze first, and then fixed it tight with masking tape.

"I'm here, you know," he said.

He had always been, hadn't he?

I sighed.

"I decided to quit, the science and all. Steve was going to propose during the EURO final, but I didn't want to wait anymore. I would resign straight after the ESRF trip – work my notice, move back to Birmingham, and start again as a business development manager. Or a patent attorney."

"I thought it was your dream to become a professor?"

I couldn't hold a bitter chuckle.

"How soon would I land a permanent position, Dan? I've had enough of the gipsy postdoc life by now. I wanted to stay with Steve, settle down together, start a family…"

"Or was it Steve who wanted it?"

I stared at my hand, where red spots emerged from the white gauze fabric.

"Of course, he did. I only wanted to be with him, and if it meant giving up my future Nobel Prize, well, hey-ho. Now he's with someone else, and nobody hands out Nobel Prizes, anyway."

The solvent in the rotavap was almost gone, leaving a crystalline white precipitate on the walls of the flask, with only a few millilitres of heavy liquid splashing on the bottom. The rest of the solvent – diethyl ether – evaporated within a minute.

"And she's a dog groomer," I added, lifting the rotavap flask from the water bath and releasing the vacuum. The air rushed inside, making the white flakes flurry like in a crystal ball. There were at least a couple of grams of AZ-2.

I detached the flask and handed it to Dan. He weighed and transferred the white powder into a small sample vial. Slightly over a gram, almost nothing on a potato scale, but on a drug scale, this amount could be enough to treat dozens of people.

High hopes.

Bleed the most.

"And I didn't tell him," I admitted, mesmerised by the reflection of lamplight in the vial glass. "About AZ-2. I just couldn't. Not there and then."

"I understand. If you're stabbed in the heart, science is the last thing you think of. Don't worry. If AZ-2 works, we will spam everyone out there. Everyone alive."

"Even Edsie's barber?"

"Especially him."

I laughed, but a gunshot broke my laughter into a hiccup. Wide-eyed, I stared at Dan, an awful feeling creeping up my spine.

"It's in the rat lab. Some equipment might have exploded," he suggested.

We don't have any equipment that can explode in the rat lab; there's only Dale in a plastic cage! Please don't do anything funny, Dan; let's first come up with a good, healthy explanation! Please!

Dan grabbed the liquid nitrogen wrench and stormed out of the lab.

I followed behind.

2.

The first thing I saw was the rat cage lying upside down on the pile of shredded paper, the rat gone. Then I lifted my eyes and met Greg face to face.

At first, I wanted to laugh. I'd seen Greg in my nightmares a few times, but when he appeared in reality, he looked cartoonish, blurry, like an episode from a distant memory, and everyone knows how flexible memory could be – removing things that were and creating things that weren't.

This Greg was real, and—

"A gun?" I uttered.

At the synchrotron? No, it couldn't be. We weren't in a bloody Hollywood movie where every headlouse swung a gun. This was reality; firearms weren't allowed in this reality!

Real or imaginary, the gun was directed at Dan frozen next to me, his hands raised in a protective gesture in front of him. He was barely breathing; his eyes locked onto the weapon.

"Oh, hello, Anna. How sweet of you to join us!"

Meh. At least, in my nightmares, Greg-Michael didn't spit out poorly written dialogue, more appropriate for a Z-movie, and didn't look like an air-balloon version of Joker. Since our last encounter, he seemed to have grown taller, gained more weight – how's that possible? what was he eating? – and become more insane. The madness now shone from his face like from an illuminated billboard.

What else could it be? Normal people didn't point guns at others with such dazzling smiles.

Or maybe it's not a real gun?

Yes, and he's come to say, "Sorry for trying to inject you with methanol before; let's start again and be friends for a lifetime".

Speaking of friends, who would make it here first – Edsie, Tanya, and Louise, who texted that they were on their way back only a couple of hours ago, or the spleen-eaters attracted by the gunshot?

"They are coming," Greg answered my unspoken question, and of course, he didn't mean the crew of ID26. He didn't look scared but... satisfied?

Hey, man, those spleen-eating guys are not your fan club! They're going to eat you!

"What are you doing?" asked Dan.

Greg shrugged, the smile glued to his lips as if it was painted. "I've had enough of playing games with you. The broken equipment and screwed samples, it was good fun, and I'd keep playing, but you guys are way too good and too stubborn. You shouldn't be doing what you're doing."

"What do you mean?" asked Dan.

I caught a nano-movement in the corner of my eye when Dan shifted his weight towards the bench on his right. Did he have a plan? He held the lab wrench, but how much use was that against the gun?

At least he has something, Anna, silly cow. What were you thinking when you left the lab bare-handed?

"Oh, I know all about your little scientific developments. A cure, huh? Against what? Against the virus? But who told you the virus is a disease?"

"What then?" asked Dan. Another nano-movement.

"It is a remedy. A liberation, a tool of revolution that brought a brand-new generation of humans! Look how strong they are, how intelligent in their hive thinking. They have cleansed the place of the leftovers of old and are now building a new society. They have evolved! They will prosper!"

Oh, well, I see.

"And you're their king!" I said, unable to hide disappointment. I thought that insanity was the epitome of grandiose chaos that couldn't be grasped by normal people to whom I assigned myself. But looking at Greg, I saw that insanity, armed or not, was only pitiful and predictable.

Greg's smile twisted into a crude shock. "How do you know?"

"I'll tell you if you tell me first where you've got the gun from," I said.

Another movement from Dan.

Gosh, if there's such a thing as telepathy, it's time for it to work. Don't do anything stupid, Dan; stay where you are, stay still, and we'll figure it out. Please, please, please, hear me! Please don't do it. You aren't a Rambo; you're a bald middle-aged chemistry lecturer!

"Campus security guys have a gun safe. Do you think this baby is not real? I suggest you do not do anything stupid to test it," Greg scowled at me and pulled the trigger.

What the fuck's he doing? Is he shooting us already? I thought he'd talk first! Don't they all do that?

A gunshot at such a distance was as loud as a nuclear explosion. I dropped to the floor, covering my head, just like the spleen-eaters who coiled away at the sound of the fire alarm.

Gods of the universe, whoever's listening, help! SOS!

The moment lasted for thirteen eternities, but when the ringing in my ears subsided, I realised there wasn't pain anywhere in my body. Next to me, Dan was also sprawled on the floor, as much as I could see – also unharmed.

"Are you okay?" I breathed out.

He blinked in agreement.

Slowly, I lifted my head. Greg stood over us, grinning like a Cheshire cat. The gun in his hand was bloody real; I got it!

"What the fuck?" I whined.

He laughed. "Do not start thinking I am a bad shot. This was not for you, either of you. This was for my friends out there," he pointed the gun at the door. "They have heard my call and know where they are heading."

The hum of steps, at first barely distinguishable, was growing louder, getting closer – the unmistakable sound of the large horde approaching.

"What do you want?" Dan asked.

"Oh, is it not clear? I want the two of you to join my army! Do you know why they are evolving? Because I am teaching them, showing them tricks on how to get the fresh flesh in. I am teaching them to hunt! No, they won't come at me. Do you know why? Because I am their father, and they are my children! They are me!"

I looked at Greg with a numb scientific interest, admitting that there was nothing human about him but pure, insatiable insanity, which – in contrast to what I'd always believed – had very little to do with chaos. Clever and organised, it had a goal, a plan and the tools to make it all happen.

And who the heck gave a shit that his goal was to kill us all?

The footsteps were much closer now – how many? A dozen? Two dozen? An army, as he said? Soon, we would discover how much truth was in his words, as if it mattered to us or the loaded gun.

The spleen-eaters had become more organised and learnt to lay low and ambush the prey, but Greg had managed to survive on his own for so long. Could that be the reason? Could his madness connect him to the monsters? A new connection on an evolutionary level? Could it be for real that they worshipped and followed him? Or was it only a convenient coincidence that he'd made it so far? Was it all in his head?

The echo of Louise's words seeped through the confused fog in my head. "The neurons in our brain have developed a unique ability to form plastic and complex connections with each other. … this is only a part of what is possible. What if your brain could reach out to the other brains just like those tiny neurons?"

Did that mean that Greg could reach out to their minds? The same way that I reached Kay's?

Goodness, what a mess!

Okay, slow down, Anna. Maybe, it's all way simpler than you think. Perhaps the sole reason he's made it so far is that the monsters just didn't want to eat him. With his brain already a slushy, they thought him rotten, and the virus didn't see him as a suitable host.

Anyway, don't you have much more urgent things to focus on? The gun? The zombies?

"What are you going do with us?" I asked. "Will you let them eat us? How will this help us join you?"

"A bite will do just enough. And then I will tell them to leave you to turn. I will be patient. I will wait."

"What if they won't stop?"

Greg shrugged. "Then you would not be able to join. Sadly."

"Ehm, how about we just join you, Greg? Skip the whole biting thing and all? We can join you and build a new world together," said Dan, getting up from the floor.

I got up, too, discovering that while I lay down, speculating over the scientific hypothesis, my legs had turned into clotted cream and were no longer holding me well. My hands were shaking, and I locked my fingers together, trying to suppress the shivering working up my body.

Stop it, Anna. This is not a good time to be scared. When the zombies come, you will not wait for them to snack on you. You will fight; if Greg wants you to stay still, he'd have to shoot you first.

Next time, please don't forget your wrench.

The distant footsteps turned into a loud hum of grunts. They were around the corner. They would be coming in any second now.

No, they won't unless Greg shoots the gun again, this time to let them know which lab to come in. When he pulls that trigger, I will have a second. A second's a lot.

"They are coming through the *door*," I said, peering straight into Greg's eyes. His pupils were unnaturally dilated, and I almost giggled. What a rookie mistake! I'd gone through funky theories in my head, and the answer was straight before me. In addition to mental, Greg was high!

Unaware of my internal revelation, Greg smiled back at me. There was some crooked kindness in that smile – kindness for the doomed. I focused on his hand, holding the gun.

"Yes, they will be here in a minute."

I saw his finger move a freckle of a moment before it pulled the trigger. When the first shot rang, I dashed to the door and twisted the lock into a closed position. The bullet wheezed somewhere between Dan and me and buried in the wall behind me, chipping paint and plaster. The next shot followed my movement – as I expected, Greg's instinct was to shoot at the moving target – but the bullet met the edge of the wooden cupboard. I squeezed against the cupboard wall, trying to get out of his shooting range. With my back pressed to the lab door, I felt it strain in the frame as the first arriving monsters tried to push in.

Distracted by me, Greg seemed to forget about Dan, and Dan jumped onto Greg from the left, his wrench aimed at Greg's head. They went down on the floor, hard and loud, with a familiar smashing sound – the skull collapsing under a blow, bones caving into the brain. Another gunshot ran, but I couldn't see where the bullet went. The monsters outside echoed the gunshot with an impatient howl and doubled their efforts at the door. It squealed in the doorframe, tugging on the hinges – another hit and it'd blow.

I grabbed a lab stand from the bench and ran towards Dan. He was lying on top of Greg, breathing heavily, and I saw that my help wasn't needed anymore. Dan had driven the wrench into Greg's brain through his eye socket. No man could sustain such an injury. A monster, perhaps, but Greg was a human.

If in a dodgy way.

"Com'on, Dan, let me help you!"

I wrapped my hands around his shoulders, trying to pull him up, but Dan cringed and slumped back with a groan.

"What's up, man?"

"I think... think he's got me."

Gentle this time, I pulled him off the body and leant to the cupboard. The blood was seeping through his clothes where he pressed his hands to his stomach, and the dark spot grew larger with every second.

"Stray bullet?" I smiled weakly.

He smiled back. His eyes were hazing, his look turning distant and unfocused.

Dan was bleeding out, and I had no idea what to do.

Come on, Anna, get hold of yourself, useless piece of shit. Think!

First, call for help. Second, work on the wound. Third, panic.

I dialled the group chat and left the rings going, praying that someone would answer soon, someone with first aid training, someone, Jeez, anyone! I grabbed the blue roll off the shelf, pulled a big chunk, clumped it into a ball, and pressed it onto his stomach between Dan's hands.

"This should soak the blood and help stop the bleeding," I told him.

He nodded, the same absent smile lingering on his lips.

I hadn't been trained for such situations. Nobody's trained to stop a bullet wound from bleeding, not unless they are a paramedic, a surgeon, or any bloody doctor in the end! But I'm not a doctor, not the proper type of doctor! I'm a useless type of shit doctor!

I screamed and woke Dan up from his beautiful reverie. The smile slipped off his lips.

"That bad?" he asked.

I closed my eyes. "Very bad."

"Gonna get worse."

We both turned towards the door, about to give up under the pressure of the monsters.

I smiled. "You aren't legging it out. You'll have to help me with those buggers."

"You can get out of the window. You know, like we did the last time?"

"I can't rappel, forgot?"

I kept changing the blue roll every minute. My hands were smudged in blood and shaking, and I could barely see anything because of the tears....

"It won't work," Dan whispered, pushing away my hand with another piece of blue roll. "Enough, Anna."

Bloody foam appeared on his lips as he spoke. I looked him in the eyes, then turned the phone off and leaned on the cupboard beside him, stretching my legs so my right toe pushed against Greg's body. I poked him with my shoe, but he remained dead. The smile still twisted his lips, a weird, ominous sign. Didn't Louise tell us that all muscles relaxed after death, including facial? Some muscles did relax alright, I noted with disgust from a quick look at the wet spot on Greg's trousers.

We are going to die, and the fucker had the audacity to smile.

The big mechanical clock on the wall was ticking off the seconds, every tick like a hit on the head in the woolly silence that settled in the lab. I could hear my irregular, adrenaline-fueled heartbeat and Dan's as it got increasingly out of sync with the clock.

The monsters? What about them?

In our gooey, stretchy world of silence, the monsters didn't exist, their groans and grunts inaudible against the loud ticking of time. The time running out for both of us.

Dan's hand found mine and pushed something into my palm, closing my fingers around it. With my fingertips, I felt a sleek glass cylinder with a plastic screw cap – a sample vial.

AZ-2.

I put the vial back into his palm, covered it with my hand, and squeezed it. His hand was freezing cold, and the cold crawled off his skin onto mine.

"Please... take care... Lesley..."

His hand in my hand went limp. His eyes were peering into Nothing, a lonely tear trickling down his left cheek, and no more breath came out of his mouth.

I shrieked.

Something shattered behind me. I spun around to see the door torn out of the hinges. The first spleen-eater jumped into the room.

3.

Most of all, I wanted to die.

It would be so easy to let them get me, easy and smart – no fight, no pain, a tasty spleen as a bonus. But my body and my instincts – bloody traitors! – had a different idea. I grabbed the wrench, wincing from the pain in my injured hand, slipped the gun into my coat pocket, and dashed to the window.

Bad idea, of course. Not that I'd learnt to rappel in the last couple of months, all those appointments in my calendar preventing me from prioritising my training. There wasn't even anything I could use as a rope.

And shit, it was high.

In death, Dan and Greg kindly gave me a couple of minutes to think. Attracted by the smell of fresh blood, the spleen-eaters rushed straight to their two bodies, paying me little attention, and dug into the stomachs with their teeth, spluttering guts and blood all over the floor.

Screw the worm king, they are eating Dan! As if dying was not enough…

Don't think about it. First, save yourself, then think.

More monsters poured into the lab through the gaping hole in the wall, but I decided I could deal with them one by one, as more monsters flooded into the lab through the gaping hole in the wall. But if I wanted them to be organised in an orderly queue, like proper Englishmen they weren't, I would have to organise them myself into a single file.

I looked around. The gap between two fume hoods on the other side of the lab was big enough to fit only a nitrogen tank, but now the space was empty, a small chiller parked next to it. I'd have to make a dash for it, past the bodies on the floor, past the blood-craving crowd.

Around fifteen of them. Can I take them on? By myself?

Well, I'd have to try.

I sprinted, and some of them turned away from the body to follow me. I squeezed into the small space between two fume hoods and pulled the chiller in front of me, obstructing the path for my followers. The fastest monsters lunged at me, and I swung the wrench without looking at his face. The wrench met the bones with a satisfying slurp, sending the monster stumbling backwards. He didn't go far. His friends shoved him away, and the next one stepped into his place.

I was strong. I was practised. I was used to smashing and smacking. I wanted to live, even if my heart was bleeding.

Would it work against the crowd of spleen-eaters? Although I'd never excelled in statistics, I could see my chances were slim.

In the end, I had a gun. One bullet wouldn't do much harm to *them*, but I could end it there and then.

Would I have a chance to pull the trigger?

I stopped thinking and kept working the wrench.

If you wonder about the logistics, it's pretty straightforward. You draw your arm back, swing, and when it's about to meet the target, put the force into it, driving the wrench in. Then, you pull away for your next hit.

Repeat.

A few monsters dove for my legs and found the chiller blocking their way. They stumbled over it, falling under the feet of their own, immediately trampled over. I kicked away those who squeezed by the chiller or smashed them dead on the heads. In an organised queue, someone would push it aside, but in this zombie frenzy, they demonstrated a stark relapse into their old, pre-intelligence days, making me wonder if Greg's claims had some juice in them. Maybe, he did teach them, and now that he was dead, they switched back to their happy, merry animal ways.

Draw back, swing, crush.

Draw, swing, crush.

The whacking and smashing obtained a distinctive automated rhythm, and my mind took off, no longer caring about the outcome. My hand started to grow tired, a familiar numbness tingling at my fingertips, blood from the earlier hand wound wetting the wrench. My lab coat got covered in brains and blood, hanging heavy on me, pulling me down like a useless armour.

Maybe, there were fifteen of them. Maybe, they were a thousand.

Did it matter?

It's alright, Anna. It's okay if you don't make it. You didn't give up to wallow in self-pity. You didn't wait for the rescue. You had a good run for it.

You had a good run for it *all*.

And then, out of the blue, the last spleen-eater fell to my feet, splashing his brains on my shoes. No hand reached out to grab me; no blooded face appeared in front of mine. The lights in the lab, suddenly not blocked by the crowd of monsters, blinded me for a moment. I dropped the wrench and covered my eyes.

Tanya stood on the other side of the pile of bodies with a fire axe dripping blood in her hand. She offered me her other hand, which I grabbed like a safety rope. I climbed over the bodies and almost fell into her arms. She pulled me into a bear hug and soaked my face in tears before I managed to wiggle out and wipe them off – hot, salty, red from mixing with blood. Edsie and Louise stepped from the side, their faces grim and determined. Louise wiped the sweat from her forehead, spreading a thick red paste of clotting blood over her face.

The lab was a massacre spot. Dead spleen-eaters lay everywhere, brains out, limbs torn from the joints. Women and men, old and young, dark and white skin – no discrimination, no regret.

All those people could be cured one day, becoming people again, not zombies, not spleen-eaters, not animals in a horde. They didn't have a chance anymore because of one stupid arse who looked human and talked like a human but was more monster than all spleen-eaters together.

My eyes found Greg's body buried under the pile of dead monsters, his guts smudged on the floor and trampled over by the crowd of his own "children". I wanted to spit on him, but my mouth was desert-dry.

This is your tomb, you, King of Worms. This is your funeral. Rot in hell; if there's no hell, I swear, it will be custom-made for you.

Then I saw Dan. My friends had pulled his body away from the spleen-eaters, but the monsters had already done so much damage that I couldn't even look at him without feeling sick.

"What's happened here?"

Did it matter now?

I kneeled down next to Dan's body, my knees sinking in the puddle of blood, and picked the vial out of his fist. Virgin-white fluffy crystals in the blood-stained glass glittered in the lamplight like fairy-tale snowflakes. I tossed the vial in my coat pocket and reached for Dan's hand. It was limp and sticky with blood, and unexpectedly warm, as if the last of his life energy remained in his fingers to keep the vial safe. I pressed his hand to my chest, closed my eyes, and let the tears run.

Thank you for keeping it safe. I am sorry, my friend.

I love you.

4.

Well, I couldn't be lucky forever.

I don't know what's more annoying – the fact that I've managed to get fucked when we've almost found the cure or the pity in their eyes when they look at me.

I hate pity.

I'm not looking at them.

I'm looking at the small cut on my arm, wondering how the hell I didn't notice it before. Or did I subconsciously ignore it? One of Greg's "children" has gotten to me. It feels different from any other wounds I had before, pulsing, living. Is my mind playing tricks, or is it how the virus starts affecting my brain?

Not impossible. It's been a few hours now.

We put Dan into a black sack and locked him in one of the empty offices. The rest of the bodies should also be packed away or tossed out of the window – that's what Louise and real Michael did. But there are so many, and we're so exhausted that this will be a task for tomorrow.

So, not my problem, hooray!

"Stop whispering," I said. *And prepare your weapons for when I turn…*

Whose spleen will I go for first? I would think Tanya's… For some reason, she looks tastiest.

Jesus, can someone take these thoughts out of my head? Has it already started?

"I'm going to scream if you don't stop whispering behind my back," I said again.

They stopped and stared in silence. It was even worse than whispering.

"What are my options?" I asked Louise because she seemed to be the only person in this room who hadn't buried me yet. "I guess amputating my hand won't make any difference."

She scanned me with her usual scientific interest. "Too late for that. Would you?"

I shrugged.

"I am afraid that is the only thing left." She pointed at the vial of white powder on the table in front of me.

"What? Test it on Anna? How do you imagine that?" Edsie's face turned white, almost the same colour as AZ-2. "Have you forgotten what happened to Chip?"

I winced at the undesired comparison. I agreed; the idea smelled rotten, and Edsie and Tanya turned away in disgust, but they weren't in my place because, in my place, I couldn't turn down my only chance because I feared needles.

"Let's do it," I said. "Unless someone has a better idea?"

"You do not have to do it. We can wait, lock you up in a room, and get you out when we know that AZ-2 works!"

Louise offered me a perfectly eligible alternative, but I thought of Dan's hand in my hand, Steve's "that's not that", and a long winding path home that didn't seem to lead anywhere. I was tired of walking and not arriving, tired of breathing but not getting any air, tired of promises of life always escaping me in the last moment.

Promises… I didn't even have time to promise Dan to take care of Lesley. Steve will have to take care of her, relieving me from any further obligations.

I'm free to go.

As a last resort, I thought of my parents, forever drifting across the ocean. I wasn't much different, was I? My safe harbour didn't exist, and my raft had a hole. I could let the wind swipe me into the grey waves or jump myself and breathe in the cold water.

"You'll need a human subject to test it anyway." I jumped. "So, let me do the honours!"

Louise nodded and grabbed the vial from the table.

"It's a bloody suicide! You can't be serious! Do you believe that it'll work?"

Tanya was crying, and Edsie hid her in his arms. I felt a pang of shame, as if I was betraying them and their faith in me. I squeezed Tanya's shoulder and said that I did believe because if AZ-2 didn't work, nothing would.

That was a lie. There could have been a million reasons for it not working, and the real cure could be only an atom away. But I made my bed, and I would lie in it.

So, I did.

5.

Day 67, 11th of April, Thur

"No."

Who would think that the last entertainment in my life would be the argument between Edsie and Louise on who gets to prick me with needles? It's a shame I had to interrupt it just before I bet on who would win it – because nobody would.

Hey, guys, I'm still in the room and in my own mind.

"No," I repeated. "I'm going to do it myself."

My motivation is simple. Have you ever seen a test subject injecting herself? While I make my own choice, although from a limited number of options, I'm still a conscious human. While my hand holds the syringe, I'm still a scientist.

On the other hand, I didn't expect to join the test subject cohort so soon.

Isn't it ironic?

"How quickly will I turn?" I asked Lou.

"No idea. I guess you still have a few hours."

So here's a good philosophical question. What would you do with your life if you had a few hours left? With so many options, I could seriously consider only one – having something to eat. Luckily, thanks to the recent food raid, we have exciting things on the menu.

Would you go and talk to your family?

And what would you tell them?

"Let's do it now," I decided, not seeing any further reasons to delay.

On death row, you're allowed to choose your last dinner. I rummaged through the dinner offering and lingered nostalgically over the SPAM tin before I realised that food no longer fascinated me. Was it the matter with human food, and was I about to cross the line to a different hunger?

Skipping dinner, I got to choose the place instead. I will stay in this room in the corner of the lab – small space, comforting temperature, fans humming, don't mind the glass walls – where I can write down my final entry without unwanted comments from people staring into the screen behind my back, Tanya!

Get out of here!

A bit selfish of me because the others will need to plan what to do with me if AZ-2 doesn't work, which is a fifty-fifty chance.

I handed the gun to Edsie a few minutes ago. One bullet left. How bloody convenient!

Maybe, that's their plan.

Lou was the last to go.

"Are you still sure you want to do it yourself?"

I nodded. She put the filled syringe on the table next to the keyboard.

"We will be watching you thr-rough the windows, so if something goes wr-rong, we will be there in a second," she said.

I looked around the room – glass walls and nowhere to hide – a plastic rat cage.

"Please don't write "Dale" in my records."

I don't know if she understood my joke, but she nodded. "Do you want me to stay?"

"It doesn't have to be a vein or anything? Just stick it in, right?"

"Pr-retty much."

"I'll manage," I smiled.

She left.

I heard the door lock click behind her and asked myself if it would be easier if she said something like "Good luck", "Do not die", or "See you in a bit". She didn't, and it feels fine. Lou has never been big on emotions, which is why she's so good at what she does.

Now it's only me.

I have a general idea of what I should feel right now. Grief. Sadness. Anger. Despair. But do I actually feel all that? Any of that?

From a scientific point of view, I'm long past the point of no return, so whatever I feel, it won't affect the outcomes. There's no use in feelings. Crying's not going to help.

From a human point of view, there's nothing left but to cry.

From a legal point of view, if I make a will now, will it be valid? Will there be anyone to execute it?

Here is a better question – will anyone be waiting for me on the other side? My mom and dad? Max? Dan? Kay?

That would be nice, but I have a fifty-fifty chance of making it through, which isn't that low, right? I've never been good with statistics.

Focus, Anna.

Let Steve know I love him. Whatever it is, I still love him. I always will, and I wish I could be there with him and not here with this.

In any case.

Here we go.

If you enjoyed this story, please sign-up at
www.rain-hunter.com
for a free short story prequel to The Synchrotron "ID 26"
or follow me on Instagram, Facebook, Tiktok:
@rainhunter.author

Thank you

Writing *The Synchrotron* was a rollercoaster ride inside an erupting volcano, and I wouldn't have made it out on my own.
I am eternally grateful to my small but mighty team of supporters and early readers.

To Ben – thank you for not divorcing me, even after having to read this novel twenty times.

To Kira and Hulia – thank you for taking the first leap of faith into this wild story.

To Olga – your scientific insight and attention to the lifecycle of the virus were invaluable.

To Selina and Jeffers – for diligently liking all my social networks posts.

To Paul – thank you for designing me a synchrotron... at least five times!

Finally, to every reader brave enough to buy a ticket for this rollercoaster — I hope you survived. If not — well, you won't be asking for a refund if you're dead, right?

— Rain Hunter

A note from the author

We've already established that the dazzling European Synchrotron is a real facility. It's equipped with all sorts of gear researchers need to run experiments on both soft and hard matter, in pretty much any state or form – though ideally, solid.

While we speculate about the next likely cause of humanity's demise, most people would probably agree that a global pandemic is high on the list. A Flavi virus would be a strong contender. These viruses have been around for ages and were even found in some aquatic spider species – before those creepy little things crawled out of the water to haunt our ancestors… So, it's totally plausible that the nasty V-2024 virus thawed out from ancient ice somewhere in South America. That could help explain its weird effects on human brain function. Modern flaviviruses, like dengue or West Nile, are definitely unpleasant (and occasionally deadly), but they've been tamed by years of evolutionary interaction with humans and don't behave anything like the one in the book.

The drug discovery process the ID26 team uses is fairly standard – just fast-tracked for fiction's sake. In real life, identifying viable drug targets (proteins, carbohydrates, etc.) takes ages, mostly due to the extensive validation needed to confirm their biological relevance. Isolating, growing, and sequencing a virus would also take much longer than shown in the story – even with solid support from international collaborators – and it would require specialised incubation facilities that the ESRF doesn't have.

Once there's enough virus material, it needs to be crystallised – frozen solid, usually with water molecules locked inside the structure. But crystallising proteins (and viruses are basically massive protein complexes with genetic material inside) is more of an art than a science. It can take years. For instance, we still don't have the full crystal structure of the SARS-CoV-2 virus.

Even after you've got crystals, taking X-ray images is no walk in the park. The real challenge is converting all that diffraction data into a meaningful atomic model. What helps? Having the full genetic sequence (thanks, Yuin!) and knowing the structures of related viruses. Then you throw a lot of computing power at the problem to build a model that actually makes sense.

Next comes the fun (and exhausting) part: figuring out which small (relative to the virus) molecules might trigger the virus to self-destruct. One could attempt this task by placing any test molecule in proximity to the virus surface (at any random place) and calculate the strength of binding of the two, based on the force fields of all interaction between the atoms of the virus and the death molecule. And don't forget that when virus interacts with the molecule, it will likely change its configuration, shape, position and environment. The task is enormous – the sheer number of calculations is impossible for a human but is fine for a powerful computer (the more power, the better). The process of placing two molecules together is called docking, and the calculation of forces involved in the interaction is a simulation process in the heart of the in silico drug discovery.

The ENZ death molecule is actually a caspase-12 protein, part of a family involved in programmed cell death (a.k.a. apoptosis). Caspase-12 can be triggered by cellular stress, which is happening all the time in our bodies. So, it's not a stretch (in fictional terms, at least) to imagine the virus reacting to a big enough wave of these death signals during the full-system shutdown of the host. There's even some real-world research linking caspases to neurodegenerative conditions caused by viruses and prions.

Synthesising the ENZ analogue, elaborately named *antizombine*, would actually be one of the simpler tasks, provided the team had access to the necessary chemicals and basic lab equipment for identifying the products and intermediates. Normally, a rigorous synthesis process would involve confirming each new compound using nuclear magnetic resonance (NMR) spectroscopy. But NMR machines need careful maintenance and constant topping-up with liquid nitrogen to keep their magnets happy – not exactly feasible in a post-apocalyptic world. So, I quietly skipped that part, assuming the ID26 team were more focused on saving lives than ticking every scientific checkbox. Sure, any chemist worth their salt wouldn't move forward without an NMR confirmation, but hey, humans made new compounds long before NMR was invented.

And yes, the chromatography column is *still* the most boring thing you'll do in a chemistry lab.

Printed in Great Britain
by Amazon

62970447R00211